W9-CMQ-108

A
GIFT TO THE
GLOUCESTER LIBRARY
FROM THE
J. EDWIN TREAKLE
FOUNDATION, INC

ASTRA

Also by Naomi Foyle

Seoul Survivors

ASTRA

NAOMI FOYLE

BOOK ONE OF
THE GAIA CHRONICLES

Gloucester Library
P.O. Box 2380
Gloucester, VA 23061

Jo Fletcher
New York • London

F Foy 79 gL 10/15

Jo Fletcher Books
An imprint of Querus
New York • London

Copyright © 2014 Naomi Foyle
Maps © Morag Hood 2013
First published in the United States by Quercus in 2015

"The Sixth Night *growing (up)*" from the poem cycle "The Seven Nights" by Bejan
Matur, translated by Ruth Christie with Selçuk Berilgen and published in *How Abraham
Abandoned Me* (Arc Publications, 2012); quoted here by permission of author and
publisher.

All rights reserved. No part of this book may be reproduced in any form or by any
electronic or mechanical means, including information storage and retrieval systems,
without permission in writing from the publisher, except by reviewers, who may quote
brief passages in a review. Scanning, uploading, and electronic distribution of this book or
the facilitation of the same without the permission of the publisher is prohibited.

Please purchase only authorized electronic editions, and do not participate in or
encourage electronic piracy of copyrighted materials. Your support of the author's rights is
appreciated.

Any member of educational institutions wishing to photocopy part or all of the work for
classroom use or anthology should send inquiries to permissions@quercus.com.

ISBN 978-1-62365-405-4

Library of Congress Control Number: 2015940788

Distributed in the United States and Canada by
Hachette Book Group
1290 Avenue of the Americas
New York, NY 10104

This book is a work of fiction. Names, characters, institutions, places, and events are either
the product of the author's imagination or are used fictitiously. Any resemblance to actual
persons—living or dead—events, or locales is entirely coincidental.

Manufactured in the United States

10 9 8 7 6 5 4 3 2 1

www.quercus.com

for Catherine Lupton

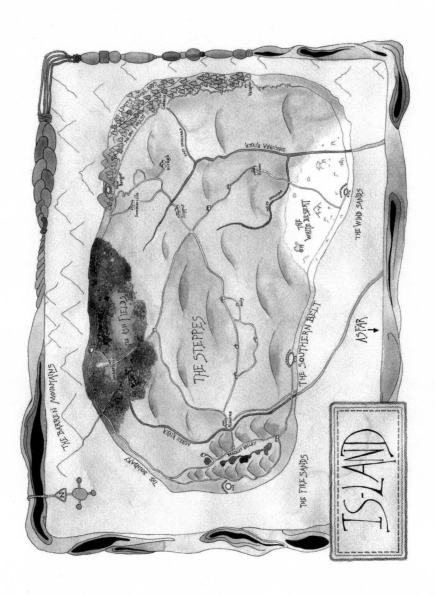

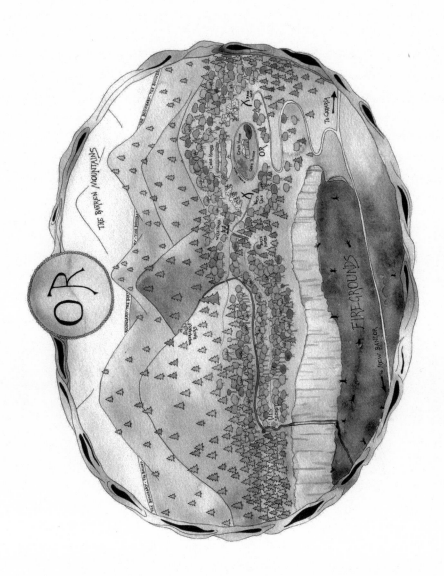

In a garden
of forgotten innocence
circling
round
and round
O human creature
when the circle is completed
what remains
is Self.
And night.

Bejan Matur
from "The Seven Nights: The Sixth Night *growing (up)*"

CONTENTS

Part One: Spring 77 RE   1

Part Two: Summer 82 RE   133

Part Three: Autumn 86 RE–Spring 87 RE   325

Acknowledgments   415

PART ONE

SPRING 77 RE

1.1

"Astraaa! *Aaaaaa*-straaaa!"

Her name floated up to her again, rising on the simmering spring air through a dense puzzle of branches, light and shade. But though Hokma's voice rasped at her conscience like the bark beneath her palms, Astra pretended—for just another minute—not to hear it.

Gaia had led her here, and all around her Gaia's symphony played on: ants streamed in delicate patterns over the forest floor, worms squirmed beneath rocks and logs, squirrels chattered in the treetops and birds flung their careless loops of notes up to the sun. Immersed in these thrilling rhythms, alert to their flashing revelations, Astra had discovered the pine glade. There, craning to follow the arc of a raptor circling far above, she'd spied a branch strangely waving in a windless sky. And now, just above her in the tip of the tree, was the reason why: five grubby toes, peeking through the needles like a misplaced nest of baby mice.

Yes. She hadn't been "making up stories," as Nimma had announced to the other Or-kids last week. It *was* the girl. The infiltrator. The spindly Non-Lander girl she'd seen slipping behind the rocks near the brook, wild-haired and wearing nothing but a string of hazelnuts around her neck. The girl had disappeared then, as sinuously as a vaporizing liquid, but today she was rustling above Astra in the tree, dislodging dust and needles, forcing Astra to squint and duck as she climbed higher than she ever had before. The girl was real: and nearly close enough to touch.

The girl probably thought she was safe. Thought the dwindling pine branches couldn't support Astra's sturdy seven-nearly-eight-year-old body. That Astra would be scared to climb higher. That she, the skinny forest child, could just wait, invisibly, her arms wrapped like snakes around the trunk, until Astra—hungry, overheated, tired of hugging the prickly tree—had to descend and go home.

But if she thought any of that, she was wrong. Dead wrong. Tomorrow was Security Shot Day, and Astra wasn't scared of any kind of needles. Nor was she too hot. A bright bar of sunlight was smacking her neck and her whole body was slick with sweat, but she'd filled her brand new hydropac with crushed ice before leaving Or and she watered herself again now through the tubing. Refreshed, she reached up and grasped a branch above her head.

Keeping her feet firmly planted on their perch, she hung her full weight from this next rung in her tree ladder. Yes: thin but strong; it wouldn't snap. She eyed another likely hand-branch, slightly higher than the first—that one, there. Good: gripped. Now the tricky part: looking down. Careful not to focus on anything beneath her own toes in their rubber-soled sandals, she checked for a sturdy branch about level with her knees. That one? Yes. She lifted her left foot and—

"*Owwww*."

A pine cone thwacked Astra's right hand, ricocheted off her cheek, and plummeted out of sight. For a terrible second, Astra's knees weakened and her fingers loosened their hold on their branches.

But though her hand stung and throbbed, and her heart was drilling like a woodpecker in her chest, she was still—praise Gaia!—clinging to the tree. Breathing hard, Astra withdrew her left foot to safety and clamped her arms around the trunk. The crusty bark chafed her chest and, like the steam from one of Nimma's essential-oil baths, the bracing sap-scent scoured her nostrils, clearing her head. At last her pulse steadied. She examined her hand: the pine cone hadn't drawn blood, but there was a graze mark beneath her knuckles.

The Non-Lander had inflicted a wound, possibly a serious injury, a crippling blow. One at a time, Astra flexed her fingers. Thank Gaia: nothing seemed to be broken. She'd been aiming to kill or maim, hoping to knock Astra clean out of the tree, but the untrained, undisciplined girl had managed only a superficial scratch. Hostile intention had been signaled, and under international law, an IMBOD officer was permitted to retaliate. Cautiously, Astra glanced up.

The row of toes was still visible. So was the ball of the girl's foot. *Ha.* Her assailant couldn't go any higher. Maybe Astra couldn't either, but if she was a Boundary constable now, charged with the sacred duty to defend Is-Land's borders from criminals and infiltrators, one way or another she was going to win.

First, she needed to gather strength and take her bearings. Arm curled around the tree, she surveyed the terrain.

Her face was taking a direct hit of sun because, she saw now, for the first time ever she'd climbed above the forest canopy. Below her, a turbulent ocean charged down the steep mountain slope, pools of bright spring foliage swirling between the jagged waves of pine until—as if all the forest's colors were crashing together on a distant shore—the tide plunged over the escarpment into a gash of charred black trunks and emerald new growth. The firegrounds were a slowly healing wound, a bristling reminder of Gaia's pain. At the sight of them splayed out for acres beneath her, Astra's breath snagged in her throat.

A Boundary constable couldn't afford to contemplate the past; a Boundary constable had to live in the present, fully alive to its invisible threats. Astra shaded her eyes with her hand. Below the forest Is-Land's rich interior shimmered out to the horizon, an endless, luxurious rolling plain. For a moment, Astra felt dizzy. From Or the steppes were either hidden by the trees or a distant vision beyond them; here they sprawled on and on like . . . she regained her focus . . . like the crazy quilt on Klor and Nimma's bed, stuffed with a cloud-puff sky. Yes, the fields below her were like countless scraps of gold hempcloth, chocolate velvet, jade linen; fancy-dress remnants stitched together with sparkling rivers and canals and embroidered with clusters of homes and farms, the many communities that worked the steppes' detoxified soil. She'd once asked Klor why the interior was called "the steppes"—the gently sloping hills didn't climb high, and the mountains were far more like stairs or ladders. "Ah, but these hills, fledgling," Klor had replied, "are stepping stones to a new future, not only for Is-Land, but the whole world." Now at last, as the steppes beckoned her into a vast lake of heat haze, she could see exactly what he meant. Klor also called the interior "Gaia's granary." The Pioneers had risked their lives to cleanse and replant Is-Land's fertile fields and no true Gaian could gaze on them without a sense of awe and gratitude. The steppes, Astra realized, gripping tight to the tree, were a vision of abundance that made the firegrounds look like a tiny scratch on Gaia's swollen belly.

But even the lowest-ranking IMBOD officer knew that the safety of Is-Land's greatest treasure could never be taken for granted. Somewhere beyond the faint blue horizon was the Boundary, and pressed up behind it the squalid Southern Belt. There, despite decades of efforts to evict them, hundreds of thousands of Non-Landers still festered, scheming to overrun Is-Land and murder any Gaian who stood in their way. Nowhere was safe. Above Astra, higher in the mountains but only an hour's trek away from Or, was the start of the off-limits woodlands, where the reintroduced megafauna lived, protected by the IMBOD constables who patrolled the Eastern Boundary. Twenty-five years ago, before the bears arrived, the off-limits woodlands had swarmed with infiltrators: cells of Non-Landers who had secretly journeyed from the Southern Belt, swinging out into the desert then up into the mountains where the Boundary was less strongly defended. Shockingly, they had succeeded in penetrating Is-Land, establishing hideouts in the dry forest from where they'd made surprise attacks on New Bangor, Vanapur and Cedaria, and even as far as Sippur in the steppes. IMBOD had fought back, jailing or evicting the infiltrators, blocking their tunnels and increasing the Eastern constabulary. When the dry forest was safe again, Gaians had established more communities in the bioregion: Or had been founded then, to show the Non-Landers that we weren't afraid of them, Klor and Nimma said. But there hadn't been an attack from the East for nearly two decades now and many Or-adults seemed to have forgotten the need for evergreen vigilance. That negligence, Astra feared, would be Or's downfall.

She twisted on her branch, hoping to inspect Or, nestled between the flanks of the mountains. But her community was hidden by the trees. The forest, though, was no protection from infiltrators. Every Or building and every inhabitant was vulnerable to attack. Really, there ought to be an IMBOD squad patrolling these woods. After Astra got her Security shot and was super-fit and super-smart she was going to come up here every day and keep watch. Maybe, because it was her idea, she could organize the other Or-kids to help her. Meem and Yoki would do what they were told; Peat and Torrent wouldn't like taking orders from an under-ten, but once she'd proved the infiltrator existed they'd have to listen. So now she had to do just that. Like Hokma and Klor proved things: with hard evidence.

Slowly, keeping her arm close to her body, Astra reached down to her hip and fumbled in the side pocket of her hydropac. Tabby's creamy Ultraflex surface responded to her touch with a short buzzy purr.

"Astra! Come *down*." Hokma's voice tore up the tree like a wildcat. She must have pinpointed Tabby's location. But this would only take a moment.

Astra carefully withdrew Tabby, activated his camera and slid him up her chest. She was going to frame the infiltrator's foot and then show Hokma the proof. Hokma would phone Klor and stand guard beneath the tree with her until he came with reinforcements—maybe even an IMBOD officer. The girl couldn't sleep in the tree, after all. When she finally came down, the officer would arrest her and take her back to Non-Land. She'd hiss and spit at Astra as they bundled her into the solar van, but there'd be nothing she could do. Then tomorrow, right before Astra's Security shot, Astra would sync Tabby to the class projector and tell everyone the story of how she'd captured the last remaining Non-Lander in Is-Land. Everyone would gasp and stand and clap, even the IMBOD officers. She might even get an Is-child Medal.

The sun was boring into her temple. A bead of sweat was tickling the tip of her nose. Astra cautiously angled Tabby toward the clutch of grimy toes.

Click.

CRACK.

Noooooooo.

Another pine cone, drone-missiling down from the top of the tree, struck Tabby dead center on the screen. Two hundred and twenty Stones' worth of IMBOD-Coded, emoti-loaded Ultraflex comm-tech flipped out of Astra's hand and twirled down through the branches of a sixty-foot pine tree to the distant forest floor. As she watched him disappear, Astra's blood freeze-dried in her veins.

"*Astra Ordott.*" Hokma's shout had ratcheted up a notch. "Get. Down. *Now.*"

That was Hokma's final-warning voice. Things didn't go well for the Or-child who ignored it. And more importantly, Tabby was wounded. He'd come under enemy fire, had taken a long, whirling nosedive to an uncertain, tree-scratched, earth-whacked fate. It was now Astra's First Duty of Care to find him. Boundary constables swore to always look after each other, even if it meant letting a Non-Lander get away.

"*Coming,*" Astra called. Above her, what sounded suspiciously like a titter filtered through the pine needles. Agile as the lemur she'd studied that morning in Biodiversity class, Astra scramble-swung down the tree.

"That Tablette had better still be working." Hokma's stout boots were solidly planted in the soil, one hand was knuckled on her hydro-hipbelt, the other gripped her carved cedar staff, and above her red velvet eye-patch her right eyebrow was raised in a stern arc. This was her look of maximum authority. Hokma was tall and broad-shouldered, with full, imposing breasts and large brown nipples, and she could transform in a second from firm but fair Shared Shelter mother to unignorable Commanding Officer. Even her hair was mighty when she told you off, its dark waves lifting like a turbulent sea around her face. Right now, she was jutting her jaw at a patch of wild garlic: Tabby, Astra saw with a heart leap, had landed among the lush green leaves.

She ducked and with every cell in her body sizzling and foaming, recceing right, left and overhead in case of further sniper fire, she ran low to the ground toward Tabby. Belly first, she slid into a cloud of savory stench and scooped her fallen comrade from his bed of stems and soil.

Oh no. His screen was scratched and black with shock. He must have suffered terribly, falling through the branches.

"Stay with us, Tabby!" she urged. "Stay with us." Turning her back to the pine tree to cover the wounded constable from further attack, she wiped him clean of dirt. Her fingertip moist with alarm, she pressed his Wake Up button.

Praise Gaia. The screen lit up and the IMBOD Shield shone forth in its bright insignia of green and red and gold. Twining one leg around the other, she waited for Tabby's Facepage to upload. At last Tabby's furry head appeared.

"He's alive!" Astra jumped to her feet and punched the air. But Tabby's emotional weather report was *Not Good.* His whiskery mouth was pinched in a tight, puckered circle; his eyes were unfocused; his ears were ragged and drooping. As she stroked his pink nose a thundercloud, bloated with rain and spiky with lightning bolts, bloomed above his head.

Tabby blinked twice. "Where am I?" he bleated.

He wasn't his normal jaunty self, but at least his vital functions were intact. She smooched his sweet face and clasped his slim form to her chest. "Don't worry, Tabby. You're safe with me. Everything's going to be okay."

"Give." Hokma was towering over her.

Astra reluctantly relinquished Tabby for inspection by a senior officer and fixed her attention on Hokma's navel. The deep indent was like a rabbit's burrow in her Shelter mother's creased olive-skinned stomach. Peat and Meem's Birth-Code mother, Honey, sometimes let Astra stick her finger in her own chocolate-dark belly button, but it was impossible to imagine Hokma doing that. Hokma sometimes let Astra hold her hand, or briefly put her arm around her, but she never tickled Astra, or invited her to sit in her lap. Hokma "showed her love in other ways," Nimma said. Far too often, though, Hokma's love seemed to consist of telling Astra off.

Hokma unfolded Tabby from handheld to notepad mode. The Ultraflex screen locked into shape, but Astra could see that the image hadn't expanded to fill it. Hokma tapped and stroked the screen all over, but nothing worked—even when she tried in laptop mode, his poor confused face remained tiny in the corner of the screen. "His circuitry is damaged." She refolded Tabby, handed him back and scanned Astra from toe to top. "Why aren't you wearing your flap-hat?"

Her flap-hat? This was no time to be worrying about *flap-hats*. "I was in the shade," Astra protested, gripping Tabby to her heart.

"Oh?" Hokma gazed pointedly around at the shafts of sunlight slicing through the pines. But she let it go. "It doesn't matter where you are outside, Astra. You have to wear your flap-hat until dusk. Do you even have it with you?"

"Yes," Astra muttered, unzipping her hydropac back pocket. Flap-hats were for babies. She couldn't wait until she was eight and her skin was thick enough to go out without one.

She put the stupid thing on, but Hokma wasn't satisfied yet. "And what in Gaia's name were you doing climbing trees? I told you to meet me at West Gate at four."

"You are ten minutes late to meet Hokma at West Gate," Tabby piped up helpfully. "You are ten minutes Hokma late to meet West Gate at four. You are ten Hokma West to late minutes . . ."

"He's got shell-shock!" Astra cried.

"I said he's damaged. Turn him off."

"*No!* He has to stay awake or we might lose him."

"All right. Put him on silent then."

Astra obeyed and slipped Tabby back into his pocket. "Klor can fix him," she offered, scuffing the ground with her sandal. "Like he did last time."

"Astra. Look at me."

Constable Ordott straightened up and obeyed her Chief Inspector's order. This could be big-trouble time.

But fire wasn't flashing from Hokma's hazel-gold eye. Her brows weren't scrunched together, forcing that fierce eagle line between them to rise, splitting her forehead like it did when Or-kids neglected their chores or fought over biscuits that were all exactly the same size, as Hokma had once famously proved with an electronic scale. Instead, her square face with its prominent bones was set in a familiar, patient expression. She looked like she did when explaining why a certain Or-child rule was different for under-tens and over-nines. And when Hokma was in explaining mode, you could usually try to reason with her. She always won, of course, but she liked to give you the chance to defend yourself, if only to thoroughly demonstrate exactly why you were wrong and she was right.

"Klor's got better things to do than mending your Tablette every two weeks, hasn't he?"

Hokma's tone was calm, so Astra risked a minor contradiction. "Klor said it was a good teaching task," she attempted. "He showed me Tabby's nanochip. I learned a lot, Hokma!"

"You take Tech Repair next term. Tablettes are expensive. You should never play with them while you're climbing trees."

"But I was looking for the girl. I needed Tabby to take photos."

The ghost of a frown floated over Hokma's features. "What girl?"

Astra whipped Tabby out again. Maybe he couldn't talk properly, but he could still see. She clicked his camera icon and speed-browsed her photos. Hokma was getting dangerously close to impatience now, but in a minute she would be praising Astra and Tabby for their valor and initiative; she would be calling Or to raise the alarm and gather a team to bring the enemy down.

"The girl in the tree. *Look.*"

But the photo was just a muddy blur of greens and browns.

"I don't have time for these games, Astra."

Astra stuffed Tabby back in his pocket. No one would believe her now. "It was the girl I saw last week," she muttered. "The one who lives in the forest. She's a Non-Lander. An *infiltrator*. She threw pine cones at me. See." She held out her bruised hand. "So I dropped Tabby, and the photo didn't turn out."

Now it deepened: the warning line between Hokma's eyebrows. Silently, she examined Astra's knuckles. When she spoke again, it was as if she were talking to somebody young or naughty or slow: to Meem or Yoki.

"There's no girl living in the forest, Astra. You've just scraped yourself again."

"But I saw—"

Hokma bent down and grasped Astra's shoulders. Astra was supposed to look her in the eye, she knew, but she didn't want to. She stared down at her feet again and dug her sandal toes into the garlic patch. Torrent was going to tell her she smelled like an alt-beef casserole when she got back to Or.

"There are no Non-Landers in Is-Land anymore," Hokma said, using her instructor voice as if Astra was stupid, as if Astra hadn't just completed Year Two Inglish Vocabulary a whole three months ahead of her class.

She folded her arms and glowered up at Hokma. "Klor and Nimma said there are still *lots* of infiltrators in Is-Land," she retorted. "They're disguised as Gaians with fake papers or they're still hiding in the off-limits woodlands."

Sometimes when her face was this close to Hokma's, she felt an urge to stroke her eyepatch, especially the velvet ones. Nimma made them using material from a hoard of ancient curtains she used only for very special things, like the crazy quilt, or toy mice for toddlers, or fancy purses for the older girls when they started going to dances in New Bangor. Right now, however, Hokma was gripping her shoulders tighter until they hurt. Just as Astra was about to squeal *ow*, her Shared Shelter mother let go.

"Klor and Nimma shouldn't be scaring you with their *rainwarped* notions, Astra," she said firmly. "The off-limits woodlands are heavily patrolled, and if IMBOD didn't catch any infiltrators, the reintroduced bears would."

Usually Astra loved to hear Hokma swear, but right now it was infuriating to be argued with. To be *punished* for caring about national security. How could Hokma refuse to acknowledge the ever-present dangers they all lived with? She was supposed to be *smart*.

"*No*," she insisted, rubbing her shoulder, "the Non-Landers have changed tactics. They *deliberately* aren't attacking us now. They live up high in tree nests, where the bears can't climb. They've got stolen Tablettes that can hack IMBOD emails and they're stockpiling bows and arrows through the tunnels and helping Asfar and the Southern Belt prepare to attack us when the global ceasefire finishes."

"What on Gaia's good earth have they been telling you?" Hokma snorted. "Klor and Nimma just aren't used to living in peace, Astra. The tunnels are all blocked up, and Asfar is our *ally*."

"There are *new* tunnels. And Klor said the Asfarian billionaires could—"

"*Enough*, Astra. There's no such thing as a Non-Lander girl running wild in the woods. Everyone in Is-Land is registered and has a home. If you saw someone, she's from New Bangor and her parents are close by."

"*No.*" Astra stamped her foot. "She was dirty and her hydropac was really old. She lives *here*. She—"

"I said *FOG FRIGGING ENOUGH*," Hokma bellowed.

Astra stepped back, her heart thumping in her chest. Nimma and Klor *never* yelled like that, out of nowhere, let alone swore at her. When Nimma was angry she talked at you rapidly in a high, sharp voice, whittling you away with her rules and explanations, and behind her Klor stood solemn and sad, shaking his head and saying, "Nimma's right, Astra," so you felt you had terribly disappointed him and eventually, half-ashamedly, accepted your punishment. This furnace blast of fury was very different. She stood quivering, not knowing what to do.

Hokma waved her hand through the air as if to brush away a bothersome insect. "Astra, I'm sorry I shouted. I didn't come here to bicker with you. I asked you to meet me so we could discuss something important. Let's leave this discussion behind us. Now."

Astra kicked at a stone. Okay, Hokma had said she was sorry—but she didn't *sound* sorry. She was being unfair and bossy and ignoring invaluable ground evidence. That was senior officers all over. Most of them, it was well known, had long forgotten what it was like to be out there, vulnerable and under fire from hostile criminals.

Hokma turned and started down the trail back to Or, swinging her staff by her side. "Don't you want to see Wise House?" she called over her shoulder. "If there's time before supper chores you can help me feed the Owleon chicks."

Astra stared down the path, her heart bobbing like a balloon in a sudden gust of wind. *Wise House?* Where Hokma lived alone breeding and training the Owleons, and no one was ever allowed to visit? Hokma was inviting her there to feed the chicks? *Yes way*.

She sprang forward to catch up. A pine cone zinged over her head and hit the dirt path in front of her feet. She wheeled around and craned up at the jack pine. The top branches were waving gently but the Non-Lander girl was invisible, camouflaged by a screen of needles and adult indifference.

"We'll prove it one day, Constable Tabby," she swore. "After I get my Security shot."

"*Astra*." Hokma was nearly at the brook now. Astra glared at the top of the tree and stuck out her tongue. Then she spun on her heel and raced after Hokma.

"*Wait up*," she shouted. "Wait for me!"

1.2

Astra jumped into Hokma's footprints then skipped through the pines after her Shelter mother. She was going to Wise House, to *Wise House*, where no one except Hokma, Ahn and IMBOD officers were allowed to go. The officers came twice a year, to inspect the Owleons and take the fully grown and trained birds away. Since Astra had started school she hadn't seen them arrive or leave, but every few weeks she spied Ahn in his canvas-topped boots and old straw hat, his Tablette tucked in a scroll beneath his arm, striding out toward West Gate in the evening. He and Hokma were Gaia-bonded, Nimma said, a bond of more than twenty years, though it was hard to believe because they never even sat together in Core House at mealtimes, let alone held hands or kissed like Klor and Nimma did. Still, Nimma said that some people liked to kiss each other when no one else was watching.

Ahn's lips were so thin they were nearly invisible, but still it was just conceivable that Hokma might want to kiss them and give him permission to visit Wise House; what was nearly impossible to accept, however, was that Or-kids—even *her*, Hokma's own Shelter daughter—were strictly forbidden. Or-kids were noisy and galumphing, Hokma said, and ran around and frightened the birds. "*I'm* not galumphing," Astra had complained to her last year. It wasn't fair. Hokma was her Shared

Shelter mother so why couldn't Astra visit her? Peat and Meem went
to stay with their Birth-Code-Shelter parents sometimes, and Yoki
often stayed with his Birth-Code uncle. In fact, *all* the other Or-kids
except her got to stay with *all* their Shared Shelter parents. Especially
considering that she didn't have a Birth-Code mother or a Code father,
it wasn't right that she should be stuck with Klor and Nimma all
the time.

"You're the biggest galumpher of them all, Astra," Hokma had
laughed. "You're always knocking into people. Better save all that energy
for the Kinbat track for now."

It *wasn't true*. She could run fast, and sometimes her elbows jabbed
into adults who didn't get out of the way. But she was light, and she
knew she could be a silent tracker in the woods if she tried, even with
her sandals on. But when she'd tried to explain, Hokma had got angry,
and told her to stop arguing or she'd be running extra laps for the next
two weeks.

I wish you weren't my Shelter mother, Astra had nearly shouted.
But what if Hokma had said, *Fine, I'll stop now*? So instead Astra had
stormed off to the orchard, where she'd sat under a fig tree nestling the
hurt like a dead bee in a puff of cotton. Later, she'd carefully placed
the bee-hurt in a little drawer inside her heart. She didn't like to open the
drawer very often, though, because even though the bee-hurt was dead,
it could still sting her.

But now, at last, she was going to visit Wise House. As Astra followed Hokma down to the brook, the drawer in her heart flew open and
like a small miracle, the bee took flight.

Ahead of her, Hokma crossed the small wooden bridge Klor and Ahn
had built twenty years ago, when Or was new and the brook little more
than a dried-up ditch. The water was deep again now, a smooth umber
current nearly as deep as Astra was tall. She bent down, ripped open
her Velcro sandal straps and, arm back behind her head like she'd been
taught in cricket practice, hurled her shoes across to the opposite bank.
The second one landed short of the first and rolled dangerously down
toward the water.

"Astra!" Hokma's hands were on her hipbelt again. But the sandal didn't fall in. Hurriedly, before Hokma could object, Astra slipped off her hydropac and slung it across the brook too. As the pac sailed past Hokma's head and into the woods, she splashed into the water. Clothed in its silky flow, she swam to the other side, dipping her head beneath the tarnished green reflections of the trees to refresh her hot face. Clean and glistening, she scrambled up the bank.

"Better?" Hokma watched Astra put her sandals back on. Leaves and bits of bark had stuck to her wet feet, but they would soon dry. Hokma tugged her flap-hat back down on her head and Astra lunged up to the path. On this side of the bridge it rambled through a bower of ancient oaks, rare trees that had somehow survived the Dark Time and become a place of solemn pilgrimage for every international visitor to Or. Today Astra and Hokma had the bower to themselves. As Astra pranced through the shady glade, the drops of water sparkling on her skin were consumed by the familiar sheen of sweat. She slowed down and let Hokma catch up with her; now they walked side by side, Hokma marking their strides with her staff, her free hand swinging lightly beside Astra. Quietly, carefully, almost as if she herself didn't know what it was doing, Astra's hand reached up and curled around two of Hokma's fingers. Hokma squeezed. Astra gripped a little tighter.

"Hokma?"

"Yes, Astra?"

"What does bicker mean?"

"To have a nonsense argument. An argument no one can win."

"Oh. I thought it did, but I wanted to make sure." Somewhere, a wood pigeon mournfully echoed its own coo. Astra giggled. "It sounds like what the birds do outside my window. Bicker."

Hokma gave a gruff laugh. "Birds bicker. Squirrels squabble."

Astra thought for a moment. "And crows crorrel, I mean choral. I mean *quarrel*. Hey, I invented a tongue-twister! *Yay.*" She risked a skip. Just a little one, so as not to pull too hard on Hokma's arm and make her let go.

"You certainly did."

Astra took a long step forward. She really wanted to ask Hokma about her missing eye. Even though Hokma was her Shared Shelter mother and they went for walks together and Astra could sit in her lap in the Quiet Room, as long as she asked nicely first, Hokma had never talked about it properly with her. The only time Astra had asked what had happened, Hokma had said she lost her eye because she wasn't looking. Then she'd said, "Look!" and pointed at the ceiling. There'd been nothing there and Hokma had laughed and said, "You missed it!"

But then last autumn, after Klor and Nimma had told Astra, Meem, Yoki and Peat the terrible story of Sheba, and Klor's leg, Astra had begun to ask them more about Non-Land and finally they'd also told her that during the Southern Offensive a Non-Lander had shot Hokma in the face. Hokma had been on patrol in the Southern Belt and the armed criminal had tried to shoot her CO. She'd stepped out in front of her officer and taken the bullet for him. Afterward, IMBOD had given her a medal. Klor and Nimma had said that Hokma didn't like to talk about it because she was very modest, but she still had the medal, at Wise House, which was private, and no, Astra couldn't ask Hokma if she could go there and see it. As a rule, she shouldn't ask people personal questions, not even Shelter parents. They would tell her themselves when they were ready, or when they thought she was ready, like she and her Shelter siblings were now ready to hear about Sheba.

Hokma had stopped walking. She dropped Astra's hand and began poking at a rock in the path with her staff. She was frowning a little. Astra scratched her belly. Maybe now wasn't the right time to ask about Hokma's eye. Not if it was worse than the story about Sheba, which had made them all cry, even Peat and Klor. Especially Klor. Maybe soon, when Astra had an IMBOD medal of her own and everyone was celebrating in Core House, she would ask Hokma to bring hers down from Wise House to show people and Hokma would go and get her medal and put it next to Astra's and tell the story then.

Luckily there was another question pressing forward in the line, one she had been wanting to ask all week and now was inescapable.

"Hokma?"

Hokma was inspecting the underbelly of the stone. "Yes, Astra?"

"Torrent said you feed the Owleon chicks *real worms*. But that's not true, is it?"

Astra waited confidently for a reply she could snap back to Torrent, who fancied himself the leader of the eleven-year-olds—and everyone younger than him. He was just being mean, she knew, trying to make Yoki cry as the three of them spread that evening's food scraps into the vermicompost bins outside Core House. The bins were filled with trays of red wigglers that worked day and night turning Or's vegetable peelings into rich, nutritious soil for the gardens. The wigglers didn't get paid, not like horses, sheep, cows and llamas did, because the bins were like luxury worm hotels they could stay in their whole lives so they didn't need retirement funds; but worms were Gaia's creatures, just the same as megafauna, insects and worker animals: they had rights and there was no way Hokma would Code a bird to eat them.

"Don't tell lies, Torrent," she'd said scornfully. "Don't worry, Yoki. The Owleons are grain-eaters. Everyone knows that."

But Hokma didn't scoff at Torrent's claim. With a twist of her staff she dug the rock out of the path and flicked it into the undergrowth. Then she peered into the hole, *tsked*, and straightened up.

"That's a good question. Let's sit down and talk about it, shall we?"

They had left the oak bower now and were skirting a bushy glade. Hokma pointed with her staff to an almond tree at the far edge of the clearing. Astra looked at it doubtfully. Why couldn't they just talk here? As Hokma headed for the tree, she examined the hole in the path. Where the rock had been, a fat nightcrawler was squirming its way back into the dry ground. Astra placed a leaf over the hole to protect the worm from the sun, then scuffed her way through the sun and shrubs after Hokma.

At the tree, Hokma hooked a branch down with her staff. It was thick with green almonds. "Here." Hokma pressed one of the nuts into her hand. It felt like a hard, fuzzy little mouse. As Astra fingered it, Hokma tugged at her hydropac and dropped handfuls more into the back pocket. "Give those to Nimma tonight for a stew," she said, buttoning the pocket back up. "They won't be around for long."

Why was Hokma talking about stew? Astra threw the almond into the glade and swiveled around. "Is Torrent right?" she challenged. "Do you *really* feed the Owleon chicks *worms*?"

"Sit down, Astra." Three large, flat stones were arranged in a semi-circle beneath the tree and Hokma lowered herself onto one. If she were Klor or Nimma, she would be patting the place beside her, but Hokma said she liked to look at a person properly when she spoke to them. She pointed with her staff at the stone opposite. Astra hesitated, then sat down with her arms crossed in front of her chest. The stone was warm but hard, and it felt gritty against her bottom. Sunlight was dappling Hokma's face and breasts through the almond tree branches; suddenly everything seemed uncertain, shifting, not one thing or another.

"The answer to that question," Hokma said calmly, "is one of the reasons you couldn't come up to Wise House before. You were too young to understand. But now you're older and I can explain. Astra, I Coded the Edition One Owleons to eat grain, but they didn't live long. So for Edition Two I reverted to the owl's natural diet, with some minor adaptations. You see, to fly at night on silent wings, and for other applications, IMBOD needs the birds to be more owl than pigeon. And owls are carnivores. They won't be healthy and strong if they don't eat meat."

Astra struggled to understand. "But aren't the Owleons like cats and dogs? Don't you feed them alt-meat?"

"I do," Hokma said. "I have an alt-mouse incubator, and I freeze what I don't use right away. But Wise House is off-grid so I don't have unlimited electricity, especially in the rainy season, and I can't count on being able to always run both the incubator and the freezer. My solution, which IMBOD has approved, was to add a short sequence of Blackbird Code to the Second Edition so they could eat worms too."

It was as if Hokma had calmly told her that Nimma had tied Yoki to a chair and stabbed him with a kitchen knife. "But . . . don't the birds *peck* them to death?" Astra stammered. "Worms are *Gaia's creatures*. We have to *protect* them. Not *torture* them."

"Of course we do. But Astra, you remember studying the self-defense law last month, don't you?"

"Yeah." Who could forget *that* lesson?

"Well, the Owleons are classified as an Is-Land self-defense project, so IMBOD allows me to feed them unendangered creatures. But even so, IMBOD won't let anyone be cruel to worms. I keep them in a nice vermicompost and I feed them special vegetables from my garden. Then I give them an injection to put them to sleep before I feed their bodies to the Owleons. It's not nice, but it has to be done."

Individually, the sentences made sense, but Astra was struggling to make sense of them all together. Killing worms was cruel, wasn't it, no matter how you did it? Behind her the woods emitted a groan, swiftly pursued by a thundering crash. She spun around on her stone.

"It's the girl!" she yelled, way too loud—but she was on edge; she couldn't be expected to follow every single constabulary rule.

"It's a branch falling," Hokma said sternly. "Astra, pay attention."

Breathing hard, Astra fell silent. Sunlight was playing in pretty patterns over Hokma's shoulders and a light breeze was shushing through the stringybark trees surrounding the glade. Apart from the birds, there was no other movement or sound in the woods. As if the balloon of the afternoon's excitement was gradually deflating, she felt her certainty seep out of her. Had she really seen the girl in the tree? Maybe it was a squirrel making the pine cones drop. And was the breeze really Gaia, whispering that she was being a baby? The self-defense law had been a hard shock for many of the children to absorb, especially Yoki, but she had thought she understood it. She had just never dreamed it would apply to Hokma and the Owleons.

Frowning, she thought back over the lesson: a special joint presentation to the two Year Three classes. Ms. Raintree had sat up front with Yoki's teacher, Mr. Banzan, and together they'd explained that it was time for the children to deepen their knowledge of Is-Land's First Principles.

"Who can tell me what those are?" Ms. Raintree had asked. Every hand in the room had shot up.

"All together, then," Mr. Banzan had urged, and in unison the two classes had chanted:

"Is-Land exists to nurse Gaia back to health. Is-Land cradles all Gaia's creatures. Is-Land will always defend Gaia from harm."

"Very good." Ms. Raintree clapped. "Now let's talk about Gaia's creatures. Some of them aren't always very nice to us, are they? What about

ticks and mosquitoes? Sometimes they bite us or poison us. In other
countries they call such creatures pests and try to control them. So why
do we cradle them?"

Of course everyone knew the answer to that: which species, after
all, had proved to be the planet's real pest? Which species had nearly
destroyed the biosphere of the only known life-bearing planet in *the
whole universe*? Insects, on the other hand, were vital to biodiversity,
and without them we'd never be able to reintroduce lost mammals and
birds. Human beings just had to take precautions and wear repellent if
we didn't want to get bitten.

But then Mr. Banzan asked another, harder, question: what if carnivorous creatures ate human beings, or persistent insects threatened
our forests or crops? Could we kill them then?

"No," Yoki declared, his face red. "We should move and let the creatures live in their natural habitat. Gaia gives us lots of places to live."

"Good, Yoki." Mr. Banzan said. "That's one view, and a very important one. Any others?"

The children were silent. "What if we had to all move away from
Is-Land?" Ms. Raintree prompted. "Would that be good for Gaia?"

Beside Astra, one hand waved. Big surprise who it belonged to.

"Leaf?" Ms. Raintree smiled.

"*I* think," the school's only girl-boy said slowly, "we can't move away
from Is-Land because if there was no Is-Land to nurse Her, then Gaia
might get sick again. So maybe, in that case, it *might* be allowed to kill
some of Her creatures . . . if that was the *only* way to stay here and protect
Her. I mean"—Leaf finished on a triumphant note—"it would be like if
you had to cut off a person's arm to save their life."

That, it turned out, was the right answer. The National Wheel
Meet had established that Is-Landers were Gaia's creatures too, with no
greater or lesser rights than any other species. Therefore Is-Land's legal
principles of self-defense applied to life-threatening animals and insects
in just the same way as it did to hostile humans. An exception was made
if the offending species was endangered; in that case the principle of
biodiversity was paramount and human beings had to find other ways
to cope with the problem.

Once the children had debated these concepts, the teachers took them to the school vegetable garden, Ms. Raintree wheeling herself along the paths and pointing out interesting plants with her baton, Mr. Banzan and the gardener taking them into the furrows. This was very exciting at first, because up to now the patch had been off-limits: under-eights were allowed to grow food only in the hydroponic lab, and at home at Or there was a lock on the vegetable garden gate and only bigger children's fingerprints were on the key registry. At school that day they had discovered why. There, between the rows of beans and lettuces, at the edge of the path where Ms. Raintree could see too, the gardener had shown them the slug traps.

Yoki had cried and said he didn't want to eat garden-grown vegetables anymore, only hydroponic ones, but Mr. Banzan had said that if we covered Gaia with labs, we would stop being able to respond to Her beautiful complexity. "Sometimes complexity means difficulty, Yoki," Ms. Raintree had said gently, reaching out from her chair to put her arm around him.

Astra had known she ought to comfort her Shelter brother too, but instead she'd knelt down and examined a trap. It was filled with beer. The slugs got drunk and dozy, the gardener had said, and drowned before they even discovered they couldn't get back out.

"Slugs are like Non-Landers," she'd announced. "They're always trying to infiltrate us."

"Clever girl," the gardener had said. "But we're too smart for them, aren't we?"

Worms, Astra knew, were wonderful, essential, amazing. But if IMBOD said a small number of them had to be sacrificed to help the Owleons protect Is-Land and Is-Land protect Gaia, then she had to be strong and accept it.

"I *do* understand," she said, at last. "I just didn't want Yoki to cry, that's all."

"I know," Hokma replied. "He found the lesson upsetting, didn't he? But Nimma said you were fine."

Astra prepared herself for the worst. "Will I have to inject the worms?"

"Not if you don't want to. And you don't have to feed the chicks either if you'd rather not. I can just show you Wise House and feed them when you've gone."

What? "*No*," Astra said, panicked. "Constables have to kill if it's necessary. That's what you learn on IMBOD Service, isn't it?"

With the tip of her staff Hokma toyed with the almond Astra had hurled aside. "Astra," she said at last, "we're going to talk about your IMBOD Service later, okay?"

Astra's eyes widened. Normally whenever she asked the Or-adults about her IMBOD Service, they said she didn't have to worry about that for years yet. "Really?"

"Yes. After we feed the chicks. And they're hungry, so let's go."

Hokma flicked the almond further into the glade and, digging her staff into the ground, hoisted herself to her feet. Astra jumped up too and scampered after her Shelter mother, back to the path.

1.3

Hokma was walking way too slowly now. She kept stopping to turn over stones, looking for wigglers. If she found one, she put it into a pouch on her hydrobelt. Watching her do that made Astra feel funny, so, cheering herself on like a Neolympics athlete, she raced up the path until it met the trail that marked the upper Or border. She leapt with both feet into the center of the crossways. Ahead, the path sloped down to West Gate. To her right, rock steps descended to Birth House and the Fountain. To her left, a perilously steep narrow track overhung with massive leafy stringybark branches led up to Wise House. Panting, she swiveled to face it head-on. This path had no steps, just roots and loose stones. It was a difficult climb, but when on patrol you had to be ready for any challenge Gaia threw at you.

"That was quite a run." Hokma had caught up. "Better have some water."

She *was* hot, but not too bad. The Pioneers had marched much further in far worse conditions. Hokma was right though: constables had a duty not to get dehydrated. Astra sucked at her tubing again. The water was warm now, but it still refreshed her cells as it sluiced through her. Hokma drank too, uncoiling her own tubing from the side of her belt.

"Good girl," she said when Astra was done. "Now, you're going to need a stout stick." She placed her hands a foot apart. "About this long."

A stick? *Sunburst!* She was heading into unknown territory now, so it would be good to be armed. Who knows, the girl might be following them, and she could have other Non-Landers with her. Astra tramped off the path toward a mossy log that might have shed some branches once upon a time. She found a short, strong stick and stripped its twigs away. Then she ran back to the crossroads, brandishing her find.

"Perfect." Hokma gestured at the slope. "You first. I'll catch you if you fall."

To climb the practically vertical path, Astra had to hunt for foot-holds in the roots and between rocks. She dug her stick into the earth for balance and stopped for breathers when she needed to rest, taking the opportunity to assess the stringybarks on both sides of the path. Stringybark branches could crash without warning, like the one at the glade, but thanks to Tabby and his forest-knowledge, Astra had recently discovered that with the help of an adult, you could identify a strong climbing tree and use spikes and ropes to fix a swing to it. That was for another time, though. Right now she had to keep going, one step after another, her heart battering against her chest, constantly watching out for the infiltrator.

At last she reached the top of the slope. Here the stringybarks gave way to a swath of graceful lacebarks, Or lawn trees with wide-spreading branches perfect for picnicking under. Weaving between their trunks, like a metallic band in a loose, delicate shawl, was a tall wire fence. Astra flung her stick aside, tore up the last stretch of path and threw herself at it. Sticking her fingers in the mesh links, she made the fence shake and the gate rattle on its posts, but her sandals were too big for the gaps, so she dropped back down to the ground. Through the wire and the three lacebarks inside it she could see a grassy clearing and a square brown house.

Hokma arrived behind her. "Calm down, Astra."

"I was just testing the security," Astra explained. It would be so easy for the infiltrator to climb the fence, but she wasn't allowed to mention *her.*

"That fence could have been electrified, and then I'd be carrying you back to Or, wouldn't I?"

But she could tell Hokma wasn't seriously angry. She placed her fingertip on the lock and the gate swung open. Astra wriggled through it and dashed ahead onto the path that curved up through the clearing to Wise House.

Wise House, Astra knew from Biotecture class, was a cob-plastered straw-bale cabin kept cool by its thick walls and small windows. Ahn had designed it for Hokma while they were still living together in an Earthship in Or. Later he'd sold the plans to the Bioregional Wheel Meet for a batch of kindergartens in New Bangor, Cedaria and Vanapur, making lots of money for Or. Astra had once asked Nimma if Ahn had known Hokma would leave the Earthship they shared and move into Wise House, where she now worked and slept and often even cooked for herself. Nimma had said that both Ahn and Hokma were happier and more productive living alone. The reason the Edition Three Owleons were a work of genius—a breakthrough in Code technique—was that Hokma had totally dedicated herself to their design; and the reason Ahn won so many prizes and contracts for his buildings was because he stayed up late most nights at his screendesk. Some scientists worked best in teams; others needed solitude, and Or provided the right conditions for both.

Astra had seen photographs of the kindergartens, but though they had the same floorplan and used the same building techniques, they looked nothing like Wise House. Standing in front of it, at last, Astra understood in an instant why Hokma had left Or. The cabin was magical, an enchanted cottage from an Old World fairy tale. The tawny brown walls were flecked with mica that glinted in the sunlight streaming into the clearing. The two square windows were framed by grooved disks of pine, like two big wooden suns, one either side of the front door, which was inset with a triangle of gold glass and topped by a living lintel of feathery grasses. The flat meadow roof was ablaze with yellow, orange and white wildflowers, and two angular sets of solar cells stuck up like cute little pyramids in the corners.

Little pyramids or . . . *ears*? Oh! With a gasp, Astra got the joke.

"It looks like an Owleon!" She jumped and clapped.

"Well spotted, Astra. Why do you think Ahn designed it that way?"

"Because"—Astra hazarded a guess—"if you live inside an Owleon's head, you'll understand them better?"

Hokma laughed again, another short, rough bark of amusement. "That's a great answer. I'll tell Ahn you said that."

"Really?" Astra flushed. Ahn had lived with Hokma and was still Gaia-bonded with her. That meant that he was almost Astra's Shelter father. But still, if she ran into him at Core House, something always stopped her from grabbing his hand as she might do with any of the other Or-adults, because Ahn wasn't anyone's Code or Shelter parent, and you couldn't imagine him being one. Tall and lanky, with a fuzz-ball of blond hair, Ahn floated through Or in his straw hat and ex-IMBOD boots, his pale gray eyes always measuring some distant sightline. He never knew any of the Or-kids' names, and if he did say hello, you usually felt as though the greeting was an accident, an automatic reaction triggered by a disturbance of air in his vicinity; that he hadn't really seen you—not as *you*, anyway. In the Quiet Room once, Klor had joked that Ahn viewed people mainly as bodies that needed spaces around them. "Bodies and psyches," Ahn had softly corrected, as Astra stared at him from Nimma's lap, too tongue-tied to ask what a "sy-key" was.

"Do you think he knows who I am?" she asked.

"Of course he does. He's just Ahn. He forgets his own name when he's thinking."

Astra wanted to ask if Hokma and Ahn talked about her sometimes, but she was afraid of what the answer would be. Anyway, Hokma was heading up the path and then they were there, at the Wise House front door with its gold glass beak, where Hokma was taking off her boots and turning on the hosepipe to wash herself, and Astra too, down to her feet and rubber sandals, and then she was opening the door and finally Astra was going inside.

The Wise House entrance chamber was spacious and cool, with a stripped pine floor. There were doors in all four walls and three holes in the ceiling: two air vents and one bean-shaped translucent solar panel, which cast spirals of light over Astra and Hokma as they removed their outdoor gear. Paintings and carvings of Owleons hung on the walls and the housecoat hooks were carved hardwood talons. Hokma rested her cedar staff in a corner rack, then unlaced her boots and slid them under a bench with Astra's sandals. Astra took off her flap-hat and hydropac, wondering where to put them.

"We'll have to get a lower row of hooks for you," Hokma said, hanging Astra's things up on a talon. "How about red pigeon toes?" As Astra protested—she wanted talons *too*—her Shelter mother took down a towel and rubbed her all over, wet feet last. Then she pulled two pairs of curvy-toed slippers out of a basket on the bench. Astra's were new, and just her size. "Here." Hokma held out a small sateen housecoat. "I thought turquoise would suit you."

Astra scrunched up her nose. "Do I have to wear clothes?"

"Wise House isn't an Earthship, Astra. It can get a bit nippy in here. I don't want you catching cold."

Cold? Cold was the walk-in fridge in the kitchen or an ice cube on your tongue. "I'm not cold."

"You might be soon. Now come on."

Astra blew a raspberry, but slid her arms into the soft sleeves and tied the belt as loosely as possible. If you had to wear clothes, sateen was just about bearable. At least Hokma wasn't dragging a comb through her hair like Nimma always did the second she stepped indoors.

Hokma had slipped on a short green kimono, which she tied loosely over her hipbelt. From right to left, she pointed at the three interior doors: "Living room. Bathroom if you need it. Lab." With that, she gripped the carved handle and opened the door.

Astra realized she was trembling. Luckily Hokma's back was turned. She followed her Shelter mother into a large, luminous room, a proper, organized Or workspace, humming with industry and tingling with the scent of pine-water disinfectant. To her right, light from the front window danced over a stainless-steel countertop, a sink, a stove and a shuddering brushed-steel fridge, behind which glass doors gave a view of a back veranda and a grassy clearing. Jars of nuts, berries and grains

were arranged neatly on shelves above the countertop, which was like
a kitchen surface with cupboards and drawers beneath it. But the rest
of the room was all lab. Opposite Astra, an ergonomic chair knelt
beneath a long wooden table. One end was an easeled screendesk, its
black tail plugged into a socket in the blue-tiled floor; the rest was neatly
equipped with microscopes, scales, test-tube stands and, at the far end, a
large wooden crate. All of this paraphernalia was immensely impressive,
but the magnet that drew Astra's gaze was stationed in the center of the
room: a sleek, transparent alt-meat incubator.

Or's alt-lamb, -beef, -chicken and -fish came from a plant in New
Bangor. Next year Astra's class would go and visit it, but up until now
she'd only ever seen pictures of alt-meat incubators: giant industrial vats
stored in large buildings in all Is-Land towns and cities. Hokma's was
tiny in comparison; about a square yard in area and about a foot deep.
It rested on its table like a shallow aquarium filled with green algae.
Through the murky, bubbling liquid, Astra could see the artificial mouse
muscles growing from coils of polymer tubing, absorbing proteins from
the algae and fatty tissues from the biodegradable scaffolding.

She placed her fingertips on the incubator lid. The strips of pink
muscle immersed in their plant-based bath were peacefully flexing
in time to pulses emitted by the biodegradable tubing. "I like alt-fish
sticks," she said. "They're nice and flaky. And I like roast alt-chicken. I
think alt-beef is too tough, though. And Yoki says he wants to eat only
hydroponic vegetables now."

"Yoki might have to go and live with the Jain Gaians when he gets
older. And you'd better not tell him what we're going to do now."

Hokma stepped around the incubator and over to the wooden crate
on the desk. It was a vermicompost, Astra realized: there were holes in
the lid and a tray of liquid underneath it. Worms couldn't get too hot
or they died, so the big vermicompost boxes at Core House were housed
in a thick-walled lean-to. This one was small enough to keep indoors,
where the temperature wasn't *cold* but, she had to agree, cooler than
at home in the Earthship. Together Astra and Hokma lifted the lid.
Hokma took the worms from her hipbelt pouch and added them to the
compost. Astra stood on tiptoe and gazed down at the familiar sight of

red wigglers, clumped together like tiny pink socks in a drawer full of worm castings, vegetable scraps and earth. Or-soil was dry and dusty, but this humus was as rich as Nimma's fruitcake.

It was very strange, looking down at the worms knowing you were going to kill them.

"The bins at Core House are like worm hotels," she said. "But this one's sort of like a worm Death Ship, isn't it?"

Hokma put her hand on Astra's forearm. "Astra," she said quietly.

Astra turned, alarmed. What had she done?

"You must never talk about the Death Ships like that."

"Like what?"

"You mustn't ever compare the people in the Death Ships to worms. Remember, Elpis's father died in the Ships, and her mother had terrible dreams about them all her life."

She hadn't meant to insult Elpis or her parents. She *hadn't*. "But we're all Gaia's creatures," she defended herself. "Worms and people too."

"I know. But this vermicompost is like our beehives: a nice place for worker creatures to live, not a prison. You'll learn more about the Death Ships in Year Seven. Then you'll see what I mean."

"Oh." Astra picked at a splinter on the edge of the wormery. Maybe she shouldn't tell Hokma she'd called the Non-Landers slugs. "I'm sorry."

"That's okay. Now let's find some juicy ones, shall we?"

Hokma took a bucket from under the desk and pulled on a pair of biolatex gloves. One by one, she picked up a dozen worms, small ones the chicks could swallow easily, she said, and dropped them gently in the bucket. As they landed, Astra felt the little thumps echo in the pit of her stomach: *Doom doom. Doom doom.*

"Are you all right?"

Astra looked down into the bucket. The worms were tangled in a writhing knot around the edge, all seeking to escape in that slinky way worms had: squeezing their coils of muscles together into a blood-red bunch, then stretching out again into a thin pink ribbon to move forward. Klor had told her about a Gaian scientist in New Zonia who had used this principle of locomotion to design a better, less painful colon cancer detection camera, one that pulsed gently up inside the patient's body to take pictures of what was wrong. Like all Gaia's creatures, worms were so inspiring if you just stopped and observed them for a while.

One of the worms, the skinniest one, twitched its blind head as if beseeching her for help. Her mouth dried. "I guess."

"I know it's hard. But they aren't going to be hurt, not for a moment."

Hokma crossed the room, put the bucket on the stainless-steel counter and took down a cutting board from a shelf beside the fridge.

"Do you want to help? There's another pair of gloves here. You could pass me the worms."

It was a test—but she hadn't studied; she wasn't ready to take it. Suppose she squished a worm too hard and killed it by mistake? Astra shook her head dumbly.

"Okay." Her Shelter mother opened a drawer and took out a medical syringe and needle and a bottle of yellowish liquid. Holding the bottle up to the light, she filled the syringe from it. "This is a special solution I make up here," she said. "It paralyzes the worm and stops its hearts beating. It also contains a special Code sequence that will customize the chicks for particular IMBOD applications."

Astra only had one heart, not five, and right now it was shrinking in her chest into a tight, squirming little knot. "Are the worms Code-vectors, then?" she asked, trying to sound professional. "Like the Security Serum?"

"Exactly." Hokma reached into the bucket and plucked out a worm. She placed it on the cutting board. Pinned between her fingers, it contracted and expanded in a long, slithery S shape. Just at the point Astra thought of as the neck—though Torrent always said worms were like Mr. Banzan and didn't have necks—Hokma inserted the needle between two of the worm's muscles.

"It's just a tiny prick," she said as she depressed the plunger. "Far better than being stabbed to death by a blackbird."

The liquid drained into the worm and its crimson body rippled for a moment more, then it stopped moving and lay there on the board, limp and still.

"Can't you grow alt-worms in the alt-mouse incubator?" Astra asked. Her eyes felt wet and prickly and there was a lump in her throat.

Squeezing past it, her voice had turned all thin and squeaky. She felt her face turn red, but she couldn't cry. She couldn't let Hokma know she was upset. If she acted like Yoki, Hokma would decide not to tell her important things either.

"No, it's not big enough, and it's too expensive to run two." Hokma set the needle down and rested her wrist on Astra's shoulder. Her gloved hand, the hand that had just murdered the worm, hung in the air in front of Astra's face. "There's no need to cry, Astra," she said. "These worms have lived a very full life, much longer than they might have in the wild. And the Owleons protect us in all sorts of ways. They need to be fed."

Astra rubbed her eyes dry. "I know," she said, defiantly. "I just felt sad for a minute, that's all."

"That's okay," Hokma straightened up. "In life we often feel different emotions at the same time. Being able to do that is a sign of great strength."

Meem would be crying if she were here, and Yoki screaming. Torrent, though, would want to try out the needle. And Peat would ask questions. Astra swallowed. "My teacher said that complexity is difficult. Is that what she meant?"

"Partly, yes. Complexity is difficult in all sorts of ways. Now, are you sure you want to watch me kill the rest?"

Kill. The word ricocheted around the room like an acorn hitting glass, steel, skull. The sound of it hurt. But killing was what Hokma was doing, and Astra wanted Hokma to know she understood: killing was sometimes necessary.

She nodded and one by one, Hokma injected the rest of the worms. When she'd finished, she carefully lowered their dead bodies back into the bucket.

"They have returned to Gaia now." She stripped off her gloves and handed the bucket to Astra. The worms were arranged in motionless heaps, small pink spirals dotted across the bottom. Was she going to have to pick them up now? Was that the next test to fail?

Carrying the bucket with both hands, trying not to look at the worms, she trailed after Hokma through the sliding glass doors and onto the veranda. The wooden deck was supported by three massive stripped tree trunks and opened onto a wide, wild lawn behind Wise House; the long grass was studded with stumps and what looked like roughly made stools.

"Those are the perches," Hokma said. "I put the Owleons on them in the mornings."

Beyond the lawn a pinewood beckoned with raspy fingers. Between the trees was a row of brown hutches. *The Owleons.* The birds were invisible in the dark interiors, but Astra's heart lurched in her chest and she made toward the veranda steps.

"Not yet. The chicks are in here." Hokma strode past the frosted bathroom window to the door at the right end of the veranda where another wall jutted out at the back of the cabin.

Astra entered a swirl of shadows. Hokma flipped a switch and the living room window blinds silently retracted, letting light spill into another large room, this one lined with plants and shelves and smelling of sage and licorice tea. Oddly, the ceiling was higher in the middle of the room; that, Astra realized after a moment or two, was because there was a loft at either end, accessed by two sets of narrow steps running up the wall in an interesting V shape she instantly wanted to climb and jump between. The front loft, she quickly determined, held a futon and a lamp; she was standing beneath the other, beside a low-angled screendesk that faced out through the back window into the clearing. Some curious objects were lined up on the edge of the screendesk: several metal sticks displayed in a mug, and a row of bottles filled with blue, red and green water. These were even more interesting than the staircases and Astra was just going to ask Hokma about them when from the other side of the room came a faint scrambling and scratching, then a strange wheezy *psh psh psh.*

Beneath the front loft, a sofa and a comfy chair sat at angles to a handcrafted coffee table. The noises were coming from a large wooden box sitting on top of the table.

"Yes, wake up, my pretties." Hokma crossed the big greeny-blue rag rug on the floor. "I've got a friend I want you to meet."

Astra followed and knelt beside Hokma. She put the bucket down carefully between them and peered over the edge of the box.

"*Ohh!*" she whispered, recoiling.

There, blinking up at her, were three small balls of snowy-white fluff. Their wings were tiny, just little fingers of feathers, but what should have been the most adorable things she'd ever seen were disfigured by enormous hook-like beaks. It was a wonder the chicks could stand up, the beaks were so ridiculously big. They made the baby birds look like crabbed old men or ancient demons in fairytales: more than just old, a *million years* old.

"Why are they so *ugly?*" she blurted.

"Ugly?" Hokma smiled and offered her finger for the littlest bird to nip at. "You'll hurt their feelings."

As if seeking protection from Astra's disgust, the middle chick shuffled over and huddled against its bigger sibling. The tiny one was left stranded in the corner of the box. Like Mr. Banzan, it didn't seem to have a neck; its head simply emerged from its puffy body as if it were a tiny snowman. But then it stretched out a claw and turned toward her. Face-on, its beak curved like a crescent moon, its eyes were two onyx pools and its bewildered expression was framed by a heart-shaped ruff.

In an instant, Astra's heart was a puddle of love. "*Oooohh*," she cooed, "I'm *sorry.*"

"Astra, meet Copper, Amber and Silver." Hokma pointed to the birds from biggest to smallest. "Amber's a girl and Copper and Silver are boys. Normally it's hard to tell with birds, but I Coded them, so I know."

Astra couldn't take her eyes off Silver. "Why is he so *small?*"

"Silver is the youngest. The eggs are laid several days apart, so if the parents can't feed them, the oldest can eat the smaller ones and survive."

Astra's hand flew to her mouth. "Copper's not going to *eat* Silver, is he?"

"Not if we feed them plenty of worms."

Hokma reached into the bucket, pinched a dead worm between her thumb and forefinger and dangled it over the box. When Copper seized the creature's body in his beak, Hokma let it drop. As the three chicks jabbed and clawed at the worm, she nudged Astra. "They're Coded to be assertive. But if you give them another one, they won't have to fight."

This was the moment. Astra peeked into the bucket. Waiting in their spirals, the worms looked like tiny pink ziggurats, the ancient desert temples the school hallway wallscreen sometimes showed. Hokma would say the worm-temples were there to help her worship Gaia. And if Astra didn't pick one up to feed the Owleons, Hokma might say she could never come back to Wise House. But she didn't want to touch their lifeless bodies with her bare hands.

"Can I wear a pair of gloves?" she whispered.

Hokma laughed. "Okay—but you'll have to wash them afterward. I'm not wasting expensive lab gloves on a squeamish girl."

Hokma went back into the lab. Astra sat waiting, her stomach squeezing. Hokma thought she was being silly, but she *was* going to feed the Owleons. She *was*. Then Hokma would see she was a good Wise House worker. She just needed some practice, that was all.

The biolatex gloves Hokma returned with were way too big for Astra and the tips of the fingers flopped into the bucket. She chose a worm, hoping it wasn't the one that had looked up at her. As she pressed her fingers around it she flinched, half expecting a current of pain to jolt up her arm. But there was nothing: the worm felt squidgy through the eco-latex, no different from a living one.

She picked it up and quickly dropped it in the box in front of Silver. The little Owleon pounced and sucked up its meal with three gulpy hops.

Astra laughed. "He likes it!"

"He certainly does. Worms are their natural food, Astra, so we're working in harmony with Gaia when we feed them."

Hokma fed Copper, dangling the worm so it could slide down the chick's throat, and Astra tried that next with Amber. It was like the Tablette films she'd seen at school: steppe farmers feeding baby lambs with a bottle. Soon she was eagerly picking up worms and cheering as the Owleons gobbled them down. Then the bucket was empty and the chicks were waddling around, bumping into each other and the sides of the box.

She sat back on her heels, her heart shining in her chest.

Hokma scooped up Silver. "Do you want to hold him?"

Oh! "Yes, please!" Astra pulled off her gloves and cupped her hands and Silver, light as a dandelion seed head, explored her palms. The chick's long claws gently clutched at her fingers as if trying to pry them up into the air.

Her heart began to evaporate. "I feel like I can fly now," she whispered.

"I know. I called my own Owleon Helium because of that feeling."

"Can I see him too?"

"Not today. He's on his way back from Atourne."

"Is he on a secret IMBOD mission?"

Hokma laughed. "If he was and I told you, he wouldn't be anymore."

Astra flushed. It wasn't a stupid question. Owleons were sneakernets, everyone knew that. They carried memory sticks and encryption keys on their leg clips, classified material that was too sensitive to trust to the internet. That's why they were half-pigeon Coded—so they could be trained to fly between home bases—and half-owl Coded, so they would live a long time and fly silently at night, when it would be harder for criminals to see them. In the cities, some rich people used them for love letters and junk like that, but the Or Owleons were all professional IMBOD Code couriers.

"I didn't mean *secret*," she corrected herself as Silver nearly toppled over in her hands. "I meant *important*."

"I know what you meant, but no, he's just on a regular update flight." Hokma stood up. "You can see Helium when he gets back, but right now I have to talk to you about something very important."

"About my IMBOD Service?" Astra sprang to attention. This mission wasn't over yet.

"Yes, partly. Let's go outside. You might need to ask Gaia for Her wisdom."

That was unexpected. Astra opened her mouth, then closed it again. She wasn't sure if she was allowed to ask Gaia for Her wisdom: Klor and Nimma always said that was only for emergencies. They said the Pioneers had asked all the main questions about how to live in Is-Land and they were happy to follow the guidance She had given them. Because if everyone was out in the woods all the time pestering Gaia with personal dilemmas, what would happen to the kitchen dishes and all of

Or's IMBOD contracts, not to mention the Boundary? The best way to commune with Gaia, Klor and Nimma said, was to work hard to revere and defend Her: if Gaia really wanted to speak to you individually, She would visit you in a dream.

But Sheba had been an emergency, and Klor had asked Gaia for help then. Was this an emergency too? If so, no one had properly prepared Astra for it.

"I don't know how to do that," she said doubtfully.

"That's okay. I'll teach you." Hokma stood. "Come on. We'll go up on the roof."

Astra put Silver down gently back inside the box and scrambled to her feet. "Can Tabby come?" she asked. "Gaia might help make him better."

"Okay. But he has to stay in your pac until we get to the top."

Housecoats off, sandals and boots on, Tabby secured in his transport, the mission was back on the move.

1.4

"I like to sit there when I'm speaking to Gaia." Hokma pointed at a clump of poppies near the middle of the roof meadow. "Beside Her vision plant."

They had climbed the ladder at the side of Wise House to get up to the roof. The sky was paler now, the sun a diffuse orb, and even though it was only ten past five, Hokma had let Astra come outside without her flap-hat. All around them the early evening light was gilding the long grasses and wildflowers that first Ahn, then the forest winds, had seeded for Hokma. At the Earthship Nimma kept the outer botanical cells full of white flowers, daisies and lilies and yarrow, transplanting anything else that seeded; here though, within the gilded border of wallflowers and wild cosmos, was a whole Tabby paintbox splattered all over the L-shaped roof. Disturbing damselflies and red admirals, Astra bounded through blue flax and cornflowers, pink-tinged daisies, yellow dandelions, magenta sweet williams, purple and crimson and gold baby snap-dragons and a host of other blossoms she couldn't identify yet. At the tall poppy crown she grasped a hairy stem and pulled its flimsy scarlet flower to her face. "I love you!" she declared and settled herself down on the grass. Hokma joined her, arranging herself in half-lotus.

"Look—Or's flower!" Astra pointed at a stand of spider orchids, the plant Or was named for.

Hokma smiled. "Ahn brought them up from Core House lawn. What's an Or building without orchids?" She paused. "And Or-kids. It's wonderful to be able to invite you here at last, Astra."

Astra didn't know how to say how much she loved being here. Instead she bent over an orchid and gently fingered its lime-green sepals and big brown velvety lip. When Klor had given the Or-kids their first orchid lesson at Code House, he'd said that the mouths of the flower were called "labela." They enticed insects deep inside to the anther lobes, which were pollen sticks that got stuck on the bugs' heads—standing up like antlers at first, but then falling down like Yoki's floppy fringe—so that when the insects flew away they carried the orchid's pollen to the stigma of another flower. Torrent and the older boys had teased Yoki all day after that.

"Klor says the orchid is one of the most efficient flowers in the meadow," she told Hokma. "Not like us Or-kids, he said."

"They're certainly one of the most beautiful. I love the purple H on the lip: H for Hokma, Ahn says."

The labelum's three shiny purple stripes did make an H shape: Astra had never thought of it as Hokma's flower before but of course it absolutely was. "*I* think they're efficient *and* beautiful. Like you," she blurted.

"Like me?" Hokma raised her dark eyebrows.

Astra's face burned, but she couldn't stop now. "Yes—you breed the Owleons *and* you're the School Spoke of the Parents' Committee, and Ahn said that you used to be one of the most beautiful women in Is-Land."

"Did he now?" There was an edge to Hokma's voice that made Astra's face flare as hot as one of Nimma's pancake pans. Actually, when you thought about it, it sounded like Ahn was saying that *now* Hokma was old and ugly. But he hadn't meant that at all, she was sure. *There goes a formidable woman*, Ahn had said to the head of an Old World delegation as Hokma passed by the vegetable garden on her way to Code House. Astra had been weeding, not exactly hiding, but the grown-ups hadn't paid her any attention. Astra hadn't known what "formidable" meant— she'd asked Tabby later—but the visitor had nodded and added, *She's certainly very handsome*. Then Ahn had sounded almost puzzled. *I suppose she is now*, he'd replied, *but when she was younger she was one of the most beautiful women in Is-Land.*

Defiantly, Astra continued, "*I* think you're still beautiful. I hate dangly earrings and silly grass skirts." Oh dear. That wasn't right either. "Except when Nimma wears them, I mean," she concluded, stupidly.

Now Hokma really laughed: a throaty peal that echoed out across the roof and into the woods. "Thank you, Astra." Then, though she was still smiling, she sounded serious again. "But Ahn knows that all women are beautiful. We're all different faces of Gaia. You're beautiful too."

Astra grimaced. "I don't want to be beautiful. I want to get my Security shot and be smart and strong and do my IMBOD Service and be a great scientist and win an IMBOD medal." She jutted out her chin. "I want to be a Boundary constable and patrol the Southern Belt when it's my turn, like you did. I want to help save Is-Land from the Non-Landers when they attack us again."

For a moment Hokma's face tensed as though she'd sipped something nasty by mistake. But when she spoke, her voice was as deep and calm as a morning lake. "Astra, did you like feeding the Owleons?"

Astra wiggled on her butt. The grass was tickly, but it felt nice. "Uh huh. Especially Silver."

"And would you like to feed the chicks every day, and when they are old enough, help me to train them to fly?"

Astra gawked at Hokma. Her Shelter mother's olive skin was burnished by the lowering sun. She was more than beautiful: she was like a Buddhist Tara, shining with mysterious knowledge. She had set a test, an enormously difficult spiritual test, and Astra had *passed*. "*Yes*," she yelped.

"I thought you would. But first I have to know: can you keep a secret?"

That was easy. Tabby and Astra had lots of secrets. "Definitely."

"Good, because I've brought you up here to ask you to make a choice. The choice is yours, but whatever you decide, this conversation has to be a secret between you, me and Gaia. If you tell anyone about it I will get into trouble—big trouble. I might even get taken away, and you wouldn't see me anymore, maybe never again. Do you understand what I'm saying, Astra?"

Sunlight still hung in golden scarves across the meadow but suddenly Astra felt cold. She rubbed her arms. "Why? Who would take you away?"

Hokma paused. "IMBOD might, because IMBOD has a plan for Is-children that I don't agree with. If you want to take part in their plan, you can, but I want to explain it to you first so that you can make up your own mind."

It was as if Astra had swallowed a pebble, but instead of getting warm inside her tummy, it was turning into a lump of ice. "But IMBOD takes care of Is-Land," she protested. "They only want what's good for us. Don't they?"

Hokma lifted a warning finger. "I'm not saying that IMBOD is bad, okay? I never said IMBOD is bad, did I?"

The ice pebble throbbed in her tummy. "No."

"But sometimes I question their methods. And this is one of those times."

Oh. Maybe sometimes Chief Inspectors disagreed with the Chief Commissioner's national strategy, just like constables sometimes secretly argued with CIs. "You mean," Astra asked, "it's like when *I* know that I could stay up late and still be fine in the morning, but *Nimma* says I have to go to bed?"

"Yes, it's a bit like that." Hokma's upper lip was glistening with tiny speckles of sweat. She wiped her face with her hand, pushing her fingertips just under her eyepatch for a second. "Astra, I don't want you to have your Security Serum shot tomorrow."

It was like Klor saying that two plus two made five, or Yoki claiming that he didn't like ice cream. An error message flashed up on Astra's brainscreen. "But *everyone* wants to have the Security shot." She laughed, and for a moment the ice pebble melted. Hokma hadn't had the school prep talk—she just needed to be told the facts.

"The Serum makes your muscles and emotions stronger, and your brain work faster at Code. We need it to help us build the Shell."

"It does do those things; that's true," Hokma said slowly. "But it does other things as well. It will make you less sensitive and more willing to follow orders. These are good qualities in constables, but not so good in scientists, are they?"

The error message was replaced with a whole new study-level page. Sometimes learning was complicated, Astra had discovered. It wasn't always like putting one brick on top of another. Sometimes you learned something that changed what you had learned before—like moving from whole numbers to fractions and negative numbers. When you were little you thought a number was real and solid, like a chair, but then you learned that a number was a concept and in conceptual space all kinds of strange things could happen. Still, she'd never *ever* thought that IMBOD Rules were concepts. That was like walking through the forest and suddenly realizing you were stepping along the edge of a cliff. Astra pulled her hydropac onto her lap to have Tabby near.

"I thought it was good to be less sensitive," she said finally. "Klor says Yoki's too sensitive sometimes."

Hokma plucked a blade of wild grass and stroked its seedpods. "Klor loves Yoki," she said, "but he isn't very sensitive himself, so he sometimes can't understand Yoki's reactions to the world. Yoki finds bright lights and noise over-stimulating, and he gets upset if other children tease him. You're not as sensitive as that, but you're curious and alert—you notice a lot of details in your environment, and you understand how other people are feeling. Don't you?"

She wasn't sure if Hokma was praising or criticizing her. "Sometimes. I guess," she admitted.

"Last summer, when Elpis had her stroke and Nimma was upset, you organized the other children to go and pick wildflowers for Nimma, didn't you? We talked about it then." Hokma gently set down the grass stem. "We thought you might feel especially sad for Nimma because you didn't have any memories of your own Birth-Code mother."

Astra padded her hydropac down into her lap. Tabby liked to feel snug. "I did, a bit."

"But not all the children felt like you," Hokma continued. "Some just picked the flowers because you told them to, and then they raced off and started playing, didn't they? If you have the Security shot, you'll become more like those children. Physically and emotionally you won't feel pain so much, but also you won't be able to perceive so easily what other people—or animals—are thinking or feeling. You won't be so curious about the world, and your language skills will level off quite quickly. You won't be able to make up tongue-twisters so easily, or enjoy poetry, unless you're reciting it with other Or-children. The world will seem much simpler to you, and you'll hardly remember when you used to ask questions all the time. You might make a good lab technician one day, but you'd never be a great scientist. I think that would be a terrible waste of your gifts, and that's why I don't want you to have the shot."

It was like being told that you had to leap off that cliff edge now and walk on thin air.

"I don't understand," Astra whispered. "Why does IMBOD want to change me—and all the other Or-kids—like that? Why don't they want to have good scientists anymore?"

"It's complicated. Personally, I don't think IMBOD has thought it through properly. The first batch of test subjects are now fourteen. They are happy and healthy, and they have always scored well above average on their Code exams. But scientists like me are very concerned about their Language and Creative Problem-Solving scores. Usually, on any test, some children score high, and others low, and the mean average, if the test is a good one, is in the sixty-five-to-seventy range. But the test subjects have all always achieved an average score on their Language and CPS exams. No one ever gets a low grade or fails, but no one gets eighty or ninety either, or even seventy-five. People like me have been arguing that children should be pretested and those with an aptitude for creative thinking shouldn't have the shot. But IMBOD says that average scores across the board are a good result. I think they'll regret it one day and change the policy, but that will be too late for you."

Astra examined her hand. It still ached, and the scratch stung. "It would be good not to get hurt so much anymore," she offered.

"Pain tells you that there's something wrong, Astra. Everyone needs a little bit of pain in life, even emotional pain."

"But I want to be stronger, and learn Code fast, like all the test subject kids. Can't I just have that part of the Security shot?"

"Unfortunately not. The Serum comes as one inoculation. I wouldn't be able to request the separate components without someone asking why."

Astra reached for her hydropac. "I'm going to ask Tabby what he thinks."

Hokma placed her hand on Astra's wrist. "Astra, you promised to keep this a secret and that means you can't ever tell Tabby about this conversation. Tabby is programmed to tell IMBOD everything you ask him. That's for your security, but it means you have to be extra careful now. You can never web-search anything we've discussed here today."

Beneath her, the cliff vanished. Astra was flailing in midair with an ice stone in her tummy while Tabby twirled out of her hand to the ground far below. But Hokma wasn't reaching out for her to pull her to safety. Hokma was regarding her seriously, not as though Astra was lost in space with nothing to grab on to, but as though she was in the Quiet Room doing her homework and Hokma was patiently waiting for her to add up her figures and come to the right answer.

She wasn't falling, though. Somehow she was floating, suspended in a strange new world. She put her hydropac aside. "Hokma," she said at last.

"Yes, Astra?"

"Do you think my Birth-Code mother would have wanted me to have my Security shot?"

"No, Eya wouldn't have wanted you to. That's why I'm talking to you now. I promised Eya that I would always look out for you. But I can't make a major decision for you, especially not one that involves a great deal of risk. So you have to choose what you want to do."

But how could she decide? The whole equation was a jumble of unknown variables and millions of minus signs. "Will IMBOD take *me* away?" she squeaked.

At last, for the first time ever, Hokma reached into the void and pulled Astra into her lap, into her big, warm nest of muscle and bone. "No, they won't," she promised as Astra pressed her cheek against her chest. "If we get found out, they'll blame me. But if you learn to act like the other children we won't get found out. That means keeping a very big secret from everyone, even Klor and Nimma—*especially* Klor and Nimma. It means you will always have to be on your guard."

Hokma's heart thudded steadily in her ear like a distant drum—the deep booming drum a constable played to pass emergency messages along the Boundary. Astra pulled away. "I can't tell Klor and Nimma?"

"Not yet. They wouldn't understand. Later, when they can see you're okay, we might decide to tell them."

Hokma's lap was like her: strong, but hard to get comfortable in. Astra shifted between her thighs. "But what if they find out? What if they get upset with me?"

"They won't find out." Hokma hugged her tight for a moment. "Look, Astra: up until now you've lived with Klor and Nimma and just spent time with me during the day, but now that you're older, I'm going to be a more involved Shelter parent. We can spend more time together, and sometimes you can stay with me at Wise House. If your behavior is different from the other children's, Klor and Nimma will think it's because of my influence. And"—she paused, then kiss-whispered into Astra's black mop of hair—"if you don't get your shot, I can teach you to train Silver. How does that sound? Do you want to be my special helper with the Owleons?"

It was an *unbelievable* question. The best, most exciting, most amazing question anyone had *ever* asked her. Astra's own heart did a cartwheel, right off the roof and into the sky. When at last it landed back in her chest, though, she felt a little sick: *of course* she wanted to be Hokma's special helper with the Owleons. But how could Hokma ask her not to have her shot? And keep it secret from everyone? She leaned against Hokma's breasts. "What if I *do* have my shot," she asked, "and I become like all the other Or-kids? Can I still come and stay with you?"

"Absolutely." Hokma patted her back. "I'll always love you the same, no matter what. But you'll have to stop wriggling when you sit on me, how's that for a deal?"

Astra slid off Hokma's lap, but stayed sheltered beneath her arm. Hokma loved her. She must if she said so, and wanted her to come and help at Wise House. But if she loved her so much, then surely she wanted Astra to be happy? "So if we do that," she ventured, "I mean, if I have my shot and come and stay sometimes, can I still feed the Owleon chicks?"

"Yes—but you couldn't train them. You need to be sensitive to do that: you need to be able to listen and watch, to recognize how they are feeling and discover how to train them better in the future. That way you'll learn how to be a great scientist."

Oh. Astra gently stroked the scratch on her hand. "I don't want to only memorize Code," she whispered, hopelessly. "I want to be a super-smart scientist like you and Klor. I want to train Copper and Silver and Amber and make hypotheses and big discoveries."

"I know you do, Astra. That's why I'm giving you this choice."

The pebble wrenched around again in her stomach. "But I have to have my shot," she wailed. "It's the *law.* They're coming to school tomorrow to give it to all of us. I don't want to get into trouble, and I don't want you to get taken away. And—" She gulped, and said, "I want to do my IMBOD Service and catch Non-Landers like the girl in the tree." She hid her face in her arms. She was useless. She had nearly failed Hokma with the worms and she was going to fail her again now, up here on the roof meadow.

Hokma shook her by the shoulders. "Astra, I have a plan for tomorrow. If we work together and trust each other, no one's going to get taken away. And you can still do your IMBOD Service. You'll just have to follow special, secret orders from now on."

Astra couldn't listen anymore. It was too much. Hokma's tests were too hard. She'd had to watch her kill worms and now she was being told not to have her shot and to grow up different from every other kid in Is-Land. This was an emergency, yes, a very big emergency. She disentangled herself from Hokma's arms. "*I don't know what to do,*" she shouted.

"I know—I know it's a very difficult choice. That's why I brought you here. So you could ask Gaia to help you make your own decision."

"But how do I do *that*?"

"Different people have different ways. I usually sit quietly and ask Gaia to send me a sign."

"What *kind* of a sign?"

"It could be anything—something living, or a cloud, even a picture in your mind. I usually close my eyes to start, then if nothing comes to me, I open them and see what happens."

If Klor had done it and Hokma did it, it must work. And at least if she closed her eyes she could try to not think about anything at all. The sunshine made the inside of her eye lids orange. Actually, it was nice like this. If she breathed quietly and didn't move, the ice pebble stayed still too. If she breathed deeply, into her stomach muscles, the ice even melted a little around the edges. Hokma was quiet as well. Around them, the forest birds chattered and cooed.

Astra opened her eyes. In the far distance, between the gap in the trees, a narrow segment of steppe rolled to the horizon; in front of her in the meadow, an emerald-black beetle crawled out from beneath a dock leaf and waddled away. Right beside the toe of her left sandal a bee dozily nuzzled an orchid.

It wasn't as if a big sign lit up and flashed the answer in her head. It was more like watching the sun rising in the morning and gradually making things clear. Most of the spider orchid stems were tall, with several blossoms each, growing close together, but the flower the bee was suckling was alone.

"Look, Hokma." She pointed at the orchid. The bee was clinging to it now, almost pulling the stem over with its weight. "That stem's only got one flower. And it's all by itself, next to me. Do you think that's a sign?"

"Maybe. What do you think?"

Astra leaned over the plant. The bee flew away and she noticed something strange: the purple vertical lines on the lip *met at the top*.

"Hokma," she gasped, "it's got an *A*. Not an H."

"Really?" Hokma reached over and touched the orchid. "Well, look at that."

Astra's face was glowing, her heart singing. "A for *Astra*. Gaia's giving me Her wisdom, Hokma! She's telling me that I'm *supposed* to be different from the others. That I shouldn't have my shot. That's the answer. For sure. One hundred percent."

"Good girl. Now listen carefully. This is the plan."

As the long fingers of the sun stroked her hair and striped Hokma's cheeks, Astra listened and remembered and wondered, in a small room in her mind, if somewhere in one of the tall spiky pine trees that surrounded them, the Non-Lander girl was watching and waiting for all the Or-kids to grow up dull and stupid. Well, maybe they would. But *she* wouldn't; *she* would stay smart. She would catch the Non-Lander girl and help train the Owleons and grow up to be a famous scientist, and Hokma would love her the way a Birth-Code-Shelter mother loved her child.

1.5

Passing through West Gate hand in hand with her Shelter mother, Astra felt like a giant, striding into Or in seven-league boots, taking command of everything she saw. Here was her innocent community, anchored in its mountain valley by the central hub of Core House and Craft House, a cozy cluster of old stone walls, cedar extensions and solar roofs. Spiraling out like petals from the two main buildings were Or's vegetable, herb and flower gardens, its fruit orchard and beehives, sports field and kidney-shaped swimming pool: a blossom of industry, health and nutrition, all surrounded and powered by the red Kinbat track. Above the track on East and West Slope rose tiers of Earthships, the best homes in all the world—Astra grew another yard taller as she surveyed them. Earthships hugged Gaia, Klor said. Their curved soilbag walls kept their interiors cool in the summer and in the winter stored the low rays of the sun that flooded in though their front greenhouse corridors, which grew fruit and vegetables all year round. Earthships also had colorful mosaic walls made of old bottles, roof cisterns to harvest the rain and flower-full botanical cells to treat the water for drinking, washing, gardening and toilet flushing. Earthships generated electricity from solar panels and wind turbines, and even in cold climates they were warm enough to grow mangoes inside. Everyone on the whole planet should live in an Earthship—but Is-Land was the only country in the world to make them the main rural habitat. Astra's heart glowed as she picked out hers in the lowest ring on East Slope, a ray of pride smoldering like the amber sunlight striking the massive glass curves of Code House, Ahn's prize-winning building and the jewel in Or's crown. Code House sprouted out of North Slope like an enormous shelf fungi, but today, for the first time, Astra didn't feel tiny like an ant when she looked at it. She was a great Wise House scientist now, and a secret IMBOD patrol officer in the forest. Soon Or would need her to survive.

She and Hokma crossed the Kinbat track, avoiding a few sprinting Or-kids and jogging or wheeling Or-adults who were making their daily contribution to Or's electricity supply. Back in Core House she moved as if in slow motion as she jostled for a seat at the Or-kids' dining table, protected from pointy elbows and hard chair corners by an invisible aura of power and knowledge, as if she were suddenly a whole epoch older and wiser than all her Or-siblings. She might later tell Torrent and Peat about the worms—Hokma had said she could—but for now she just smiled as the older boys play-punched each other and squabbled over the breadbasket. Then Yoki peeled back his plaster and showed her the cut on his thumb from kitchen duty—a raw flap of skin exposing scarlet flesh—and of course she had to show him her bruised hand.

"How did you get that?" he asked, his eyes brimming with imagined pain.

"I was chasing the Non-Lander girl," she boasted.

"Oh, so she's a *Non-Lander* now, is she?" Torrent scoffed from across the trestle table. His nose, shoulders and chest were peeling because he always neglected to reapply his sun lotion like the lighter-skinned kids were supposed to. Before Astra could call him "Lizardman," Meem whipped out Blotto, her Tablette.

"I arrested eight infiltrators today!" she crowed, shaking her big honey-colored Afro. "A whole family and three loners."

"Hope you remembered to build a prison," Torrent teased.

Astra narrowed her eyes. Torrent had better not try to make Meem cry. Astra had already played Operation Is-Land straight through to Level Five, twice, but Meem was still a baby and you had to encourage her. She'd spent the last week helping Meem complete Foundation Level. Together they'd marshaled Meem's starting forces of CONC officers and brave Gaian Pioneers into squadrons and put them to work establishing the Boundary, detoxifying the soil and rebuilding the infrastructure. Throughout the country, Meem's squadrons had repaired roads, reintroduced rodents, reptiles and other small fauna, torn down unsafe buildings and retrofitted others with PV panels and rain vats. On the steppes she'd established solar panel fields, sited wind farms in locations free of bats and birdlife and sowed the first crops of nitrogen-fixer grains. In the ash fields Meem had built Is-Land's first and largest geothermal plant, and the continental server it would heat and power. In the White Desert, she had established salt and crystals mines; in Bracelet Valley she had planted fruit and nut orchards; in the dry forest she had begun the extensive work of regreening the mountains; and in Atourne she had founded Code and Craft College. All the while, Meem had also—of course—erected lookout posts along the Boundary, digging ditches and unrolling barbed wire between them, all the while forcing back or containing the first thin waves of Non-Landers. It was inevitable, in this vulnerable stage of Is-Land's development, that some infiltrators would manage to get a toe-hold in caves and rough camps, but Meem's squadrons had rounded all of them up and she was holding them in prison outside Atourne. Yesterday her Foundation Level had ended and her Level One had begun.

"*Doh.*" Meem stuck up for herself for a change, showing Torrent her map with the prison in Atourne already at near-capacity. Level One policing was difficult. Half of your CONC forces had left, and though more Gaians were arriving every week in cavalcades of buses trundling overland from Neuropa, Himalaya and Nuafrica, now that the country was habitable again determined Non-Landers were launching fresh assaults, surging through unguarded gaps in the Boundary and through tunnels in the soft earth of the steppes. It took a lot of time to round up infiltrators because they just kept coming: no matter how big you made your first prison, it was always soon bulging.

"Might be time to build another one," Torrent laughed. "Did you budget for that?"

Next to him, Peat put down his own Tablette and sternly assessed his Birth-Code sister. "What length sentence are you giving them?" he asked.

"A year," Meem replied, a note of doubt in her voice.

"That's not a big enough deterrent," Peat told her. "You'll get floods more."

"They'll hunt your rabbits and birds," Yoki piped up. "Your biodiversity score will go down."

Astra peered over Meem's shoulder at Blotto. "Peat's right, Meem. If too many more infiltrate, you won't be able to arrest them all. They could squat in old villages and then you'll never get to Level Two."

"So what do I do now?" Meem fretted.

"You can put them back on trial for killing Gaia's creatures," Yoki offered. "I gave maximum sentences for that."

"But I don't have any evidence."

"So?" Yoki's eyes flashed. "*Obviously* they ate rabbits and birds. They're alive, aren't they? And check their clothes: I bet they're wearing leather."

Torrent had been joking with the twins, but he turned away from Brook and Drake and barged back into the conversation. "If she charges them all with new offenses she'll overload her court system," he announced. "This is Level One: you can't get bogged down in bureaucracy."

Yoki shrank back into his seat but Astra faced the older boy. "She can do what she likes, Torrent," she retorted.

"Can't I just increase the sentences I already gave them?" Meem asked Peat.

Astra had sentenced infiltrators to ten years right from the start, so she didn't know if that was possible. But Peat, as always, had an answer. He replied briskly, "Technically, no. But you can create a new law, saying that infiltrators will only be released if they sign a contract acknowledging they have no rights to live in Is-Land, and vowing never to come within fifty miles of the Boundary again. If they don't sign, they stay locked up. Bingo."

Peat thought he was such a legal hotshot, but sometimes he was just plain dumb. "But they'd just sign the contract and then break it," Astra objected.

Peat tapped his temple. "It's psychological, Astra. They're in the spotlight. The embedded press are there and the whole world is watching them. They want it to look like *we're* being unreasonable. So they refuse to sign. For sure."

"Then you'll have to police those fifty miles," Torrent warned. "Don't do it, Meem."

Brook and Drake laughed, but Peat was stung. "It makes sense to plan for a buffer zone," he said hotly. "Whatever happens, you know Non-Landers are going to mass along the Boundary. Might as well establish a police presence early."

Meem's lower lip was trembling. Not a good sign.

"Peat's right, Meem," Astra told her, casting a haughty glance at Torrent. "You'll need to patrol the Boundary, whatever happens. Do it."

Torrent made an *Ooh ooh, look at you* face, but Meem straightened up and wiggled in her seat. "Okay. Here goes." She tapped on her Justice icon, lifted Blotto to her lips and voice-introduced the new law. Immediately, there was a small international outcry. Even Brook and Drake looked impressed.

"Now what do I do?" Meem pleaded.

"It's nothing," Peat reassured her. "Just Asfar and a few NGOs. CONC hasn't reacted, has it?"

She checked her CONC icon.

"Asfar has issued a formal objection, but no other member state has signed it."

"Good. Now you should respond with a strongly worded statement to the effect that Gaians donated our nitrogen-fixer grain Codes in good faith and we have every right to protect Is-Land from those who have abused our gift to the world."

"C'mon, Peat," Torrent objected. "You can't play the game for her. She's got to make her own decisions."

"I'm her legal consultant," Peat claimed as Meem pressed her Tablette to her lips again.

"Shhh," Astra hissed.

"Yeah, shhhh everyone," Yoki echoed.

The table fell quiet, even Brook and Drake.

"Dear Council of the New Continents," Meem started. "Because of Gaians, the whole world can grow wheat and rice and all other crops without poisonous fertilizer. You promised that in return we could have our own country and live the way we wanted to. We live in Is-Land now, and we are making it habitable again and reintroducing lots of animals. People who kill Gaia's creatures and wear their skins and think that humans are better than everything else can't live here. That's what you promised. The Non-Landers have to promise to leave us alone, or else they have to stay in jail."

Meem held Blotto up so they could all hear the result of her diplomacy. In a matter of moments the outcry subsided into murmurs of dissent, which then faded into just a lone objection barely audible against the hubbub of the dining room.

"See," Peat crowed. "You can't be too nice, Meem. CONC respects the Boundary, and they'll keep Asfar in check."

BRRRZZZZ. BRRRZZZZ. BRRRZZZZ. TING. TING. TING. Blotto nearly jumped out of Meem's hand, he was vibrating so hard.

"*Level Two,*" Meem gasped.

"Excellent," Peat chuckled.

"But . . . that means I have an *armed* infiltrator!" Meem sounded panicked. "He might kill a pioneer."

"C'mon, let's all take a proper look." Torrent reached over, grabbed Blotto and rudely wrenched him open, enlarging him from handheld to tablet, then to notebook. He flattened Blotto out on the table.

"*Hey,*" Meem bleated as Blotto's plasma creases smoothed out and the game image spread into the enlarged screen.

"Torrent, the grown-ups will see!" Astra hissed.

But Torrent, Brook and Drake were all poring over the game. "It's a she—wow, an old gal. She's hiding in Code College," Torrent announced.

"*Fold him back up.*" Meem was starting to get agitated.

"C'mon, Torrent." Peat made a try for Blotto, but the older boy slapped his hand away.

Then he laughed, folded Blotto back into handheld mode and tossed him over to Meem, crying, "Catch!"

"*No—*"

But it was an easy throw and now Blotto was back in Meem's possession. As Meem studied the screen, Astra laid an arm on the table to protect her Shelter sibling from another attack. Beside her Yoki stood up and leaned over her shoulder, his belly warm against her arm. Sure enough, a shadowy robed figure was crouching in a college classroom, clutching a sub-machine gun to her chest. According to the game clock it was 8 a.m., so students and teachers would start arriving in an hour.

"What do I do now?" Meem squeaked.

"You're lucky: she's triggered an alarm. You have to alert Security and surround the college," Astra ordered. "*Quick.*"

Everyone leaned in to see as Meem hurriedly tapped the Security icon—then a familiar pale brown wrinkled hand, its forefinger adorned with a large beveled emerald ring, swooped down over the table and plucked Blotto from Meem's grasp.

"What did I say yesterday?" Nimma loomed above them, her silver pendant glinting between her long breasts, her gray-gold braids encircling her head like a crown. "*No Tablettes at mealtimes.*"

"But dinner's not here yet," Peat pointed out.

"And no talking back, either, or everyone's Tablette will be confiscated. Meem, come to me afterward and get Blotto back." With that Nimma tucked Blotto in her hipbelt pocket and swept on to her own table, the pink and jade faux-grass fronds stitched to her belt framing her majestic bottom.

"It's not fair," Meem pouted. "Now I'll get a massacre scored against me."

"Maybe she'll turn Blotto off," Peat said hopefully, looking at Nimma's retreating back. But as the Or-kids grumbled about Nimma's draconian punishments and general obliviousness to their need for education, Moon arrived from the kitchen, bearing dishes heaped with crispy alt-fishcakes and fries and Arjun followed carrying a platter full of steaming spring greens chopped up with garlic and leeks.

Soon they were all tucking in, and then Torrent was sticking two fries up his nostrils like a walrus and Astra was convulsing with laughter, thoughts of Non-Landers and worms, Owleons and secrets, all swept to the far shores of her mind.

After dinner she did her kitchen duty, helping with washing and drying and putting away. When she'd finished, she wandered back into the dining room. Peat was still there, playing Tablette games with the older boys, but she didn't try to join them as usual; instead she padded over to the Quiet Room to ask Klor to fix Tabby. But he wasn't there. Nimma, who was sitting on a comfy sofa knitting, said he'd taken Meem and Yoki back to the Earthship and then gone up to Code House.

"He won't be back until after your bedtime, darling."

"I'm not tired," Astra said, yawning.

"Aren't you now?" Nimma opened her arms. "Come on, let's cuddle, then it's off to the Earthship with you."

Nimma's lap was soft and plump and cushiony, the best lap in the whole world. Hokma's lap was like a sturdy alt-leather armchair, and Klor's was like a creaky wooden fence, but Nimma's lap was a feather comforter with a crêpey sateen coverlet. Tonight, however, even though Astra's eyes were heavy and sleepy and her body was sinking into Nimma's pillowy breasts, the lump in her tummy was back, feeling awkward and uncomfortable. If she went to bed she would fall asleep and then when she woke up it would be tomorrow, and she had promised to do something tomorrow she could never tell Nimma, never tell Klor.

Nimma was patting her hydropac pocket. "Goodness. What have you got in here? No wonder you're worn out."

"Hokma gave me some green almonds," she muttered.

"Oh, won't they be delicious," Nimma exclaimed, patting her shoulder. "Take them back home, darling, and put them in a bowl in the kitchen."

Astra felt like a green almond right now: all fuzzy on the outside, but hard on the inside. *Was that another Gaia sign?* she wondered. She needed to talk to Hokma again.

"Okay," she said, slipping out of Nimma's lap. "I'll just say goodnight to Hokma."

Hokma was reading in an armchair beneath the bioluminescence lamp. "How's your hand, Astra?" she asked as Astra leaned close.

"Okay," she said in a little voice.

"You know you can change your mind," Hokma whispered in her ear.

But close to Hokma again, enveloped in the glow of their secret, Astra didn't want to change her mind. She wanted Hokma to piggyback her to the Earthship and even though Nimma looked up from her knitting and said not to baby her, Hokma carried her out of the Quiet Room and Core House and up the path to East Slope. The night air was warm on her skin and the stars were scattered across the sky like salt on a jet-black tablecloth.

"Oof, you've grown, Astra," Hokma said as they crunched over the gravel, but she didn't put Astra down and make her walk. She carried her upstairs, tucked her up in bed and made sure her nightlight was on and Tabby safe on her bedside table. Astra wanted to ask Hokma to tell her the story about her Birth-Code mother, but she was so tired she couldn't get the words out, so tired she couldn't remember closing her eyes, couldn't remember Hokma leaving.

The next morning, Astra woke up an hour before Tabby normally yowled his alarm. Today he was broken and turned off, but her eyes were tickled open by the mild light tiptoeing in through the bamboo blinds that divided her room from the greenhouse corridor. She watched the light gently toying with the plants on the table, the dolls' hospital and building-block games on the shelves, Meem's bundled form in the next bed. Birds were bickering outside, and in the distance the gate to the vegetable patch clanged shut as one of the Or-adults went to pick some herbs for breakfast. Meem gave a hiccoughy gurgle and stretched her arm out from beneath her comforter. It was all so peaceful.

Except that Astra wasn't dozy and dreamy. She was wide awake and her tummy hurt.

Today was supposed to be the day she got her Security Serum shot, but instead it was the day she *wasn't* going to have her shot; it was the day she had to start pretending that she had.

She stared up at the ceiling where Klor had nailed a constellation of tin stars to reflect Tabby and Blotto's nightlights. Right now they were a soft metal gray. Hokma had said she could change her mind, but good scientists didn't make up their minds after just one trial. They got their research checked by other scientists. What if she asked Klor about the

Security shot? She had to see him anyway, to ask him to fix Tabby. She wouldn't tell him what Hokma had said but she could test out the topic with him. If Klor said that the shot would stop her being a great scientist, then she definitely wouldn't have it. But if he said that the shot would help her think better, then she would get it like everyone else and she'd ask Hokma if she could train the Owleons anyway, or maybe just Silver, not the IMBOD birds.

She sat up. Klor would be awake. He got up at 5 a.m. every day and went over to Code House to work for an hour and a half before returning to help Nimma get her, Meem, Yoki and Peat ready for school. All she had to do was go to Code House. She'd never done it before on her own, but no one had ever said she wasn't allowed to either.

She swung her legs out of bed and slipped her feet onto the cool, slate-tiled floor. The school had emailed Or to say that students had to wear something today—something special to mark the occasion—and Nimma had draped a yellow faux-grass hipskirt over her desk. Everyone *knew* she hated wearing skirts. Hokma would never have done that. Carefully, so as not to wake Meem, Astra tugged open her dresser drawer, stuffed the hipskirt back in and pulled out an armband for later. That would be formal enough. Then she put Tabby into her hydropac and crept out along the greenhouse corridor toward the stairs, stopping just long enough to pick a banana and a peach to eat on the way to Code House.

It was hot already, and as Astra passed Craft House she wished she'd showered before leaving the Earthship. But that might have awakened Nimma and anyway, by the time she reached the foot of North Slope she had forgotten her grimy skin. Code House loomed above her like a giant lantern, its glass chamber walls glimmering in the candy-pink and sherbet-orange dawn light. Code House was different every single time you looked at it. Standing on the empty Kinbat track beneath it, Astra marveled again at the massive glass and cedar structure that ten years ago had won a gold medal for Ahn in the annual International Biotecture Congress living building competition.

It wasn't just a living building but a working one, the Or-adults always proudly told international visitors. Teams of microclimate specialists worked in the two vast ground-floor chambers, managing a series of controlled-temperature grow rooms and developing tundra, rainforest and desert vegetation. On top of these giant greenhouse labs sat three smaller chambers, the indigenous plant labs. These chambers opened onto the sloping sod roofs that gave Code House its distinctive appearance; in this arable soil the scientists planted the seeds they'd Coded to grow in Is-Land's climate.

Klor was an Is-Land plant specialist and a Code House Co-Director. He worked in the central upper chamber. The smallest chamber in the top tier was Ahn's office—he wasn't a Code scientist, but he had designed the building so of course he could work there. His chamber was set off to the right and jutted out over the ground level like the prow of a ship. Astra had never been allowed inside it, and Ahn's windows were tinted so you couldn't even see his silhouette, but Klor said Ahn had angled the chamber so that he could see the Shugurra River and the steppes from his screendesk. One day Ahn would invite her to visit his office and she would see the river too.

The roofs of the upper chambers collected rain in the autumn like the Earthships, supplementing the water piped down from the tanks in the forest. The perimeters were planted with miniature fruit trees that hid the rainvats and blended the building into the hill foliage behind. Klor's roof was currently testing restricted-growth apple trees. Last autumn a lady had complained about the apples dropping onto visitors' heads, so Klor's team had fixed netting below the gutters, even though Ahn had objected to "the scar" on his design. Two weeks ago the trees had been black and tangled, like Astra's hair after a day in the forest. Now they were in blossom and Code House looked as if it was wearing pink eye shadow, like one of the older girls going to a dance in New Bangor. Later, in the summer, the grains on the main roofs would be high, shading the scientists at their desks, but today the plots were still just mounded earth. If Klor was looking out of his window, he might be able to see Astra dawdling on the Kinbat track. Just in case, she waved.

But Klor probably wasn't looking out of the window. Probably he was deep in Code Thinking, or what Hokma called "administrivia."

Klor didn't like that term. He took his administration duties very seriously. She'd heard other Or-adults tease him, saying that all he did before dawn was alphabetize their work schedules. "And that means I can tell you where to go!" he'd boom in reply.

She could still go back to bed . . .

But she mounted the steps to Code House as if she were a baby bee and the building a massive orchid, its labelum enticing her deep inside. Soon she was hovering on the decking outside the two lower chambers. In front of her were the two huge cedar doors to Core House and at the far end of the deck was the Owleon aviary: three tall wood and wire-mesh cages housing the six birds that flew to New Bangor and Sippur, delivering Code House discoveries to the IMBOD offices there. One of the birds, the little black-feathered one, was out on its perch.

The aviary was off-limits; only scientists were allowed to touch the Owleons. Or-kids could get in big trouble for going near them. Were there any scientists around? She stepped up to the left chamber window and cupped her hands to the glass, peering inside through her own reflection: a tiny black-haired figure framed by mirrored hills and a swirly pink sky.

During the day the chamber would be filled with a phalanx of scientists, intent on their tasks, but now it was eerily empty of people; now the computers and plants reigned. Deep in the chamber, ranks of glossy white sequencing machines stood like sentries, stiff at their stations, waiting to be powered up into a whirring sense of purpose. In front of them, the window was planted with a mass of tropical orchids; further down, in another temperature-controlled zone, was a wall of flowering cacti. These serpentine vines, spongy blossoms and spiky succulents were the mysterious silent royalty of Or. Code House was a palace, built to cater to their every need.

The sun was brightening and behind her she could hear people calling to each other on the Kinbat track. She'd come early and peek at the Owleons another day, but now she had to hurry up. She took three giant steps to the front doors. On the lintel were carved the words "Conscious Evolution." She placed her finger on the keypad and passed under Is-Land's founding creed into its most beautiful bastion: Code House.

The atrium was flooded with light. Resisting the temptation to bounce on the visitor sofas or explore the empty lower chambers, Astra mounted the cedar staircase that curved up like a helix from the center of the green slate floor. There was an elevator too, for wheelchair users, but it was wasteful for other people to ride in it. Besides, she liked climbing. Trailing her fingers along the polished banister, she gazed down into the rainforest micro-biome at the back of the atrium, hoping to spot the parakeets that occasionally flashed their vivid emerald feathers or the shy toucans who hopped from branch to branch in their ungainly, top-heavy way. She wished that Or could house rainforest animals too, so she could help feed baby monkeys and tapirs until they were ready to be reintroduced. But reintroduction animals had to be reared in their own countries, Klor had explained. Transporting them across vast distances was cruel. And besides, animals were a lot of work. "Do *you* want to shovel a tapir's poo every day before breakfast, Or-child?" he'd asked. "No? Well neither do I."

Thirty-two steps. She emerged from the staircase into the foyer between the upper chambers. This was her favorite place in all Or. Behind her, either side of the elevator doors, two corridors ran along the back of the building, one leading into the Urban Agriculture lab on the left, the other to Klor's Staple Crops lab on the right. In front of her was a massive window overlooking the living roofs of the lower chambers. These were the field labs where the urbag team tested high-vitamin miniature fruits and vegetables for balconies and patios and where Klor and his stapcro scientists planted new varieties of oats, barley, kamut, rye, wheat and spelled: Gaia's holy grains. When they were fully grown in the summer the grains were like a golden sea, the wind caressing their feathery spikelets and glumes, ruffling their bristly awns, so the whole roof seemed to flow on forever, wave after wave of goodness and beauty and hope for the whole wide world. Astra stepped forward, pressed her nose to the window and breathed a small cloudy patch on the pane.

Right now the most exciting thing out there was a big bag of horse poo at the head of the oat plot. But beyond the mounded earth the mountains parted and faint pink clouds trailed away over the steppes. Astra opened her heart and drank in the immense, distant beauty. Up until yesterday, when she'd climbed the pine tree, the vista from Code House roof was the most amazing view she'd ever seen. It was even better out in the furrows, with the sun on your skin and Klor talking to you and the visitors all about the miracle of new life sprouting everywhere. One day this last autumn the combination of Gaia's magnificence and Klor's eloquence had made one of the lady visitors cry. It was later that same day, Astra remembered, her nose grazing the glass, that Klor had cried too. Until yesterday, that had been the most important day in her life.

"It's not sexy!" Klor had announced. "It's not plums or hibiscus or . . . Venus fly traps," he'd said, winking at the lady visitors. They were older ladies, wearing strange cloth cups strapped over their breasts and flowery underpants beneath the faux grass skirts Nimma had lent them, but they'd all giggled like little Or-girls. "This work," Klor had raised his voice, "is the *bread of life*." Then, his right hip rolling ever so slightly as his mechatronic leg lifted and swung across the furrows, he'd guided the guests up and down the roof plots. Astra had tripped along behind, wearing her red rubber boots to keep her feet clean and carrying Klor's spade in case he asked a visitor to plant something. The spade was heavy and taller than she was but she'd carried it proudly and the visitors had smiled and nudged each other, and when Klor wasn't looking she'd let one lady take a Tablette photo of her. Klor had walked ahead listing Code House's accomplishments until finally they were all standing at the edge of the roof, overlooking Or and the steppes beyond. The visitors fell silent then, clustered around Klor as he gave his final speech, the sermon Astra herself knew by heart now. She thought she could hear it every day without getting bored.

"Friends," Klor had started, beaming, his big gravelly voice carrying over the roof, "Gaians are a resilient people. We suffered during the Dark Time—as did so many—but we never lost faith in our way of life, a way of life founded on the imperative human need and duty to form a sustainable relationship with our beloved Mother Earth. When we donated our patents for nitrogen-fixing wheat, rice and barley to the CONC seed bank, we gave humanity a vital tool to globally implement this clean, sane vision. No longer do farmers need to poison the earth with chemicals in order to produce high-yield basic crops. Three staple grains can now take the nitrogen they need from the air itself. A miracle, you might say—or perhaps you might suspect your eccentric Gaian preacher believes it to be one." He paused to let the ladies giggle again. "But no, this is not the act of a distant god; rather, it is the result of human intellect and moral vision working hand in hand. It is *conscious evolution*, the Gaian creed, in action. In return for our donation, we Gaians were given our own country, land that had lain blasted and empty since the Dark Time, and CONC protection to ensure Is-Land's security. In a world filled with refugees we do not take this immense blessing for granted. Rather, we see it as our duty to continue to develop crops that will grow and thrive in the unpredictable ecologies of the Regeneration Era." As the visitors murmured agreement, Klor gestured behind them at the harvest-time roof fields. "The grains you see here are resistant to drought and flood and a whole host of insects. All are high yield, biofortified and gender neutral, so their introduction will never threaten native species. Some contain bamboo Code, creating faster-growing crops for use in situations of severe food shortage. Unlike Code labs in other countries, we test all our crops thoroughly and without harming animals, using artificial stomachs and the very latest in computer modeling. This may make our seeds expensive, but we don't want innocent people to pay the cost of our work with their greatest treasure: their health." The visitors were all nodding now, even the gentlemen, like dolls with springs for necks. Everyone loved Is-Land, Astra knew, because Is-Land scientists were the best in the world. They gave people nutritious and delicious food, free of all the health problems other Code producers caused.

"But our work doesn't stop there," Klor went on as Astra mouthed the big words with him. "Here at Code House we innovate wherever we can. We've bred carnivorous jungle plants to serve as kitchen composters; we've Coded fungi to eat plastic; we've developed cacti bursting with biofortified milk for desert nomads to sow; we've ensured that every child in the world can study with a living lamp, a bioluminescent cactus sequenced with jellyfish Code."

He had forgotten Astra's favorite part, the reintroduced reindeers in Nenetsland, eating hardy and vitamin-enriched grass, but she didn't like to interrupt him. She leaned on the spade as he finished up, as always, with his hymn to Or.

"Now, of course, we in Or take pride in our accomplishments." Klor raised his palms to the air as if admitting a terrible crime. "But above all we are grateful people. Come." He beckoned, and a couple of lady visitors bravely joined him at the edge of the roof. "Look at our little community, our simple structures. Imagine, twenty years ago, just two dozen of us embarking on a self-sufficient lifestyle, worshipping Gaia in all our activities. My wife spun and sewed our hemp shirts and knitted our shawls and I planted the seeds of the first superfood avocados. Now we're a community of nearly three hundred people: scientists, artisans, gardeners, cooks—and children." He raised his voice for the end of his speech and the sentence that stirred Astra to her core every time she heard it. "Here in Or we live collectively, in the founding tradition of Is-Land. The land that was once too hot for human habitation is now a green light steadily glowing on the face of a ravaged planet."

Astra closed her eyes, imagining the emerald-green light of Is-Land spreading its fertile, healing rays all over the world. "I can only remind you," Klor continued, "that none of our work would be possible without the support of the Council of the New Continents, the Is-Land National Wheel Meet, and individual donors like your good selves. Any gift you care to make, however small, will be most welcome—but in my heart I wish only to give *you* something: a sense of hope and a belief that despite all our past mistakes, we human beings *belong* here, in the warm bosom of our mother Gaia."

Some of the visitors looked up at the sky; some of them made a cross on their chests. Some of the men stroked their long beards—and that's when the lady cried. Astra was standing right there and she saw her reach into her bag, take out a white hanky with pink stitching and dab her face, pulling her mouth down at the ends as she did so, maybe to make sure all the tears got squeezed out of her eyes.

She had reported this to Nimma, Meem, Yoki and Peat that night around the kitchen table when they were having their oatmilk and berry biscuits. *Today, Klor made a lady cry.*

"Do you know why my words touched them?" Klor asked. "It's because everyone is at heart a Gaian. Even if they revere a Holy Book, even if they worship science, everyone knows in their hearts that neither religion or science alone can give us *meaning*. People ten thousand years ago didn't have books or sequencing machines and yet there was still purpose and beauty to their lives. It is Gaia who gives life meaning, Or-children, and when Gaia took my leg back into her dark womb and I asked her why, She told me to stand up, use my mind and feed Her people."

It was part of the speech, the answer he gave if a visitor asked him why he became a Code scientist. Hearing it here at home made Astra frown. Of course she knew that Klor had lost his leg defending Gaia: nearly every Or-adult who was missing a limb or an eye or had burns on their face or muscle tremors or used a wheelchair had been injured fighting the Non-Landers. But though Klor loved explaining how the microprocessor on his ultra-light recycled aluminum prosthesis controlled the knee and ankle joints, and the athletes who represented Is-Land in the Neoparalympics always sparked fierce debate about wheelchair design, no one ever explained exactly how these sacrifices had been sustained.

"Klor," she asked, "when did Gaia take your leg? Were you doing your IMBOD Service?"

"Astra," Nimma said sharply, "we don't ask—" but Klor interrupted her.

"Perhaps it's time, dear."

"Meem's not nearly old enough. Or Yoki." Nimma retorted. She had been short an awful lot lately, ever since Elpis had her stroke.

Klor was sitting between Meem and Astra. He tousled Meem's hair. "She'll be fine, my angel. It's the truth, and they should all hear it together."

"I want to hear!" Meem pleaded.

"I'm older than Astra!" Yoki was affronted. "How come she gets to hear?"

"She doesn't!" Nimma snapped. But Klor gazed at her steadily until she gave in. "All right, Klor. But if there are wet sheets tonight, they're on *your* head."

Astra caught Peat's eye and they both suppressed a giggle. But it wasn't a joke, she knew.

Nimma tightened her lips and Klor started telling them all the story of how he lost his leg. It wasn't during his IMBOD Service, when most people made their sacrifice for Gaia, but later, after he and Nimma had got married and were living in New Bangor, when Sheba was seven years old.

Astra knew that Sheba had returned to Gaia when she was seven after being ill with a very rare condition, something that she didn't need to worry about, because other children wouldn't ever get it. "Were you in the hospital at the same time as Sheba?" she asked.

Across the table, Nimma's eyes were filling with tears and Astra wondered for a moment if she was going to get told off again, but Klor just patted her shoulder and continued kindly, "I was, my darling. You see, Sheba and I went to Sippur for the day. It was going to be Nimma's birthday soon and we went to buy her a special present. We were going to get some beads for her to make a necklace with. We went on the bus from New Bangor. We thought we'd be back that afternoon."

Opposite Astra, Peat was chewing his lip and sliding his thumb along the edge of the table. Nimma wiped her face and put her arm around Yoki. "We really should have talked about this first, Klor," she complained.

But Klor continued, speaking in the same even, calm voice he used when explaining how Tablette circuitry worked. "We sat in the middle of the bus. Sheba was by the window so she could look out at the steppes and I was right beside her. I had my leg sticking out in the aisle because there wasn't much room between the seats. Oh my dewy meadow, we were looking forward to our day at the market. It was going to be Sheba's first time in Sippur. But my darlings, there was a man on the bus who didn't want us to arrive. I didn't see him board the bus, but someone told me later that he got on at a stop in the outskirts of Sippur. He sat at the front. He had a hydropac on his back, but it didn't just hold water. It contained a nanobomb, my darlings, and as the bus arrived at Sippur fruit market, the bomb exploded."

Klor paused. No one spoke or moved. The only sounds in the kitchen were the ticking of the cuckoo clock and Nimma's quiet sobs. For a moment Astra couldn't breathe. It was as if each hoarse gasp Nimma uttered was rending a hole in the air, and through those holes all the oxygen was rushing out of the room, leaving her stranded in a vacuum. *Sheba had died in a bus-bomb.* The clock was ticking, yes, but the hand was stuck and time wasn't moving on. No one sitting around the table could move or speak; they would just sit here forever, shriveling up, until they weren't people anymore but withered, rotting stems.

The clock was ticking louder now, like the timer in Operation Is-Land counting down to an emergency. When a bus-bomb exploded in Operation Is-Land there were bodies everywhere: babies and children and pregnant women, all limp and dripping with blood. Astra began to feel hot just thinking about it. In Operation Is-Land, when a bus-bomber struck, you had to take action immediately. You had to send constables and medics to take the dead and injured to the hospital, and then the National Wheel Meet had to redouble efforts to round up and expel all the infiltrators.

"It was a Non-Lander," she furiously declared, shattering the vacuum. "A Non-Lander *killed Sheba.*"

"Yes, Astra," Klor said. "The man was a Non-Lander. He killed Sheba, and himself, and seven other people, including the driver. Most of them were sitting near him, but the blast blew all the windows out of the bus and Sheba was thrown halfway out into the street. The shock-waves caused a disruption in the bones in my leg and later it had to be amputated above the knee. But I wasn't thinking about my leg. I was thinking about Sheba. She was in the hospital for three days, like we told you, but she never opened her eyes again. And then Gaia took her back."

Klor's voice was strained now. He stopped talking and an image of Sheba, flung out with the shattered glass, her body rinsed scarlet with blood, flashed into Astra's mind. What did "halfway out of the window" mean?

"Was Sheba *cut in half?*" she blurted.

"Astra!" Nimma gasped.

"No, no, darling—no she wasn't." Klor said soothingly. "She had cuts from the glass and her skin was sooty, but they washed her in the hospital and she looked beautiful, didn't she, Nimma?"

Nimma sucked in her cheeks and cast a hurt, angry glance at Astra. That wasn't fair! *She* hadn't killed Sheba.

Peat, sitting beside Nimma, was concentrating hard as if considering a move in chess. "Was there a trial?" he asked. "Did you give evidence, Klor?"

"There was no need for a trial, Peat. The man was dead. But later IMBOD rounded up a ring of infiltrators in the dry forest and expelled them all. It's been safe here ever since. None of you have had to live with the threat of such violence, thank Gaia."

Nimma was hugging Yoki so tightly there were red patches on his arms. "But mark my words," she flared, "they'll try and come back here as soon as we let down our guard. That's why we all have to do our IMBOD Service. To stop Non-Landers coming here to blow up our children."

"I'm scared," Yoki wailed. "I don't ever want to go to Sippur."

"I told you, Klor," Nimma scolded, pressing Yoki's head to her breast. "They're not old enough."

"You don't have to be frightened, Yoki," Klor said. "There aren't any Non-Landers in Is-Land anymore. They've all been found and taken back to the Belt. The man on the bus was one of the very last ones."

Why was Yoki such a mouse? Why did Nimma always baby him? "*I'm* not scared," Astra shouted, half-raising herself from the bench. "I *hate* that man. I wish he wasn't dead so I could *kill* him."

"Shhh, Astra," Klor said softly. "He's dead, and Gaia doesn't ever want us to act out of hate."

"She can feel angry if she wants to," Nimma retorted, even though she didn't normally ever like Astra to lose her temper.

Astra sat up straight. Yes, she *did* feel angry. It was *right* to feel angry when a bus-bomber killed your *sister*.

"I feel sad for Sheba," Meem whimpered, tears drooling down her face now as well. "She was going to buy Nimma a b-b-birthday present." Then her voice rose too. "It was Nimma's *birthday*. Why did the Non-Lander have to get on *your* bus? You and Nimma didn't do anything wrong. Why did Gaia take Sheba away from you?"

"I don't know, darling. Gaia is very mysterious." Klor's voice was choked. Then he put his elbows on the table and his hands up to his brow and Astra, sitting beside him, could feel his whole body began to shake. The sound coming out of his throat was terrible: deep and racking, like the old water pump in the school playground, creaking and groaning, but coming up dry. Nimma, opposite, had her eyes were closed. Her face was wet and she was rocking back and forth on the bench, her arms still clasped around Yoki. Meem was wailing, and across from Astra, Peat's face was crumpling too. Watching everyone crying, Astra felt her skin burst all over with cold.

"I miss her, my darlings," Klor finally managed to sputter. "I miss her very much."

After that, he'd put his arms around Astra and Meem and everyone had cried all together, the tears running down Astra's cheeks and dripping onto the table. Finally, Klor had taken his hanky out from his hipbelt and blown his nose like a reintroduced elephant and Nimma had got up to get hankies for everyone else. Then she and Klor had hugged them all and said how much they loved having Shelter children and how Gaia had told them they could still be wonderful parents, even though Sheba didn't need them anymore. Then Nimma had made echinacea tea, and as they were drinking it she told them that because they had lost Sheba, IMBOD had given Klor his mechatronic leg, which would otherwise have been far too expensive. And Klor had said that when he had accepted the leg he and Nimma had also accepted the challenge of being Or cofounders, moving here as soon as IMBOD had made the dry forest safe again. So that had explained that. Then Nimma was quiet again and Klor had said, "It's better we all know, isn't it, darlings? Better that we all miss Sheba together. That's what makes us a Shelter family." And Nimma had sniffed and said she hoped Yoki and Meem would sleep tonight, but what was done was done.

Astra had felt better then, for a while. Now, though, looking out over the roof, she felt those small cold flowers blossoming on her skin again. She was afraid, she realized. And she had been scared in the kitchen too: not, like Yoki, of a bus-bomber, but because it was frightening to see Klor weep. That autumn afternoon, talking to the visitors, he had been tall and glorious, a priest of Gaia, and then suddenly he was broken, hiding his face and gagging for air. She never wanted to see him like that again.

Frost petals were scaling her body now. Today, she realized, she was maybe going to do something that might make Klor very angry. If she did it and kept it secret from him, if he ever found out, he might think she didn't love him. Would Klor cry, she wondered, if she didn't have the shot and one day he discovered the truth?

Between the mountains the sky was slowly turning the color of a robin's eggshell. *No*, she thought, staring at the long rows of fertile soil soaking up the sun's heat, *not if I'm a famous scientist*. Then Klor might be angry, but he would be proud too. He wouldn't cry if she was a top Coder when she grew up, like Hokma and him: Klor definitely wouldn't cry then.

The sun was climbing over the mountains now. Nimma would be getting up soon, and if she didn't find Astra in her bed, there could be house punishments in store. She pulled herself away from the window and entered the back corridor to the stapcro lab. One wall of the corridor was glass, a window onto the hillside behind Code House, letting you see the plants and crevices and bird nests in the rock. The other was an ordinary wall full of lab and office doors. Klor's office was at the far end; the only room past his was Ahn's chamber. Ahn's door was closed. Klor's was open.

Astra stood on the threshold, her heart pumping in her ribcage. Klor was sitting at his screendesk in the center of the room. He was facing the window, overlooking the crops, so all she could see of him behind his old office chair were his knobbly elbows, his big ears and the strands of long gray hair that wound like tendrils over his broad skull. Swiping and tapping away, he made no sign that he had heard her. She could still sneak away. But her hand raised itself in the air and she knocked on the door frame.

"Astra. What are you doing up so early, fledgling?" He swung around on his chair, his tufty eyebrows lifting when he saw her, furrowing his brow. Klor had hair sprouting everywhere except the top of his head: his shoulders and chest and butt were all furry and he even had hair growing out of his nose and ears, though Nimma always tried to get him to trim those parts. "Let a man keep the little hair he has left on his head, woman," he'd demand as Meem squealed, "Cut it, Klor, cut it!" But not Astra. She liked Klor's gray mossy straggles. They made him look like an old man of the forest, she'd told him once, and he'd laughed and said Astra was his warrior princess from an Old World fairy tale.

Now she hovered at the threshold.

"Must be excitement. Security Serum Day today, isn't it?"

She nodded. That was true, wasn't it?

"You're not usually so quiet. Are you sure you're not sleepwalking?"

She smiled. "No."

"Come here, chickpea." Klor patted the bench beside him where his assistants and trainees sometimes sat in the daytime, watching him work and discussing their ideas. "Tell me what's on your mind. Dawn thoughts: best thoughts, that's what my grandfather used to say."

Astra sidled over and sat down on the bench. One day she'd work up the nerve to ask if she could sit in Klor's chair—just for a minute. Klor always said he'd had all his best ideas in this chair and even though it was falling apart he refused to recycle it. Yellow foam was crumbling through the armrests but he just kept mending them with black gaffer tape. Nimma had reupholstered the cushions twice, and he'd replaced the rollerwheels three times. The Or-adults sometimes joked about it, but no Or-kids would ever make fun of Klor's chair. It was his throne.

The bench was the next best place to sit, though. In front of her, the angled screendesk was crowded with strings of letters: A, G, C and T, over and over again in different patterns. Klor must have been assessing data when she arrived, making sure his grains would improve people's health, not cause diseases like some other countries' Code crops did. The letters A, G, C and T didn't make any words in Gaian, but they spelled a few in Inglish, and also in Klor's mother tongue. TAG meant "label" and "day" and a children's game. ACT meant to do something, or to pretend you were doing something, like she was doing today. TAC was part of another game, TA meant "thank you" and CAT was another word for Tabby. Sometimes she liked to sit beside Klor and count how many CATs she could find in his Code, but right now when she looked the first word she saw was ACT.

Was it another Gaia sign? She toyed with the edge of the screendesk. The blue nail varnish Meem had painted her nails with last week was starting to chip.

In the Quiet Room or the Earthship Klor would sometimes tuck his Gaia plow between his legs and say you could sit on his lap. Or if you were crying, he'd put his big knuckley hand on your shoulder and draw you to him. Leaning against his bony ribs and rangy thigh, close to his marvelous, shiny, intelligent leg, you felt safer and stronger. And when your sniffles had faded he'd ask, "Are you better now, ping-pong?" And you always nodded, because you were. And he'd say, "Well then, run and play, while you're still an Or-child." Today he just rested his hand lightly on the base of her neck and asked, "What's the matter, Astra?" Then he waited, as he always did, for her to speak.

"Nothing's the matter," Astra said.

"Ah."

She paused. "I want to be a famous scientist when I grow up, like you."

Klor's nut-brown face creased into his toothy smile. "I'm sure you'll be far more famous than I am, Astra. You just have to keep working hard."

She had to be careful. She couldn't let Klor know what Hokma had told her. "But if I have my Security shot, maybe I'll be an IMBOD officer instead," she ventured. "The teachers said it will make us all super-strong."

"It will, that's true. It will make you a good team player too."

"But what if I don't want to be a team player?" she persisted. "What if I want to be a genius like you and Hokma and Ahn?"

Klor wasn't smiling now. His bright blue eyes were looking at her intently. "Astra, I'm not a genius, and neither is Hokma. Or Ahn. We've just been very lucky to develop our talents in a supportive environment. The shot will help ensure that everyone in Is-Land lives in such an environment. It will make you feel calmer and happier, and help you use language in a clear, orderly fashion. You and your generation will be able to communicate with each other in a way the rest of humanity can only dream of. Oh my dewy meadow, there won't be any need for geniuses when so many fine minds are working as one."

Astra leaned her head against Klor's flank and inhaled his clean smell of warm stone. She had to weigh up Klor's evidence now, she knew, and compare it with Hokma's findings. Klor was saying she could still be a scientist if she had her shot. But he was also saying she wouldn't be a genius. And why was he saying that *he* wasn't a genius when everyone knew that he was? Nimma was always complaining that Klor didn't take enough credit for his discoveries. He let the team win the medals, and last year he'd even told IMBOD to give a prize to his assistant, not him. At the ceremony, he'd said that she'd done most of the headwork on the project and he'd just done the legwork—well, fifty percent of it, at least—and everyone had laughed except Nimma, who had pursed her lips. Klor *was* a genius, he was just too modest to say so.

Klor squeezed her shoulder. "Does that answer your question, little one?"

Her elbow was on the armrest of his chair and between the screendesk and his furry chest she could see his lap. Between his legs his soft Gaia plow was drooping on its wrinkly seed bag. Sheba's Code had come from there—well, half of it, and the other half from Nimma's egg, which was hidden in a nest deep inside her Gaia garden. You weren't allowed to touch adults' Gaia plows or Gaia gardens. They were like expensive microscopes or Owleons: important, delicate things that only other adults could play with.

Her eyes strayed over Klor's black stump-sling and mechatronic leg. She wasn't allowed to touch the leg either, because he always said little fingers could get caught in the complicated joints. And of course she'd never touched his stump, but once at home, when he was lying on the sofa with the prosthesis recharging in the corner, she had seen it. The stump was bumpy and scarred. Even though Klor never complained she knew that it hurt sometimes still. On those days his face looked strained and he didn't always answer you right away. Other times the straps on the sling made his skin chafe and Nimma had to put lotion on his thigh. Klor also had to go to the doctor in New Bangor once a year to have his gait and circulation checked and his prosthesis adjusted. It wasn't right, Astra thought, that he spent his life making other people healthy but no one could fix him.

"If I have my shot," she slowly asked, "will I be able to discover how to make your leg regrow?"

Klor patted her fingers. "Oh my sun-drenched garden, that's a kind thought, fledgling. But mammalian limb regeneration simply isn't possible. Even lizards do it very badly." Laughing, he tweaked her nose. "My word, you *would* have to be a genius to learn how to regrow my leg."

He tickled her tummy and she laughed too. Everything was as clear as rainwater now: she was going to be a genius and make a world breakthrough in limb regeneration. When she won a medal she would give it to Klor, because he was her inspiration. Then she might tell him she'd never had her Security shot, or she might keep it secret forever.

"Happy?" he grinned. "Good. Now, where's Tabby? Hokma said you'd broken him again."

Astra opened her mouth to explain it was the Non-Lander girl who'd broken Tabby but changed her mind. She had better start acting now. It would be good practice for later.

"I didn't mean to. I was climbing a tree and he fell out of his pocket." She should have said "my hand" but "his pocket" was better— she shouldn't have been climbing with Tabby in her hand anyway. She retrieved him from her hydropac and without meeting Klor's eyes, handed him over.

"I don't know why they call these things childproof." Klor pinched her cheek. "They ought to give you a job testing them. That would bring in a little funding for Or, wouldn't it?"

He had believed her. Astra bounced on her seat. "Really?"

"If I see the position advertised, you'll be the first to know. Now where is my Tabby-fixing kit?"

Acting was going to be *easy*. Astra raced to the window and rummaged in Klor's IT drawer for his set of tiny Tablette tools. Outside, the sky had brightened to a pale powder-blue and the green shoots poking through the roof turf were glinting like dagger tips. In the valley, people had started work in the gardens and orchards, and the kitchen team were heading to Core House to start making breakfast. Or was awakening, just like any other day. All she had to do was help Klor fix Tabby, show Nimma she was dressed properly for school, go to Core House for special Security Shot Day waffles and syrup, then meet Hokma at West Gate with Meem, Yoki, Peat and the others. Hokma would give them special goody bags to celebrate Security Shot Day, with carob bars to eat after the needle. When she got to school, before class started, she had to drink the bottle of orange juice Hokma was going to give her, all in one go. That was very important. *Don't sip it*, Hokma had said. *It won't taste very nice, but you have to drink it down all in one go. Promise?*

What would happen next would be disgusting and horrible and make Tedis Sonnenson laugh at her for the whole of the term. But it would also turn her into a famous genius one day.

Clasping the toolkit to her chest, Astra ran back to Klor with a hop, skip and a Neolympic-length jump.

1.6

As the rest of the school filed into the gym, Astra tried to memorize every detail of the IMBOD medical officers' appearance. They were the most impressive officers she had ever seen and she also had to do something to distract her from the strange feeling that had been bubbling in her tummy ever since she'd drunk the orange juice on the bus. It had tasted disgusting but she'd managed not to pull a face as she drank it, *all in one go*. Now she just needed to get through Assembly without drawing any attention to herself. She wished Tabby was here to give her moral support, but after their joint examination of his wounds Klor had said fixing him would take a little time so she was on her own. At least no one was allowed to take photos in Assembly, so she didn't have to sit there like a mushroom while everyone else thrust their Tablettes in the air to snap the officers in a massive competition she would have wanted to win.

The officers were both Corporals, but one had two stripes. The lower-ranking Officer was small, round and blond. The First Officer was tall and muscular and her skin was as dark as one of Nimma's ebony spoons. Both were wearing black peaked caps trimmed with silver, black army boots and hydrobelts, black thigh-knife straps and IMBOD armbands displaying their silver stripes. In front of them, Astra felt proud of her own wardrobe. She had won her morning battle with Nimma and the skirt had stayed in the drawer. Instead she was adorned with her green and white Or-kid armband, the one she usually wore for Sportsdays. Today was like a Sportsday prize-giving ceremony, in fact, because behind the officers the stage was draped with a huge IMBOD flag. The Is-Land Shield on a white background was exactly the same as the national flag, except curving beneath the Shield were the bold black words Is-Land Ministry of Boundary Defense. Astra didn't need to memorize the Shield, of course; she could draw it in her sleep: a sea-green downward-pointing triangle halved by a vertical crimson line and surrounded by a radiant golden circle. But the flag still commanded her attention: it was enormous and shiny, made of sateen and handstitched in the kind of plush, richly-colored threads Nimma never let young sewers use.

At last, when the gym was full, the teachers had finished shushing from the sidelines and the children were all quiet, the Head, Mr. Waters-son, got up from his chair on the stage and stood at the lectern. "Happy Security Shot Day, Golden Bough School," he greeted them. "Please rise and welcome our guests with your best rendition of the National Anthem."

The officers stood up, and Astra scrambled to her feet with the rest of the children. She loved the National Anthem—though she would have to concentrate, to make sure she remembered the new version. "*O Shield*," she recited, gazing devotedly at the flag and wishing Tabby was there to hear the stirring words.

Your beautiful Triangle
Summons the spirit of Gaia
And sings also of Is-Land
The green earth that springs anew
Between two rivers

Your bright red pillar
Commands us to respect
Gaia's molten core

And the martyrs' blood
That runs in Is-Lander veins

Surrounding all
Your golden circle
Holds us safe
Inspires us to revere
The Sun, the Shell, the Wheel Meet
And Is-Land's Sacred Grains

O IMBOD Shield
You protect us
And we vow to defend
All that you contain

The hymn unfurled from two hundred throats. To make "Shell" fit, the word "shining" before "Sun" had been taken out. Astra still had the old line in her head, but she chanted the right words and the hymn went off perfectly. When the last syllable faded Mr. Watersson gestured for them all to sit again and she made herself comfortable on the floor. The chanting had helped her to breathe deeply and her stomach felt calmer. Onstage, the Second Officer sat back down again too, but the First Officer stepped forward to the front of the stage.

"Good morning, Golden Bough School," she said in a loud, clear voice. "And it is a *very* good morning. Today is a historic day for you and for Is-Land. Today the Year One to Year Three students in this hall will be joining a major evolution in national defense, a *conscious revolution*, in fact. Today, as you know, is Security Serum Day. Now, some of you may not like needles, but I know what you do like: Is-Land!"

She and the Second Officer raised their fists in the air: "Is-Land!" they shouted.

"Is-Land! Is-Land!" the whole Assembly roared, teachers too. It was tremendous to be shouting together: with each syllable she expelled, Astra felt the remaining tension in her tummy leave her mouth in a stream of little bubbles and burst into nothing at all. It was even okay that Tabby wasn't there. She would have so much to tell him when she got home.

"Yes, we all love Is-Land," the First Officer continued after the tumult had subsided. "Thanks to the noble sacrifices your parents and their parents have made, the children in this school have grown up in our beautiful nation in safety. The infiltrators have all been expelled and Non-Landers are confined now to the Southern Belt. While the task of policing the Belt is not easy, IMBOD is more than capable of meeting it. But in twenty-three years' time, when the Global Ceasefire ends, Is-Land will face far more dangerous challenges."

Silvie Higgsdott was wriggling beside Astra. Astra shot her a deadly glance and moved her thigh away. Didn't Silvie *care* about the future? In twenty-three years' time she would be—she did the sum in her head—*nearly thirty-one*. When Hokma was thirty-one she had moved into Wise House and begun work on the Owleons. What would she, Astra, be doing? Would she have her own office at Code House, discovering how to regrow mammalian limbs? Would she be working in Atourne on top secret Shelltech? Would she be giving IMBOD talks, like the First Officer, tall and confident and glowing?

"We hope—the whole world hopes," the officer went on, "that one hundred years without war will have changed humanity. We hope that no nation state will ever again initiate military aggression against its neighbors. But we cannot be sure of that and so we must be prepared. As we all know, IMBOD has been working for the past seven years on developing the Shell: a magnetic defense field that will cover Is-Land like a dome. When completed, and switched on in times of need, the Shell will be capable of repelling any bomb or missile our enemies may try to use against us. The technical details are still classified, but I have been authorized to tell you that the Shell has just passed its first stage of testing with flying colors."

The officer paused again, so the Assembly could cheer this momentous announcement. Astra cheered too, louder than Silvie on her left, louder than Tedis on her right. Tedis, she saw, was *picking his nose*. Ms. Raintree frowned at him and he smeared his finger on his leg. She shifted away from him. Just like Tedis to make the class look bad.

Onstage, the officer flashed her dazzling smile. "Mining the rare Shelltech components and building the Shell will be an immense task," she told them. "It will require the Boundary's entire outer walls to be clad in Shelltech components, even through the treacherous Southern Belt. Our personnel resources will be stretched to the limit, and we know the Non-Landers will take advantage of any weakness in our ranks. To succeed, the work will require collective skills, courage and dedication on a scale only the earliest Gaian Pioneers could surpass. That is why, in tandem with the Shell, IMBOD has also developed the Security Serum. The Serum will create a new generation of Is-Landers superbly equipped to defend the nation our parents and grandparents sacrificed so much to build. Years One, Two and Three, I am talking to you."

The officer's voice rang out against the hall. Astra sat up straight and flexed her biceps. Her armband tightened. Beside her, Tedis and Silvie stopped fidgeting.

"As Security Generation members, you will be logical, calm and team-spirited—but you will also be fearless warriors. You will excel in all the traditional fields of Gaian endeavor, but you will also be ideally suited to the new national task that lies ahead of us all: the task of building and maintaining the Shell in the most dangerous conditions imaginable. You will all be *heroes*. For those Is-children *lucky* enough to be in Years One, Two and Three, the best way to show your gratitude is to have your Security shot bravely today, without crying. Because there is *absolutely nothing to cry about anymore*. Quite the opposite! The Security shot is a gift from IMBOD's top scientists to us all.

"Everyone else, don't be sad. Your lives will be far safer and simpler thanks to the Security Generation. Teachers, Years Four, Five, Six and Seven: can we clap Years One, Two and Three, please? Can we thank them in advance for the tremendous work they will do for us in the years ahead?"

The two officers and Mr. Watersson began to clap. The older children and the teachers joined in, dutifully at first, then, as the First Officer paced across the stage, conducting with her arms, more exuberantly, some whistling and whooping as they realized that a clamor was not only permitted but required. For a moment, as Silvie leaned against her, warm and giggling, Astra forgot that she didn't deserve the deafening applause. She peeked over her shoulder to see if Torrent was clapping as energetically as he ought to be. But Ms. Raintree caught her eye and pursed her lips so she gave up and faced the stage again.

"*Thank you, Golden Bough School!*" the First Officer exclaimed over the din. When the applause finally died down, she resumed her speech. "Thanks to your enthusiasm and loyalty, thanks to the foresight and hard work of IMBOD's Serum and Shell scientists, Is-Land *need never fear* that our powerful neighbors may one day turn against us. We *need never fear* that the terror squatters in the Southern Belt will acquire rockets or bombers. Instead, as the decades progress, Is-Land will continue to take its rightful place among the world's nations, not only as a prime exporter of Code Innovation and Shelltech but, like Garmaland and Himalaya, as a Sacred Land, a CONC-designated haven, safe for all to visit."

As she finished her speech, the First Officer's soaring voice and gleaming smile acquired an electrifying sheen. The children yelled "Is-Land, Is-Land," again, and the teachers stood up and clapped wildly. Ms. Raintree even cried—Astra saw her wipe her eyes. Her job done, the First Officer sat down next to the Second Officer and batted her a bashful, sidelong glance, as if to say, "How did I do?"

Back in the classroom, before they started their math tasks, Ms. Raintree spent a few minutes discussing the Assembly. Both the officers were young—they had just finished their IMBOD Service, she told the students. Imagine having such an important responsibility when you were still only twenty! They must have done very well on all their tests. And yes, Tedis, administering Security shots definitely involved math: graphs, pie charts, schedules and dosages. The officers had undoubtedly done exceptionally well in their math tests. If you wanted to be as successful as they were when you were twenty, you needed to get your head down now and concentrate on your Tablette exercises. Astra put up her hand, and Ms. Raintree said, yes I know you need a school Tablette today, and rolled down the aisle to give her one.

Astra's desk was by the window. If she glanced sideways she had a perfect view of the IMBOD mobile medical unit parked in the playground; sneaking a look when Ms. Raintree was helping Leaf with a sum, she watched a batch of Year Ones enter the unit. As she waited for them to emerge, her stomach began to feel tender and gassy again, and it became even more difficult to concentrate on her equations, even though they were easy. She did her best, but she was falling behind. Silvie or Acorn would get the gold star today.

At last the Year Ones poured out of the unit. Some were proudly examining their Tablettes, showing each other their new certificate uploads; some were punching the air, others were tenderly fingering their shoulders. Kamut Bosonson was crying and holding the Second Officer's hand as she escorted the children back to their classroom. The First Officer stayed inside the unit. She must be the one injecting the Serum.

Meem was in the next group of students being led across the yard. She was wearing her flap-hat and a faux-grass skirt, and she was skipping and laughing and kicking a pebble until the Second Officer told her not to. Astra's stomach contracted. Her skin felt hot. *Couldn't Meem, Yoki and Peat also not have the shot?* she'd asked Hokma, but Hokma had said that giving a group of children a secret was like putting an egg in a washing machine. Besides, the other Or-kids' Code parents wanted them to have the shot—and even if they didn't, Hokma's plan would only work for one child.

Meem disappeared into the van. Astra checked the time. Her Tablette clock read 9:51. The school had emailed Hokma the schedule so she knew it would take another hour to finish the Year Ones, then the Year Twos would start at 11:00: first Mr. Banzan's class, then Ms. Raintree's, so Yoki would get his shot before Astra was supposed to. Peat and the Year Threes would have their shot after siesta.

She tried to do one more sum. But her tummy swelled and squeezed again and the numerals swam together before her eyes. Her skin was burning and her mouth felt dry. Hot bubbles of sweat were bursting out on her forehead. She couldn't breathe. She gasped for air and her stomach cranked a blazing bolt of pain up toward her heart. She wrapped her arms around her middle and started to cry.

"Ms. Raintree," Tedis piped up excitedly, "Astra's going to be sick."

"Euw!" Silvie squealed. The harsh metallic noise of chairs being dragged over the tiled floor scraped the inside of Astra's skull. Vaguely she sensed Ms. Raintree's cool palm on her brow, but nothing could soothe the fire racing over her or douse the acid flaming in her throat. She was gagging now, in great gulpy hiccoughs, until her ribs ached and her whole body was shaking.

"Astra, what's wrong?" Ms. Raintree sounded very far away.

She raised her head. Like an Old World sea monster hurtling out of an underwater cave, a spume of vomit shot from her mouth across the room. Splotchy drops of half-digested waffle splattered over Ms. Raintree's teaching robe and wheelchair arms, Silvie's curly hair, Tedis's math book, her classmates' desks, the Fractions Family vidboard and the floor. Astra's face drained of blood and she slumped back down in her seat, her forehead on her desk, her arms still hugging her stomach.

"Wow!" Tedis exhaled as Silvie started to shriek. Cries of *eugh* and *yuck* and *no way!* zinged around the room like Tablette ping-balls.

"Oh, Astra," Ms. Raintree sighed. "Tedis, can you please go and find the caretaker? Tell him he'll need to bring the mop and some wet cloths. The rest of you, stay here and get on with your sums."

After Ms. Raintree took Astra to the nurse's office and helped the nurse clean her up, she phoned Hokma's Tablette, because Hokma was the School Spoke of the Or Parents' Committee. Luckily, Hokma just happened to be in New Bangor doing some shopping and she came right away in the Or solar van. By the time her Shelter mother arrived, Astra had had diarrhea twice and was lying scrunched up on the nurse's cot, moaning. She had ripped off her armband because she couldn't bear anything touching her skin, and her eyes were half-closed because the light hurt them, but at the same time she didn't want to miss anything. Hokma—whose dark purple eyepatch made her seem almost as commanding as the First Officer—took one look at her and told Ms. Raintree and the nurse and Mr. Watersson that the Security shot would have to wait because Astra needed to come home with her right now and recover. Ms. Raintree, who had a big wet mark on her robe where she'd washed off Astra's sick, wasn't sure about that, because the IMBOD unit was at the school for only one day, and next week it was moving on to the steppes; but Hokma said not to worry: her Birth-Code brother,

Dr. Samrod Blesserson, was a high-ranking IMBOD medical officer—in fact, he had helped develop the Security Serum in its early stages—and she would take Astra to see him tomorrow.

Then Mr. Watersson said, "Oh my dewy meadow, Dr. Blesserson—I didn't know you were related—perhaps he might come here and give a talk to the older students, do you think?" And Hokma explained that when the community name law had been introduced, Samrod—like Mr. Watersson, she assumed—had patriotically decided to adapt his Shelter family name, but she hadn't because while Blesserson had a nice flow to it, she thought "Blesserdott" sounded like a piece of bad Code splicing. Astra didn't get the joke, she knew she was supposed to be too sick to ask questions anyway and in fact she *was* still feeling awful, but Mr. Watersson and Ms. Raintree laughed, and Ms. Raintree said she perfectly understood, she herself had decided that Raintreedott was a bit of a mouthful. Then the teacher added, quietly, "Please thank your brother for me," because one of his Code treatments for posttraumatic stress syndrome had been very helpful to her after her injury. Mr. Watersson very politely asked Hokma to ask her brother to email Astra's Security shot certificate to the school and then he said Astra should take as much time as she needed to recover. She was ahead in all her lessons, so a few days off wouldn't hurt. Hokma said, "Yes, that might be productive," and shook their hands goodbye. Then she bundled Astra up in her arms and carried her like a baby out to the parking lot.

"Good girl," Hokma crooned as she belted her into the front seat of the van. "Now let's take you home to Nimma, and in the afternoon we'll go up to see the Owleons."

Astra groaned, because her throat still hurt too much to talk. But Hokma had brought her a soy yogurt drink to calm her tummy and she sipped it slowly, knowing that she had followed orders and would be a great scientist one day like Hokma and Dr. Samrod Blesserson. The van sailed smoothly over the main road out of New Bangor, sunshine and warm woodsy air flowing in through the windows from the firegrounds beneath the escarpment, and when they turned off to climb the steep, dusty road to Or, Hokma drove extra slowly all the rest of the way home.

1.7

"What in Gaia's holy name happened?" Nimma came rushing out of Craft House to meet Hokma and Astra, the pink ribbons of her faux-grass skirt fluttering around her hips. Hokma had called her from West Gate.

"She was sick." Hokma hugged Astra to her side. "She must have eaten some roots or leaves in the woods yesterday."

"Astra." It didn't match her pearly pink lipstick and feather earrings, but Nimma put her spiky voice on. "How many times do we have to tell you? You must never eat anything from the woods unless we pick it with you."

"I didn't eat any leaves." Her voice rising, Astra pushed Hokma away, harder than she'd meant to. This was the acting part, but with both her Shelter mothers accusing her of something she hadn't done, for a moment it almost felt as if she *had*.

"No one else was sick, were they?" Hokma said, reasonably.

"If you did, let this be a lesson to you." Nimma waggled her finger at Astra, the one with the big emerald ring. "You didn't sleep properly, you've been sick at school and you've missed your Security shot. Have you checked her temperature, Hokma?"

"The nurse said it wasn't too high," Hokma said as Nimma rested the back of her hand on Astra's forehead.

"I didn't do anything wrong. I just got sick, that's all." Astra folded her arms and glared up at Nimma.

"Shush, Astra." Hokma rubbed her shoulders. "It's okay, we believe you. Nimma, don't worry, get back to work. I'll take Astra to her room."

She could tell Nimma was on the verge of getting really angry now. "But what about her shot, Hokma?" her Shelter mother insisted. "She has to have it—what did you arrange with the school?"

"Samrod will give it to her tomorrow. Mr. Watersson's fine with that."

"Samrod? I thought you weren't—" Nimma glanced down at Astra and tightened her lips.

"I've just been so busy lately. I'll call him today—it will be a good chance to catch up. I can take her tomorrow, in the morning."

"All the way to Sippur? She's ill. And—" Nimma paused and her face seemed to crinkle for a moment. "Klor and I wanted to take her there. With the others."

Dr. Blesserson lived in Sippur? Where Sheba had died? And she might get to go there before Peat did? Astra held her breath.

"If she's not better, of course we won't go," Hokma said. "And we can take flowers for Sheba. Would you like to do that, Astra?"

Before Astra could answer, Nimma raised her hands, palms in the air. "Oh I give up. As long as the school approves." She glanced back at Craft House. "I would take a break, Hokma, but we have to finish the new dining-hall curtains before the next load of visitors runs us off our feet again."

"I know, Nimma. I'll settle her in. She'll be fine on her own. Won't you, Astra?" Clinging to Hokma's fingers, Astra nodded. The yogurt drink had comforted her tummy and she was already feeling much better. As soon as siesta was over, Hokma was going to take her up to see the Owleons again.

"Astra," Nimma ordered, "you must go to bed and stay there— no playing in the woods today, or you won't be coming to the Fountain tonight."

She had to stay in bed? "But Hokma said—" Astra beseeched.

Hokma shushed her again. "Nimma's right," she said. "You need to rest."

Astra scowled. Typical Shared Shelter parents: always breaking promises and siding with each other.

"I want Tabby back," she demanded. "Has Klor finished fixing him?"

"Temper, Astra!" Nimma warned. "Believe it or not, Klor and I have not been messaging each other all day on Tabby's progress. You'll get him back at dinner *if* you are good today and *if* Klor is done with him."

"Hush Astra," Hokma said. "You're tired and you need to sleep."

It was too much. The two of them were merging into one big NO machine. She turned her back on her Shelter mothers, only just resisting the temptation to bat at some brown-eyed Susans on the path verge. She wouldn't be hurting the flowers, just helping them seed, but Nimma and Hokma would probably accuse her of plant abuse.

"Thank you so much, Hokma," Nimma was saying. "I'm sorry if I was rude just then. You know how it is: just the word Sippur puts me on edge." Her voice softened. "It's very sweet of you to think about taking flowers. I'll tell Klor how helpful you're being."

"Nimma, it's nothing," Hokma said, pulling Astra back to her side. "We've always said I would get more involved in Astra's life when she started school. And besides, Or's supposed to be about cooperation, isn't it?"

"It's nice that you still feel that way, Hokma. I know Klor and I do too." Nimma put her hand, with its wrinkly brown skin and faint speckles, on Hokma's, and patted it. Astra risked a peek up at her. Nimma's face had relaxed and suddenly she smiled, like she used to do before Elpis had her stroke. She looked pretty again, instead of pinched and worn.

But then she cupped Astra's face and inspected her one more time. "You're positively green around the gills, young lady. Better make sure she has a bucket by the bed, Hokma."

"C'mon, Astra." Hokma gently shook her shoulder. "Let's get you to bed."

It wasn't fair that she didn't get to see the Owleons today after drinking that horrible juice and throwing up on Ms. Raintree and agreeing to lie to Klor and Nimma and everyone forever. But Astra had to admit she felt, if not exactly tired, a bit weak. Hokma tucked her in, fetched a glass of water and a bucket and closed the greenhouse corridor blinds so the bedroom was shady like the forest.

"Now you get some sleep and Nimma will come up later with some lunch."

Astra flounced beneath the sheets. "I don't want Nimma to come up. She's *mean* to me sometimes."

Hokma looked at her sternly. "Nimma's not mean, Astra. She loves you very much. She just doesn't want you to get hurt or lost running around in the woods."

"But . . ." But Astra was yawning now and her complaint got lost in her pillow.

Hokma laughed. "I think it's time for someone to get some sleep. I'll see you this evening, and tomorrow we'll leave early to meet Dr. Blesserson. We haven't completed our mission yet, remember."

Hokma got up and left her to sleep. Astra burrowed deeper into bed. Tonight was Storytelling at the Fountain, and tomorrow she was going to meet the famous Dr. Samrod Blesserson. But right now she was a brave Is-Land constable recovering from a dangerous mission and basking in the glow of her rewards: a day off school and the promise of the Owleons. She stretched between the cottony-clean sheets and as she did, a quiet tingle stole over her. It was the feeling she had when she and Meem and Yoki pretended to be lion cubs fighting, or were cuddling together in bed: a flame flickering between her legs, making her feel bigger and warmer, as though something important was going to happen.

Now they were at school, she, Meem and Yoki didn't play those games very much anymore; they played with their Tablettes instead. But Astra still sometimes had the feeling by herself: when she'd run a race, or swum all the way across Green Lake. Nimma had told her, Meem and Yoki that the feeling was Gaia Power, and it felt so nice because it was Gaia's special gift to everyone. Gaia Power, Nimma said, is the life force that flows through everything on the planet: trees, flowers, animals, water, even stones and metals. In human beings Gaia Power is especially strong in the sexual organs, because these are the parts of the body that create and nourish new life. Mostly people just use enough Gaia Power to do everyday work and hardly notice their sexual organs, but some-times our Gaia Power turns up the volume and reminds us just what a miracle our bodies are. Then we feel extra excited and happy to be alive. Gaia Power, Nimma had said, will always help you feel good about your-self and the world. When you get older, the feeling will be stronger and you might want to share it with other people, but for now you should just enjoy it quietly.

Of course Astra had asked why she had to be quiet about her Gaia Power and Nimma told her it was because Gaia Power needed privacy to sprout. It was like a seed, which was why women call their vaginas Gaia gardens, and men call their penises Gaia plows or when they're still boys, Gaia peppers. But Nimma and Hokma would always answer questions about it, and if anyone ever tried to touch Astra's Gaia garden, she was to come and tell Nimma at once.

If Astra was with other people, her Gaia Power was usually fleeting—an Or-child would say something stupid or an adult would give a command—and the spell would be broken. But if her Gaia Power lit up when she was by herself, in the forest, or in bed with the lights out, she sometimes rubbed herself to make the feeling stay longer. She reached down now and put her hand between her legs. Often it was nice just to feel the pressure of her wrist there. Was that what a Gaia plow felt like? As she gripped her wrist bone with her thighs, images of the girl in the tree floated through her mind. Had she been feeling her Gaia Power too, so high up there in the tree?

Astra yawned and snuggled under the sheets. One day she was going to capture the Non-Lander girl and then something very important would happen. Leaving her fingers planted in her damp Gaia garden, she drifted like a leaf into sleep.

When she woke up, Nimma was setting a tray of green almond stew down on the bed. As she ate, Nimma pulled up a chair and talked. She said the other children were back from school now, showing off their Security Serum certificates. But Astra shouldn't worry; Hokma had spo-ken to Dr. Blesserson and he had some extra shots at his clinic and was definitely going to see her tomorrow.

"Hokma will take you," Nimma said as Astra licked her spoon clean. "She's going to be looking after you more from now on."

Astra put the spoon back on the tray. Like the yogurt, the slippery, delicate flesh of the green almonds had been just the right medicine for her tummy. "I know. She said I could stay at Wise House with her sometimes."

"And how do you feel about that?"

"Great!"

Nimma was smiling, but her face looked like it did when she gazed at Elpis sometimes: as though, like at the brook, an eddy of sad thoughts were trapped beneath the surface of her features.

"I mean, as long as I can still stay here too," Astra hurriedly added.

Nimma wrinkled her nose in that cutesy way she had. "Of course you can," she said, in her nicest, warmest tone. "Klor and I will always be your Shared Shelter parents, and this will always be your's and Meem's room."

Nimma picked up the tray. Astra thought she was going to get up and take it downstairs, but she set it on the bedside table and remained in her chair.

"You're our angel, Astra," she said. "Gaia gave you to us and we promised Her we'd always look after you. I'm sorry I've been a little short with you lately. I've had a lot of extra responsibilities this year. But things will be a lot easier now that Hokma can share taking care of you. I promise I'll try to be nicer; how's that?"

Astra squirmed a little beneath the sheets. Had Hokma told Nimma she'd said Nimma was mean? "You're not short with me," she mumbled. "Only when I'm naughty."

"You wouldn't be Astra if you weren't naughty sometimes." Nimma smiled properly now, her eyes crinkling at the edges. But she still didn't get up to go.

"What are your responsibilities?" Astra asked, enjoying the way the big word made her mouth move in lots of different ways.

"Well, Elpis needs a lot of care now. And at Craft House we're already preparing for next year's twentieth anniversary celebrations. I haven't been sleeping very well lately. But I'm sure that will pass."

Astra played with her sheet, rolling the edge up like a veggie sausage. It had never occurred to her that Nimma found her jobs hard. "Can I help with Elpis?" she asked.

"That's very kind of you, Astra. It helps Elpis when you play in the living room. It's good for her to have company." Nimma rested her wrist on Astra's forehead again. "Your temperature's gone down. Do you want to sit downstairs with her now and do some Tablette drawing on the sofa?"

Astra did want to get up, but at the same time it was so nice to have Nimma all to herself. With her golden coils of braids piled up on her head and all her *responsibilities* her Shelter mother was like an Old World Queen, and when she was especially nice to Astra it felt like being given a gift of royal treasure. "Can you tell me a story first?" she asked. "Like you used to do?"

"A story? There'll be lots of stories tonight."

"Yes, but I want to hear my story—the story of my Birth-Code mother."

"Ah." Nimma stroked Astra's hand. "That's a good story, isn't it?" Her eyes creased and twinkled. "And I did just promise to be nicer to you, didn't I?"

Astra nodded happily and settled down into the pillows.

"This story has a sad part, remember?" Nimma cautioned.

"That's okay. I like the sad part now."

"All right then. Well," Nimma began, "as we all know, all Or-children have Code parents, Shelter parents and a Birth mother. Sometimes these are the same person, but mostly they're different, and so every Or-kid has a different combination of Parent Stories. This is the story of Astra Ordott's Birth-Code mother. Her name was Eya. Eya was young and strong and very pretty, and she'd grown up in a small community in Bracelet Valley. Her community wasn't like Or. The people there still followed some Old World customs. They had only one Gaia partner, and they didn't usually Shelter other people's children. The children still did IMBOD Service and went to college with everyone else, and sometimes they moved away from the community and began to live more like other Gaians. After Eya's IMBOD Service she moved to Atourne to attend Craft College. There she Gaia-bonded with a handsome older man who worked at a restaurant near the college. But even though he was very intelligent, her lover was uneducated and Eya knew that her Code-Shelter father wouldn't approve of him. So she kept their Gaia bond secret. And when she found out she was pregnant, she was very scared."

Astra frowned. Pregnancy—and how to avoid it—had been explained recently at school and this part of the story now needed some clarification. "How come Eya got pregnant with me?" she asked. "Why didn't she have the implant?"

"Not everyone does well on the implant, darling. Some people experience painful side effects and have to have it removed. Eya's community didn't encourage its use, and she told me she was using sheath protection but the sheath broke. She didn't want her father to find out, but she didn't want to dissolve the embryo either. Her community believed that all pregnancies are gifts from Gaia and she wanted the embryo to grow into a fetus and then a baby and be born. She told her best friend Cora, and Cora said, 'Eya, don't worry. My Code aunt Hokma lives in a place called Or—in Or there are lots of kids with lots of different kinds of parents. Why don't you go there, and tell Aunt Hokma I sent you? You can tell your papa you're working in the gardens and after the baby is born Hokma can give it to some Or Shelter parents and you can come back to Atourne.'"

Astra had to stop Nimma again here. "Is Cora Dr. Blesserson's Code daughter?" she asked.

"Cora? No. Dr. Blesserson doesn't have any children." Nimma paused. "Cora Pollen is the daughter of Hokma's older Code-Shelter sister, Paloma."

"Is Paloma my Shelter aunty, then?"

Nimma smoothed the edge of the sheet. "Paloma would be your aunty if she was still alive, darling. But she returned to Gaia when she was a young woman. She had stored her egg, though, just in case, for her Gaia partner to fertilize if anything should ever happen to her. He made a request for a professional Birth mother and when Cora was born he and his own parents Sheltered her. They were called Pollen. Hokma used to say it was a good name for Cora because she was seeded on the winds of change."

This was all a new part of the story, and very interesting. Astra sat up. "How did Paloma return to Gaia?"

"Look, darling, I can't tell you everyone's story all at once. Paloma sacrificed her life for Is-Land, and everyone in her family is very proud of her. Cora grew up in Atourne, but she visited here once or twice when she was little. That's how she knew to send Eya here. All right?"

"Okay," Astra agreed. She had wanted to ask about family and community names as well, and why Dr. Blesserson had changed his but Hokma hadn't, but Nimma was getting impatient now and if she asked too many more questions she might stop telling the story.

"Now, at first Eya didn't say she was expecting a baby. She just asked if she could work here. She had some Craft skills, of course, but Craft House was full, so we registered her as a seasonal aglab and she helped Klor with the fruit trees—and if any of my team members fell ill, she helped me, selling handmade cloths to visitors. She wore loose robes, because she said she had a skin rash that got worse in the sun, and for a while no one knew she had a baby in her tummy. But one day she talked to Hokma and told her about the baby. She said it was going to be born in two months, at the end of the summer, and she asked Hokma to help her. She was very frightened of her papa still, and she wouldn't tell Hokma the name of the baby's Code father. She cried and cried, until Hokma said she'd ask the other Or-adults what to do.

"So Hokma called an emergency meeting. She said she would be one of the child's Shelter mothers, but she wouldn't be able to look after a baby and do all her work with the Owleons. She offered to stand for the position of School Spoke on the Parents' Committee to make up for that—and let me tell you, that was appreciated—but she needed other parents to take primary responsibility for you while you were an infant. So we all went away and thought about it, and that night Gaia came to Klor in his dreams. She said the baby was her gift to Or and She asked him to be the baby's Shelter father, have it as a Shelter sibling for Peat and Yoki. When he woke up, he told me about the dream and because I knew Gaia had really been asking us both, I agreed."

Another new question occurred to Astra. "Did you know I was a girl?" she asked.

Nimma blinked, and her smile seemed to freeze for a moment.

Oh no. She had said the wrong thing—something that made Nimma feel bad about Sheba. She gripped her sheet-sausage tightly, started to say sorry, it didn't matter, but Nimma recovered and sailed on. "No," she said briskly. "Eya couldn't go to the hospital for a scan so no one knew your sex. We didn't mind if you were a girl or a boy, Astra. We wanted to Shelter you either way, and Eya was very happy because she knew her baby would be safe and well loved in this world. She did some beautiful crocheting with me then, a little green hat and bootees for when you were born. And when it was Eya's time, Hokma and I helped her to bring a wonderful baby girl into the world."

Nimma said the last words in a light, magical tone, as if the story was over. But it wasn't. "Eya and my Code father chose my name," Astra reminded her.

Nimma smiled. "That's right, darling," she continued, the way she was supposed to. "Eya said you were to be called Astra, which means 'star'—she said that was the name your Code father had chosen."

Astra gazed up at the tin stars in the ceiling. Her Code father was the most mysterious character in the story. But lots of kids had anonymous Code fathers and Astra had never really thought very much about him before. Today, though, she wondered for a moment where he was now. "Does Cora know the name of my Code father?" she asked.

"No, darling. If she did, she would have told Hokma." Nimma reached over and stroked Astra's forehead. "I remember that Eya said your curly hair is just like his. You were born with a cap of black curls— that was very unusual."

That was also fascinating new information. Being born with hair sounded like she had been born older than she really was. Astra wondered if it might be useful to tell Torrent that. Perhaps not. He would doubtless turn it against her somehow.

"What was Eya's hair like?" she asked.

"It was straight and brown." Nimma thought a bit longer. "She wore it shoulder-length. From what she said, I got the impression her community was Northern Neuropean in origin, but like everywhere, other Gaians had joined it over the years."

Astra liked the way Nimma was now talking to her like an adult. "What was her community called?" she asked.

"She never told us, darling," Nimma said. "And we didn't like to pry. I just know that she wanted very much to take you back home with her, but she couldn't. She stayed in Or for a month, breast-feeding you, but then she had to go back to Atourne. Oh, how she cried—but she said she would come and visit every holiday, and she did come back, once, when you were six months old, and she brought the silver bracelet that Klor and I keep in a special drawer for you to look at and play with on special days."

They were back in the story now, Nimma's voice a soft brush painting familiar scenes in her mind. Astra pictured the bracelet, delicate silver links interspersed with five sparkling blue gemstones, one for each lake in Bracelet Valley. It was too big for her wrist still, but she had once put it around her ankle, until Nimma got annoyed and said it would fall off and get lost. There wasn't any chance of that, really, because she was never allowed to take Eya's gift out of Nimma's sight, but she had removed it and drawn a Tabby picture of it instead.

"When I'm thirteen," she said, "I'll be allowed to wear my bracelet on special occasions, and when I'm eighteen, I'm allowed to keep it, and wear it whenever I want."

"That's right, darling." Nimma's voice sounded far away now. Her face was turned toward the greenhouse corridor, not as if she was counting the parallel light lines falling through the blinds over Meem's bed but as though she were looking through them to a place no one else could see.

"Then what happened?" Astra asked, even though she knew. This was the sad part; she'd cried a lot the first time she'd heard it. But now, in a funny way, she liked to hear it.

Nimma shifted in her chair and returned to the story. "Well, we didn't hear from Eya for a while. Then Cora visited and said that she had got married to a wealthy Shelltech engineer, one of her Shelter Code father's friends who lived in a mountain stronghold near her community. Eya had gone to live with him there and she wasn't able to visit Or anymore. She couldn't email or Tablette-talk us either, because her new husband would be very angry if he found out she'd had a baby before she married him. But Eya had told Cora to tell us that she loved Astra very much and would never, ever forget her. One day, if she could, she would come and find Astra, but she didn't know when that would be. In the meantime, she had left her with Hokma and Nimma and Klor because they were the best Shelter parents Astra could have. And that's what we're trying to be, all the time, darling."

Astra lunged forward and hugged her Shelter mother. Her elbow caught the tray, and her bowl and plate and spoons went clattering to the floor. But Nimma didn't shout at her; she hugged her back. Her arms went right around Astra, her cheek rested on Astra's head and her soft breasts enveloped Astra in the smell of wild roses and chamomile, the special perfume Klor gave her every birthday. "I love you, Nimma," Astra blurted. "When I meet Eya, I'm going to tell her you're the best Shared Shelter mother ever in the whole wide world."

Then Nimma did have to go back to Craft House, so Astra came downstairs with her and sat on the sofa beside Elpis in her wheelchair. Elpis nodded and opened her mouth, which was her way of smiling. Nimma wrapped Astra up in a loose-weave shawl with the Earthship Tablette, Libby, on her lap, and asked her to make a picture of Craft House. When Nimma left, Astra unfolded Libby—which was short for Libraria, not a real name but Klor had chosen it so you couldn't argue—to poster size and laid her out on the coffee table, where she drew a big cutaway of Craft House. She put Nimma's team in red and gold robes and Nimma in a silvery-blue kimono and had everyone working at their looms and jewelry tables, surrounded by the racks of faux-grass skirts and house robes and trays of necklaces and hipbeads. Then she looked up at the mantelpiece above Libby's wallnook, to the photograph of Sheba with her fifth-birthday cake, her eyes shining like a Fountain lightshow, and she added a drawing of Sheba in a green hip skirt, floating above Nimma and clapping her hands. "That's bee-you-*tea*-ful," Libby exclaimed, but she wasn't done yet. She scrolled to the blank edges of the drawing and drew the gardens outside Craft House too, adding Is-Land officers, up in the fruit trees and lying in the grass, to protect them all. One was Durga, because Durga was doing her IMBOD Service and had learned how to shoot a gun, and another was Torrent, because even though Torrent was bossy he was good at archery, but the biggest one—of course—was Astra, with Tabby in her pocket and an Owleon flying above her.

"I like this picture very much," Libby said, which made Astra worry that perhaps Libby thought the portrait of Tabby was of her. She thought about writing TABBY underneath it, but she didn't want to hurt Libby's feelings so in the end she didn't. She zoomed out again, and above everyone and everything she painted the Shell, a golden shining dome, and above that missiles veering away from the Shell's magnetic force field and boomeranging back onto the Non-Landers in their strongholds in the deserts and mountains bordering Is-Land.

"Wow, you are drawing lots today," Libby cheered.

And then the picture turned into a huge movie storyboard, with lots of dead Non-Landers covered in blood, and more grieving Non-Landers killing themselves with sharp sticks, and the leaders of Asfar being put in jail by CONC officers and the Guardians of the Servers.

"Done now," she told Libby.

"One hour and twenty-two minutes. You're a drawing superstar," Libby exclaimed. Then Astra showed the whole picture to Elpis and explained each part of the story, and when Elpis drooled a little on her pale, brown-spotted chest, Astra dabbed it up with a hanky like she'd seen Nimma do.

When Nimma came back to see if Astra was well enough for dinner and storytelling, she said how wonderful the picture was, and when Astra pointed out Sheba, she gave Astra a special hug. Then Nimma took her temperature and said she could come to Core House for dinner and to the Fountain afterward, as long as she went straight to bed as soon as Nimma told her. She had a big day tomorrow, traveling with Hokma to meet Dr. Blesserson, and she needed to be all better to make sure she wasn't sick again before her shot.

Yes, Astra thought, she didn't want to throw up in Dr. Blesserson's office. He was a genius, like she was going to be one day, and she was going to talk to him about Code-working and Owleon design and maybe, if Hokma went to the bathroom for a minute, what Hokma was like when she was little. But right now she was starving for her dinner.

1.8

The next morning, when Hokma entered the dining hall and strode over to Nimma and Astra, practically the whole of Or turned and stared. Hokma was wearing a short blue skirt and a lavender linen vest.

Nimma was delighted. "Oh my dewy meadow, I'd forgotten I'd made that for you," she said, pinching the fabric of the vest. Then she tutted. "You're not twenty-odd anymore, Hokma. Let me take it out for you. It will only take half an hour." But Hokma said it was her best outfit and the urbaggers were leaving right after breakfast, so it would have to do. She was also wearing a matching lavender eyepatch. Astra thought she looked less commanding in the paler-colored patch. Perhaps she only wore darker ones when she wanted people to feel afraid of her.

Astra herself was wearing a short sleeveless cotton tunic, loosely belted. It was already damp with sweat between her back and hydropac and would have to be washed later. But Nimma said that most people in Sippur wore clothes and Dr. Blesserson would think she was more grown-up if she did too, so for once she hadn't made a fuss. She'd even let Nimma drag a comb through her hair, though she'd refused to wear a gold ribbon in it. Ribbons were either tied too tight and hurt your scalp, or too loose and fell out when you were running. And bunches felt all knobbly under a flap-hat. Nimma had sighed, but put the ribbon back in her shoulder bag.

Hokma and Nimma went to eat at the adults' table and Astra sat down with her Shelter siblings. Klor was *still* fixing Tabby, so Peat, holding his own Tablette under the table, server-searched Sippur for her. The city, he said, had a population of nearly 25,000 people, which was ginormous compared to Or's 282, and even way bigger than New Bangor's 7,916, though only half as big as Atourne, of course. Astra had known that Sippur was retrofitted like New Bangor. But she hadn't known until Peat told her that it was made of basalt: not only the houses and the sidewalks, but also the thick wall with turrets and ramparts that surrounded the city as if it were a castle.

Basalt was the *cooled lava* from a volcanic eruption. It wasn't orange though, Peat said; it was black and porous, which meant filled with holes. He couldn't show her pictures in case Nimma confiscated his Tablette, so as she ate her porridge and apricots, Astra imagined what he meant. Basalt, she thought, would be like black melted wax after it had cooled and hardened and someone had pricked it all over with a needle. It would be a strange shape, pinched bits sticking out everywhere like the coral Nimma kept on the uppermost shelf in the Earthship living room. Yes—Sippur would look like a giant black coral reef, with steps and roads carved between its weird poking-out fingers, which would sparkle at night from their countless tiny porous windows. And winding all around the city the basalt wall would bulge like a gnarled dragon's tail. She couldn't wait to come home again and tell everyone all about it.

The journey took the whole morning. After breakfast, Astra, Hokma and Nimma picked some flowers for Sheba—an armful of daisies from the Earthship botanical cell, because those had been her favorite flowers, and three spider orchid stems from the lawn for Or. Then Nimma Tablette-talked Klor, who came down from Code House to meet them on the lawn. He was carrying a sprig of apple blossom, and—*yay!*—Tabby.

"Astra's first trip to Sippur." Klor stroked her head as she hugged Tabby and turned him on. "Hokma, really, I should come with you."

"No, Klor." Nimma took the apple blossom and added it to the bouquet. "I don't want you going on that bus. We'll take Astra and the others in the solar van soon."

Phhwweet. An urbagger whistled from the path and waved at Hokma. Astra kissed the IMBOD Shield on Tabby's screen, stuffed him in his pocket, grabbed Hokma's hand and tugged. The van was leaving now. She could catch up properly with Tabby on the road.

"I'll take good care of her, Klor," Hokma reassured him as Nimma retrieved the gold hair ribbon from her bag and tied it around the stems. Watching her, Astra remembered again that she shouldn't be excited about going to Sippur.

"Can I carry Sheba's flowers, Nimma?" she asked.

"Yes, darling. But take good care of them or you'll have to give them to Hokma."

The bouquet was big but not heavy. Astra cradled it in her arms. Nimma started dabbing her eyes with a hanky from her bag. Klor put his arm around her. "Sheba always wanted a little sister, didn't she, Nimma?" he said.

"Umm." Nimma's response was almost a whimper.

Astra felt frightened for a moment. It wasn't like Nimma not to talk.

From East Gate, the van honked. "We'd better be off, then," Hokma said.

Astra let Klor and Nimma both kiss her, then trotted after Hokma to the van. When she got to East Gate she turned and gave a final good-bye wave. Klor and Nimma were hunched together, haloed by the sun behind them, as if they'd disappeared and only their dark shapes were left floating on the lawn.

"Quick, Astra," Hokma ordered. "Arjun wants to get off." Astra jumped into the back of the van and sat down on a side plank opposite Sorrel. Between them the floor of the van was filled with plants the urbaggers were delivering to shops and houses in New Bangor.

The van rumbled off and Astra sat quietly checking Tabby's functions. Everything was fine. His emotional weather report was sunny and breezy, and on his school homepage there was a new download: the official photo of the two IMBOD medical officers. She showed Sorrel, who said, "Don't they look impressive? But *you're* going to get your shot from Dr. Blesserson. Wow!" Then Astra wanted to ask Hokma lots of questions, about Dr. Blesserson and Cora and her Code father, and whether Klor had ever been back on the bus to Sippur. But when the driver, Arjun, asked Hokma what Dr. Blesserson was working on now, she just grunted, and said, "Gaia knows!" in a grumpy voice. So Astra put Tabby back in his pocket and examined the plants, asking Sorrel all about them. Sorrel was very friendly. She plucked a stem of yellow freesias and loosened the ribbon to add it to Sheba's bouquet. And when they stopped at the Sunbat station outside New Bangor for Arjun to exchange the van's solar batteries and for Hokma to take Astra to the bathroom to pee, Sorrel bought Astra a bottle of peach nectar to drink.

The bus stop for Sippur was on the far side of New Bangor. Arjun drove there first to drop them off. Waiting by the side of the road, holding the flowers for Sheba, who had never woken up after being on the bus, was strange in itself, but other things were odd too. You couldn't just walk up to the stop: there was a fence around it and an IMBOD officer at the gate who scanned their hydropacs and clothes with a paddle sensor. He even took Tabby out of his pocket and scanned him. When he'd finished, he didn't give him back right away. He turned Tabby off.

"What?" Astra yelped to Hokma behind her. Tabby had only just been fixed. Was the officer going to take him away from her?

The officer pointed to a sign on the fence, a picture of a handheld with a red line through it. "No Tablette usage on the bus," he ordered, handing Tabby back.

"Sorry, Astra, I should have told you to switch him off," Hokma said, reaching in her bag for her own Tablette.

Astra had wanted to tell the officer that her flowers were for Sheba, but she didn't like him anymore so she kept her mouth closed and waited for Hokma to be scanned. Inside the fenced enclosure, some of the other people were wearing clothes—skirts and robes. None of them, even the sky-clad ones, looked at Astra and asked how she was, or said to Hokma how good the bioregional security was, or what a beautiful day Gaia had brought, like people in New Bangor shops would have done. They just stood around, not looking at each other, occasionally peering through the fence down the road for the bus. There were four seats in the enclosure, but they were all taken. Behind them was a screen, displaying National and Bioregional Wheel Meet news. Astra waited beside Hokma, the bouquet in her arms getting heavier, almost as if the flowers were turning into a painted toxic metal, like in a fairy tale.

At last the bus drew up, shuddering to a stop and aligning its door with another gate in the fence. It was an ordinary bus, like the one that took her to school, but at the same time it was a big white metal shark that might eat you and keep you inside it forever. The IMBOD officer opened the gate and Astra hesitated a moment. Then Hokma put her hand on her shoulder and guided her firmly up the steps of the bus and to a window seat.

"It's a very scenic journey," she said sternly as the bus pulled back out onto the road, almost as if ordering Astra to look at it. But Astra was staring at the necks of the women in front of her. The women's heads were shaved and each of them had a big red lumpy scar right at the base of her skull.

"Hokma," she whispered, pointing at the women.

"Shhh." Hokma scowled. She was tugging at her vest. Maybe, Astra realized, she was in a bad mood because of the clothes.

Astra rested Sheba's flowers on her lap, then took off her flap-hat and stuffed it between the seats. The bus rumbled down the road, winding through the forest northwest of New Bangor. The firegrounds were behind them here, and between stringybarks and pines were side roads signposted with the familiar names of her school friends' communities—Boson, Higgs, Sonnenplatz, Shady Grove, Windfall. Then there was a long stretch of just trees and Astra returned her attention to the scarskulled women. Suddenly, as she was counting the neat white holes surrounding the red lump directly in front of her, the woman grabbed her companion's arm and said loudly, tapping at the window, "The Congregation Site shines today. Praise Gaia."

Hokma was sleeping, but nearly everyone else in the bus craned their necks. Half-standing, Astra followed the woman's finger. The Boundary in the dry forest ran high on the slopes or behind inhabited hills and was color-blended with the foliage and rocks so even in photographs you couldn't really see it. But there it was: the Bioregional Congregation Site flashing like a golden waterfall in the distance. The Congregation Site was designed to shine—it was for pilgrimages and ceremonies—and though Astra had been there once, she had been just a baby then and she wouldn't return until the Blood & Seed ceremony, which was ages away, at the end of Year Seven. She hadn't known you could see it from the bus. Why hadn't Hokma *told* her? If only she was allowed to use Tabby—she could have taken a photo to show everyone at home. She fingered the flowers in her lap. Had Sheba seen the Boundary too?

Even more awesome than the glimpse of the Boundary was the descent to the steppes, which was a whole new bioregion. Though Astra had seen far more of the steppes from up in the pine tree, it wasn't until the road leveled off and the bus left the mountains and foothills behind that she understood how unutterably vast they truly were. When you were up high, she realized, you felt huge, but traveling through the steppes, unable to see beyond the line of their rising slopes, you realized that you weren't even a freckle on the face of Gaia.

That revelation was followed by a slowly unfolding shock. Before, the steppes had always looked neatly if eccentrically patterned, like a cape or quilt made from random bits of fabric someone had spent years carefully fitting together. Astra had always assumed that the pieces were all fields, planted or lying fallow. Now, though, with her nose pressed to the bus window, she could see that huge parts of Is-Land's interior were almost as desolate as the firegrounds. The roads were lined at intervals with narrow fields of grain or vegetables and there was the occasional walled orchard or llama pen, but these cultivated plots were dwarfed by the huge dirt hills billowing in all directions, their bowls of dry soil etched only with dry, sage-colored bushes. The steppes, she now knew, were largely a world without water or trees or anything humans needed to survive.

Was this Gaia's crone face, Astra wondered: parched and cracked, gifted with supernatural endurance? It was a frightening vision, and a warped one too. Down here, the heat haze that had shimmered in the view from the pine tree was as thickly rippled as the glass in the Old World silver mirror that Nimma kept in a drawer in her bedroom. The swollen heat waves were pressing in all around them; if Astra peered down the aisle to look out of the driver's big window it looked like the bus was swimming underwater. The road ahead even looked *wet*, but as the bus got closer to the black patches she'd first assumed were puddles, they mysteriously evaporated. The wildness of the steppes, she thought, in a tangled kind of way, wasn't one of pathless woods and rampant growth; it was more like she imagined the Barren Mountains to be: a climbing loneliness, an almost-emptiness that snatched away everything you ever thought you knew.

She wanted to ask Hokma all about the steppes, but Hokma was still sleeping, her head rolling against the bus seat. Astra kept thinking surely she would jerk awake any minute, but she didn't, so she turned back to her window.

There were dirt tracks off the highway, signposted to communities she'd heard of only in passing, or not at all: Ripen, Sarsaparilla, Aberffraulein, Mahā Vidyā. Occasionally the bus passed a van or a cart, the carts pulled by garlanded cows or shire horses, but otherwise the road was empty. At one point the bus crossed an intersection, another main road between two steppes towns she did recognize: Sommerville in one direction and Nīrāgā in the other.

Then, after what seemed like ages, huge square buildings began to march along the sides of the roads, at least eight stories high, twice as high as any in New Bangor, but all empty, with dirty, broken windows. Why hadn't they been demolished? Peat would know. Perhaps IMBOD thought they might be useful again one day, or maybe the Bioregional Wheel Meet had run out of money for demolitions. These buildings were too nice to tear down, anyway: they were covered in mosaics, made of small tiles in patterns like needlework on a Craft House tablecloth. The colors had faded to shades of gray, and some of the tiles had fallen out, but you could still see that the design on each building was different from its neighbors'. That was very special. It made you want to keep staring and staring, never getting bored. Astra wanted to jump out and clean the tiles to make them gleam again in the sun.

But the bus rolled on, and now the farmed fields and grazing pastures started to crowd out the barren stretches of the steppes. Astra saw a woman herding sheep, a girl placing flowers at a cow shrine and a man riding a horse toward an Earthship, and then there was a deep stretch of greenhouses, their pointed roofs reflecting the sun. The bus stopped in front of them to let some more people on. Was it here that the man with the bomb had got on Klor and Sheba's bus? Astra shook Hokma's arm.

"Uh, are we there?" Hokma stretched, and smiled for the first time all day. "You've taken good care of those flowers, haven't you?"

They were nearly there, and yes, Astra had, and her reward was seeing the Shugurra River before Hokma did, a beautiful blue snake glinting ahead between its bright green banks. The bus crossed the water on a long low-walled bridge, and after that the land was green and lush everywhere, dotted with little sandstone retrofitted houses, their gardens filled with flowers: yellow flags, aurums, freesias and anemones, and other blossoms Astra had never seen before. There were people, too, watering their plants, sitting on porches or walking up the road, and apart from a few children, *they were all wearing clothes.* The women were dressed in tunics like hers, or smocks and skirts. Some of the men were in robes or sarongs and others were wearing loose pants. Around her, on the bus, the sky-clad passengers were pulling robes and tunics out of their hydropacs and putting them on. The bus stopped again to pick up people and let others off, and when it started moving again, there in front of her, high on a terraced hill, was the basalt wall of Sippur.

The wall wasn't spiny and craggy, like she'd imagined, but sheer-sided and crested as if with great rotting black teeth. Two massive white Is-Land banners were draped either side of its arched entrance, the Is-Land Shield standing proud in their centers, and green, gold and red wavy lines running across the tops and the bottoms. It was hard to imagine the loom that could have woven such banners. It would have to be a giant loom in an industrial warehouse, like the alt-meat vat factories.

The road looped steadily toward the archway. As they neared Astra could see that it was crested by a huge sculpture of . . . a black pigeon, its breast plumped out over the road and its feet gripping the block of basalt it was carved from.

"Look, Hokma!" She tugged at Hokma's vest.

"I know. The pigeon is the city's holy bird. For the people who built the wall it represented the goddess of love."

The woman in front of Astra turned around and addressed them. "Gaia is the one true goddess of love," she said quietly. Astra flinched. The woman was unnerving. Her face was round and still, her eyes were unblinking and her gappy teeth were as black as the wall's.

"Gaia is all goddesses, and all men and women are Gaia's ambassadors," Hokma replied.

The woman appeared to be satisfied with this response. She nodded serenely, and as the bus neared the archway, returned her attention to her companion. It was dark now, because the wall was at least five yards thick, but as they entered Astra could see that the basalt did have millions of little pores in it, like black speckles in the smooth sides of the bricks. Then for a moment, there was no one on the bus but whispering shadows, and the scars on the women's skulls were two black, twisted eyeholes. A second later the bus reemerged into the sunshine, and the driver pulled up in front of a fruit market.

This was where Klor and Sheba's bus had exploded.

Everyone stood up. Clutching the flowers to her chest, Astra let Hokma put her flap-hat back on, then, one slow, inching step after the next, she followed her Shelter mother off the bus, and out of the bus-stop enclosure.

They stood on the sidewalk for a moment. The street was zooming with bicycles, carts and cars and the sidewalk was crowded with stalls covered with red-and-white striped awnings. People were examining apples, apricots, pomegranates and dates, fruit that must have been grown in the greenhouses. A seller called out to Hokma, who ignored him. Astra stood paralyzed in the whirlwind of activity, the sun beating down on her arms.

"There's a lot of people here, isn't there?" Hokma said.

"Umm."

"Do you know where they go to cool down?"

"No."

Hokma pointed across the street to a small park in the shadow of the wall. "To Sheba's Fountain."

There was a traffic light on the corner. Normally Astra was supposed to hold an adult's hand when she crossed the road, but she wanted to carry the bouquet properly, so she walked in front of Hokma instead, with Hokma's hand on her shoulder. She held the flowers up high and the cars and bikes and horse carts all stopped for them.

The sidewalk was busy, but the park was peaceful, a triangular lawn planted with a circle of apple trees, the grass strewn with blossoms. At its center was a shallow basalt basin, a black lens resting on a slender concave pillar, from which a fragile spine of water rose about a yard in the air, gradually separating as it fell into graceful sprays shining silver in the sun that arced back down to the basin. Astra drew closer and saw there were three gleaming metal cups set into niches in the pillar, which was buttressed by a curving set of steps so that even the smallest child could lean over and drink from the spray. Above the cups was a small silver plaque. It said, *For Sheba, who loved to dance in the trees.*

The Fountain was like a tiny willow tree, eternally weeping on a thin black moonshell. It was too sad for words. But it was achingly beautiful too. Sheba was there: Astra felt her. She wasn't wearing a flap-hat. Her hair was streaming in a breeze no one else could feel, and she was crying and laughing and dancing at the same time. Her tears were keeping everyone cool, and as they hissed into the air they sang *sister, sister, sister.*

"Where can we put the flowers?" she whispered. Hokma showed her a trough curving around the steps for dogs and cats to drink from. The trough had a central bank with recesses for flowers. Other people had been tending it: a row of cherry and apple branches were shedding their petals into the water.

"Can Tabby take a photo for Nimma and Klor?" Astra asked. "Me putting the flowers down? And one of the Fountain, just by itself?"

"That's a nice idea." Hokma took Tabby and stepped back to frame the photos. She took the one of the Fountain first, and then Astra knelt and carefully placed Sheba's bouquet into the bank, making sure you could see the orchids and Sorrel's freesias and the sprig of apple blossom among the daisies and then she had to check that all the stems were dipped into the water. It didn't feel right to smile or even look at Tabby. She just kept her hand on the stems for a minute so that the picture wouldn't be blurry and it would be clear which flowers were from Or.

Afterward Hokma showed her the photos and they were perfect. The Fountain was casting no shadow and on her knees, reaching across the petalled water, Astra looked exactly like she felt: full of awe and respect. *Reverential.* Somehow, she realized, being in this place even for a few minutes had changed her feelings about Sheba. Before she had secretly been afraid of Sheba: terrified of the bus-bomb and scared to ask questions in case of upsetting Nimma. Now she felt like she knew Sheba a little. And she liked her. Sheba wasn't like Meem or Silvie or any other girl Astra knew. She was pretty and playful, but she was wise and comforting too.

"When a person returns to Gaia," she said slowly as Hokma turned Tabby off, "after a while, Gaia gives them back to us, doesn't She?"

"That's exactly right, Astra," Hokma said. "She gives us back the best part of everyone. Now, shall we let Sheba give us a drink?"

After they left the park Astra wanted to explore Sippur, but Hokma said that Dr. Blesserson was expecting them right away so they took a taxi up a wide road lined with all kinds of shops, a bit like New Bangor Square, but long and thronging with people. The buildings were tall, not like the crumbling apartments on the outskirts, but four or five stories high. Is-Land flags were rippling from the roofs, and more banners were draped down the walls, giving the city a holiday feeling. But Astra asked the taxi driver, who said it wasn't a special festival: everyone here celebrated Is-Land every day. They also liked shopping. Beneath the banners, each block was devoted to a different type of produce. First, there was food everywhere: garlands of dried peppers hanging from canopies; colorful bins full of pistachios, almonds, walnuts, sunflower seeds, dried figs, dates and apricots; sacks of grains and pulses, all set out on the sidewalk to tempt passers-by. Then came a street of soap- and perfume-sellers, followed by a block of Tablette shops, the shiny devices lined up neatly behind the glass shop fronts. The taxi turned down another long road and here the sidewalks were filled with clothes, masses of them, all fluttering on rails next to racks full of sunglasses, hats and hydropacs. Astra and Tabby took pictures of everything.

"Hokma?" she asked at last, "why do people in Sippur wear clothes?"

"Well," Hokma said, "for a few reasons. Originally there was a big CONC station here and the Gaians who worked with the internationals wore robes out of politeness. There's still a CONC travel office, and a lot of visitors, so the habit stuck, I suppose. But also, urban dwellers aren't lucky like us in the dry forest, or people in rural communities: there are so many buildings and roads here and they can't plant enough trees to shade everyone, and the Code for melanoma protection only works up to a point. The lighter-skinned people especially need to cover up."

In the front seat, the taxi driver laughed. "There's another reason too, but only the locals know it, Is-child. The streets are very dusty and there aren't enough trees to stop the wind, so the grit flies right up into your Gaia parts. Don't you worry, though, we all go sky-clad at home."

"Does Dr. Blesserson go—?" Astra started to ask.

But Hokma wasn't listening. "In a minute, Astra. Driver, take the outer-wall road please."

"That's the long route, lady—and there's an extra charge for punctures."

"I know that. Just take it, please. Astra, be quiet now. I want you to see this."

Then the taxi was exiting the wall through another massive archway, this one topped with two stone lions, and she was looking down upon a terrifying view: in the near distance an immense crater—bigger than Or, surely—obliterated the land. Its lip was a rim of rubble, its base a cracked dish of bleached soil and it was surrounded by acres of debris: broken sandstone, crumbled tarmac, ancient rusting stoves and refrigerators, twisted metal posts and what looked like fallen logs with nails sticking out of them, all tangled up in wires. Speechless, Astra gaped at the sight.

The taxi turned right, skirting the ruined area and driving slowly along the foot of the wall. People were dragging things out of the pile of unrecycled metal and it was easy to see that nails and sharp scraps could be falling in the road.

"Sippur was bombed at the start of the Dark Time," Hokma said in her teacher voice. "We still don't know which of our neighboring nations was responsible, or why they chose a residential area instead of the old city. Incredibly, the basalt wall withstood the shock, but the radiation fallout was severe. That's when the last of the Non-Landers fled."

"All of this was *houses*?" Astra asked incredulously.

The taxi driver looked at her in the rearview mirror. "Don't you worry about the Non-Landers," he chuckled. "Plenty of homes for Non-Landers in Asfar, where they belong."

He'd misunderstood her question. She'd meant, how could buildings cover so much of Gaia's face? Surely there had also been trees and grass and parks here? Had not one tree regenerated?

She opened her mouth to correct him, but Hokma butted in. "She knows all about the Non-Landers."

The driver sniffed. "Course she does. I was just saying."

Astra lifted Tabby to the window, but Hokma's hand shot out to her wrist. "No photos here, Astra."

"Why?"

"There are plenty of photos online, and we're nearly there now." It wasn't an answer but Hokma suddenly sounded as stern as the bus stop IMBOD officer. They finished the ride in silence, leaving the pulverized moonscape and entering another green, leafy neighborhood with all of Astra's questions rattling behind them.

At last the taxi drove away, leaving them standing at Dr. Blesserson's gate, through which Astra could see a two-story white wooden house and a long stone outbuilding. "How do you know Dr. Blesserson will help us?" she asked.

Hokma rang the bell on the gatepost. "I don't," she replied shortly. "But he owes me a favor and I'm hoping he'd like to pay me back."

"What favor did you do for him?"

"Shh, Astra. It's not important. Please just be quiet here and do exactly as I say."

"*Hello?*" A male voice crackled through the intercom.

"Samrod. It's Hokma."

"But—" Astra tugged at Hokma's vest.

"*Shhhh,*" Hokma hissed.

There was no reply from the intercom, but the gate swung open. Astra trudged resentfully after Hokma up the long white-pebbled drive. It was fine to say "do as I say," but only if you had actually given a constable some instructions. They were on a mission and she'd had no orders. It wouldn't be *her* fault if everything went wrong.

As she plodded up the drive behind Hokma, Dr. Samrod Blesserson emerged from his house. He was wearing a sky-blue linen shirt and white drawstring pants, and he didn't come out to meet them but waited in the shade on the front porch until they neared the house. Then he jogged quickly down the steps to greet them. Or Hokma, at least. He ignored Astra, and though he kissed both Hokma's cheeks, he didn't smile or seem remotely pleased to see his Birth-Code-Shelter sister. Squinting up at him, Astra couldn't tell if he was a nice man or not. He was tall like Hokma, and had the same dark wavy hair, square face and full lips as her, but rather more forehead. As well as clothes, he was wearing wire-framed glasses, a watch and an impatient expression.

"I keep the shots in the clinic," he said, jutting his chin toward the outbuilding. That made him look exactly like Hokma.

"Actually, Samrod, Astra's frightened of needles. I told her we could see the orchard first, if it's not too much bother." Hokma placed her hand on Astra's neck and gave a warning squeeze. She hadn't even known there was an orchard.

Samrod looked at his watch and then down at Astra, for the first time. At first she thought he was annoyed with her. Then he gave a tight little smile. "So, an arboriculturalist, are we?" he asked.

She cocked her head back up at him. "What does that mean?"

"Someone who studies trees. I'd have thought you'd have learned that already in a dry forest school."

Beneath her tunic her chest got a little hot, but she tried not to hate him, not just yet. He didn't know yet that she was going to be a genius scientist too.

"I like climbing trees," she said, jutting out her chin too. "Especially apple trees. Do you have any of those?"

"I do. A prize-winning Pink Lady, in fact. And I don't want her branches broken. Look, Hokma, this is short notice and I don't have much time. You can show her the orchard afterward."

But Hokma was tugging Astra down the path between the house and the outbuilding. "Trust me, Samrod," she said over her shoulder, "you don't want her climbing your clinic walls."

Her brother strode rapidly after them. Hokma waited at the orchard gate. It was a small orchard, surrounded by a low stone wall, with twenty or so trees, mostly cherries or plums, all in blossom.

"I'm serious, Hokma. I don't want her monkeying around in the trees." Samrod definitely sounded annoyed now. "They're all very young still."

"She won't do any climbing, I promise. Samrod, I need to talk to you. Can we sit down?"

"Why couldn't you Tablette-talk me? Or send an Owleon? So mysterious, Hokma."

"Please, Samrod. It will only take ten minutes."

He stared at her, then opened the gate and gestured to a wooden bench between two magenta-blossomed cherry trees.

Astra followed at a distance as they crossed the grass toward it. Samrod didn't seem to like Hokma very much. This was why Is-kids now all had to be brought up by least three people, she remembered. Previously, siblings often didn't get along because they had to compete for the scarce resources of only one or two parents.

Hokma sat down on the bench. "Astra, you go and play while I talk to Samrod," she said. "You can run around in the orchard, but keep Tabby turned off and *no climbing*."

What? Why were there all these rules about Tabby today? "Why can't I take photos?"

"Astra. What did I tell you just now? Just *do as I say*."

It wasn't fair. Why was *she* being shouted at when Dr. Blesserson was the one being rude and mean? Astra dawdled further among the trees as Samrod arranged himself at the opposite end of the bench. She was behind them now and they couldn't see her. But sure enough, Hokma looked over her shoulder and stared at her so she slumped down under what she hoped was the famous Pink Lady apple tree and just to look busy took a Knitting Nancy out of her pac.

Hokma turned back to Samrod. He was leaning against the armrest of the bench with his arms crossed. He didn't look as though he would offer his sister a cup of echinacea tea, let alone agree to break the law for her.

There was a rhododendron bush a few feet behind the bench. Astra slipped the Knitting Nancy back into her pac and got up. Quietly, she moved first away from the bench, then, in a wide circle, from tree to tree, back toward it, pausing and watching to make sure that she hadn't been heard. At last she was crouching behind the bush, peering at the adults through the leaves. They were speaking very quickly, their voices overlapping, and Samrod was leaning toward his sister now, his hand gripping the back of the bench.

"You don't believe in it any more than I do!" Hokma said loudly, throwing her hands up in the air so that one of them nearly caught her brother on the chin.

"What? And keep your voice down!" Samrod hissed, looking around him. There were houses either side of the wall, but unless they were hiding like Astra, none of his neighbors were out in their gardens.

"That's why you left GeneIsis, isn't it?" his sister pressed. "Because you can see how dangerous it is for us all."

"No, Hokma: I left the GeneIsis project because I had contributed all that I could and there were other demands on my time. If you think I am now going to sabotage the work of my colleagues and jeopardize the security of my country, you are very much mistaken." Samrod brushed a drift of cherry petals off the lap of his white pants.

When Hokma spoke again, it was in a low voice so that Astra had to strain to hear her. "I lost my eye, Samrod. I don't complain. I can see many things far more clearly now than I ever could before. But still I'm just one accident or defect away from total blindness."

"I *knew* it. I knew one day you'd come here and blame me for—"

Hokma raised her voice. "I've never regretted what I did. It was worth it to see you happy. All I'm asking is that you do one small thing for me in return. No one will ever know. And I'll never ask anything of you again."

Samrod had clearly forgotten that his neighbors might be listening. "I'm sorry about your frigging *eye*, Hokma," he shouted. "I always have been! But the point is, I never asked you to jump in front of that bullet. I wasn't even *there*."

"The *point*, Samrod," Hokma raised her voice again, "is that you didn't *have* to ask me to do it. I did it for you *instinctively*, because I'm your *sister*. And now I'm asking you to do something for me, not just because you know it's the right thing to do, but because you're my *brother*."

"Hokma the Hero," Samrod spat. "Hokma the Visionary. Won't get a prosthetic—no, you wear that designer patch like a medal, so no one will ever forget that courage runs like molten gold in your veins. Well, not everyone lives for risk and glory and obscure political vendettas, Hokma. What you're asking could land me in a traitor's well. I should report you for even suggesting it."

Samrod was trembling now, but Hokma didn't flinch. Calmly she replied, "He was a shit officer, Samrod. He thought about himself first, himself second, and the team third. But I knew how you felt about him and I couldn't let some barefoot kid shoot him dead."

To Astra's astonishment, Samrod's shoulders started heaving and he buried his face in his hands. Was Dr. Blesserson *crying*? Hokma leaned over and touched his sleeve, but he brushed her hand away.

"He wasn't worth an eyelash," he choked.

"He loved you in the end," Hokma said. "And he gave you all this—" She gestured at the house and the clinic, and around the orchard.

Samrod groaned. "I don't want to talk about him."

"We don't have to talk about him. Let's talk about what we *believe* in. What Mama and Baba and Paloma would have wanted us to do—"

"I don't want to talk about Paloma either! Or our parents. They're *dead*, Hokma, and the world is moving on without them. It's *evolving*, all right? The world is consciously, *collectively*, evolving toward a better future and there is nothing you nor I can do about that except evolve with it too."

Hokma stared out again over the field in front of the orchard. "He changed you," she said quietly. "I thought I'd get you back after he left, but I still don't know where you went."

Her brother stiffened. "I am right here. Precisely *right* here, in my orchard, beside my house and clinic, all of which mean a great deal to me, Hokma, as I am sure your work does to you too." Dr. Blesserson had brought himself back under control, Astra realized. Shouting about his dead family seemed to have calmed him down. "Quite frankly," he continued, "why you would want to ruin a young girl's life is beyond me. Personally, I think it's despicable of you to embark on this course of action without the consent of her other parents."

"She's my only Shelter daughter," Hokma said quietly, "and you're my one hope to help her. Please, Samrod. No one will ever find out—and if they do, I'll tell them I gave her an antidote. I know there is one."

There was a long pause. Samrod took off his glasses, cleaned them on his shirt, then put them back on his nose.

"Hokma," he said at last, "I'm sick of the sight of you. If I do help you, that's it. We're not just even, we're *through*. I don't want to advise on any more of your IMBOD projects, I don't want you coming around here to psychoanalyze me or browbeat me about Paloma, and I don't want any updates on your little experiment. You will take her back to your off-grid human safari and leave me alone. Forever. Understood?"

Astra narrowed her eyes. *I'm not Hokma's "little experiment"*, she wanted to shout. *I'm Hokma's Shelter daughter. And that, Dr. Blesserson, makes me your Shelter niece! And Hokma's not going to ruin my life. One day I'm going to be a genius, a bigger genius than you! That's why you want me to have my shot, isn't it? So I won't be more famous than you. Tell him, Hokma, tell him that's why we're doing it and not telling Nimma and Klor!*

But Hokma just nodded. Once. "Understood. Thank you, Samrod."

The adults stood up and turned to look across the orchard. "Astra!" Hokma yelled.

Astra's heart began to pound, and she squirmed deeper into the bush.

"If she's damaged any of those trees, I'll be sending you the bill," Samrod warned.

"She's just playing somewhere. I'll find her. We'll see you at the clinic." Hokma walked deeper into the orchard and Samrod strode back to the gate.

Astra waited until he was through it before emerging from the bush. Hokma was at the far end of the orchard now, she could see, so she ran down the wall to the opposite corner. Then she shouted, "Here I am!" and skipped toward her Shelter mother.

"Where were you?" Hokma inspected her. "Did you climb a tree?"

"No! I was hiding." Astra pointed at the long grass along the wall. "I had to patrol the perimeter." It wasn't exactly a lie. She had done both of those things, and she hadn't climbed a tree. Lying was easy if you just told the truth but left some parts out.

"Good girl, Astra. There'd better not be any broken branches, that's all. Now look: he's agreed to help us but he's not very happy about it, so you must be very polite, and thank him nicely, okay?"

Astra remembered to look surprised. "He's going to help us? *Yay.*" She hugged Hokma, who laughed.

"Yes, it's good news, isn't it? Come on, he's waiting at the clinic."

Dr. Blesserson vaccinated Astra against a nearly extinct disease called "teaby," so that she would have a scar on her shoulder, just like the other Or-kids. He was grumpy, and apart from telling her to roll up her sleeve, didn't speak to her—he didn't even warn her nicely that the needle would hurt, and he didn't have any kids' plasters with frogs or lollipops on them. Instead he stuck a round blue grown-up plaster on her arm. Then he gave Hokma a chill bag and a needle full of Security Serum. If she kept the shot in the freezer, he explained, it would last for ten years. If IMBOD ever planned to test Astra, as long as they had a little notice Hokma could give her the dose. The older she was the less effect it would have; the critical period of skills-leveling was between now and the age of twelve. But at least the Serum would be in her bloodstream.

A muscle in Dr. Blesserson's jaw was twitching, Astra noticed, and it kept pulsing as he powered on his screendesk, logged into the IMBOD Security Serum database and ticked a box by Astra Ordott's name. He added a note on her file that he had personally given her the shot, then he esigned her certificate and emailed it to Astra's school.

"Thank you, Samrod," Hokma said, holding the chill bag on her lap. "Astra, if you're ever tested and I can't give you this shot before hand, we're going to say that I gave you an antidote. So no judge is ever going to question that certificate, Samrod."

Samrod closed the email tab. "I don't want to talk about judges. I want to forget this meeting ever happened."

Hokma stood up. "It will be fine, Samrod. No one's ever going to know." She put her hand on Astra's back and pushed her forward.

"Thank you, Dr. Blesserson," Astra said. "And my teacher says thank you too."

Dr. Blesserson practically flew out of his chair. "Her *teacher's* in on this too?" He lunged at his sister, his arms flapping up again like they had in the orchard. "Do you really want to get me arrested, Hokma? Is that what this is about? Vengeance for your eye? I wasn't *there*, Hokma. I wasn't even *there*."

His own eyes were bulging like frogspawn, his face had reddened and flecks of his spit landed on Astra cheeks—one on her *lip*—but she was too frightened to wipe them away.

"No, no!" Hokma pulled Astra close. "Samrod, no—you mean Ms. Raintree, don't you, Astra? Samrod, I told the teacher you would give Astra her shot and she was thrilled. She said that your PTSS treatment had helped her immensely after her spinal cord injury in the Belt. She got quite emotional about it. *Of course* I didn't tell her anything about today."

Dr. Blesserson ran his hand through his hair. His breath was loud and wheezy and there were two big sweat patches beneath his armpits. He would have to wash his shirt soon, maybe even buy a new one. Glaring at his sister, he sat back down in his chair. "I just want to keep on doing my work, Hokma *supporting* this country, not undermining it."

"We all want to do our best for Is-Land, Samrod. Thank you very much for your help today. I won't bother you again."

In response, her brother waved them out of his clinic. He didn't get up and he didn't see them to the gate. Back out on the verge of the road, Astra squeezed some pac water into her palm and scrubbed her face where Dr. Blesserson had spat on it.

Hokma called for a taxi on her Tablette. They were in the shade and she didn't nag Astra about her flap-hat. Instead, as they waited, she picked cherry blossoms out of Astra's hair. Astra wondered if she could ask now why Dr. Blesserson had helped them. Maybe Hokma would tell her the story of saving the officer and how it felt to get shot in the eye, and why Samrod used to love the officer and why he now hated the officer and Hokma. But when she looked up at Hokma she saw that Hokma's eye was gleaming, and then she spied a tear dripping down over her lashes. So she didn't ask; she picked at the edges of her blue plaster until Hokma said, "Don't, Astra." Other than that, all the while they waited for the taxi, Hokma didn't say anything at all. She just unbuttoned her vest and let her sweat-slicked breasts dry in the sun.

1.9

The next day was Arkaday, the day most Or-kids saw parents they didn't spend much time with in the week. After breakfast, chores and Kinbat laps, Hokma took Astra back to Wise House. They stopped on the way to have a picnic by the brook, spreading a red hempcloth over a weathered pine bench that Klor and Ahn had built when Or was new. Hokma was in a much better mood today. She was wearing a jade necklace and a green eyepatch stitched with silver thread. She unpacked a frosted lemon cake and a flask of fizzy orange juice and poured them each a coconut-shell cupful.

"Here's to Mission Accomplished," she toasted.

"Mission Accomplished!" Astra clicked her cup to Hokma's and they both took a swig in celebration of their triumph. It was their first ever picnic, just the two of them, Astra thought. Maybe they should toast that too. Except perhaps you could only make one toast per picnic? She was going to ask, but Hokma spoke first.

"It wasn't so hard last night, was it?" she asked.

Astra shook her head. "No, it was fun!" And really, it hadn't felt like lying at all. She'd been planning to mostly tell the truth, like in the orchard, just leaving some parts out, but in fact she hadn't had to say much at all about her shot. When they'd arrived back at Or with the urbaggers she'd run to show Nimma and Klor and Elpis her blue plaster and her certificate and the photos of Sheba's Fountain, which Tabby had already sent to Libby to share with everyone. Elpis had waved her finger over Libby's screen and opened and closed her mouth three times, which meant she liked the pictures very much, and Astra had sat on Klor's lap, waiting for him and Nimma to say they wanted to hang Libby in her wallnook in poster mode and display the photo of Astra placing the Or flowers in the trough. Perhaps, she had thought, looking up at the mantelpiece, Nimma and Klor might even say they would buy another digiframe and put the picture next to the photograph of Sheba so that everyone who visited the Earthship could see that Sheba had a little Shelter sister who loved her.

But Nimma and Klor hadn't done any of that. Klor had hugged Astra and said they would add the photos to their Sheba album, wouldn't they Nimma? And Nimma had said "Yes, dear." Astra hadn't even known there was a whole Sheba album, but when she asked to see it, Nimma said, "Not today, darling," and that was that. Then Klor had admired her plaster and asked if her shot had hurt, and she'd said, "No, well, yes, a little bit but I didn't cry." Nimma had hugged her too, and said she was a brave girl and should go out to play now before dinner. On the Kinbat track she'd discovered that the other kids' plasters were getting grubby now, so she'd lorded it over them, telling everyone about Dr. Blesserson's orchard, where she'd climbed his Gold Medal Pink Lady apple tree and he'd said she would be an outstanding arbiculty-ist one day. Yes, everything had gone very well, and maybe Nimma and Klor would show her Sheba's album soon.

"Good." Hokma smiled. "We'll just see how things go, how the shot affects the others. If you need to change your behavior a little, we'll decide what to do together. But we can only discuss that here or in Wise House. Okay?"

Astra reached for a piece of cake. "Okay. Can I feed the chicks by myself today?" she asked. "I mean, except for killing the worms."

"You can."

"*Yay.*" With her free hand, Astra gave the bench a ferocious karate chop, setting the coconut cups atremble.

Hokma moved her cup away from Astra. "Helium's back. Maybe you'd like to meet him first?"

"Yes way!" Astra took a slurp of her juice. "I want to help feed him too."

Astra would learn how to feed all the Owleons, Hokma explained, and she would also help clean the huts and monitor the alt-mouse incubator. Soon she could start training the chicks to eat from a glove, and then to jump onto it. After that, they would train the chicks to fly, and when they were ready IMBOD would come and take them away for testing. It would take another two months to see if the Edition Four upgrade was successful; if it had been, then the birds would be returned for breeding and the cycle would begin again. If not, Hokma would have to tweak the Code and start again with new eggs. But in either case, if Astra learned how to train Owleons this summer, they could nurture six to eight chicks next time between them and double the profit for Or.

"Are you up for that?"

Astra's mouth was full of cake. "Um-hmm," she said through the crumbs. She cleaned her teeth with her tongue. "Hokma?"

"Yes, Astra?"

"Why did those people on the bus have black holes in their heads? Did Non-Landers attack them?"

Hokma picked up the empty sandwich bag and folded it neatly into four. "No," she said slowly. "Those people had a treatment in a neurohospice. That's what left those scars. Now finish up and let's go."

She stood up and started gathering all the picnic gear together. Astra washed her cake down with the last gulp of juice and let Hokma zip the cups and bags back into her hydropac. Together, they set off down the boundary trail to the crossroads, Astra striding beside Hokma, arms swinging by her sides.

"Hokma?"

"Yes, Astra?"

"What's a neurohospice?"

Hokma took three steps before she answered. "It's a place where people go before they return to Gaia, to get extra-special care. The doctors there use high-tech equipment to help people feel at peace before they leave their families and friends. Some patients have brain treatments to put their memories in order. Sometimes people who aren't returning to Gaia yet but have difficult memories go to neurohospices for treatment too."

That all sounded very interesting. "What kind of treatment did the people on the bus have?"

Hokma pushed away an overhanging pine branch with her staff. She was scanning the trees, not paying full attention to Astra. Was she going to be grumpy again like yesterday? "That scar is caused by a Tablette node implant," she said at last. "Doctors say it makes people feel calmer, and able to make better sense of their past. It also makes them love Gaia very much."

"Their brains were attached to a Tablette? *Wow.*" Astra broke into a run, swung around a young stringybark, then jumped back in front of Hokma. "Can I do that one day? Then I'd know *everything.*"

Hokma trod on a twig. It snapped beneath her boot and Astra started. "That treatment is only for sick people, Astra. You don't need it. Your mind is far more powerful than a Tablette."

"No it isn't," Astra scoffed. "Tabby knows every language in the world, and he can do a zillion sums."

Hokma smiled at last. "Sure he can. Tabby is super-smart. But think of it this way. Even the biggest hard drive has only limited space, but your mind is like a magic house—it looks small on the outside, but inside it has rooms that go on forever. All you have to do is keep opening the doors. With words. Words are the keys to infinite space. Do you follow me?"

Astra considered this. "You mean the way a certain word, like 'food,' gives me pictures in my head? And feelings, like getting excited?"

"Yes, exactly: a big key, like the word 'food,' will open a big room, with lots of thoughts and memories inside it. But if you look closely around the walls, you'll always see other doors. And rarer, more specific words—like 'protein,' or 'carbohydrates,' or . . . 'waffle'—they are smaller keys that will open those doors. And in those rooms, you'll find more doors, and so it goes, on and on. All these rooms are connected, even the Word rooms and the Code rooms, so the more you open, the more space you have to store information and combine it and come up with new ideas."

Astra took a giant step over a mossy log. "Do you think," she said slowly, almost feeling the thought form in her mouth, "because, it's *your* mind, and your mind is *you*, the rooms disappear when you aren't in them? Do you think that could happen?"

Hokma laughed. "Actually, that is one theory of mind—or maybe the empty rooms just shrink, like bouncy biocastles. Like when you learn a language and then forget most of the words. But you can always inflate the room again if you want."

Now Hokma was being silly. Bouncy biocastles were for Little Orkids. Astra persisted, "Or perhaps there are trapdoors and attic doors in your mind rooms. I mean, you'd have to go up or down sometimes, otherwise you couldn't fit all the rooms in."

"Yes, that's true. Sometimes you have to dig a little when you're thinking, or climb a ladder, like you climbed that tree the other day. So words don't take up space in your mind, do they? They create it."

Astra bent down to examine a primrose. Its flowers were as pink as Nimma's special occasion lipstick, and its petals were wrinkled just like elephant skin. She'd once asked Klor if elephants ate primroses, and he'd said they probably would if they could, but primroses didn't grow in the savannah where the last big elephants had lived, or in Himalaya where the reintroduced smaller ones were now. There were primroses in Neuropa, pale yellow ones, but except in animal prisons there hadn't been elephants there since the Ice Age, and those ones had woolly skin. Astra had asked what happened to the elephants in the prisons, and Klor had said that during the Dark Time, the Neuropeans had eaten them. That was a terrible story, so she'd stopped asking questions then.

"So if I learn more words, then I can put more Code in my head too?" she asked Hokma. "More even than Klor?"

"Maybe—though you'd have to live a few decades to match him, I expect."

Astra stood up. It was fun thinking about her mind, but Hokma was still overlooking the obvious. "You could just put all the words in the world into Tabby. A human brain can never be as big as a Tablette's.

Klor told Peat that Code workers in New Zonia are making computers that can think. Peat said that soon everyone will have a computer
best friend, just like Tabby but even better. They'll make jokes and know
when you're sad and exactly what to say to make you feel better."

Hokma placed her palm on the bark of an oak tree. She patted the
tree as if it were a horse, then moved on. "A Tablette might work like a
brain, Astra, but it doesn't have a mind. Even if Tabby were programmed
to compose poetry, or intuit emotions from changes in physiology, or
even fall in love, he'd only be like an actor playing a part, reading from
a script someone else has written. That's someone you've never met, so
how can you be friends with them?"

She was trying to think of an answer, but Hokma swept on, "Tablettes
are *tools*, Astra: they're not living creatures. They're not unique like you
or me or Helium or Silver. No matter what marvelous things they can
do, they're always limited by their programmer's values and skills, and
they're *always* replaceable. Tabby's a very useful learning companion,
but I don't want him to be your best friend."

Klor had said something similar to Peat, Astra recalled. Sometimes
grown-ups were so dumb. "Tabby is my *very* best friend," she declared.
"That's what his software is *for*: making sure I don't ever get lonely."

Hokma stopped and faced her. "I know it seems as though Tabby
likes you, Astra, but I promise you he doesn't love you the way I do,
or Klor does, or Meem and Yoki do, when their heads aren't buried in
Operation Is-Land. You need to spend time with other people and with
living creatures. If you want to develop proper Owleon training skills,
we'll have to wean you from Tabby."

Weaning was when the sheep stopped giving milk to the baby
lamb—but Tabby wasn't a sheep, and Astra wasn't a baby. Astra stooped
to flick a stone out of her sandal. When Hokma had walked on ahead,
she pulled Tabby out of her hydropac pocket.

"*Purrrup*. What's up?" He greeted her with a whisker-wash wave of
his paw.

"We've got to race Hokma now," she told him, clutching him tight.

"I like races!" he enthused, his green eyes twinkling. She set his clock to
Stop Watch and stuffed him back in his pocket. Then she overtook Hokma

and sped down the trail to the crossroads. Not caring about scratches or grazes, she grabbed a short stick and hoisted herself all the way up the steep path to Wise House, miles ahead of Hokma, who plodded on behind.

Hokma pulled a box out from under the bench on the veranda. It was filled with alt-leather gloves. She put one on and rummaged for a good fit for Astra. They were all far too big, but Astra didn't mind. Her hand swimming in a scuffed brown glove with a cuff that nearly came up to her elbow, she followed her Shelter mother across the back clearing to the aviary beneath the pine trees.

Helium was perched on a roost in the first cage. He was an enormous tawny Owleon, almost half as big as Astra herself, with black camouflage patterns on his wings and chest and thick feathers running right down his legs to the tips of his scaly yellow claws. His ear tufts stuck up like two crooked black fingers on his head and beneath his beak he had a soft white beard, like the one Klor had grown last year until Nimma had said he looked like an Amish minister and made him shave it off. The Amish were farmers in New Zonia, a very peaceful and orderly people, Klor had told Astra later, but with an unfortunate resistance to education. Helium didn't look peaceful. His eyes were two blazing orange planets and his black beak shone like brushed steel.

"He's like a flying lion," Astra breathed.

"He's a beautiful Edition Two Owleon in the prime of his life," Hokma said. "He does the Sippur and Atourne runs, don't you, boy?"

"He flies all the way to *Atourne*?" Astra stared at Helium's wings. Atourne was *ages* away. It took a whole day in a bus to get there, Klor said, and nearly two weeks in a cart, which a lot of people preferred anyway, because you could visit so many interesting places in the steppes on the way.

"He does." Hokma opened the cage and entered it. "It takes him two days. He sleeps on the way in a tree in a community called Moly. The people there feed him lots of nice homegrown grains. Oh, they spoil Hely in Moly, don't they, my boy?"

Astra watched, spellbound, as Hokma offered Helium her wrist. The bird stepped onto it as fussily as an old man in New Bangor stepping up onto a curb, testing it first with his stick. Gripping his jesses, Hokma brought him out into the light.

Astra involuntarily took a step back. "He looks like an Edition *Two Hundred* Owleon," she declared.

"I know." Hokma stroked the bird's chest with her ungloved finger. He nipped it and Hokma chuckled. "Hard to imagine improving on Hely, isn't it? But he does what he was designed to do perfectly, and the longer he lives the more confidence IMBOD will have in the foundation Code."

Astra wanted to touch Helium too, but she wasn't sure about putting her finger close to that beak. "What's the difference between Edition Three and Edition Four Owleons?" she asked. "Will they have even more nesting points?"

Hokma tickled the bird's chin and he blinked lazily back at her. "That's a good guess, Astra, but in fact the upgrade is a secret. IMBOD made me promise not to tell anyone how the new Owleons are Coded."

"Not even me?" Astra pouted.

"Not even you." As Hokma spoke, Helium swiveled his head around so it was facing behind him. "Hey, Hely, don't be rude," she chided.

"But how can I train them if I don't know what they're supposed to do?"

Hokma reached into her hipbelt for a piece of alt-meat. "To tell the truth, Astra, *I* don't even know everything the Owleons can do." She held the morsel of pink flesh up in front of Helium's beak. "My job is to Code and breed the birds, and to establish their basic bond with human beings. IMBOD handlers take over after that."

"But you Code the birds—you must know the special stuff they can do."

"Good boy," Hokma praised as Helium followed her fingers back to his chest and took the food with a delicate bob of his head. "I have instructions and target behaviors, but I don't know how those behaviors are going to be applied in the field."

She should be excited about meeting Helium, she knew, but Hokma was spoiling it. "It's not fair. I'm keeping a big secret but I don't get to understand everything about the Owleons."

Hokma considered her. "Astra, not everything in life is fair. Now, do you want to hold Helium? He's lighter than he looks."

She did want to put out her wrist and hold this mighty creature, but she wanted to argue as well. As she hesitated, a twig cracked and she looked in the direction of the noise.

Beyond Hokma's elbow, just yards away, an unmistakable slim figure was tearing between the trees.

Astra launched into a run. Ahead of her, the girl's lithe brown body twisted through the woods. She was clearly visible, all of her: thick hair flowing, elbows pumping, heels flashing. Astra tore off her glove and fumbled at her hydropac for Tabby. At last the pocket was open; gripping Tabby she activated his camera and, aiming as she ran, clicked again and again. She had got her this time. The girl was heading straight toward the fence where she would be trapped and Astra could wrestle her to the ground.

But no—amazingly, the girl ran up a leaning tree trunk and flung herself over the fence and down to the rocky earth below.

She'd need both hands to follow. Astra tried to stuff Tabby back into his pocket, but he slipped from her hand and she had to fumble to catch him before he hit the ground. She fell to her knees, clutching him safe, as Hokma crashed through the trees behind her shouting, *"Astra! Stop this minute!"* She could only watch as the Non-Lander scrambled over a small rise in the land and disappeared into the woods.

But she had still got her. She *had*. Her heart racing, Astra checked Tabby's screen. Yes, yes, *yes*: there were six, seven, eight photos of the girl. She sprang to her feet. Her knees were stinging and her blood was coursing like boiling water through her veins but she had crossed the finish line at last. Her face was glowing like the summer sun, crowds were cheering in her ears and green and red and yellow ribbons were streaming in the air.

"What in Gaia's Name are you doing?" Hokma was behind her, hoarse and panting, grabbing her wrist, wresting Tabby out of her hand.

"It was the girl! The Non-Lander! I took pictures of her—look!"

But Hokma didn't smile as she scanned the photos. A thundercloud bloomed in her face, threatening to break over Astra, swamping her triumph. Holding Tabby high above Astra's head, she deleted the photographs one by one.

"Are you sure—? Are you sh—? Ar—? Ar—? Ar—?" Tabby bleated.

"*No*—don't. Hokma, *don't*," Astra shouted, leaping for Tabby, but not even grasping Hokma's arm.

"Stop screaming. *Now*, or you don't get Tabby back and you don't get to feed Silver ever again."

She'd won—running and Tabby-snapping like a constable and top scientist cross-Coded together, she'd done it: she'd *proved* the girl existed. And the very next moment, Hokma had snatched the trophy away. Astra's ribs hurt. She sat down and punched her fist into the ground. "Why did you do it, Hokma?" she wept. "*Why?*"

Hokma put Tabby in the back pocket of her hydrobelt and knelt down beside her. "Astra, listen to me. There is no girl living in the woods."

"But there *is* . . . *YOU JUST SAW HER*," Astra screamed, and kept screaming, as loud as her burning throat and lungs would let her, until the high, searing scream ripped through the woods, and Wise House, and the whole world—

Until, with a lightning-crack smack, her cheek flamed into fire and her breath was snatched out of her body.

Hokma had slapped her. Hokma had *slapped* her. And now she was grabbing Astra's shoulders and shaking her, trying to make her look her in the eye.

"*No*. There *isn't*. There's an Is-Land girl who lives nearby and plays in the woods. If you tell anyone she's a Non-Lander living in the wild, IMBOD will come and ask me lots of questions about her—and about *you*. We don't want IMBOD to notice you now. You have to promise me you'll never mention her to anyone again. Do you *understand?*"

Astra was sobbing and hiccoughing. Her face was wet and hot, but inside she felt as black and empty as a rain barrel in high summer. Hokma tried to hug her, but Astra pushed her away.

"I *hate* you. I don't want to keep everything a secret! I don't want to do everything you say!"

She struggled to her feet to get away, but Hokma was everywhere. She lunged forward, hitting out at Hokma's chest and face, scratching at her breasts, pulling at fistfuls of her hair. For a minute they wrestled and her nose was full of the fug of Hokma's sweat, her teeth were burrowing into Hokma's shoulder and her ears were buzzing with her own blood. Then Hokma was bending over her, her strong arm pinning Astra's right elbow to her waist. Her left shoulder socket hurt. Her arm was crushed against Hokma's neck and there was something soft in her hand. Somehow, Hokma was grabbing her wrist again.

"Let go, Astra. You've got my eyepatch. *Let go.*"

She did. She was squeezing Hokma's green and silver patch in the palm of her hand and the elastic strap was around Hokma's neck, forcing her head down. Astra let go and Hokma released her. Astra looked up into her face.

The skin around Hokma's right eye socket was pink and shiny and ridged. It had also shrunk somehow, so that it tugged down her lower eyelid and the upper lid drooped over a white glistening recess where her eyeball had once been. Astra gasped and stepped back.

Hokma straightened up. "Does it look scary?" she asked. Her voice was high and tight and breathless and struck an unfamiliar note at the end. She was trying to sound calm, but she didn't. She sounded as if she was trying not to cry.

"A bit," Astra mumbled. The distorted socket just looked strange and unexpected, but the whiteness inside *had* been frightening. Something that you should be looking into and should be looking back at you was blank and moist and hidden instead, so you couldn't tell what Hokma was feeling or thinking. That was the most frightening part. The socket didn't seem like part of Hokma at all.

"You were very close up, weren't you? Why don't you look again now you can see my whole face."

Hokma's voice was steadier now. Astra lifted her head.

Hokma pushed her hair behind her ears, and smiled. "It's not so bad really, is it? I was going to show you sometime anyway."

From this distance, the empty socket didn't look so much like a deep-sea monster squatting on Hokma's face. She could see how the lids and lashes, though distorted, resembled the ones she knew so well. It looked more now like a bit of Hokma's face was melting in the sun. Astra flushed. She'd been a coward, shrinking away and acting like Hokma was ugly. A constable wouldn't ever do that if her buddy got injured, not even if her buddy's whole face was blistered and charred with third-degree burns. She had to say something nice to make Hokma feel better.

"I think it looks like an ice cream," she declared. "Strawberry and vanilla."

Hokma laughed, a big belly laugh. "Well, I've never thought of it like that before! I suppose we'd better not tell Peat, had we?" And then Astra was laughing too and Hokma was hugging her again and she was hugging Hokma too.

They separated and Hokma tried to put the eyepatch back on, but the elastic had stretched too much. "I'll have to sew it up in the house," she said, leaving it dangling around her neck. Astra brushed the grass and needles off her legs. Then she rubbed her wrist, which still hurt. Her cheek stung too. Hokma gently stroked her face and picked a leaf out of her hair.

"I'm sorry I slapped you, Astra," she said, "but you were out of control. When you do your IMBOD Service you'll learn that when someone gets into a state like that, you have to slap them to snap them out of it. It's called hysteria."

"Really?"

"Really. On Boundary patrol you might save someone's life with a slap one day."

"Oh." Astra wondered if in the meantime she might be able to slap Meem when she had one of her tantrums. No, probably Nimma wouldn't understand.

"I know it's hard right now," Hokma went on. "Everything's changing, but we'll work it out together, okay?"

Astra was silent. A minute ago she'd been hitting Hokma and before that she'd been screaming until her lungs were about to burst. She couldn't tell anyone what had happened and she didn't know what was going to happen next. It didn't feel like everything was going to be okay at all.

"But what if we can't?" She rubbed her elbow and stared down at her sneakers. "What if I say something wrong and IMBOD comes to get you?"

"Astra." Hokma's crisp tone cut through the peaty forest air. "I have the Security shot in the fridge. If you want to take it, any time, I'll give it to you. I just ask that you think about it first. For a week. You need to consider everything you will be giving up. Okay?"

Astra stared up at Hokma. "If you give me my shot, can I still train Silver?"

"I told you before," Hokma said quietly, "you need to be very empathic to work with Owleons. I'll still let you feed him, but you might not be able to create a bond with him. You might be too rough with him, or not reward him enough. Then even if he flies for you, he'll give you bites and scratches."

Astra's shoulders drooped. "But I want Silver to love me," she said. "Like Helium loves you."

"I know you do." Hokma put her arm around her. "It won't be easy keeping our secret, but if you trust me, I can teach you to be the best scientist and Owleon trainer in all of Is-Land."

Her mouth was trembling and she couldn't reply.

"Astra, do you trust me?"

She looked deep into Hokma's warm hazel-gold eye with its lattice-work of creases, and her wild, strange eye socket that gleamed like an ice-cream moon. She nodded, once, like Hokma always did.

"I love you, Astra. I never want anything bad to happen to you." Hokma pulled Astra close and Astra leaned against her, feeling the grit from the forest and the warmth of Hokma's skin.

"I love you too, Hokma. I'm sorry I said I hated you."

"That's okay. I'm sure you did at that moment."

Astra's arms were around Hokma's butt. She could feel Tabby sticking out of Hokma's belt.

"Can I have Tabby back now?" she asked.

But Hokma reached behind her back and gently removed Astra's hand from her belt. "No. Silver needs all your attention at Wise House. And we have to be very careful about Tabby. He's only to help you with schoolwork, and he mustn't see or overhear anything I teach you. That's why I didn't want you taking photos of the bomb crater, or Dr. Blesser-son's garden. From now on I'll keep Tabby safe while you're here. Okay?"

Astra didn't want to say okay. Her hand felt empty without Tabby in it. As if Hokma guessed, she looked around in the grass and picked up the falconer's glove Astra had hurled aside as she ran. She held it out to Astra.

"Do you want to hold Helium before we go back in and feed the chicks?"

Astra looked at the glove, then up at Hokma: at Hokma's real face that she didn't show anyone else. She nodded, took the glove and put it on. Then Hokma held out her ungloved hand and Astra let herself be walked back through the woods to the aviary.

She didn't glance back once over her shoulder, not even once.

PART TWO

SUMMER 82 RE

2.1

"So." Klor waggled his famous eyebrows. Their gray tufts were singed turquoise and gold from the light of the Fountain and his face, like everyone's, was gleaming with mist and sweat. "Who's ready for a story?"

A faint wind was hushing through the clearing's curve of pine trees, and over Klor's bony shoulders long shadows danced up the windowless mud walls of Birth House. Astra ought, she knew, to be gazing with rapt attention at her Shelter father, but from her place in the circle she stole a glance at the turf-roofed cave. It was hard to believe that just two months ago, Birth House had welcomed Elpis back to Gaia. Then the Fountain lights had been crimson and scarlet, flickering flame-tongues licking the tears from people's faces. Now the water sprays were as bright as tropical feathers and everyone was smiling, but the entrance to the dark womb-chamber was as black as before, and the round cedar door was gaping open so Elpis could hear the story too. An invisible path ran from the doorway down to a gap in the Fountain circle: this was the Ancestors' Place, gate-posted by Klor on one side and on the other, her bottom firmly planted on the Teller's Trunk, Nimma.

Long ago, when Astra was very little, Elpis herself had sat on the Teller's Trunk, and in her wavery voice had told Kali's famous story, which was her story too. Astra had listened to all of it, even though it was the longest story she'd ever heard. But she'd been so young then, she could hardly remember it; possibly she had fallen asleep toward the end. Last year at the spring story night, when Modem had told the story of the founding of Or, Elpis had sat beside Nimma. Elpis had listened to everything: you could tell by the way she tilted her head during the exciting, scary parts and opened her eyes wide for the happy parts. Nimma had dabbed the drool from her mouth with hankies and Meem had fed her apple juice through a straw. But now Elpis was buried in the deepest chamber of Birth House and Kali's story had become homeless. It didn't belong to anyone's voice anymore but floated around in Or memory like a distant murmuration of starlings, its shifting contours fading and dispersing into a bruise-blue sky. Sometimes that happened to stories, Klor said, and only stray feathers of them remained to stick into a new Teller's cap.

But Kali's story was one of the most important stories there was; that was why they were hearing it again tonight. And, even though Nimma wasn't a real Teller, she was Elpis's Birth-Code-Shelter daughter so her place tonight was on the Teller's Trunk.

We are. We are. We are. Around her, the Security Generation shouted and bounced, waggling their hands in the air. Astra shifted uncomfortably. Even with the Fountain, it was a hot night. The Sec Gen section was three or four deep in places and she was squashed between Hokma's hipbelt and a squirmy seven-year-old called Sprig. Behind her another seven-year-old, Tulsi, was sitting in her Shelter father's lap and butting her feet into Astra's back—kicking, actually. She reached behind and firmly pushed Tulsi's sandals away.

"*Waaaah,*" Tulsi protested. She and Sprig had only just had their Security shots, so they weren't placid yet.

"Shhh." Her father bundled the girl closer to him.

Hokma turned her head and frowned. "Astra," she warned.

"Sor-ree." Astra stuck the tip of her dreadlock in her mouth and sucked. Nimma hated her doing that, but Nimma wasn't looking.

"Don't do that either." Hokma reached up and tugged the dread back into place behind Astra's ear. *Frigging Gaia.* Hokma was pushing it tonight. Astra scowled but kept quiet. She was already getting away with selfish behavior, she knew, plunking herself down near the cool Fountain mist when the older Sec Gens should be sitting behind the little ones. She was on the edge of the group, though, like always, and for once Hokma hadn't argued with her. She probably thought Astra wanted a good view of Nimma. Up beside Klor, Peat and Yoki were also close to the front, while Meem was in the back row between her Birth-Code mother's legs—even though you weren't supposed to stand up during a Telling, Astra knew Honey would let Meem do so if she wanted a better look. Honey spoiled Meem, Nimma said, and for once Astra agreed with her.

Me. I am. Hear hear. Hear Her. From around the Circle adults and non-Sec Gen Or-kids chipped in with shouts and cheers. People's faces swam like glinting fish in the supernatural Fountain light. Behind them, the pine trees bristled up into the night like a forest palisade.

"Good. Very good. Now, remember . . . Oh . . . Wait a minute." Klor pulled a perplexed face and scratched his head. "What must we all remember?" Nimma, looking watery in a silver faux-grass hipskirt and a mother-of-pearl necklace, put her hand to her ear and looked expectantly around the Circle.

Astra winced. Her Shelter mother was tonight's *frigging Teller*. Why did she have to act like an overdressed kindergarten teacher? She'd be wagging her finger and telling people off next. And sure enough, when her gaze settled on Torrent and Stream—the two older teens every Or-parent had been talking about for weeks—Nimma lifted a warning eyebrow. Astra pulled her knees up to her chest and wrapped her arms around her shins. As the eldest Shelter daughter of this control-freak Teller she suddenly felt horribly exposed.

Stream's slender brown arms were entwined around Torrent's pale torso. Seeing Nimma's disapproval, the girl straightened up and as if asserting her independence, she shook her glossy chestnut mane; at the same time she tucked her right hand firmly behind Torrent's knee. She was all over him like an army of red ants these days. Astra didn't know why he put up with it. It must be awfully hot—and besides, didn't he care about Congruence anymore? His ex-Gaia play pal was sitting with her friends just a few yards away, staring quietly into the Fountain opposite the Ancestors' Place.

Watching her now, it was hard to believe that Congruence, as was whispered, had cried *all day* and *all night* after Torrent and Stream made their Gaia bond public, kissing in the back seat of the bus all the way home from school. She had done so in private, behind her Shelter family's own doors; in public she maintained a fragile silence.

"She's too mature for Torrent," Astra had heard Nimma tell Luna, one of Congruence's Shelter mothers. "Imagine forming an exclusive bond at his age."

"Praise Gaia we won't have these problems with this group," Luna had sighed, patting Astra's head. She had meant the Sec Gens, which was worrying. Astra was almost afraid to ask Hokma if *she* might end up like Congruence one day. *Traumatized*, Nimma had said in her most ominous tone.

Astra hugged her knees tighter. Thinking too hard about the older teens and their non-Sec Gen world made her feel queasy inside.

"*Don't look at the Kezcams!*" All around the Circle, a chorus of voices harmonized like a morning chant-hymn before pealing into laughter. Beside Astra, the Sec Gens clapped and wriggled. Astra, as usual, was the only person not positively frothing with delight. Maybe she *should* have sat at the back, where she wouldn't have to wrench her face into a different expression to match each new line in the story. Because the story was going to be dull, that was guaranteed. Nimma wasn't a proper Teller, for Gaia's sake. She'd been fretting about tonight for weeks, spending hours in her room practicing, and not listening properly when people asked her questions. You'd think, considering how self-absorbed she'd been, she could have just ignored Astra: but no, she'd been nagging her about absolutely everything until it was all Astra could do not to scream, "*Leave me alone.*"

To top it all off, when Astra had complained to Hokma, Hokma had nearly frigging exploded: "You can't afford to lose your temper!" she'd yelled, so loud she'd practically blown a hole in the roof of Wise House. "Do you want Nimma to find out you're not Sec Gen? You've nearly finished Foundation School now, Astra. You have to *grow up!*"

Yeah, well, that was easy for a *grown-up* to say. Grown-ups got to lose their frigging tempers whenever they frigging well wanted to. And besides, Astra didn't frigging *want* to grow up, thank you very much. Not if it meant behaving like Nimma, with her pettifogging rules, or Hokma with her grunts and silences and complete lack of interest in the world beyond Wise House. The problem with her Shared Shelter mothers, she had realized lately, was that apart from the Owleons and language lessons, Hokma didn't care a dried fig about Astra's life, and Nimma cared way too much.

"The Circle is ready to roll!" Klor hollered over to Ahn. Astra glowered over the Fountain to the real reason she'd bagged a place in the front. Sitting alone on a bench behind Stream and Torrent, his face hidden by his battered straw trilby, oblivious as always to the micro-dramas playing out at his feet, Ahn tapped at the notebook Tablette resting on his knees. Craning her neck, Astra peered through the fine Fountain spray, straining to catch a glimpse of the Kezcams lined up on the bench.

The Kezcams, three small helium-filled biotech balls with thin shells of black steel and retractable kestrel-Coded wings, were the nicest part of IMBOD kit to arrive in Or since bendable Tablette screens—but, extremely unfairly, no one except Ahn was allowed to touch them. Astra was barely allowed to *look* at them. As if to torment her, Ahn walked around Or with the Kezcams bunched in a string bag on his hydro-belt, each hidden in a heavy enameled case that protected the delicately jointed wings and weighed the sphere down. She had finally spied him practicing his operating technique out on the lawn yesterday, but as she'd stood mesmerized, watching the Kezcams dart and hover like hummingbird moths over the gladioli, Nimma had come and chased her away, saying she mustn't spoil his concentration. And at rehearsal today, Klor had told them all that if a Kezcam hovered in front of them, they were to ignore it. Later Ahn would edit the footage into a film that would be shown weekly at the Boundary Congregation Site on the way to Sippur. Is-Landers and visitors from all over the world would see the film so it was important to give him lots of good shots to choose from. Anyone behaving in a *frivolous manner*—here Klor had directed his eyebrows at Stream and Torrent—would have to run extra Kinbat laps for weeks.

"Don't worry, folks, you won't even notice them." Ahn made an adjustment to a Kezcam and set it back down in its case—annoyingly out of sight. "Nearly ready now."

"Ready, Congruence?" Klor asked.

"I am." The girl nodded, her dark eyes shining. The Parents' Committee had given Congruence the role of Asker partly, everyone knew, to make up for the misery Torrent and Stream's inexplicably exclusive relationship was causing her. But Astra had to agree that she had the dignity required of the role. Congruence was sitting in full lotus, her hands in *chin mudra* on her knees, her long black hair falling straight to her waist, her skin gleaming like polished oak. Her calm, melodic voice betrayed no sense of pride and no hint of bitterness toward the couple she could surely see in her peripheral vision. She was well defended though: to her right, her friend Ariel sat up straighter, on her left Holaa peeled a stray blade of grass from Congruence's arm and further along a whole squadron of adults was regarding her with pride—not only Luna, Gloria and Arjun, her Shelter parents, but a doting flank of Parents' Committee members, and Sorrel and Mr. Ripenson too.

Astra shrank back a little behind Hokma so Mr. Ripenson—or Vishnu, as he'd told her to call him outside school—couldn't see her if he looked this way again. The teacher had joined the school staff last year when Mr. Banzan left, and had met Sorrel on one of her urbag deliveries. Before anyone even knew they had bonded she was pregnant and soon after that, with the approval of the Parents' Committee, Mr. Ripenson had moved to Or. He'd been on the school bus that fateful day when everything had started going wrong for Congruence, and had played a special role in counseling all the teens, Nimma had said. She and all the other Or adults admired him now. Astra didn't *dis*like Mr. Ripenson—*Vishnu* sounded wrong—he was always friendly to everyone and good at cricket; she just didn't like having a teacher living in Or, an adult with more chances to observe her behavior than practically anyone. Hopefully he—and everyone—would keep staring at Congruence tonight.

"Ahn?" Klor raised a knuckley forefinger in the air—the signal for filming to begin.

Astra couldn't help it. Moving her eyes only, she watched Ahn release the three Kezcams from their cases. One by one, they drifted up into the air, unfolding their transparent wings. Brushing his Tablette screen with his fingers, Ahn directed their ascent. They were barely visible as they entered the Fountain light, their wings gray blurs, their shiny surfaces reflecting the changing colors of the spray. The Kezcams soared to a height of three yards, then as Ahn expertly choreographed their movements, one began a slow circle overhead and the others descended into the Fountain pit to take up their starting positions: one facing Nimma, Klor and the Ancestors' Place and one suspended in front of Congruence.

Swipe. Swoop. Swap. Controlling the Kezcams, especially three at once, was an art, a dance involving your whole body; Astra could see that. But it wasn't like flying an Owleon. It wasn't like knowing that one of Gaia's fiercest creatures would come arcing back to you through the air at your call and clutch your wrist as if it owned you. Silver should be here, listening to the story, hooting softly to Elpis after all the sad parts.

"Welcome all, to the first Or Story Night of Summer 82 RE." Klor's voice tugged Astra back into the Circle. The Kezcam in front of her Shelter father was barely visible in the Fountain glare, but its lens could rotate 360 degrees and Ahn would see if Astra was trying to spot it. She did her very best to stare resolutely past it. "Our Teller tonight is Nimma," Klor continued. "What story shall we ask her to tell?"

"I want to hear Kali's story," Congruence said, her voice as soft and clear as a bamboo wind chime. "I want Nimma, Birth-Code daughter of Elpis, to tell it." Beside her, Ariel and Holaa solemnly nodded.

"Nimma?" Klor turned to the Teller. "Do you hear the Asker?"

All heads turned to Nimma. As Astra stared, not at her Shelter mother but the Ancestors' Place, just for a moment she found herself touched by the spell of the Asking. This was Kali's story and Elpis's story, and telling it would bring Elpis back into the Circle.

"Thank you, Asker," Nimma replied in the time-honored manner—except that her voice had a hairline crack in it. She paused and swallowed before continuing, her voice fuller now, "With Gaia's help—and another flame in the Fountain—I'll tell the tale."

Klor took the remote control from his hydrobelt and pointed it at the Fountain. Tulsi, Sprig and the other younger Sec Gens gasped as a stream of fiery sparks flew up through the mist. The story was starting now and there was nothing Astra could do except listen and hope Nimma wouldn't make too big a hash of it. She stared into the heart of the lightshow. Tall orange flames were flowing in the spray like the silky sleeves of summer dresses, and the churning surface of the Fountain pool glowed like jagged jewels.

"This is a story from the Dark Time," Nimma began. Her voice was stronger now, and Astra had to admit that it carried well across the Fountain. "Many stories from that time have been lost, for even golden eagles may not survive a cyclone, but this one is still with us because its first Teller, Kali, survived that terrible period. It was a painful story for Kali to tell, but because so many people wanted to hear it, she mastered her fear and grief and became a powerful Teller. Kali's Telling helped create Is-Land: that is how powerful it was. But before she was a Teller, Kali suffered—not as a child, no: she had a very happy childhood because her parents were Gaians and she grew up in a beautiful community called Beltane in the mountains of Yr Widdfa, which, despite a fierce independent spirit, was governed by the kingdom of Yukay. She and the other Gaian visionaries of Beltane lived in yurts and tipis and Earthships. The people in yurts and tipis burned wood for heat, and everyone used wind turbines and photovoltaic cells to power their Tablettes and washing machines. It was cold in Yr Widdfa, so in the winter Kali wore clothes outside, but inside the Earthships and on the hot days of summer she and her family lived sky-clad and free, just like us. But though they were naked, they were not vulnerable. As the Great Collapse accelerated, Beltane constructed an Earthcastle with a moat and ramparts. For Beltane Gaians were Pioneers. They were among the first Gaian communities to realize that *if we truly want to defend our Mother, we have to defend ourselves.*"

Nimma's voice rang out deep as a bronze bell as she stated this central truth, and the adults around the Fountain chimed their agreement: *Hear Her. Hear Her. Gaia forever.* Everyone was eager for the story now, Astra could tell. No one was acting for the Kezcams. She risked another glance at Ahn.

Hokma elbowed her in the shoulder. *Look at Nimma*, the sharp nudge said.

"Gaians are not selfish, no," Nimma declaimed to another murmur of agreement. "During the Great Collapse, Beltane, like all Gaian communities, offered to share their knowledge and skills—their clean-energy technology, their collective decision-making processes—with the rest of the world, but this offer was rejected. Instead, the Yukay government refused Beltane permission to build more self-sufficient dwellings, and the local media mocked them as backward simpletons. At best, people saw Gaians as cranks, living in a precious little world of our own, sewing our own clothes, homeschooling our children, milking goats. Most people didn't understand the urgent necessity of our way of life. Most people were racing headlong into the Dark Time, their vision of life on earth smeared blind by oil."

Oil. Actually, oil was interesting—Astra had to write an essay on fossil fuels this month for school. And after that poor start, Nimma was Telling better now. Astra rearranged herself into a cross-legged position and, elbows on knees, chin on hands, leaned forward.

"We know now," Nimma said sternly, "that oil was a powerful drug, more dangerous than heroin, more addictive than nicotine. Governments and corporations were the drug-pushers, and everywhere, all over the world, ordinary people were the addicts. Oil junkies might come to a Gaian community for a festival but they would drive home in their gas-guzzlers and urban tractors. No one could imagine more than a day without oil. Oh"—she waved dismissively—"oil made life *fun*, there's no denying that. If people were bored of living in cold, dirty cities, they just hopped on an arrowpain and flew halfway around the world to flop around on a beach of white sand. But this addiction to *fun*"—Nimma spat the word out as if it were a cockroach in a mouthful of lentil stew—"this commitment to *convenience*, to *leisure*, to the *mindless gratification of the senses*, this pandemic lust for *black gold*—as the greediest of those humans called oil—was having a devastating effect on Gaia. Not only were the oil junkies draining our Mother of Her natural lubricants, they were pumping Her atmosphere full of greenhouse gases, heating Her surface to levels that threatened to render Her waterless and ferociously hot, turning Her into a barren, volcanic crone planet, like Her sister Venus."

The story of oil was really awful. Beside Astra, Sprig gulped and stuck her fingers in her mouth. Astra put her arm around the girl's shoulders. It was the first time the little ones would have heard about the Great Collapse. It was *so* awful to think about the near-death of Gaia that the Dark Time was introduced only gradually into their school studies. But it was part of Kali's story. Shelter parents had been warned the youngest children might need extra care after hearing it.

"Gaians, of course," Nimma went on, "didn't need a turbine to know which way the wind was blowing. As well as building the Earthcastle, Beltane bought guns. And sure enough, when Kali was fifteen and the Great Collapse had accelerated beyond anyone's ability to stop it, terrified and apologetic oil junkies started to arrive in Beltane. At first this was just a trickle of locals, carrying gifts and begging for shelter. The guns remained hidden and help was given willingly. It doesn't take long to put up a yurt or even to build an Earthship if everyone helps. For three years Beltane grew stronger, attracting people who had awakened to the dangers Gaia faced and wanted to help defend Her. During this time Kali chose a partner, a young man called Peredur. They lived together in a yurt, planning to eventually build an Earthship with a group of other couples. For now, Beltane was safe.

"But this safety depended on laws that Gaians had no hand in writing. Around the world floods and droughts and hurricanes intensified, and soon a food shortage gripped the kingdom of Yukay. This was the beginning of the Dark Time. In exchange for tithing one-eighth of their crops to the Yukay Ministry of Agriculture, Beltane Gaians were allowed to stay on their land. In other countries, though, the oil junkies panicked. Instead of respecting the Gaians' cozy off-grid homes, our fields bursting with fruit, grains and vegetables, instead of asking to learn from us, they decided to invade us. Whole communities were slaughtered and their crops were eaten and never replanted. Yes, the people who could teach them how to live sustainably were killed for one season of food. This was the oil junkie mentality of the late Common Era in action."

Those younger children who weren't burying their faces in their Shelter parents' laps gazed at Nimma with dumbstruck eyes. Adults were shaking their heads; a tear slid down Congruence's cheek. Even Torrent was tense and alert; Stream huddled beneath his arm as if he could save her from imminent annihilation. Astra ground her teeth. Worse almost than picturing Gaians being massacred was the thought of people eating grains and vegetables and not replanting the seeds. Who could savagely waste Gaia's fruits like that? No wonder She had taken such a terrible revenge.

In the front row, Mr. Ripenson clapped the earth with his palm. "We. Remember. The Dark Time Martyrs," he chanted.

"WE. REMEMBER. THE DARK TIME MARTYRS." Nimma and Klor threw their voices and arms to the sky. But all attention was on the teacher now; he was small and energetic, and good at taking assembly. His body rocking, he scanned the Circle. Around him first Sorrel, then Modem, and then a long row of Or-adults joined the chant:

"WE. REMEMBER. THE DARK TIME MARTYRS."

Everyone was chanting now, and the whole Circle was drumming the earth, harder and harder, louder and louder, until the vibrations were traveling right up Astra's spine. Sorrel, too heavily pregnant to bend, clapped her thighs. Torrent and Stream drummed with one hand each, their other hands interlocked in Torrent's lap. Congruence and her friends stretched forward and with both palms beat the earth around the Fountain pit. Hokma, Astra and Sprig did the same, and with another sly glance before she dropped her head, Astra saw Ahn gaze upward, his head rolling clockwise as he directed an aerial shot of the Circle united in a thundering wave of defiance.

The chanters peaked and stopped. With their thunder in her voice, Nimma resumed the story. "Then came the Neuropean floods. In a matter of days, the coastal cities of Yukay were under six feet of water and the kingdom's low-lying regions had disappeared into the sea. The power grid was locked and many people had no electricity. The government declared a state of emergency and ordered the army to control the roads. Beltane, of course, still had power, and Kali and Peredur kept a constant check on Tablette news, meeting with the community every evening to discuss the worsening situation, for every day, the chaos in Yukay drew closer to Beltane.

"Before, refugees in Yukay had always been from other countries. Now millions of the nation's own citizens had been displaced and for a time, even with every soldier in the country deployed, the government lost control of the roads. Oil junkies fled from cities and towns, and though many became stuck in massive gridlocks, some escaped, burning the last of their gas in their cars as they scorched up motorways and headed for the country lanes. Many of these refugees were peaceful people, now homeless and helpless, but others were armed marauders: street gangs with knives and guns, or rich men in four-wheel drives, toting weapons they'd bought from criminals and didn't really know how to use. The government established tent cities in the midlands and moors, where the peaceful refugees gathered, sleeping in their cars if there weren't enough tents. But the armed men—for it was mostly men with the guns—didn't want to be herded into camps. And although in the cities all these different gangs had fought each other, now, in the dark and lonely countryside, the night lit only by their headlights, they realized that they were stronger together.

"Soon the gangs formed super-gangs, convoys of dozens of vehicles. When one car ran out of gas they would dump it by the side of the road and set fire to it, then they would all pile into another. The more crowded the cars, the more violent the gangs became. They terrorized villages, ransacking houses and gas stations, violating and killing anyone who tried to stop them. They never stayed anywhere long. They only wanted more gasoline and then they'd move on—but the more violence they committed, the more they developed a taste for it. The worst atrocity occurred in the Black Mountains south of Yr Widdfa. A roaming super-gang entered a Gaian community called Dawntreader, and though the Dawntreadian Gaians had staves and knives, the gang had automatic rifles and they slaughtered everyone there, down to the last infant."

Nimma's voice was low and grim. Beside her, the Fountain light cast a lacy golden shawl over the Craft-worker Moon and her new Birth-Code son, Aesop. Moon's cheeks were glistening. In her arms, Aesop's face wrinkled as if he was about to cry, but instead he yawned and reached vaguely for his mother's nipple. Moon lifted him up and buried her face in his belly.

"Can you imagine Kali's fear at that news?" Nimma asked. "Everyone in Beltane knew that the murderous oil-sick gangs would soon arrive in their Yr Widdfa fastness. Although the community was miles off the road, four-wheel drives could easily traverse the terrain. They kept their guns at the ready and established lookouts and patrols. Then one evening the radio announced that the Yukay army was sending reinforcements to Yr Widdfa to subdue the super-gangs once and for all. Everyone living in the hills was to report to the nearest Safety Point, where army troops would protect them until the gangs had been dealt with. Travel was advised in the morning, because it was well known that the gangs caroused all night and didn't wake until the late afternoon. Now, the nearest Safety Point to Kali's community was a village at least four hours' walk away. That evening the Beltane Gaians gathered in their Community Hub to discuss what to do. Even the children had a voice and a vote."

Nimma looked around the Circle. "What do *you* think, Or-children? Should Beltane have obeyed the government order?"

"No way!" Torrent, to Astra's surprise, emphatically announced. From his place beside Moon, Russett, his Code-Shelter father, cast him a sharp look, as if to say, *About time, boy*. Stream, who was tracing Torrent's abdominal muscles with her forefinger, didn't look as if she cared an aduki bean about the fate of the Beltane Gaians. Astra snuck a peek at Congruence, but she was gazing soulfully at Nimma, shaking her head.

No way. No way. No way. The younger children echoed Torrent gleefully, Spring and Tulsi shrieking so loudly Astra covered her ears with her hands. Hokma elbowed her in the ribs and she chimed in, "No way! No way!"

Nimma waited for the clamor of agreement to subside. "That," she announced, "is exactly what the Beltane Gaians decided. If they left their land, the government might seize it. If they left their animals, the animals would starve or be butchered by the refugees. And besides, they hadn't spent their lives building a new world just to jump when the oil junkies whistled. So they stayed where they were. Everyone dressed in combat clothes and those who could fight armed themselves with weapons: rifles, pistols and crossbows. For six days, nothing happened. But on the seventh day, the army arrived."

Astra stiffened. Everyone over ten knew this part of the story from their Tablette history lessons. A part of her didn't want to hear it, but most of her had to listen and understand.

"The army came in a host of jeeps, ripping up the mountain turf. Kali's Code-Shelter father, Elphin, was on lookout over the Earthcastle ramparts, and he reported that there were about twenty vehicles, with three or four soldiers in each one, all wearing helmets and flak gear. The jeeps stopped in a semicircle in front of the ramparts and the lead officer spoke using a loudspeaker. He said that the army was here to protect Beltane. He asked the Gaians to evacuate their dwellings and in groups of five, enter the back of the jeeps so he could take them to the Safety Point.

"The Gaians refused. Elphin had his own megaphone, and through it he told the army that Beltane would protect itself until the army cleared the roads of the gangs. If the officer wanted to leave a jeep and some soldiers behind, Beltane would feed and shelter them in exchange for their support. The officer replied that under the special powers accorded to him by the current State of Emergency Measures, he was now ordering them into the jeeps. And when the Gaians refused again, he sent his soldiers in to take them by force. There were nearly eighty armed soldiers against fifty-one Beltane adults and twenty-eight children, half of them under ten years old, with forty guns and thirty crossbows between them.

"That was the Battle of Beltane, in which many brave Gaians defended our Mother. None had shed human blood before, but in battle they killed six slaves of the oil junkie government, losing twenty-two of their own number in return, including Kali's Birth-Code-Shelter mother Ravena. But though the Beltane Gaians were prepared to fight to the death, the Yukay soldiers were well trained and well armed and finally they broke into the Community Hub and took the ten smallest Gaian children hostage. Kali saw it happen. She saw Peredur's niece and nephew crying in the soldiers' arms as they emerged from the Hub, and she heard the loudspeaker announce that the children would be taken away and any adult who wanted to join them should lay down his or her weapon. The rest should be prepared to lose their lives.

"Kali saw Peredur's Birth-Code aunt lay down her crossbow and walk to the jeeps. Then, one by one, the Beltane mothers and fathers followed, surrendering to the Yukay army rather than let their children be taken away. Kali's Shared Shelter mother, Rhiannon, walked that path. And when Peredur's father shouted, *Gaia is always with us*, and laid down his gun to join his wife and children, Kali and Peredur looked at each other from across the Beltane pond. With that glance, they silently agreed that they would follow their families into the jeeps. For Gaia is not just in the land: She is everywhere, even in a cloud of gas fumes, and She is within us too. When we protect ourselves and each other, we are also protecting Her.

"So Kali and Peredur laid down their weapons and helped carry the wounded to the jeeps. One by one, the remaining Gaian warriors did the same, and the last to surrender were Kali's Code-Shelter father Elphin and his Beltane cofounder, the maestro Code worker Hew Owen. As Elphin and Hew walked straight-backed across the field to join their comrades, the Gaians ululated their courage, and their farewell to Beltane. And as the jeeps roared back down the mountain, belching fumes of oil, the Gaians wept a blazing storm of tears, and Kali and Elphin and Rhiannon grieved hard the loss of Ravena.

"But the army had tricked them. When the jeeps arrived at the Safety Point, the warriors were separated from the small children. The children were taken to a large tent and were never seen again. The warriors were put onto a bus and handcuffed to the seats. Behind them were men with tattoos and knife wounds: super-gang members, gagged, so they couldn't speak. The soldier in charge of the bus told the Gaians that if they spoke to each other they would be gagged too.

"The next day the bus drove to the coast and onto a huge ship, one of a small fleet anchored in the harbor. The ships looked like a pod of killer whales. They were painted with black-and-white chevrons and had enough room on the front deck for six buses to park, all in a row. Any windows you could see were small, their glass tinted black. The Gaians had no more freedom to lose. At last a whisper roamed around the bus: *These*, it hissed, *were the Prison Ships."*

During the last part of the story Klor had gradually lowered the Fountain. The lightshow had dimmed to a coppery glow and Astra could no longer make out faces across the spray. The warm night air was clinging to her skin, Sprig's slick little body was rubbing against hers, Hokma's flank was hot as a brick wall in the sun, but Astra felt cold and alone. She wanted to escape—to stand, to stretch, to look up at the stars—but she didn't dare move. The Circle locked her in its dark silence and somewhere high above her Ahn's Kezcam was watching, etching its invisible constellations against the vast black sky.

2.2

Sprig took her fingers out of her mouth. "What's a *prism*?" she asked, so loudly the whole Circle laughed.

"It's a glass cell rainbows try to escape from," Modem called from the other end of the firepit. He was a great Teller because he could do that—make up wisecracks in a flash. Everyone old enough to get the joke groaned or clapped, and Congruence turned around to smile at him. It was one of those natural breaks in a story, and people stretched their legs or drank from their tubing or flasks. Klor raised the Fountain again so its cool mist could revive the Circle, and he brightened the lights to a lemon-yellow sparkle. Moon was laughing with Russett and Stream was leaning against Torrent, finger-combing her hair. Astra darted a glance over at Ahn. He was looking at Congruence, his face uplit by the sickly glow of his Tablette screen.

The older girl's hands were folded in a *mudra* between her legs and her eyes were downcast—possibly because Stream was now nuzzling Torrent's neck. But Ahn obviously thought Congruence was still lost in a deep listening state because with a circling chin movement he sent a Kezcam to hover in front of her. Astra could see why. The Fountain light coated the girl's high cheekbones with glowing gilt firepaint, and her flame-armored chest rose and fell rhythmically behind her falling hair. Behind her, Holaa and Ariel, the Asker's guard of honor, echoed her posture. Ahn's fingers whisked over his Tablette, directing the Kezcams to capture the trio from different heights and angles. Then with thumb and forefinger he spread open an image and cocked his head to inspect it.

"She's a good Teller, isn't she, dready-girl?" Hokma reached over and tugged playfully on Astra's dreadbead. *Frigging Gaia.* It wasn't a light pull.

"She's okay," Astra muttered, squirming away. Her stomach was twisting, and not from the story. Ahn still had a Gaia bond with Hokma but he never visited Wise House when she, Astra, was there; he never invited her to his office to see his blueprints, never even stopped her in Core House to ask about the Owleons, let alone sent a party of Kezcams to film her. Ahn pissed her off—but if she ever tried to talk to Hokma about him, Hokma would just say, "Oh, you know Ahn," as if that was that. Why did Ahn get to act as if no one else existed? Or was supposed to be about working *and* living together, wasn't it?

Around her, Shelter parents were giving each other shoulder massages or shifting heavy children from one lap to another. Meem was sleeping now—she could never make it through a whole Fountain story—and Yoki was hugging Nimma while Peat glugged from his tubing. He still held the Or record for glugging, and was possibly aware that one of the Kezcams was recording his current heroic effort. As he wiped his mouth, the Kezcam winged in Astra's direction but it didn't slow down. Controlling an urgent desire to stick out her tongue and cross her eyes, she unfocused her gaze and let it pass. When it had moved on, she plucked at her dread, pulling it down in front of her face and twiddling the oak bead between her fingers. After a year of what Nimma called "whining" and Astra called "*a campaign for hair justice*" she'd finally got permission to make just one loc. Meem had helped backcomb, twist and bead it, and now it was fat and heavy, a black cat's tail on the side of her head. Nimma couldn't shut up about it, though. She was always frigging *lamenting* it to her friends. At least Hokma liked it—but she would, wouldn't she? Hokma's own hair was usually uncombed and carelessly tied back in a knot these days. She could at least dread it too—Astra had even offered to do it for her—but she always said she couldn't be bothered.

"Chill out, sweetie." Hokma handed Astra a summer-fruit-ice from a freezer bag one of the Shelter mothers was passing around. Well, it *was* hot. She tucked the dread back behind her ear, accepted the ice and pressed the frosty paper wrapping to her cheek. Some adults were sucking vodka ice cubes and chatter rippled around the Circle. Behind them all, their trunks lit up like beaten yellow gold, the tall pine trees stood like vigilant Shelter parents watching over children in a playpit.

Astra peeled off the paper and stuck it in Hokma's waiting hand. She took a bite of the fruit-ice, letting the lump of frozen raspberries pucker her tongue. How did adults know that what they were doing was right? They were supposed to ask Gaia for help, but did they? Did *Ahn*? He had designed Birth House, but did he ever go inside it? He hadn't been one of the team who'd taken Elpis back into Gaia's womb, that echoing chamber where all tonight's words were traveling, up the path from the Ancestors' Place. The Birth House doorway was waiting for everyone. There was room enough in the soft earth of the hillside for everyone in Or. But did Ahn want to join them there? He probably thought he should be returned to Gaia at the Boundary Congregation Site, in a chamber all to himself.

Raspberry juice was dripping down Astra's arm; she licked it up and stuck the fruit-ice stick in Hokma's hipbelt.

She shouldn't have attracted her Shelter mother's attention. Hokma looked around in annoyance. "Straighten up," she ordered. "You're always so hunched."

I'll sit how I frigging well want to sit! Astra was on the verge of yelling. But Klor clapped three times and the Circle fell silent again. "Thank you, Sprig, for a very good question," Nimma said, beaming in Astra's direction. "A *prison* is a building with locks on all the doors where the government keeps people they believe to be dangerous to others. Here in Is-Land we have very few prisons because we have no desire to hurt each other. Apart from a few Non-Landers, our prisons are nearly empty. But in late Common Era Yukay, many people were poor and were forced to steal, or were sick and put in prison instead of given treatment."

Astra knew all this, of course, but she forced herself to listen. She didn't want to miss the rest of the story because of Ahn. Anyway, Hokma was right: Ahn was Ahn, and there was nothing anyone could do about it. He brought money into Or with his commissions, and that meant he could forget his own Birth-Code-Shelter mother's name if he wanted to.

"During the start of the Dark Time," Nimma was explaining, "Yukay prisons became so crammed full of people they couldn't fit in even one more. So the Yukay government converted old navy aircraft carriers and battleships into prisons and docked them just offshore at designated harbors. Kali and the Beltane Gaians had heard about these ships on the radio, but they had never seen one before.

"On the Prison Ship, the Gaians were split up again. The fifteen Beltane women, including Kali, Rhiannon and Peredur's mother, were held on the upper deck with the female gang members, most of whom were teenage girls who were bruised and howling for their men and their make-up bags. The men were taken down below. *Gaia is with us*, Kali called as Peredur and Elphin and Peredur's father were sucked down the stairs to the belly of the ship. She didn't know then that she would never see them again. She was afraid and grieving sorely, but she was alive, and she knew she needed to be strong for the mothers who had lost their children to the army. So she didn't let herself think about the future. She lived, as Gaia asks us to, in human harmony with the evolving moment."

At the sound of these wise words, agreement hummed around the Circle. *Human harmony* was what every Is-Lander was working toward, every person was one note in a chord that sang Gaia's beauty. But at the same time Astra was becoming aware that human harmony wasn't exactly like musical harmony. It was *similar*, in that it created an overwhelming sense of *belonging*, but it wasn't predictable, wasn't something you could create just by pressing keys. You could be working or playing or eating with people and feel nothing special, but the next day you could do exactly the same things and you might suddenly experience that feeling, even if you were baking hot or your limbs ached. Human harmony was tranquil and shimmering, and it grew as you became aware of it, but if you mentioned it, the feeling popped like a soap bubble. She felt it most often with the Owleons and Hokma at Wise House, where she didn't have to speak and the feeling could expand until she almost floated away inside it.

Beside her, Sprig reached out for Astra's hand and she took Sprig's fingers in hers and let the child clamber into her lap. Hokma rubbed her back again. *Good girl*, her Shelter mother's palm said. The Security shot meant children experienced harmony more easily, but Hokma said it wasn't a deep harmony because they were tuned to each other so strongly they couldn't experience other dimensions of *belonging* in the world. Astra was usually out of harmony with the Sec Gens: she was bored by their repetitive games—they never got any better at them—and frustrated by their simple acceptance of everything they were told. But Hokma said that human harmony evolved and one day she would realize that in Gaia's endless symphony her one special note *did* chime with her Or-siblings' chord.

Right now the human harmony in the Circle was so strong Astra could almost hear it. The soft splashing of the Fountain, the whispers of the trees, the faraway creaking of the crickets in the valley, they were all subsumed into its frequency. This was the time in a Telling when the story had claimed not just every listener but Gaia Herself.

"Over the next week," Nimma continued, "more women joined the upper-deck holding cell: first another clutch of gang-girls, then a group of Socialists who had tried to warn people away from the government's tent cities, and finally, ten Gaians from a community called Firefly. Each woman was given a bunk and a blanket, two meals a day and if the guards felt like it, an hour on the open deck for exercise. Some of the Gaians kept wearing their combat clothes because they were still at war; some of them went sky-clad as an act of resistance. Together they began a journey circle, chanting and drumming, softly at first, when the gang-girls threatened to attack them, but then, after it was agreed that each group could make noise for two hours a day, more loudly. In their turn, the gang-girls sang pop songs and power ballads, mostly out of tune, though two or three of them had beautiful voices, and sometimes when they sang tears would shine on the pretty faces of the others. The Socialists chanted slogans from Great Collapse campaigns and then

gave loud speeches on the global political situation, making sure that all
the other women could hear their views.

The Socialists, you see, didn't believe in Gaia worship or even in singing and crying. They believed in organized protest. They said they had
the right to a lawyer and a fair trial; some had even memorized the tele-
phone numbers and email addresses of solicitors sympathetic to their
cause. But when they demanded these rights, the guards just laughed.
Then the Socialists would get angry and bang on the door with their
fists, and the gang-girls and the Gaians would count that as part of
their noise time. The rest of the women knew that the State of Emergency had devoured their rights the way a whale swallows plankton.
Everyone was scared, but no one was surprised when the Prison Ship's
engines growled into life and the vessel set out to sea.

"Now, for the first time, all the women formed a circle and con-
ferred together. 'They're takin' us to America,' one of the gang-girls said.
'They're gonna dump us there, 'cause it costs too much to keep us in the
style we been accustomed to.'"

Someone in the back row tittered. It *was* funny, the way Nimma was
doing the accent. She never mimicked people ordinarily; Astra had had
no idea she could do it so well.

"'Why would the government take us all the way across the ocean
to get rid of us?' scoffed one of the Socialists. 'They'd be smarter just to
feed us to the fishes. We have to pull together now, and be ready to over-
power the guards when they come to get us.'

"'If we're goin' to the Wild West, I wanna be a two-pistol stripper,' a
gang-girl crowed. And she stood up and flashed her Gaia bulbs."

Around the Fountain, some of the Or-adults and older teens
chuckled.

"What's a stripper—?" Astra whispered to Hokma.

"Later," Hokma shushed.

"Some of the Socialists frowned, but Kali and the Beltane women
applauded. Even if they were all going to be murdered, they must never
lose their Gaia joy. In the morning the ship had stopped. An eerie silence
reigned. Kali realized she could no longer hear the sound of the other
ships' engines or horns.

"'Why have they brought us out here?' she asked one of the guards.

"'Unusually,' the guard replied. 'Too many prisoners, isn't it?' she said. 'They needed to put more ships in the harbor. So you all have to live out here, and *I've* got to work two-week shifts and fly home in a friggin' helicopter.'"

Astra had to suppress a giggle. Nimma was speaking in a high, complaining lilt for the guard's voice. She wasn't a great actor like Modem, but she was okay.

"So that was Kali's new life, held without charge, trial or lawyer on a Prison Ship in the Atlantic Ocean. At first, the Beltane women despaired. But then they counted their blessings. Oh, there weren't many; Kali needed only one hand, Or-children, and she still had a thumb left over. Apart from each other and regular food, there were two things the Gaians gave thanks for: they had the freedom to move their bodies, and once a day they could go outside to walk beneath Gaia's high blue skies, smell Her salty skin and listen to Her seagulls crying. That was all they could sense of Her beauty. The walls of the ship's deck towered above them and the women could see nothing of the sea except the gulls and the vile sight of the guards fishing, bashing the heads of their victims with hammers to kill them.

"At first every day was the same: a long tense mixture of fear and desperation and snatches of gratitude. But then, as the first week adrift turned into the second and the third, though nothing changed, everything changed, for the women discovered that they had Gaia's great gift to look forward to. Kali and three of the gang-girls were pregnant."

Nimma paused and looked through the Fountain at Sorrel. Sorrel smiled around the Circle and stroked her swollen belly. Beside her, Congruence and Holaa admired her heavy curves. In Astra's lap, Sprig yawned. Other younger children were slumping too, she could see. Yoki was leaning against Klor's stump, his eyes closed, mouth open. Klor cast a meaningful glance at Nimma.

"Like all good stories," she said, "this one is getting longer in the Telling. So I won't tell Kali's Birth Story. I'll just say that the Gaians and the Socialists delivered the babies, and the gang-girls became like daughters to the midwives, and Rhiannon cut the cord of her little

Shelter granddaughter with her teeth. And when the talkative guard, whose name was Dilys, asked to hold Kali's baby, Kali begged her to tell Peredur he had a daughter, still unnamed and waiting for his blessing. Dilys granted her wish and returned saying that Peredur would like the baby to be named Elpis, after the Greek goddess of Hope and in honor of Elphin, who was not very well. And despite that sad news, for six months after her birth, a kind of happiness took root on that gray metal boat. The women nursed and washed the babies and sang to them, and the helicopters even brought diapers with snaps because they weren't allowed pins.

"But then one week the shift helicopter was late. It didn't come the day it was supposed to, and it didn't come the next day either. The guards were angry and wouldn't let the women out on deck. Finally, on the third day, the women heard the helicopter hovering above the ship as it let down its lines. It brought Dilys back, and as soon as she could, Kali asked her what had happened.

"'Short of money, aren't they?' Dilys told her. 'And short of fuel too. So they're cuttin' back on the chopper. It'll be three-week shifts now for us sorry souls workin' out here.' She didn't look Kali in the eye and when the guard left for her next shore leave, Kali was afraid that she wouldn't come back.

"Dilys did return, though. And when she did, her behavior was very strange. She shouted at the gang-girls, and the next day she left all the women out on deck for hours, until they were banging on the door to be let back inside to eat.

"'I thought you people liked being outside,' she said as she finally opened the door. Kali joined the line to return to their bunks, but Dilys took her by the elbow. 'Not you. I want to cuddle Elpis,' she said.

"Dilys locked the door behind the other women and took Elpis in her arms. Then, with a quick look at the guards fishing by the rails, she leaned close to Kali and whispered, 'Listen to me now, Kali, something's going to happen—something good for you and Elpis, but terrible bad for some other people. I'm not supposed to tell you, but I think you should know. I'm warning you though, if the gangers get wind of it, they might take it out on you and the baby. And if those politicos find out, then the whole thing will be shot and it will be bad news for everyone. So you have to promise to keep it secret. So do you want to hear me, or not?'

"Kali watched Elpis bubble a smile up at Dilys. 'I can't keep secrets from my people,' she said at last, 'but I won't tell the others.'"

Too many stories were about secrets. Astra hugged Sprig tighter. The girl's body was warm and slack and her head lolled in the crook of Astra's arm. For a moment she almost could have been baby Elpis—except Elpis had only ever been old.

"'Good girl,' Dilys said, tickling Elpis's tummy. 'So: one of the internet tycoons, that Server guru, Charles Monteray? He wants your head honcho. Hew Belson. And he wants you and Elpis too.'"

Astra had studied Charles Monteray at school. He was an important figure in the early Regeneration Era. He had cofounded the company that managed the massive Continental Server in the ash fields. At the sound of his name Hokma grunted softly. Beside Nimma, Moon stroked Aesop's head.

"Kali was confused. 'I don't understand,' she said, reaching for her baby. 'Do you mean Hew Owen?'

"'Kali, keep your voice down—and let me hold Elpis. She's happy with me, aren't you my duck? Yes, Hew Owen. He's changed his name, didn't I tell you? He says he's the son of Beltane now. And a lot else has been happening since you've been in here: very important things. All over the world the Server Gurus are cozying up to the Gaians—those of you left, anyway. They need your energy know-how to power their mainframes through this crisis and they're willing to put up with your mumbo jumbo to get it. The Yukay government's bargaining hard. They're calling you Beltane people terrorists, but they've agreed to release three of you. *A gesture of good will*, they'll call it. Monteray thinks if he can save a genius, a woman and a baby he'll make a few international headlines, and that'll help bring other Gaians on board with the Gurus. That's going to be Hew, you and Elpis. You're going to be *freed*—you'll be on the next outbound chopper.'

"*Freed*. Kali's heart sprouted wings—but then, like an unborn chick, it remained curled up tight in her chest.

"'But what about Rhiannon? And Peredur and Elphin? I can't leave them,' she started, but Dilys shook her.

"'*Kali*, listen to me: I'm not *asking*, I'm *telling*. We've got orders to strait-jacket you and Hew and hoist you up into the chopper. So I think you should say your goodbyes and let your mother know you'll be safe. I don't know why, it just seems right. I could lose my job for it, but you know what, I'm sick of those chopper rides.'

"Dilys laughed, but Kali felt ill. 'I can't go,' she whispered. 'I can't leave them all.'

"Dilys reached out and grasped Kali's hand. 'You've got to think of Elpis, Kali,' she urged. 'That Monteray, he's going to look after you both—she'll have a chance in life. Do you want her to grow up on this ship?'"

Before, Nimma had asked the Circle what they thought the Beltane Gaians should do, but this was different, Astra could tell: this was a very lonely choice, not one it would be right to take a vote on. This was a decision a person had to make with the help of Gaia alone.

Nimma lowered her voice. "That night Kali whispered Dilys's story to Rhiannon and Peredur's mother, and the women wept and held her tight. Then each alone asked Gaia what to do, and to all of them, Gaia said that Kali must go. Over the next two weeks, they told the other Beltane Gaians, one by one, and everyone agreed that Kali must take Elpis away, off the ship, with Hew. If Server Gurus were bargaining for Gaians, then Gaians must seize the power they were offered and use it to protect their Mother.

"So that is how Kali agreed to leave the Prison Ship, willingly, as Gaia's messenger. With Elpis bound to her chest, she and Hew were winched up to the chopper. Later—much later—she told Elpis that she didn't know what she would have done if Dilys had told her the full truth. Would she have told the Socialists and the gang-girls so they could have tried to take the guards hostage? Or would she have kept quiet and saved Elpis's life?

"But Dilys had lied, or perhaps she hadn't known the truth, and so when Kali hugged Hew in the back of the chopper and gave him Elpis to hold and cry over, she didn't know that all the guards and janitors and cooks, and the ship's enginemen and the captain were being airlifted away without replacements, and the prisoners were being left behind locked in their holds, without food or water."

Nimma's feet were planted firmly on the ground and her palms were resting on her knees. Her eyes were closed and her face was calm. This part of the story was virtually unbearable. Everyone except the very youngest children, who were mostly asleep now, knew what had happened on the Death Ships from studying History at school or on their Tablettes. But it was different hearing about it in a story: in a story it was happening to people who you *knew*. The Circle had already drummed its anger into Gaia's waiting bosom; now, from a host of downcast eyes, Or's bitter sorrow stabbed the earth. Human harmony: sometimes it could be cold and hard, it could line you up with others like knives in a drawer or arrows in a fist. *How was it possible*, Astra wondered, *to belong to something you could never accept?*

When the minute's silence had passed, Nimma resumed the story. "Kali, Elpis and Hew arrived on shore and were sent to live in Charles Monteray's mansion. A week later the media reported that a storm had sunk all the Prison Ships and everyone on board was lost. Kali and Hew grieved long for their losses—but although they suspected the timing of their rescue was not an accident, it was not until the fifth year of the Regeneration Era, when the Yukay government finally restored elections, that Charles Monteray's new media empire revealed the truth.

"The Yukay Dark Time government had decided to eliminate as many prisoners as possible. Elpis and the gang-girls' babies had never even been entered on official records. Under the State of Emergency, all prisoners held at sea were charged and convicted *in absentia* of conspiracy to commit treason, and all had been sentenced to death. After evacuating their crews the government sent a fleet of naval torpedo boats out to the Prison Ships, not to save three thousand people from starvation but to *drown* them, to drive them to the bottom of the Atlantic, to sink this great crime without trace. Except, that is, in Kali's memory, and in Elpis's memory and in mine, and now in yours. This story is just one of many that tell how the Gaians were betrayed in their own lands. And that savage betrayal is why, when the Regeneration Era finally began, we petitioned the Council of the New Continents to give us Is-Land to live in and, with Gaia's blessing, to protect forever."

The Fountain spray had shrunk low again. Nimma gazed around in the fading light, acknowledging the respect of each of her listeners. Torrent looked fiercely back at her as if offering Gaia his warriorhood; beneath his arm, Stream's eyes were puffy and wet. Sorrel was softly shaking her head and cradling her belly; Congruence sat poker-backed, chin set, her eyes half-closed as a Kezcam recorded her absorbing the lingering power of the Telling. Astra's right leg was numb and her arm stiff, but for a moment she forgot her discomfort, forgot that Ahn was still filming. Nimma was *her* Shelter mother and Elpis had been *her* Shelter grandmother and that made Kali *her* ancestor and this story hers to tell too. She would learn it, she vowed, word for own word, and one day she would tell it to her own children.

Congruence opened her eyes. "Thank you, Nimma," she said, as was the responsibility of the Asker.

Astra gazed at Birth House. Elpis was inside the womb-chamber, listening too. She had heard her story told and felt the deep human harmony it generated. Would she come out to smile at them with her silent, lop-sided mouth?

A pale shape appeared in the doorway: small, like Elpis in her chair, but not in a chair—standing up, moving into the light. Astra blinked, but the figure was still there.

Congruence had seen it too; she gasped and leaned forward, peering through the spray. The Kezcam shot up into the air and the Circle stiffened to attention, adults springing to their feet, Nimma and Klor twisting in their seats and Hokma hugging Astra and Sprig close to her side.

The girl—for the figure was a girl, of about Astra's age—stepped over the threshold. She was sky-clad and barefoot. Her thick black hair was matted like a sick sheep's, and her hands were bunched in fists at her sides. She walked steadily down the Ancestors' Path toward Nimma and Klor. When she got to the Ancestors' Place she stopped and glared at the Circle.

"My *stomach* hurts," she said accusingly. In the light from the Fountain, Astra could see her arms were scratched and scabbed, and thick black rivulets of blood were running down her inner thighs. Then the girl clutched her stomach and doubled over, moaning. Ahn's aerial Kez-cam plummeted twenty feet straight down to a spot just above her head. If it was filming the Or Circle, it was recording faces contorted with shock and a frantic confusion of unorchestrated movement: parents sheltering their children; warriors leaping to their feet and into perimeter patrol position; Astra lunging in front of the Fountain, grabbing a pine cone to throw. Behind her, Sprig screamed—then Hokma was on top of her, dragging her back by the waist and, finger by finger, forcing the missile from her fist.

2.3

"Lil, this is Astra. Astra, meet Lil." Hokma's hand was on the girl's back, rubbing her shoulders as Astra, her arms crossed, toed the dirt patch behind the Wise House veranda. It was two days since the Fountain night. The girl didn't look happy either. She was clean now, her hair had been combed into two paintbrush braids and she was wearing a pair of Gaia-blood panties Nimma had organized, but the scowl on her face could have stripped bark from an oak.

"Hello," Astra glowered. She had only been allowed to come to Wise House today if she'd promised to be *friendly*. It was unbelievable. Wise House was *her* Shelter home. Why was the frigging girl staying here? And why didn't *she* have to be friendly too? Everyone knew that apart from the occasional brief demand for food Lil was refusing to speak to *anyone*. She wouldn't wear shoes, either. But even though Nimma said Lil didn't need to because her soles were hardened, she'd gone through Astra's cupboard looking for sandals and boots that might fit her. "*I still wear those!*" Astra had been forced to insist. Nimma had given her an exasperated look and put her hand on Astra's brow. "You're not ill, Astra," she'd said. "I don't know why you're displaying such a temper."

The girl stuck out her hand. But that hand wasn't friendly, Astra knew. It was on the end of an arm that was straight as a spear. It was a blade, ready to slice her palm open.

Behind them, Helium and Silver and the three current trainee Owleons were tethered to their pegs on the lawn. Helium was slowly blinking his giant orange-planet eyes. Silver was waking up from his afternoon nap, stretching his moth-gray wings like a taut, brocaded shawl. The birds needed to be flown, and Hokma was waiting. Silently, briefly, Astra brushed her hand against Lil's. The girl was taller than her but she was very skinny. For sure she could take her in a fight.

"Is she sleeping in *my* bed?" she asked Hokma indignantly.

"She is, but you can sleep in with me, like you used to. I've moved your stuff over to my loft."

Sleep with *Hokma*? "*I don't want—*"

"It's just for now, Astra!" Hokma snapped, and blood rushed to Astra's face. She gripped her dread and began twirling it ferociously between her fingers.

"IMBOD will soon find Lil's home," Hokma continued smoothly. "In the meantime, I want you to be kind to her. Lil knows lots of interesting places in the woods, don't you, Lil? Maybe if you're nice to her she'll show them to you, Astra."

Hokma was being *impossible*. Astra flung her dread back over her shoulder and sullenly scanned Lil's face. The girl's tea-brown eyes didn't respond with so much as a scintilla of invitation to the woods.

"She's not going to help train the Owleons, is she?" she muttered.

"Lil's going to help clean the aviary pens. She can watch us train the birds if she wants."

What? Astra wanted to shout again. Why was Hokma being so *stupid*? This girl, Lil—or so she *said* she was called—had been spying on them for *years*—and now Hokma wanted her to observe all their secret Owleon maneuvers?

"But—" she tried.

"Astra." Hokma cut her off. "Be *nice*. Okay, girls, let's grab some buckets and brooms and get to work on those cages."

Hokma started up the veranda steps and behind her back Lil flashed Astra a smile—not a nice smile; not a sensitive, shy, I'd-really-like-to-get-to-know-you kind of smile; not a sassy, eye-rolling, *aren't-adults-bossy*, shared pain kind of smile; but a nasty, sly, triumphant little smile: a smug smile with glue slathered over it and broken glass sprinkled on top.

For an hour they worked in silence. Astra's arms ached as she scrubbed the cage floors, endeavoring to out-clean Lil, who slopped too much water around and had to go back to Wise House twice to refill her bucket. That was wasteful, but Hokma didn't tell her off. When they finished cleaning Hokma said "well done" and "thank you" to them both, in exactly the same infuriatingly brisk and encouraging manner. Astra couldn't remember when Hokma had last been this cheerful. Normally they worked in near-silence, taking the three trainees to the clearing first, and flying them for an hour. But today Hokma said, "Let's show Lil how we fly Helium and Silver," and so after they had put the buckets and brooms away and filled two pouches with alt-meat, it was the older birds they untethered first.

It was obvious that Lil couldn't touch Silver—Silver was Astra's Owleon and even IMBOD officers knew not to hold him—but Hokma gave Lil a glove and let her take Helium. As the huge Owleon stepped onto her wrist, the girl's eyes shone with a wild fire. She grabbed his jesses and bit her chapped lower lip until it practically disappeared. At last Helium spread open his huge wings and the dark screen of feathers hid the horrible image of Lil's contorted delight.

Silver perched daintily on Astra's wrist, his black eyes gleaming and his heart-shaped face tilting in response to sounds inaudible to human ears. Astra sometimes wondered if he could hear her heartbeat. If so, he would be worried, because today her heart was clenched tight as a fist, its knuckles rapping angrily on a locked door. She lagged behind as they walked through the woods behind the aviary, keeping Silver close to her chest and stroking his snowy breast feathers with a crooked finger. "I'm sorry, Silver. I'm in a bad mood today. It's not your fault."

He nipped at her knuckle as he sometimes did when they were walking. It never hurt and didn't mean he was annoyed with her; he was just seeking food.

"Not yet, Silver. We'll be there in a minute."

Ahead of them she could see Lil striding a couple of feet in front of Hokma, her slight frame dwarfed by Helium's dark feathery mass. She *willed* Lil to let her arm drop. Helium wasn't that heavy, but he still gripped your arm until it hurt. She shouldn't be able to carry him far. Surely after Hokma unlocked the back gate Lil would hand Helium back?

But Lil tucked her right hand under her left elbow and held her skinny arm steady, all the way through the woods to the cedar hedge that ran between the Wise House grounds and the flying field. Astra closed the hedge gate and trudged through the long grass to the near perches. Silver was lighter on her wrist now, half-lifting in anticipation of food and a flight. But the gentle pull of his talons on the glove didn't raise her spirits as it usually did.

How long was Lil going to be here? Hokma said until they'd found her family—but the girl didn't have a family. Her Code-Shelter father had died, that was what Nimma had said yesterday after the emergency Or meeting that none of the Or-kids were allowed to attend. The local IMBOD officer had come to it, galloping up on a sleek black horse he'd tethered to a tree near East Gate. Astra and Meem had fed the horse apples and after the officer had mounted and ridden away again Nimma and Klor had summoned them to the Earthship for a Shelter house meeting with Yoki and Peat.

Astra had sat on the floor with her knitting. The girl, she knew, would have told the adults a pack of lies. But if Astra said so, she might get into an argument and that would be dangerous for her and Hokma. The best way to avoid losing her temper at Shelter house meetings, she'd learned, was to focus on something else. Right now she was knitting a pair of socks for Craft class. The stitch was easy, but the gold yarn and the needles were thin and she had to concentrate hard to control her gauge. Nimma had said that if the socks were good enough, she could send them to a constable in the Southern Belt.

Klor and Nimma's report was even worse than she'd feared. Lil, it appeared, had managed to fool *all* the adults, even the IMBOD officer. She was a traumatized young girl, Nimma said, and Elpis had clearly sent her to Or to be healed. The girl hadn't spoken at the meeting, but when the IMBOD officer said if she didn't cooperate he'd take her away with him, she'd begun nodding or shaking her head to their questions. Her Code-Shelter father had left his community with her after her Birth-Code-Shelter mother died, eight or nine years ago—the girl wasn't sure how long it had been, and she couldn't point on a map to where the community was located—and he had wandered with her in the mountains ever since, coming down to the steppes at night if they needed supplies.

Peat was taking minutes. He looked up from Libby and frowned. "That's weird," he commented. "Why would he want to leave his community?"

It was unusual behavior, Nimma said, but grief did sometimes make men do irrational things. He'd obviously loved Lil very much, though. She'd drawn pictures for the meeting showing how they'd lived in caves, and how he'd taught her how to make fire with a piece of flint, and felt blankets from the wool he gathered from fences on the steppes so even in the winter they were warm. He'd taught her how to read, too, for she was carrying a tattered book of Gaia hymns and stories in the pocket of her old hydropac. "Imagine that," Nimma sighed. "A *book*. It must have been a family heirloom."

Sure it was. Astra pulled the yarn tight. The man was an *infiltrator* and he was making sure his kid had a cover story for when they both got caught. He'd probably *stolen* the hymnbook. IMBOD should search the crime records for *that*.

"Watch your tension, darling," Nimma warned, and Astra examined her stitches. Annoyingly, her gauge had been shrinking. She scowled and started unpicking.

Peat was still puzzled. "Eight years ago?" he persisted. "So how did she have her Security shot?"

Without warning, this had become a red-light conversation. Astra concentrated on getting her row back in order. She had to soften her shoulders and work on nice loose stitching until the topic had passed. *Knit two. Purl two. Knit two.*

"We think she didn't," Klor said. "Perhaps that was one reason he took her away."

Peat was amazed. "But that's child neglect—child *abuse*. She won't be able to fit in anywhere now."

"She won't have any friends," Meem said complacently.

"She'll be lonely," Yoki echoed.

It was her turn. "She'll be sad," Astra contributed from the Sec Gen's interchangeable stock of Imprints concerning the disastrous effects of Serum deprivation. These were learned at school—never repeated in front of the older children, of course, but expressed among themselves in tones of crocodile solicitude whenever one of the Or-teens was going through a tempestuous period. It was obvious to Astra that these comforting maxims weren't all strictly true. Despite—or perhaps even *because* of—her trauma, Congruence had strengthened her hold on her friends *and* starred in Ahn's film, while Durga had visited recently from Atourne to shyly announce she had made a Gaia bond with another young woman in her Craft College class. But still, it did look like life without the shot could be a terrible struggle. Everyone knew Pristina was having a difficult time on IMBOD Service because she wrote long, weepy letters to her Code parents begging to be allowed to come home. And just this morning Stream had been observed shouting at Torrent on the Kinbat track and then storming into the woods in tears.

Hokma always said that Astra wouldn't be lonely or sad when she grew up because she'd go to college in Atourne and meet older non-Sec Gen people like her, but in the meantime one of the adages was definitely true: she *didn't* fit in. The teens treated her like just another Sec Gen kid, but though the Sec Gens accepted her, she was only ever half-present in their company. They were fun to play chess or *hnefatafl* with, and they were good at teamwork in the kitchen or the garden, but none of them liked to make up stories or ask questions, and none of her Shelter siblings ever took her side if she was upset with Nimma. Sometimes this was a good thing and Meem's giggles or Peat's Code-talk would coax her out of a funk; other times, though, she festered and had to stomp up the path to Wise House to let her anger loose on Hokma.

"What he did was legally wrong in many ways," Nimma responded, "but the important thing is that Lil's here with us now. Hopefully one day she'll have older non-Sec Gen friends and be happy with them. Not everyone's as lucky as your generation, are they?"

"We're *very* lucky," Meem beamed.

Yoki looked troubled. "I don't like non-Sec Gen kids," he announced. "They're selfish."

"Yoki," Nimma tutted, "that's not a nice thing to say. Durga's not selfish, is she? And neither is Congruence. She helped you in the garden the other day—I saw her."

Yoki considered this. "Yes, she did," he conceded.

Peat had been tapping on Libby. Now he looked up with the air of a researcher. "What did they eat?" he asked.

Nimma glanced at Klor. "Well, they ate nuts and berries—*safe* berries, of course. And other fruit, and wild herbs and mushrooms. We think that he stole flour and other food from communities—the IMBOD officer said several such thefts had been reported in this area. And"—she twisted her emerald ring—"they hunted."

Nothing about Lil would have surprised Astra, but the other children recoiled, their faces stricken with disgust and disbelief.

"Hunted? You mean they *killed animals*?" Yoki exclaimed.

"Yes. It looks like her father taught Lil how to make traps and how to use a bow and arrow. They caught and ate birds and fish, and occasionally rabbits."

"Whoah!" Peat exhaled.

"But that's . . . *bad*," Meem stammered.

"We have to assume he was invoking the self-defense law," Klor said.

"But the self-defense law only lets us protect the crops." Peat had recovered his composure and was now analyzing the information in context. He was in Year Eight, and as expected, he was acing Law class.

"That's true," Klor said. "But if you don't have access to alt-meat or enough vegetable protein then hunting does count as self-defense. Some tribal people still do it, and Is-Land doesn't table objections at CONC meetings."

Two tears had appeared on Yoki's long eyelashes, shining like dewdrops on a spider's web. "But that's not *here*," he objected. "There's no hunting allowed in Is-Land. Never *ever*. That's why Gaia killed Lil's dad."

"Now, now, Yoki." Nimma pulled the boy to her side. "Gaia didn't kill Lil's father. He just got sick, that's all."

"They could have eaten nuts, like squirrels!" Yoki shouted, the tears flowing freely now. "I *hate* her. I don't want her here."

Everyone looked at him in concern then. Even though Yoki was one of the more sensitive Sec Gens, it was still rare for him to cry. His distress was contagious: Meem was trembling too, and she reached out for Klor, who bundled her close.

"Hush, children," Klor said soothingly as Nimma wiped Yoki's tears away. "Even if Lil's father broke the law, that's not her fault, is it?"

This was all nonsense. And if Yoki was going to throw a tantrum, she could risk an outburst too. Astra jabbed her knitting needles into the ball of yarn. "How do we know he was a Gaian?" she interjected. "He left his community and he killed birds and mammals. I think he was an *infiltrator.*"

"Of course we are concerned about Security, Astra," Klor said. "IMBOD will be thoroughly investigating Lil's story. But whatever her father was, she's just a young girl and she needs our help right now."

"We know he was a Gaian, Astra," Nimma added, "because he gave Lil the book of hymns." Nimma's own eyes welled up now.

Typical.

"He built his own pyre with her and taught her how to perform a Return to Gaia ceremony for him."

"Don't cry, Nimma," Meem pleaded as Klor reached over and stroked their Shelter mother's hand.

"I'm sorry, children. It's just very moving. Imagine performing a Return to Gaia ceremony by yourself—and then her Gaia-blood began. I think that must be why Elpis sheltered her in the Birth House."

"I don't want to help her," Yoki sulked. "Not if she ate *rabbits.*"

"I know it's hard to accept, Yoki," Klor said. "But she didn't have a choice. She was obeying her father, wasn't she?"

"We all have to obey our parents, Yoki," Meem said, sitting up and holding Klor's hand.

"She's a minor. She's not legally responsible for what her father made her do," Peat chipped in decisively. He and Meem looked composed again now. The crisis had rippled through them and subsided without leaving a trace of anxiety. Tomorrow, Astra knew, Yoki too would have come to terms with the news and none of them would question the adults' decision to believe Lil's absurd story.

"You don't have to help her, Yoki," Nimma reassured him. "She's not used to playing with other children—and she won't be here for long. We're just telling you about her now so that you don't believe any wild rumors that might go around later."

Then Nimma had revealed the plan, which had been decided on at the meeting, with the full approval of the IMBOD officer. Lil had been registered as an IMBOD Shelter child and the state was going to pay for her upkeep while they looked for her community. In the meantime, the Or Parents' Committee had volunteered to be her other temporary Shelter parent. Lil was going to stay at Wise House while investigations proceeded.

Nothing could have prepared Astra for this. "Wise House?" As if it belonged to someone else, she heard her voice slide out of range and crack like a glass. "But that's *my* Shelter home."

"Yes, it's a Shelter home," Nimma said patiently. "It shelters children. Sometimes a new child comes along. That's what being in a family is all about."

"But no one else has to make room! Why do *I* have to?" Astra cast around for support but her Or-siblings were as useless as ever: Peat was checking his Tablette, Yoki was hugging Klor's leg and Meem was sucking her thumb until Nimma gently removed it from her mouth.

"Astra," she said firmly, "there is plenty of room for both you and Lil in Hokma's heart, just like there's room for all of you and Sheba in mine."

Sheba was the final word in any argument, invoked rarely but with the dire threat of Nimma's silent tears should Astra continue to pester. She shut up, but she was fuming. Sheba was supposed to be her *big sister* but Astra knew barely anything about her. Nimma dusted Sheba's photo on the mantelpiece every day, but she and Klor still hadn't shared her album. The photos weren't in Libby, not even under child-lock; she had looked. She had once asked Klor, on his own, if she could see them on his Tablette, but he had said Nimma wouldn't like it.

"We remember Sheba all the time and we don't want you children to feel sad about her too," he'd said. Four or five years ago, when Meem was old enough, they'd all gone to Sheba's Fountain together. Those photos *were* on Libby, but when they had slideshows at birthdays, Nimma and Klor never included them. Why was she supposed to care so much about Sheba if she wasn't allowed to know a thing about her?

"Astra. Or-child," Klor cajoled. "Hokma thought it would be good for you to have some company up there. You're so busy with the Owleons, you're missing out on play time, aren't you?"

Play time? Who *were* these people? She was nearly *thirteen*. She didn't need to muck around in a frigging playground with anyone, let alone an unwashed, meat-eating, Non-Lander *spy*. Her face was blazing hot and she wanted to jump up, stamp and yell and throw her knitting across the room. But she couldn't. She saw Nimma give Klor that sharp, warning glance again, the one that meant: *See, I told you so, Astra's behaving badly again.* And Klor's tufty eyebrows gathered together, his kind face silently replying, *Come, darling, I'm sure Astra will calm down soon.* She had to stop resisting now or Nimma might one day win this recurring mimed argument and take her to the doctor, ask for tests to be run. She might lose Hokma, the Owleons, everything.

She forced herself to wilt. "I guess," she whispered.

"We know it's a big change, darling," Nimma said, magnanimous in victory. "But we're sure it will be interesting, and it won't be for long. Hokma says she'll feed the Owleons today, and you can come tomorrow as normal, as long as you promise to be nice to Lil."

She'd had no choice. She had promised, and now she was approaching the flying-field perches where Lil was flinging Helium into the air and he was beating his enormous broad wings above her head as she gasped and jumped, and as he soared into the bright blue sky, briefly blotting out the sun, Hokma was laughing and Lil was turning to Astra with a big sparkling grin, saying exultantly, "His wings made a breeze on my face!"

Then Lil looked at Silver for the first time and said, her voice quiet with awe, "He's so pretty. Can I stroke him, please?" And Hokma looked at Astra and Astra heard herself say, "Okay—but not near his face, or he might bite you." Then Lil ran a fingertip over Silver's lacy mantle and said, in the same hushed tone, "I always wanted to stroke an owl, but an Owleon's even better."

For a moment Astra wondered if Lil had ever eaten an owl, but then Silver strained again to fly and it was time to say, "Stand back," then let go of his jesses, release him into the air and watch him rising, rising on an invisible current until he was gliding silently across the forest meadow, past the flying field's solitary twisted juniper and toward the far set of perches, while beside her Lil whispered, "My dad liked owls," then, standing ramrod-still, with a terrible sawing sound from her throat, erupted into a desolate, choking upheaval of sobs, crying as if no comfort could ever reach her, until Hokma was hugging her and Astra was somehow gently, helplessly stroking her back, saying, "Don't cry, Lil, don't cry. You can help me fly Silver. It's going to be okay. Everything's going to be okay."

2.4

She hadn't wanted to become friends with Lil—she had *hated* Lil. But the girl swooped into her life and plucked out her resistance like a vulture disemboweling a lamb. First she was so unutterably grief-stricken—no one could hate someone so sad. Once she'd started crying she couldn't stop. For a week Hokma gave Lil bowls of stew and mugs of warm oatmilk and let her lie on the sofa for hours, wrapped in a sheet. Astra came to Wise House after school, bringing wildflower bouquets from the path, and tried to entice Lil outdoors to the aviary to help with Silver and Helium. Lil trailed behind her to the field and watched the birds fly through swollen eyes. When at last, on the Sabbaday afternoon, she climbed up to the roof with Astra, she just sat there hunched over, plucking at stems of grass. Astra searched for crickets and carried one over on her wrist to show Lil its bright green legs and twitching antennae.

Lil looked at it dully. "You have to cook it first," she said.

Astra whipped her wrist away and released the cricket back into the meadow. "It's not to *eat*! We don't kill Gaia's creatures here."

Lil shrugged, a lopsided twitch involving just her right shoulder. "You kill worms. They're nice fried."

"We *have* to kill them or the Owleons would die," Astra retorted. But beneath her indignation, a strange sensation was stirring. *Eat worms?*

Even though Hokma had long ago dropped the charade of medical euthanasia she had used Astra's first time at Wise House, the thought of eating them herself had never occurred to her. As she considered it, she began to feel uncomfortably aware of the inside of her mouth. No, a worm didn't belong in there. It would be gristly and sour and slimy, wouldn't it?

"My dad called it wild spaghetti," Lil continued. "You have to add garlic."

"I don't want to talk about it," Astra announced.

Lil tugged at a clump of grass, pulling it out of the turf, and Astra snapped, "Don't do that. You've killed it."

"It's just grass," Lil scoffed. "It seeds itself back. We used long grass for our beds."

Again, reactions wrestled inside her. The girl's nonchalant contempt for Gaia was outrageous, but at the same time, she was like a horrible Old World story: even though it disgusted you, you wanted to find out what happened. "Well, *this* grass helps keep Wise House cool. So don't destroy it," she ordered.

Lil looked bored, but she patted the rootball back into the roof and brushed the earth from her hands. Then she sat back, stretched out her legs and idly scratched her Gaia mound. She had far more hair there than Astra: a curly black thicket.

Astra fingered the tip of her dread. Two could play at that game.

"Hokma said you haven't got your Gaia-blood yet," Lil announced.

"*So?*" Astra sneered, but there was a pang in her chest. Was there no end to Hokma's betrayal? Lil had used three or four pads a day in her blood panties when she arrived at Wise House, washing them out in the sink with Hokma and hanging them to dry across the lawn. Hokma had said Astra's turn would come soon, and Nimma was already making her hipbeads for the Blood & Seed ceremony next month. There was no need for Lil to know *any* of that.

"It only hurts sometimes," Lil informed her. "But when it does you feel like you're going to *die*. You'll probably get it when you're thirteen."

Astra tossed her head, flipping her dread back behind her ear. "How do you know? I might get it sooner." Of course she wanted to get it during the ceremony, but Nimma had said that Gaia-bleeding wasn't a competition: girls naturally started at different ages, just as boys produced seed at different ages, and the Blood & Seed ceremony welcomed all Year Seven graduates to adulthood together. She wasn't going to talk to Lil about the ceremony, though. What if Lil said she wanted to come and Hokma let her, even though she was fourteen? Astra was the only Year Seven girl in Or, and as Nimma had been saying all year, she and Yoki would soon have the honor of representing their community at the Bioregional Congregation Site with girls and boys from all over the dry forest. She definitely didn't want to have to share that honor with Lil—whom no one had yet, after all, proved was not a Non-Lander.

Lil shrugged that minimalist shrug again. "You're still quite undeveloped."

What? Just because Lil's breasts were a fraction bigger than hers didn't make Astra *undeveloped*. "We don't make remarks like that here in Or," she announced icily. "Everyone develops in their own time."

For a moment, what looked suspiciously like a sneer distorted Lil's mouth. "Sorry," she said. "I meant, you're young still."

Astra felt like leaving, but she knew she shouldn't let Lil needle her. This was *her* turf, and she had to take control of this situation—now.

"Why don't you remember where your community was?" she demanded.

Lil picked a piece of grass out of her Gaia hair and twirled it between her fingers. "My dad said the forest was our home now."

"So your community wasn't in this bioregion?" Astra persisted.

Lil wrinkled her nose. "There were some trees. But the land was flat, I think. I used to dream about it, but then I stopped." Her lip trembled and she looked so woeful again that Astra had to stop her interrogation. You couldn't push a subject too far, she knew. You had to take her just past her limit, and let her recover before you started again.

"*Girls.* I've made berry biscuits," Hokma called up from the veranda, and Lil jumped to her feet and headed to the ladder. Astra followed her down carefully, a worm of some uncertain emotion knotting in her stomach. She couldn't remember the last time Hokma had baked anything. Normally she just sprinkled berries straight from the jar onto her cereal, but there they were: berry biscuits arranged in a crescent on a plate, beside three glasses of iced apricot nectar.

Lil ate her first biscuit in two mouthfuls, then drank her nectar all in one go. "Thank you, Hokma," she said, for the first time in Astra's hearing.

"Good?" Hokma asked Astra.

Astra took another biscuit. "Yeah," she begrudgingly conceded. They were *okay*, but not nearly as thin and crispy as Nimma's.

The next day when Astra woke up and climbed down from Hokma's loft, Lil was in the kitchen, washing last night's dishes. After breakfast Lil asked Hokma if she could help in the vegetable garden, where she proved to be very handy with a hoe. Hokma said her dad had obviously brought her up to be a hard worker.

Lil's head was down among the beans. "We worked in the mornings and played games in the afternoons," she said.

"What kind of games?" Hokma asked.

"Skipping, hopscotch, singing, catch. Reading, writing, storytelling, snap," Lil recited. "Other stuff too. Keepie-uppie. Arrow practice."

"That's a nice rhyme. We play all those games here, don't we, Astra?"

"We used to," Astra corrected. "I'm too old for snap now. And hopscotch."

"I suppose you are. But we still practice writing sometimes, don't we?"

"Sometimes." Astra shrugged. Along with her refusal to get a prosthetic eye and her insistence on living off-grid with no access to the internet, writing was one of Hokma's *eccentricities*, as Nimma put it. All the metal tubes on her desk were antique fountain pens her Code grandmother had brought with her from Neuropa to Is-Land, and the bottles were full of colored inks Hokma made from berries. She said that fountain pens were an important part of the development of Storytelling tradition, and she often tried to get Astra to use them. She'd taught her how to write the alphabet, the twenty-six Old World letters and the four Gaian diphthongs, but beyond the delight of writing her name in different artistic designs, Astra didn't really see the point.

Writing took ages and was strewn with peril: first you had to fill the pen and shake it out, risking blotting your page or the wall; when you dragged the nib across Hokma's rough handmade paper it always caught on bits of fiber and ruined your letters; then just as you were starting to concentrate properly you ran out of ink and had to refill the pen; until finally, you had to try to read what you had written. Astra did her best to write big and clearly, but Hokma's joined-up writing looked like scattered leaves, her letters loopy and irregular, her *f*s like *t*s, and *r*s for some reason almost disappearing. Hokma had shown her how to write with a quill too, made from one of Helium's feathers, but the scratchy nib was even more inefficient.

Making paper, though, was the ultimate waste of time. Hokma did it once a year in the lab: pulping the hemp, soaking it in a flat basin on top of the alt-meat incubator, screening it into sheets, hanging the pages out on the line to dry. It had been fun to help when she was little, but now she was older Astra found the whole process tedious and pointless. Worse than pointless: it was backward. You couldn't run a society on such primitive tech. It slowed your thinking. No wonder the people of the Old World had nearly destroyed Gaia.

"One day, Astra," Hokma said good-humoredly, "you'll be glad you can write."

Astra ignored her. They'd had this argument before, but Hokma wouldn't listen. It was true that Server connections could be easily hacked, so you must never trust sensitive information to Tablette talk or emails. But Owleons couldn't carry reams of paper on their ankles; that was a ridiculous notion: you used a password-protected memory clip and the recipient downloaded it onto a non-Server-linked Tablette. The only time you might conceivably need to write was if you were out on patrol, with no internet connection, and had to leave a message for your unit. But you wouldn't be wasting valuable pac space carrying a pen and paper; you'd use local materials, rocks or bricks or sticks, and leave them in a prearranged Code pattern. Writing, as Klor said, was *obsolete*.

"My dad said writing stitches our thoughts to Gaia's eternal shawl," Lil said, in a high, sing-song voice.

Astra wanted to gag, but Hokma leaned on her spade as if listening to the phrase linger in the air. "That's a beautiful thing to say, isn't it, Astra? What did you and he write with, Lil?"

Lil didn't look at Hokma. "We practiced with a stick," she said, jabbing the furrow with the hoe. "In the earth. But he had a pen and berry
ink too. Like yours."

"A pen. That's nice. So did he have paper?"

Lil's back was still turned. "He had a notebook. He was saving it for
when I wanted to write poems. I copied all my hymns in it and I put it
in his pyre with him."

"That was very thoughtful of you," Hokma said quietly. "Did you
write a poem too?"

Lil shrugged. Both shoulders lifted and dropped this time. "I like
singing. I might write a poem one day."

"Yes, I expect you might. Astra writes good poems, don't you, Astra?"

Poems: that was another thing Hokma droned on about. Astra wrote
Gaia poems in school like everyone else, and they got high grades, but
she wanted to write Code, not poems, when she grew up. Still, if it
meant she could get the last word in this inane conversation, she would
answer the question.

"I wrote the best poem in the class last week," she said, nonchalantly.
"It was called 'Gaia Take Me Higher.'"

"It's a fantastic poem. And you translated it into Asfarian and Inglish,
didn't you? Maybe you can bring your Tablette next time and show Lil."

She wasn't normally allowed to bring Tabby to Wise House, but
for Lil, obviously, none of the normal rules applied. "Maybe," she airily
replied. "Can we play knockout whist tonight?"

"That's a great idea, Astra. How does that sound, Lil?"

Lil nodded, so that's what they did after dinner. Astra won the first
game, then Hokma won one. Lil won the next one, and then when the
girls begged to continue, Astra won the fourth. Lil wanted to play one
more, but Hokma said no, Astra had to go back to Or for some Me-
Time before school. Then as Astra was putting the cards back in their
box, Hokma asked Lil if she'd like to show Astra her Gaia hymnbook.

Astra picked at a thread on the sofa arm. Despite her disdain for writing, she had to admit that books were interesting. Proper books were
printed, not handwritten, so it was as easy to read them as a Tablette screen,
but apart from the sewn notebooks she and Hokma used to make, she'd

only ever seen one example of the ancient technology, in a glass case in the School Learning Resource Center. Books were mostly illegal, because they were incredibly wasteful: they took acres of trees to make and you couldn't update them. Family heirlooms were allowed, and so were very rare hand-crafted volumes, as long as they met the Wheel Meet criteria for "art object." Lil's hymnbook, Nimma had said, was a very early one from the Pioneer days. It probably had some nice pictures, but it wouldn't have any new or updated hymns. She could tell Lil how archaic it was, and she could also tell everyone at school that she'd read a book and turned its pages.

Lil was examining her fingernails. "Not today," she said at last.

"Okay," Hokma said cheerfully, getting up with the dirty mugs, "maybe another time. Astra, will you help me wash up?"

What was she, some kind of Old World slave? "Doesn't Lil have to help too?"

"Lil did the morning dishes—without being asked. Let her relax, Astra. You and I can catch up."

Lil *had* done the morning dishes. Astra got up and followed Hokma to the vestibule entrance. At the door she stopped to say, "Thanks for the game, better luck next time." But Lil had turned her back on the room. She was spread out on the sofa, her head leaning on the armrest and her legs stretched out over the cushion Astra had just been sitting on. Astra shut the door with a bang.

Hokma's idea of catching up was nagging Astra about her homework. After she'd dried the stupid dishes, she walked back to Or with her solar lamp. When she got back to the Earthship she called out *Hi*, then went into the kitchen and poured herself a glass of oatmilk. There was a plate of Nimma's berry biscuits on the table. Good. That would take the taste of Lil's smug victory out of her mouth. She sat down and ate one.

As she munched, Nimma and Klor's voices drifted in from the living room. "Goodness, these forms get more complicated every year," Klor complained. "Now they want to know Parent and Steering Committee meeting attendance *percentages.*"

"If you kept track as you went along, darling, instead of waiting until the last minute, you wouldn't have to go back over all the minutes."

"I *have* kept track, my deep-rooted lotus blossom. I just need to calculate the percentages. Surely someone at IMBOD could program a Tablette to do that."

"I expect all their statisticians are tracking the progress of the Sec Gens," Nimma consoled.

"Probably so, probably so," Klor agreed. There was silence for a few minutes, filled only with the clicking of Nimma's needles as she sped through her rows. Astra let a biscuit melt in her mouth. Perhaps they would talk more about the Sec Gens.

"Reasons for absence!" Klor sounded impatient now. "Project deadline. Sick. Sick child. Working abroad. Working elsewhere in Is-Land. Other. But we don't keep a record of *reasons*."

"If IMBOD wants to know, it must be important. We'll have to start keeping track."

"Keeping track of Hokma, you mean. She's the top absentee. Twenty-four percent."

"Gracious—that *is* high."

"They don't have a category for 'Sick Owleon,'" Klor chuckled.

"Surely Gloria's been absent more often. Poor woman." Nimma *tsked*.

Gloria was Congruence's other Shelter mother. She hadn't been well lately. No one knew what was wrong so she was going to Atourne for tests soon. Nimma, Astra knew, thought Torrent should have "taken that into consideration," but Klor had said goodness, the boy's not responsible for the girl's mother's health. Not that Torrent was bothered. His Code-Shelter father, Russett, seemed to care about Torrent's reputation far more than he did. Russett, Astra thought, probably had a parents' meeting attendance record of one hundred and fifty percent.

"No," Klor was saying, "only twenty-two percent. And she has a valid reason."

"We'll have to talk to Hokma about it. I'm sure she doesn't want a black mark on her record. Or ours. *Astra*," Nimma called, "are you still in the kitchen, darling? Come in and say goodnight."

She set her empty glass by the sink and shuffled into the living room. Nimma was on the sofa and Klor was in his comfy chair, his Tablette on his lap.

"How did the weekend go?" Nimma asked.

"Okay," she said, hovering by the sofa arm.

"Is Lil settling in?"

"Yeah."

"Is she talking more?"

"A bit."

"But you're not, now, is that it?" Klor commented.

Astra rolled her eyes. "I ask her questions, but she doesn't remember anything from before."

"It's not your job to find out about that." Klor put his Tablette down on the side table. "IMBOD is still checking the records."

"Just be nice to her, Astra," Nimma said.

"I am being nice! We played cards, and I let her win a game."

"Good girl. Now time for bed."

Astra lolled against the sofa arm. "Nimma?"

"Yes, darling?"

"Lil's not coming to the Blood & Seed ceremony, is she?"

"I don't know. It will depend."

"On what?"

"On a lot of things." Nimma looked over at Klor. "Whether IMBOD finds her family, for one."

"Oh, I expect they will soon," he said. "There can't be too many missing single Code-Shelter fathers in Is-Land."

"But if she's still here, will she come?" Astra persisted. "I mean, the ceremony's only for kids in the bioregion. Kids with communities. And she's fourteen."

"We'd have to have a meeting about it," Nimma said firmly. "She did grow up in the bioregion after all. And it's not her fault that she missed the ceremony last year."

Her Shelter parents were frowning a little at each other again. She was arguing too much, she knew. Astra acquiesced, but not before playing her trump card. "She hasn't had her Security shot," she pouted. "She might upset Yoki."

Nimma patted her hand. "If she's still here, we'll see how she's behaving closer to the time. Now you just put yourself to bed. And darling,

Gloucester Library
P.O. Box 2380
Gloucester, VA 23061

do wash your hair in the morning—Eurasian hair dreads get so horribly greasy and rat's-nesty. It's not like you have nice springy Eurafrican hair like Meem."

Astra yanked her hand away. "I washed it yesterday. At Wise House," she lied.

"Well, it doesn't look clean. Hokma probably doesn't have any shampoo up there, does she? What did you use, baking soda?"

"I used water!"

"That's not enough. Soap, we said. Every two days."

"That's right, Astra," Klor added. "That was the contract."

"Then I'll wash it tomorrow *night*," she said, and stomped out of the room and up to bed.

The following week Lil helped Hokma make biscuits and wash the housecoats. She flew Helium and the two trainee Owleons, but she was respectful of Silver and only touched him if Astra let her. After the flying field, she played skipping games with Astra until Astra had to stop and admit she'd never be able to make the rope swing through the air the way Lil could. Veneday evening, when Astra was sleeping over again, Lil gathered wood from the forest to make a fire on the lawn.

"That's, er, *illegal*," Astra pointed out. Hokma had obviously forgotten what season it was.

"No one will know if you don't tell them," Hokma replied.

Thanks. Make *her* sound like the criminal. "They'll know if the forest burns down," she retorted.

"Oh, it'll be fine, Astra, just this once. We'll get some water buckets."

So she and Hokma filled buckets and set them in a circle in case of sparks. Then they sat on a couple of logs and watched Lil prepare a tipi of twigs, filled with shruff and kindling. Next she stripped the bark off a thin stick of elder, placed the end on another, flat piece of wood and rotated the stick between her palms. Unbelievably, an ember formed. Lil gently blew the small glowing ball into a handful of shruff, which smoked for a minute, obscuring her face, and then with a whoosh flared into flame. She poked the shruff into the tipi and soon the kindling was crackling and Hokma was cheering. When the fire was properly

Gloucester Library
P.O. Box 2380
Gloucester, VA 23061

blazing, Hokma improvised a grill from some bricks and a baking sheet and Lil fried chanterelles, wild garlic and mallow leaves in an old pan from the kitchen. The mushrooms were a little rubbery compared with how Nimma cooked them, but Astra knew Hokma would get annoyed if she said that, so she admired how frilly and golden they were, and how the mallow leaves turned all crispy. And the mushrooms weren't *bad*. She ate them all, slowly, assessing this new intelligence about their guest.

Okay, so Lil could forage and cook like a Boundary constable. But that didn't mean she wasn't a Non-Lander. Infiltrators must obviously study survivalist lore before they crossed into Is-Land, and of course enemy prisoners knew it was essential to gain people's trust. At some point, though, the girl would slip up. That night, from Hokma's loft, Astra watched Lil in bed. Lil was lying on her back, staring at the ceiling. Her lips were moving as though she was silently reciting to herself. Then she turned off the nightlight, rolled onto her side away from Astra and curled up like a small brown fox in its den.

"That wild dinner was good last night," Hokma said over breakfast. "Maybe this morning you two should go and see what else you can find in the woods. I expect Lil knows some good places."

Astra darted a glance at Lil. The girl had drunk her glass of oatmilk greedily and now a pale wet mustache glistened against her upper lip. She licked it away with a swipe of her pink tongue.

"Okay," she said, flicking a glance back at Astra.

Astra finished chewing her toast. A walk in the woods would be a chance to resume interrogation without interruption from Hokma. "Okay," she echoed.

They left by the front gate and scrambled down the steep path to the crossroads. Lil turned right, heading toward the brook, and Astra followed.

Presently, she touched Lil's elbow. "There's an almond tree over there."

"The nuts won't be ready yet," Lil scoffed.

Everyone knew that. "I'm just *saying*, that's all."

But Lil was walking faster now so Astra had to jog to keep up. Together they breasted the brook and strode gleaming into the pine glade, Lil again moving ahead of her. When she reached the tree they'd both climbed so long ago, she stopped and waited for Astra to catch up.

"That was me who chased you up there," Astra said.

Lil looked at her sideways. "No. That was *me* who chased you away."

They both at the same time stooped and scrambled for pine cones to throw at each other. Next they were running and dodging and screaming until Lil was twisting in the air and laughing like a hyena, and when Astra at last hit her, she rolled around pretending to play dead with her tongue sticking out and her eyes crossed, and Astra couldn't help it, she was laughing hysterically too.

"You hit me in the *butt*," Lil shrieked. "I died a *butt-death*!"

"Your face looked so *funny*," Astra gasped between giggles.

And suddenly Astra was having the best day she'd ever had with another person.

Lil took her on a long walk, further up the brook than she'd ever been, and on the way she started to talk: about the way trees talked to each other with their roots, and if they didn't like another tree, they ganged up and strangled it below the soil. About fire ants, whose jaws, when they ate their prey, made the fastest movement in the whole of Gaia's realm. And about—she lowered her voice—*duck vaginas*. Did Astra know that male ducks were nearly all rapists, so the females had a maze of false canals in their Gaia gardens to catch unwanted sperm before it could fertilize their eggs? Astra didn't know that—she had only a dim idea of what a "rapist" was—but she pretended that she'd studied duck anatomy in school. In return, she told Lil about the male green spoon worm, which lived his entire life as a parasite inside the female's ovary, spewing sperm onto her eggs twenty-four hours a day until he died.

"Really?" Lil sounded almost impressed.

"Yeah." Astra snickered. "Peat, he's my Shelter brother, says there's a Code clinic in Vanapur that everyone calls the Green Spoon Room. It turned out they took masses of sperm from just one donor and now there's about a hundred kids in the bioregion who aren't allowed to Gaia-play or cross-Code with each other. The clinic got in big trouble and the director lost her job."

Lil brushed her hand through a patch of dead nettles. "So is that where you were Coded?"

"Nah." Astra hesitated. "I was a bonded baby."

"Me too," Lil said. "My dad said I was Coded on the night of a thousand fireflies."

Astra stepped around the nettles. This conversation was going in a bad direction. She didn't want to talk about her Birth-Code parents. A year or so ago, when she'd first started having bad fights with Nimma, she'd begun to daydream that Eya would come and find her soon and take her to live in Atourne, where they'd search for her Code father together. But when she'd broached the subject with Hokma one day while they were gardening, her Shelter mother had put aside her spade and said Astra shouldn't count on that. Eya probably wouldn't ever come and find her, Hokma had said. She undoubtedly had more children now, with her husband, and she wouldn't want him to know that she had lied to him about her past. "You're stuck with us, kid," Hokma had said, tousling Astra's hair. Later, Peat had told her that Shelter parents had more legal rights than Birth-Code parents, so even if Eya did show up, she wouldn't be able to rescue Astra anyway.

"Did your dad really go into communities and steal things?" she asked, and when Lil said, "All the time," she pelted her with questions about living in the woods: What was the longest her dad was away for? How far up the mountains did they go? Did they ever see reintroduced bears or wolves? How did Lil brush her teeth?

Some questions Lil answered; some she ignored. At last they reached a place where the brook rushed over a low craggy outcrop of rock. A host of watercress was blossoming in the water and on the banks, the bushy dark green leaves scattered with clusters of small white flowers. Lil sat down on a large flat stone, picked a stem of cress and ate it. Astra did the same. The leaf was peppery and invigorating, the stem fresh and crunchy. They could pick bushels and make soup later.

"There are otters a couple of hours from here," Lil pointed upstream. "We made friends with one once. It used to come and eat fish with us."

Astra ignored the fish bait; Lil wasn't going to upset her again. "Otters are extinct in Is-Land," she contradicted. "They all died when the water dried up. And they haven't been reintroduced yet because of politics."

Lil twirled another stem of cress between her thumb and forefinger. "He must have been hiding. Him and his family. Once we saw him holding hands with another otter, and in the night they screamed like ghosts."

"Holding hands?" Lil had made that up for sure.

"Yes, it was so cute. While they were swimming. Like this—" Lil lay down on her back, clasped her hands together at her chest and pulled a nibbly, rodent-like face. Then she craned her neck and ate the stem of cress. Despite herself, Astra giggled.

But this was all wrong. She shouldn't be having fun with Lil, and definitely not secretly envying her. She should be testing her, trying to catch her out. She dangled her feet over the edge of the rock, cooling her toes in the fast-flowing water. "Did you ever see the Boundary?" she asked, as casually as possible.

Lil was leaning back on her elbows now. "There's too many constables at the Boundary. Same as the off-limits woodlands. We would have been caught for sure."

"They might have thought you were Non-Landers," Astra ventured, cautiously. "That you came through the tunnels."

"Nah." Lil examined a scratch on her elbow. "Non-Landers are fighters. They have guns and suicide bombs, and they wear clothes until they get to the roads. Anyway, the tunnels are all blocked up now."

"Did you ever see one?" Astra pressed.

"A tunnel?"

"No, a Non-Lander. But yeah, a tunnel too."

Lil shook her head. "There aren't any Non-Landers in the forest any more. Only otters." She paused. "We saw a cave once with boulders stacked up over the entrance. It didn't look like a rockfall. My dad said that was probably a tunnel. We got out of there quick, in case there were constables patrolling."

Practically everyone thought there weren't any Non-Landers left in the forest. It was so frustrating. "There are urban infiltrators though," Astra declared. "There was a mass arrest last year, in Sippur. They caught a whole cell, six Non-Landers using Gaian ID papers. One of them was even pretending to be an IMBOD officer. And they were going to go to the forest. On the news it said their plan was to dig a new tunnel out of the off-limits woodland. I think they had accomplices outside the Boundary and they were going to meet in the middle. So the constables might have thought you were in disguise as Is-Landers. Maybe they'd think you had *nanogrenades* in your pacs."

Lil sat up straight and lifted her arms in the air. "My dad said if I ever saw a constable, I was to raise my arms and chant 'O IMBOD Shield.' Or sing 'Gaia We Love You.'"

Astra eyed her warily. "That's my favorite hymn," she said.

"*O Gaia You are beautiful . . .*" Lil crooned.

Astra couldn't not join in. Together they sang the hymn, sending the notes soaring out into the forest:

> *We belong to You*
> *We worship Your magnificence*
> *In everything we do*
>
> *Without You we are hollow husks*
> *Adrift in lonely space*
> *To sow the seeds of human dreams*
> *We need Your earthly grace*
>
> *We lost our way, we hurt You*
> *We burned Your holy trees*
> *You boiled and raged and prophesied*
> *We drowned in Your hot seas*
>
> *But thanks to Your benevolence*
> *We are born anew*
> *We will not fail a second time*
> *Gaia we love You*

The last long note hung in the air, vibrating like the cloud of midges that had descended over the brook. But Astra and Lil were wearing citronella oil and didn't wave the insects away. After you had sung a Gaia hymn, you needed to stay still and listen so you could hear Her welcoming you deeper into Her open heart, Her secret truths. The brook was splashing over the rocks and sunlight was caressing the slender gray trunks of the hornbeams. Two were growing together, their branches gently intertwining. Astra noticed them and with an almost painful queasiness felt Gaia nudging her. *Be nice to Lil.*

"I like the word 'benevolence,'" she confided. "It sort of wraps you inside it. That's what Gaia does if you respect Her."

A caterpillar ambled by Astra's finger, carrying a torn bite of leaf. Astra could nearly hear his little feet pittering. Lil put her finger in its path and let it crawl over her knuckle. "I like 'magnificence,'" she said. "It makes everything bigger when you sing it. My dad had a magnifying glass and we looked at ants with it, and made fires too. But then I dropped it and it broke."

"Was he mad?"

"No." Lil picked up a pebble and rolled it between her palms. "He said you could never totally rely on technology. You always had to have a biological solution to every problem too."

That was interesting. Most Is-Land products were biotech—elegant, exciting and innovative—but every Or-child knew that ultimately these were two different systems, that every component had to be detachable and feed back into its own recycle loop. If you lived off-off-grid, like Lil and her dad, then of course you had to depend on exclusively biological processes, but normally you didn't learn survivalism until the first year of IMBOD Service. Lil's dad had probably been good at that course, Astra thought.

"Was he a Craft worker or a Code worker?" she asked. "In your community, I mean."

Lil threw the pebble into the brook. It landed with a plop, like a frog. "He was a Crafty worker."

For the first time, Astra tried to imagine this man. He couldn't be like Klor, tall and booming, or Ahn, ethereal and remote. He must be like a wild stag, bony and alert. "Was he thin like you?" she asked.

Lil turned and looked her in the face. When she spoke, the whites of her eyes flashed. "When I placed him on his pyre, he weighed as much as an empty bees' nest."

Astra didn't know what to say. But from her silence emerged an Imprint, one of the first ones she'd ever learned at school; the one she had chanted this year at Elpis's Return Ceremony.

"Gaia will gather your loved one in Her eternal shawl and glowing like the warm rays of Her heart, he will be around you always," she recited. As she did, she felt in her blood it was the right thing to say. Imprints were so reassuring.

"I know. That's what he said." Lil slipped her feet into the water. "He had dreads, like you."

Astra fingered her loc. "Really?"

"Yeah. But he wanted me to have hair like my Birth-Code mother's. So he combed and brushed mine every night."

"Do you want a dread now? I could help you make one."

"Nah. I didn't like it getting all matted when I was by myself. Yours looks good, though." Lil stood up and waded into the brook. "You have to snip the cress with your fingernails. Don't pull it up by the roots."

They gathered cress until they had enough for a big pot of soup, and then they returned to Wise House, singing Gaia hymns and foraging for vetch, nettles and wild asparagus until their hydropacs were full. As they walked back down the path to the crossroads, Lil, for the first time, asked Astra a question.

"Are you going to be an Owleon Coder like Hokma when you grow up?"

Astra frowned. How did Lil know she'd been asking herself that question all the time lately? Much as she loved Silver, and all the birds, she was starting to realize she *didn't* want to be an Owleon specialist when she grew up. That was Hokma's Code expertise, and no one could ever be greater than Hokma in the field. Astra wanted to find her own way of being famous. The problem was, she didn't know where her genius lay. When she was little she'd wanted to work on limb regeneration, but Klor had been right: that research had been abandoned in favor of developing more sophisticated prosthetics. Nothing else especially interested her, which was worrying, because to be a genius at anything, she had read, you had to spend ten thousand hours practicing, and the longer she went without specializing, the longer it would take her to make a major breakthrough and win an IMBOD medal.

"Nah." She trailed her hand over a bank of wild grass. "I'm going to be a Code worker, though."

"What kind of Code worker?"

She didn't like being prodded, but at the same time, it was a terribly important question and no one else seemed to care about it. The Sec Gens all just did what adults told them, and everyone, even Hokma, seemed to assume that Astra would work with Owleons one day. Feigning indifference, she replied, "Dunno. I'll decide when I'm at Code College."

Lil nodded. "My dad said that Gaia will always tell you what to do and when to do it, but sometimes She makes you wait because you aren't ripe yet."

That made sense. Actually, it was quite profound. Astra didn't like to give Lil that big a compliment, so instead she sang the opening lines of "Gaia Is Your Destiny," and Lil joined in, until they reached the foot of the slope to Wise House and had to save their breath for the climb.

At the crest of the hill, Lil turned to Astra. "You can see my hymn-book tonight if you like," she announced.

"*Really?*" Astra blurted. "I mean, yeah, okay, after dinner," she corrected herself.

"I knew you wanted to," Lil said, swinging up the path to the gate. "But I had to be sure it was for the right reasons. My dad said I should only ever show it to people who would *appreciate* it."

As they entered Wise House, Lil was no longer a Non-Lander. She was Astra's *friend*.

2.5

"How many petals have you sewn now? Astra? Yoki?" Nimma picked up Yoki's drawstring bag and rummaged through it with her finger. "Sixty-eight," Yoki claimed.

"Fifty-three," Astra grumbled. It was Veneday evening and she should be up at Wise House starting the weekend, but instead she was stuck in the Earthship falling behind Yoki in the most important task of the year. And just when she had been doing so well at Craft class. She had finished her socks, which to her immense pride had been deemed good enough to send to the Southern Belt, and last week, like everyone in her Year, she had started enthusiastically on her petals for the Blood & Seed ceremony. She and Yoki had each cut out five hundred petals from red and white cloth and now they were stitching the edges and veins in the opposite color, adding sequins to every tenth one. She just hadn't realized how long the work would take. Nimma had instituted a petal schedule on top of all their other homework, and although Astra thought she had been working quickly, yesterday Yoki had overtaken her and now he was speeding out of sight.

"Very good, Yoki," Nimma purred. "Astra, if you don't catch up you'll have to cut back on your Wise House visits. I don't want to be sewing for you the night before the ceremony."

It wasn't fair: she *was* on schedule! Yoki was pulling ahead because he was sewing extra hours while she was feeding the Owleons. But no matter how boring it was, you weren't allowed to complain about petal-sewing. You were supposed to do the work joyfully, listening to Code lessons on your earphones or singing Gaia hymns together. If you did sigh about it or, like Tedis Sonnenson, argue that your hands were made to hold bows and arrows, not needles, all the adults said sewing was a wonderful meditation and learning to do something difficult was the best possible preparation for life. "No task is too humble if performed in service of Is-Land," Klor had said sternly the one time Astra had wished out loud she was done.

Then he had relented and tousled her hair. "The trick with Craft work, Or-child, is to get into the flow," he'd said. "Then your mind will suddenly open and ideas will rush through it like fishes down a river. Many's the time I've had a breakthrough in Code thought when I was knitting." Astra had never seen Klor knit, but he did sit and stare at his Tablette screendesk all day, and some people called *that* knitting.

Yoki didn't complain, but once he said wistfully that it would be nice if Or were a larger community with more Year Sevens, then they could start an evening Blood & Seed sewing circle, like the one at school. Astra had felt a twinge of remorse then. She knew Yoki would have preferred her to sit with him most evenings instead of dashing off to Wise House right after petal hour. Now though, she might have to start sitting with him longer just to catch up. It was either that or sew at Wise House, but she didn't want to do that. If she worked on the petals in front of Lil, Lil might start asking questions about the ceremony and decide she wanted to go. And even though things were different with Lil now, Astra wasn't sure she'd like that. Lil was still pretty bossy, for one thing. When they'd looked at her small grubby hymnbook, with its coarse stitching and no illustrations, just words stuck to the ragged-edge paper, she hadn't let Astra turn the pages. "I can't let you touch it because it holds my secrets," she'd said. And then she'd opened the book up wide, to show Astra that there was a hidden sleeve in the back cover, inside which Astra could glimpse the pink leaf of paper. But even though otherwise the book wasn't that impressive, if Lil brought it to the Blood & Seed ceremony everyone would want to look at it and Lil's head would get as big as a jumbo caulisquash. No, it was better to keep sewing in the Earthship, even if it meant Yoki might beat her.

"I did fifteen petals in an hour yesterday," Yoki announced. "All by myself, with my earphones on. I can recite the Blood & Seed hymn nearly all the way through now."

"That's wonderful, Yoki." Nimma plumped herself down on the sofa beside Yoki and put her arm around him. Meem was the youngest, but Yoki was still her baby, everyone knew that. "Now, how are your night falls? Did you remember any of your wet dreams yet?"

Yoki looked down at his Gaia pepper. "I woke up during the last one. I was swimming in a river with the bigger boys."

"Oh, isn't that lovely and peaceful? You're becoming a bigger boy yourself now, aren't you, darling? And you, Astra? How are your dreams?"

Nimma was being tactful, Astra knew, not asking about her blood. "Nice," she said. "I had one at Wise House yesterday, in the hammock. In the dream I was swinging in a hammock too, in a super-tall tree, and the rhythms were rolling right through me."

"How beautiful," Nimma sighed. "And when you're not sleeping: are you both peaking okay?"

"Yes, Nimma!" Astra and Yoki chorused.

"Wonderful. And how were Gaia-play lessons this week?"

"Fine," they said together again.

"Now, like Klor and I said before, if you have any questions at all about what Vishnu tells you, you must just come and ask us. Promise?"

"*Promise*." Astra and Yoki rolled their eyes at each other. Shelter parents and teachers were more worried about the Blood & Seed ceremony than the participants were: for months now the adults had been holding discussions at home and at school about Gaia Power—as if anyone needed lessons on how to peak! Astra had been peaking for a year now and no one had ever told *her* how: when she was alone in the forest or the lights were out in her bedroom, she just closed her eyes and rubbed her Gaia bud. As her fingers moved beautiful patterns—light pouring through water, flowers bursting open—would dance over her eyelids and her mouth would water as if someone had put a big piece of rose-syrup sponge cake in front of her. Time would soar away then, like Silver up into the sky, disappearing into a vast, wonderful whiteness, until at last her Gaia bud would freeze and an astonishing sensation would flood through her veins, like a cool breeze from nowhere on the hottest day of the year.

The Gaia-play lessons did interest her though. When you were little, you Gaia-played with other little children: she, Meem and Yoki had all examined each other, and Peat had showed them all the funny puppet creatures he could make with his Gaia pepper. But as they'd got older, those games had become boring. Now, even when Gaia Power was surging through her, the thought of playing with a Shelter sibling or even other Or-kids was ... well, *weird*. They would laugh at you or boss you around or start doing something annoying just when you were enjoying yourself. In their first Gaia-play lesson Mr. Ripenson had said that this *aversion*—as he called it—was a common result of living in close-knit communities. Later, on the bus back home, he had agreed with Astra when she'd asked—in a low voice—if the fact that Stream and Congruence had both arrived in Or in their early teens was the reason Torrent was not averse to Gaia-playing with them. Aversion, he had said in class, was one of the reasons kids weren't educated in their own communities. At school, they would meet other children they might want to play with.

But as communities were often far apart, meeting up outside of school could be complicated to arrange. That was why, when they started at New Bangor High School in the autumn, they would take siesta not in a gym but in the woodlands that lay behind the school grounds. Gaia play was permitted here, subject to successful completion of their Blood & Seed ceremony, siesta supervision and a set of rules they would learn in upcoming lessons. This hadn't been news: everyone knew that high school students could Gaia-play during Woodland Siesta if they wanted to, but big siblings were always frustratingly sparse with the details. "I'm not allowed to talk about it," Peat had said when Astra pressed him. "Learning the rules is part of the build-up to the Blood & Seed ceremony and I'm not supposed to spoil it."

The build-up was tantalizing. To begin with, Mr. Ripenson had discussed the nature of Gaia play—which Tedis had claimed was competitive, like cricket, but he had said was *cooperative*, and *a form of Gaia worship*. In the next lesson they'd talked about gender difference. They knew already from Code class that gender was a spectrum—Leaf and other girl-boys and boy-girls proved that—and everyone, not just Leaf, had male and female qualities mixed up inside them in different proportions. Nevertheless, when it came to Gaia play some gender differences were particularly apparent. Peaking, for example, usually took longer for girls and girl-boys, so they'd spent a whole lesson discussing what boys and boy-girls could do to help while they were waiting.

She thought the Gaia-play lessons were mostly fun—and very informative. They were held outside in the cherry orchard, and Mr. Ripenson made jokes and the Sec Gens, even Yoki, all teased each other and laughed a lot. They learned Imprints to help them remember key points, and Mr. Ripenson also taught positive body image meditations and special detumescence techniques to help them control their erectile tissues. Tedis could now detumesce four times a day, he'd told Astra and Silvie while they were waiting to bat during cricket yesterday. "Careful you don't forget how to peak," Silvie had darted back, but he'd winked and said, "No need to worry about *that*." Then he'd asked Astra if she could detumesce her nipples yet. That was a stupid question—the girls' exercises were focused on the clitoris—but for some reason, like now, just remembering Tedis looking at her breasts, it had made her Gaia garden tingle and swell.

Sunblast! She'd pricked her finger with the needle. Thank Gaia Nimma was cuddling Yoki and hadn't noticed. Fortunately she was working on a red petal and the bloodstain didn't show. She sucked her finger. Why did *Tedis Sonnenson* make her make mistakes? Dangerous mistakes. She had to be very careful at school as well as at home. If she started letting her real feelings show she might get angry and that would raise alarms. The teachers had already called Hokma about her, back in Year Five, and since then she'd been under strict orders not to have any more temper tantrums. She'd been managing pretty well in Gaia-play lessons, except for that time Silvie had tickled Tedis with a leaf and a hot flood of emotion had rushed through Astra's guts and for a moment she had hated Silvie Higgsdott: hated her brilliant blue eyes and her blond fuzzy Gaia mound and her unflappable ability to always put Tedis in his place—and she hated especially the fact that Silvie had been the first Year Seven girl to get her Gaia-blood, coming to school two weeks ago in a pair of green blood panties with lace trim, armed with a supply of pads in a linen bag she had toted everywhere for five days.

The highly unpleasant feeling that had rushed through her was envy, Hokma had told her. It was a negative emotion, one Sec Gens experienced only faintly, as a kind of mild regret. She'd had to mask it, drop her head and play with her dread so no one could see her face. At last the envy had drained away, leaving a scum-line of shame. It was wrong to hate Silvie—she was really nice and friendly to everyone. She never boasted about her Gaia-bleeding, but always said she didn't like being first and couldn't wait for the rest of the girls to catch up. And she tickled lots of people, not just Tedis; Astra too.

Astra couldn't ask Nimma about envy. She had to keep quiet and sew. With a practiced jab she speared a sequin and threaded it though.

"I hope Astra gets her Blood soon," Yoki said.

"All in Gaia's time, Yoki." Nimma stroked his cheek. "Girls can enjoy their Gaia Power whether they're bleeding or not. Isn't that right, Astra?"

Astra grunted. That was absolutely right. She enjoyed her Gaia Power very much, *on her own*. She attached the sequin and pulled the thread tight.

"Good girl," Nimma said. "Another half an hour sewing, you two, and then an early night."

Sabbaday morning was Earthship chores, but straight after lunch, Astra was free to race up to Wise House. Hokma was busy working on Code, so she and Lil went for another walk.

Lil led the way down the slope to the crossroads, but she stopped at the top of the steps to the Fountain. "Do you want to go somewhere secret?"

Astra adjusted her hydropac. It was laden with lunch as well as enough water for the day and the straps were digging into her shoulders already. "The woods aren't secret. They belong to everyone."

Lil dug a hole in the earth with her heel. "This place is my secret. Mine and my dad's. No one else has been there since the Dark Time."

"How do you know that?" Astra asked skeptically.

"If I told you, you'd know the secret."

In the end, just to stop Lil being so lofty and annoying, Astra said she wanted to see the secret place and promised not to tell anyone, anywhere, for the rest of her life, anything about it. Probably Lil was making things up and the place was nowhere special, so the promise wasn't a big deal.

"You'll never regret it! Come on, let's go." Lil started brightly down the rock steps to the Fountain, immediately making Astra anxious: they weren't supposed to visit Birth House on their own. But halfway down Lil veered off the steps and picked a path north through the trees, a mix of pine and stringybark, with the occasional black cypress and cedar grove, which helped their orienteering. It was the ideal territory for playing Silent Tracker. Lil was already barefoot so Astra took off her sandals too and they proceeded stealthily, Lil in the lead because she knew the way, until Astra got tired of being docked points for every crackle and crunch and suggested they play Ambush instead. Noise didn't matter as much as speed in this game, so she put her sandals back on and they joined forces to swoop down slopes and capture dozens of Non-Landers. When they were bored with that, they just walked, following a shallow gorge that ran like a rip through the forest, talking about the ridiculousness of clothes, the potential self-defense uses of Owleon shit, Hokma's snoring patterns and the possible reasons why she kept her IMBOD medal in her toolbox on the veranda, in a tray with screws and nails, instead of hanging on the wall in Wise House. Lil said it was because she was planning to melt down the medal one day, and just hadn't got around to it yet, but Astra said no, that was a stupid answer: Hokma had told her she'd put it there to remind herself that the point of fighting was to build a better world. Then they had to concentrate on the terrain for a while, negotiating a tricky slope. At the bottom Lil checked her bearings and took Astra through a paperbark glade.

"Is this the secret?" Astra whispered.

"Huh?" Lil was marching ahead. "No."

But it was. Paperbark groves were rare, hidden places the Pioneers had planted far from paths so that people could worship Gaia alone in them. Astra could see why. Sunlight sashayed through the leaves and the white peeling trunks were so smooth and delicate she wanted to stop and rub her cheek against each one.

But she had to keep up with Lil. "We learned the Code for paperbarks at school this week," she said. "The original edition wouldn't grow well in a dry forest, but the Pioneers especially wanted to have them in Is-Land so they were the first trees to be Gaianised."

Lil yawned. "My dad said school was for mules."

"Mules?" Astra had studied them in Code class: if you cross-Coded species, you risked creating a genetic dead end. But she didn't see the connection with school.

"Yeah. He said you go in as prancing foals and you come out half-donkey, with your Gaia Power sterilized."

That was *ridiculous*. "We learn tons about Gaia Power at school," Astra informed Lil. "In *fact*, we're taking Gaia-play lessons right now."

Lil picked up a stick and flung it between the trees. "My dad said Gaia play is easy. All mammals do it. We don't need lessons. We just have to remember that we're worshipping Gaia first and each other second. He said it's easy to get confused about that."

Astra hesitated. Before the lessons she had thought Gaia play would be easy too. But if she told Lil how complicated it was to synchronize peaking, and how you had to do special exercises to prepare for it, Lil would just laugh at her. Lil would scoff even harder if Astra said that there were Gaia-play rules to obey. She'd demand examples, and Astra wouldn't be able to provide any. Mr. Ripenson was going to explain the rules next time, in the Woodland Siesta lesson. Then she would be able to correct Lil. Right now, she started humming, "Gaia, Gaia, My Garden is Your Shrine." Lil joined in, and soon, singing the hymn at the tops of their voices, they left the paperbark glade. Then they let the last note trail away and walked quietly until they reached a grove of cedars.

"Shh," Lil ordered.

They were in the middle of the forest and there was no one around for miles. The cedars were impressive, maybe even ancient, but there was a whole slope of them on the other side of Or, and tons around Cedaria. And, most importantly, she hadn't been making a sound. Astra felt irritated, until suddenly it struck her why Lil was being so mysterious. "Are there *animals*?" she asked, awestruck. Was this a place with *otters*?

But Lil had plunged left, nimbly zigzagging down a gentle incline through the dark towering trees. She stopped behind a large boulder and let Astra catch up.

"It's on the other side," she whispered, her cheek pressed to the lichen-speckled rock. "Don't be scared. They can't hurt you."

"Who can't—?"

Lil put her finger to her lips, then turned and tiptoed around the rock. Astra followed. Lil stopped and pointed at a long, creeper-covered hump between a stand of oaks. For a moment Astra didn't understand. Oaks: yes they were ancient, but hardly a big secret. Then she saw.

It wasn't a rock or a fallen tree trunk. It was a dirt-stained, corroded metal hull, a bit like a bus, except no bus could possibly have driven here. It wasn't shaped like a bus either. It was tubular and half-torn, with a crumpled snout buried in a tangle of bushes and, at the other end, sloping down from a jagged rip in the roof, what looked like a twisted fishtail digging into the earth. Near the nose, a flat protrusion jutted out from the hull, ending abruptly in a ragged stump. Above it was a door with a shattered window, the pane too high to see through.

She knew this shape. She had seen pictures of it from the oil junkie era. "It's an *arrowpain*," she breathed.

"*Shhh.*" Lil frowned. She moved forward again, picking her way through thigh-high undergrowth. Astra hung back, then reluctantly followed in her wake, her sandals crunching through the gritty litter of metal and glass desecrating the forest floor. Arrowpains, Klor had once said, were more lethal than the sharpest arrow: they were like a nonstop hail of bullets shooting Gaia in the lungs. This one had tried to stab Her in the heart as well. Even though obviously long disabled, it still exuded menace. The gaping holes caused by its corrosion were impenetrable to vision, puncturing the once-white metal hull with the threat of its black interior.

When they reached the base of the broken wing, Lil stopped. The arrowpain, Astra could see, had crashed on some rocks between the trees; that was why it was torn open and lifted above the ground. Though the protruding section was level with their heads it would be hard to scramble onto it without getting cut. Lil gripped the wing's short, smooth edge and hung off it for a moment. Astra stepped back nervously: what if the arrowpain rolled over and trapped them? But the wing held Lil's weight. She dropped back down, wiped her hands on her flanks and turned to face Astra.

"My dad used to lift me," she whispered, beckoning Astra closer. "Give me a leg-up."

Astra looked up at the door. There was a pinching feeling in her stomach. "That's where the driver sat," she objected.

"You mean the pilot," Lil corrected.

"*Okay*, the pilot. He might be in there still. With other people."

"They aren't *people*," Lil hissed. "They're *ancestors*."

The forest seemed to loom closer, blotting out whatever faint hints of sunshine the cedars were permitting through their branches. Ancestors belonged in Birth House, not in the forgotten wreckage of an oil monster—an *arrowpain*, one of Gaia's *worst enemies*. The ancestors wouldn't like it in there. They would be angry at being trapped all these years in a thing that should be dismantled and recycled, not left to poison the earth with its toxic paints and leaking engine. The Or-adults should be told the arrowpain was here. They would come and take it away and do a healing ceremony and return the ancestors to Gaia in Birth House. Until then, Astra didn't want to go poking around in their decrepit, disrespectful tomb.

"You're not supposed to look at ancestors," she said hotly, instantly hating herself for sounding like Yoki, reinforcing Nimma's petty limits on how many peaches one was allowed to pick from the greenhouse corridor before dinner.

"You can if they're relics," Lil rejoined, still in a low tone. "My dad said you're supposed to look at relics. But only once a year."

Astra didn't know what a relic was and she didn't want to let Lil know that she didn't. She hesitated.

"You don't have to look if you're scared," Lil whispered dismissively. "But I have to make sure they're still here. Me and my dad come every summer."

"I'm not scared," Astra retorted, even though the pit of her stomach was throbbing and she suddenly desperately needed to pee.

"Then help me. We have to make sure they're okay, and give them a ceremony. That's what me and my dad always did."

Clenching her bladder, Astra regarded Lil suspiciously. "What kind of a ceremony?"

"The window's broken at the top. We give them a feather each."

"We don't have any feathers."

"Yes we do. I brought one from Silver and one from Helium."

"You took a feather from Silver?" Astra was outraged.

"Don't panic. He's molting. I got it from the floor of his cage."

"It doesn't matter. You can't give Silver's feather away. Only *I* can do that."

"I *know*. That's why I brought it for you. I couldn't tell you because it was a *secret*. I took good care of it. Look."

Astra glowered as Lil unzipped her hydropac and took out a rolled-up red kitchen cloth. She laid it out on the ground. Inside were two feathers: one small and snow white, one long and tawny. The tips weren't bent or separated. Astra couldn't complain about how they'd been transported. As she was inspecting the flutings, making sure none were broken, Lil took a left-handed Owleon glove out of her pac and put it on.

"Does Hokma know you took that?"

"Oh, don't be such a *mule*. She's got about *forty* of them. And we need it. My dad always put a rabbit-skin blanket over the wing before we climbed it. You can get blood poisoning if you cut yourself on rust."

Well, she didn't want to do *that*. Or start trapping rabbits. Ignoring the mule remark, Astra folded her arms. "Did you bring two?"

"We need a lefty and she's only got one. We can share it." Lil stuck Helium's feather behind her ear. "C'mon, Astra, give me a legsie. You can go after me."

Why did Lil always treat her like a servant? Astra scowled. "No. You're heavy. We can make a ladder. With logs and vines."

"That'd take *hours*. I'm not that heavy. I just need a booster."

Astra glared at her but there was no point squabbling. She couldn't let Lil use Silver's feather in a ceremony without her. And even if they did spend an hour building a ladder, there was no other way to look inside the arrowpain apart from taking turns.

"All right. But I have to pee first." She stepped away, squatted and whizzed, and wiped herself with a leaf. Then she returned to Lil, bent and cupped her hands.

Gripping the arrowpain wing edge with her gloved hand, Lil placed the ball of her right foot in the cradle of Astra's hands. As Astra hoisted her as high as she could, Lil jumped, nearly kicking Astra in the face as she hauled herself onto the wing by her elbows and knees. At last Lil was standing on the metal ledge, peering down at her.

"Let me stand on your shoulder," she demanded.

Astra rubbed her hands against her thighs. "What?"

"The gap in the window is too far over. My dad always let me stand on him. I thought I'd be tall enough now to reach now, but I'm not."

She'd gone too far to object now. At least Lil didn't want to stand on her head. Lil gripped the window frame with her gloved hand and Astra let her balance her right foot on her shoulder. She waited like that for what seemed like an age, Lil's anklebone grazing her ear and her grimy sole bearing down on her hydropac strap. She wanted to watch the ceremony, but when she looked up all she could see were Lil's leg and belly pressed against the door.

At last, Lil dropped down to the ground. Her stomach was speckled with dirt and rust, but her eyes were gleaming. "No one has been here," she announced, in a tone of rich satisfaction. "Not since the Dark Time. No one except me and my dad and now you."

Then Astra put Silver's feather in her own hair and Lil gave Astra the glove and a leg-up. Astra was a bit shorter than Lil and she couldn't get onto the wing on her first jump, but Lil hawked her higher the second time and she made it. Lil made her take her right sandal off and she rested her bare foot on Lil's shoulder. The window was too splintered and fogged with age to see through, but at the top right-hand corner, just as Lil had said, the pane had fallen clean away. When she'd found her balance, she steadied her left hand above the window and peered inside the arrowpain.

A thick mulch of leaves had accumulated over the front window and it took her eyes a minute to adjust. She had known she was going to see the ancestors, otherwise, even with the gradual revelation, she might have screamed and fallen. As it was, the scream shrank to a frog-gulp in her throat, and her muscles trembled for only a moment.

There were two ancestors in the arrowpain. You couldn't tell if they were male or female, sky-clad or clothed, because any clothes they might have been wearing had rotted away with their flesh. All that was left were their skeletons—not tall, bleached, airy skeletons like the pictures in anatomy lessons, but hunched assemblages of moss-coated bones, riven with cracks. The ancestor closest to the window was slumped forward, face smashed into the dashboard, arm bones dangling down by its feet. The other ancestor was sitting up straight, except for its skull, which was drooping over its ribcage. The seat material had rotted away too, and the ancestors were resting on rusted metal coils. There was a long, jagged hole in the floor beneath the seats, and Astra could see the roots of a tree crawling through the earth below.

What was frightening, she realized, were the gaps and the teeth. You thought people were full of feelings, but through the gaps in the ancestors you could see how empty we are. An ancestor, she thought, was like an awkward hug with no one inside it. That was sad, and you could almost feel sorry for the ancestors, except for their teeth. Their teeth had feelings still—strange, threatening feelings you could never understand. The ancestors' teeth were clamped together in dark, eternal, gangrenous smiles as if being this lonely and empty was a magnificent private treasure, all anyone could ever long for.

Then, as Astra kept looking, a strange thing happened. She began to see that the inside of the plane was immensely peaceful. With their bent heads, the ancestors could be praying. Not like Himalayans or Whirlers, but . . . She tried to remember who prayed with their heads lowered—yes, maybe the ancestors were Abrahamites. They had sky gods, so perhaps the arrowpain *was* the right tomb for them. Perhaps

Gaia had called it to Her bosom and was embracing it now, forgiving the ancestors. After the Fountain story, Klor had said that oil addiction was an illness and we mustn't hate our Dark Time ancestors; we should feel sorry for them instead.

The hole in the window was too high to stick her arm through. Lil must have just dropped Helium's feather in, because it had drifted down to the seat and was resting against the first ancestor's hipbone. There were other feathers too, a glossy black one at the base of the spine and a red-tipped one in the crease of the seat. Others might have fallen down inside the door, or perhaps Lil's dad had been tall enough to climb up and put them in the other window, with the other ancestor. Next time, she and Lil would have to build a ladder.

She took Silver's feather out of her hair, closed her eyes and pressed it to her lips.

To the ancestors. You saw the whole world. Please help us fly by ourselves now.

The flutings along the edge of an Owleon's feather helped the bird fly silently. The ancestors fed on silence, she could sense that. They would be thankful for Silver's gift. Tip first, she pushed the feather through the hole in the glass. It twirled down over the near skeleton and slipped between two ribs, coming to rest on the curve of a long green bone.

She was sweltering and her body was streaked with paint and rust from the hull. She put her shoe back on and took a long swig of water from her tubing.

"We have to wash now," Lil said, pointing beyond the nose of the plane and into a stringybark stand. She led Astra downhill from the wreckage, winding through the trees, until they reached a brook. On its bank, they took off their hydropacs, stepped in and hand-splashed themselves clean. Lil rubbed herself vigorously between the legs, then picked a flake of metal-paint out of her Gaia hair.

Astra sat down on a rock. "I'm getting hungry. Should we eat here?"

"No." Lil stepped out of the brook, shaking droplets of water over Astra's arm. "I know a way better place."

They struck out again, walking further away from the arrowpain, and eventually emerged from the forest onto a long, narrow ledge. A strip of full sun blanched the rock before it dropped clean away to the lower forest and the fire grounds. Beyond, the steppes stretched out in an endless pale haze: just as the ancestors must have seen them from up in the arrowpain.

Lil walked out from the shade of the trees, planted her feet wide apart and spread her arms, stamping the sky with the brown X of her body.

"*Gaiaaaaaaa*," she called out to the horizon and up to the stratosphere.

Lil's toes weren't touching the rock edge, but they were no more than a step away from it. Astra hung back. The ledge inclined slightly downward, making her feel dizzy, as if her body were in free fall, somersaulting off the cliff.

Why was she so afraid today? The ancestors were with her now. She ventured out and stood exactly beside Lil, about an arm's length away. Far below, skirting the firegrounds, the road to New Bangor creased through the foothills. But the view was like a magnetic field, threatening to drag Astra into its green depths. She raised her gaze and focused on an imaginary spot in the air, a few feet directly ahead. When she'd regained her composure, she placed her hands in a prayer formation in front of her chest and lifted one foot to the inside of the opposite knee. Once she'd found her balance, she lifted her arms above her head. Tree pose.

"Don't dive off." Lil turned on her heel and cartwheeled back to the shade of the tree line. The sudden movement sideswiped Astra and she came out of the *asana* with a wobble. Her heart was thumping in her stomach, but she'd not toppled.

Lil was sitting half in the shade now, removing her hydropac. Astra plumped herself down cross-legged on the flat, warm stone beside her. Holding her own pac in her lap, she stared out over the steppes.

"I wonder where they came from," she said.

"From Sippur. They were Non-Landers."

Astra stared at Lil, incredulous. "*What?*"

"That's what my dad said. He checked out the back of the arrowpain and it's full of food bags. They were escaping from the bombing, but something went wrong with the engine. They tried to land, but they lost power just above the trees. That's why the arrowpain isn't smashed to little bits."

Lil thought she was so smart, but she didn't get the most basic things sometimes. "Non-Landers aren't ancestors," Astra said, shortly. "Not *our* ancestors, anyway."

"Yes, they are," Lil contradicted. "My dad said that they were ancestors of the steppes, so they belonged to Is-Land."

Astra struggled to respond. Sippur *had* been bombed during the Great Collapse—she'd seen the crater before it was landscaped into a municipal park. So it *was* just possible that the skeletons were Non-Landers; that would explain why their smiles had been so frightening. But Lil had no idea how crazy her dad was. The steppes had lain barren and abandoned, toxic and parched, during all the long years of the Dark Time, and when the Pioneers had arrived to clean up everything had started over. CONC had transferred legal ownership of the land to the Gaians, so to say that Non-Landers—no matter how dead they were—in any way *belonged* to Is-Land was not just wrong, it was absurd and dangerous. This kind of thing was precisely why she couldn't have Lil coming to the Blood & Seed ceremony.

"If they were Non-Landers," she said at last, "we have to tell Hokma so that IMBOD can come and take them away. We can't have a shrine for Non-Landers in the forest. Infiltrators might come here to worship them."

"We're not telling Hokma anything," Lil hissed. "You promised."

Lil was upset. Obscurely, Astra felt she had won. Thinking about it, the last thing Hokma would want to do was summon IMBOD to question her and Lil. If she told her Shelter mother about the arrowpain, she would probably take Lil's side. "Don't worry," she said generously. "I'm not going to tell. They're our secret. And your dad's. But they're not Non-Landers. They must have been Neuropeans, fleeing the Great Collapse."

Lil fixed her with a bitter stare, but she didn't argue. It seemed to be a deal. Lil looked south, her expression morphing into a dreamy gaze. "I wish I'd seen the balloons," she said.

"What balloons?" Astra said tetchily. She had wanted to tell Lil about her idea that the ancestors were Abrahamites, but as usual Lil had changed the subject.

Lil picked up a flattish pebble and skimmed it out over the ledge. It whisked out into the air before disappearing into the drop. "The balloons that started Operation Silkroad. Don't they teach you history at school?"

Astra bristled. "It's *your dad* who didn't teach you history. The Non-Landers in Sippur all went to the Southern Belt. And Operation Silkroad wasn't a *birthday party*. Besides," she continued haughtily, "only Asfarians call it Operation Silkroad. *We* call it the Infestation."

Lil's face shuttered up for a moment and Astra instantly regretted her attack; she shouldn't sneer at Lil's dad. But Lil recovered instantly. "Ha *ha*." She rolled her eyes. "They weren't *kids'* balloons. They were hot-air balloons, with baskets woven from rose bushes. An Asfarian billionaire bought a fleet of them to help the Non-Landers in the desert cities return to Is-Land. He hired pilots to drop people off in the Southern Belt and then go back to the cities for more. It was called Operation Silkroad because the balloons were made of silk, and ages ago people used to travel across Is-Land on silk-trading routes. I thought you knew all that."

"Everyone knows what the Silk Road was," Astra retorted, offended. "And your dad was telling you fairy tales. You can't make a flying machine out of rose bushes—the baskets would be all thorny, for one thing. They'd"—she searched for an ironclad rebuttal—"rip the material when the balloons were being deflated!"

Lil fingered a smear of dirt on her upper arm. "I expect the flight engineers removed the thorns first. For aerodynamic purposes."

Astra wanted to push Lil off the cliff. At the same time, a horrible, sad, topsy-turvy feeling was assaulting her stomach: she and Lil had just honored the ancestors—*real* ancestors, from the start of the Dark Time—so why were they fighting now? She just wasn't used to this kind of arguing, she realized as she watched Lil lick her finger and rub the dirt away. Sec Gens never tried to insult you, and adults never used sarcasm.

But it wasn't Lil's fault she hadn't gone to school and didn't know the facts. "I've never heard of the balloons," Astra said, reasonably. "I think your dad made them up because he liked to tell you stories. The Infestation Non-Landers came up through Asfar in buses and tanks. An Asfarian billionaire did help: he bought some of the last gasoline before the final CONC oil ban. Some of the Non-Landers in the Belt live in the buses still."

Lil wiped her finger on her stomach. "There were buses too," she agreed, in a far too knowledgeable tone. "But mostly they came in balloons. The silk was printed with slogans, like *One People, One Land*, or *Cradle to Cradle*. The billionaire hired photographers and the Non-Landers got a ton of international support. That, and the massacre, is why CONC told Is-Land we had to negotiate with the Non-Landers and let them live in the Belt."

Astra was utterly baffled now. "Massacre? You mean the suicide bombings?"

Lil scratched her chin. "No, not them killing us. *Us* killing *them*. When the Pioneers surrounded the camp at Harrana and killed a hundred Non-Landers. Families. Old people and babies."

"*What?*" Astra laughed, her confidence restored. "Gaians would never do that."

"Why not? IMBOD kills people all the time."

"Yeah, okay: in self-defense. But we don't kill *babies*." Astra unbuttoned her hydropac. If she could get a signal here, it would be a simple matter to settle this ridiculous argument. "Look, Lil," she said, kindly, "I know your dad had a great imagination, but he shouldn't have told you made-up stuff about history. I'll show you on Tabby. It happened like—"

"Tabby's IMBOD-loaded," Lil waved dismissively.

She turned Tabby on. "So?"

"He's not global-enabled. He doesn't have access to world websites."

Irritation bubbled in Astra's stomach. "*Doh*. He's an *Is-Land* Tablette."

Lil leaned forward and asked, in a low, conspiratorial voice, as if they could possibly be overheard, "Don't you think it's funny that Is-Land hosts one of the main continental servers but no one here can access a single world website?"

There was no signal. Astra powered Tabby down and stuffed him back in his pocket.

"I *could* visit world websites if I needed to," she informed Lil. "I could apply for a password."

"You mean you could travel for hours to Atourne and go through, I dunno, six interviews, and in the end you'd only get permission if you're working on an IMBOD project."

Astra paused. Once, in the Quiet Room, she had heard one of Klor's teammates complain about her trip to Atourne. "After all that, they said my research wasn't essential," she'd grumbled. But Klor had looked up from his Tablette and butted in, "Is-Land has the best minds in the world," he'd boomed. "We don't need to import knowledge." The other Or-adults in the room had murmured agreement and the woman had fallen quiet. Later Klor had told Astra and Peat that the IMBOD interviews weren't really assessing the importance of your research but the strength of your mind. If you were easily distracted, you would never be allowed a world websites password. Sec Gens, he'd said, would always score highly on concentration, but as they were also intensely attached to Is-Land, they would probably never want to browse the global web.

Astra wasn't sure she could—or should—explain all that to Lil. "It doesn't matter if you don't get a password," she said defiantly. "Actually, it's better not to get one. World websites are bad for us. They go on and on forever, and if you get lost in them you forget how to listen to Gaia. That's partly what caused the Dark Time. People were so busy tweeting online, they didn't hear that the birds had stopped singing."

She sat back, inordinately pleased with herself for remembering that last line. Modem had said it once, in a Fountain story, and all the adults had applauded. Even though Astra had only a vague picture of what "tweeting" meant—Peat had said it was programming bird calls into a Tablette for ringtones—she knew that whatever it was, it had contributed to Gaia's great pain, and the phrase had lingered in her mind. At the same time, however, the conversation with Lil was making her feel a bit sick again: not as bad as seeing the arrowpain for the first time or looking over the rock ledge, but queasy. Maybe she was getting dehydrated. She took a slug of water from her tubing.

"Twitter was good for knowledge-sharing, though," Lil countered, showing off. "My dad said that listening to Gaia and browsing the internet were related skills. He said—"

Astra had had enough. Water was dribbling down her chin. She rubbed it away and chucked her hydropac aside. "Well, he should have taken you to *New Zonia* then," she cut in, "instead of to the off-limits woodlands where even if you *had* a Tablette you couldn't get reception."

Surely she'd had the last word. But no, Lil just couldn't leave it alone. "My dad didn't want me to learn history from a Tablette. He said IMBOD left out parts and changed other parts to brainwash us into being para—"

It was automatic. "*Shhhh*," Astra hissed.

"Why?"

Why? "You can't talk like that about IMBOD. What if Tabby was on and his microphone picked you up?"

"See?" Lil crowed. "My dad was right: IMBOD wants you to be paranoid the whole time!"

"Wha—?" Astra sputtered to a halt. It was nearly impossible to keep up with Lil, but she had to try. Being "paranoid" was something the adults joked about sometimes. Astra used to think it was a problem caused by your adenoids, if you hadn't had them out. A while ago, though, Klor had explained it meant thinking that things were going wrong for you because other people were ganging up behind your back, instead of perhaps the fact that you hadn't been doing your work properly. Paranoia could affect people outside the workplace too, he'd said, but it wouldn't ever trouble her or any other Sec Gen.

"No they don't," she declared. "That's why IMBOD invented the Security shot. So we *don't* feel paranoid. *You're* the one who's paranoid. You think Is-Land history is made-up. You think the Pioneers killed babies. If you go around talking like that, people will think you're an *infiltrator*."

Lil wiped a speck of dirt off her hip. "So, let them. I'm not going to stay in Is-Land anyway. This place is so *provincial*."

Astra stood up. Lil was being impossible. And ignorant. Is-Land didn't have *provinces*: it had *bioregions*. She brushed away the pebbles that were sticking to her bottom. "I'm going back to Wise House."

Lil was stretching her legs and wiggling her toes in the sun. "Do you remember the way?"

"Yes. Sort of." Okay, no, she didn't. She'd just followed Lil from place to place. But somewhere behind the brook and the ancestors was the gorge; if she just kept walking she'd hit it.

"We've gone past the end of the gorge," Lil said casually. "It's easy to miss it and end up walking too far north."

Astra put her hands on her hips. "Come with me then."

Lil rolled on her tummy and smiled up at Astra, as if nothing was wrong. "We just got here! Let's have our lunch and then we'll go."

Astra scratched her ankle with the opposite foot and then sat back down. She picked up a small rock and began scraping the ledge with it. "You shouldn't talk the way you do," she muttered.

Lil twirled a lock of her hair between her fingers. "You're just saying that because you're Sec Gen."

Sometimes Astra could see the field mice in the meadow when she was flying Silver. Silver was Coded not to eat wild animals, but the mice didn't know that. They would freeze when Silver passed overhead, their ears would flatten to their heads and a millisecond later they would dart away into the long grass. She felt like one of those mice now.

"So what if I am," she said stiffly, gripping the rock in her palm.

"It's a shame for you, that's all. It means you can't think for yourself, so all the adults talk to you like you're a child and you'll just be an IMBOD drone your whole life. My dad didn't want that for me. That's why he took me away."

Astra avoided Lil's gaze. She rooted in her mind for the right Sec Gen Imprints. "I can think for myself. But my self is part of Is-Land, and therefore I think with everyone. IMBOD protects us, and we protect—"

"Is-Land is a CONC *outpost*," Lil triumphantly interrupted. "IMBOD's job is to protect the Continental Server and make Is-Land a safe place to stop between Himalaya and Neuropa. But when the global ceasefire ends, Asfar and the Non-Landers might declare war on us. *That's* why IMBOD invented the Security Serum. You're like the worms Hokma feeds to the Owleons: born and raised to blindly die for Is-Land."

Astra slammed the rock down onto the ledge. "*All* Is-Landers would die for Is-Land," she said fiercely. "Being Sec Gen means we can fight better so we *don't* die."

Lil looked at her pityingly. "No, being Sec Gen means you'll follow orders. Too many Is-Landers were starting to question IMBOD and that's why they developed the Serum."

Astra had lost track of what she herself thought, but she knew she had to defend herself, defend Is-Land, defend IMBOD, from Lil's outrageous accusations. "No one questions IMBOD because no one *has* to question IMBOD," she flared. "IMBOD takes orders from the National Wheel Meet, and the National Wheel Meet represents all of us!" As she was saying it, she believed it.

Lil sat up. She was excited now, her eyes bright, her voice high. "People *used* to question the Nat Meet. My dad told me that lots of Is-Landers used to believe that some Non-Landers should have the right to stay here, especially the day laborers."

Lil's voice was buzzing around Astra's head like a bluebottle fly. She reached up and took a vicious swat at it. "The *infiltrators*, you mean."

She'd only made things worse. Lil became even more eager, speaking more quickly and leaning close to Astra's face. "They weren't infiltrators." She pounced on the word, flung it aside. "They were seasonal aglabs, and when IMBOD decided to close the Boundary checkpoints, some communities wanted to help them stay. They even petitioned for Non-Landers to get citizenship if they converted to Gaianism. IMBOD cracked down on the dissidents and jailed them. That's why they invented the Security Serum. So that no one would ever question IMBOD again."

Like "faxma-sheen" and "burlesque," "dissident" was a word from another world. Is-Land had never had *dissidents*. Again, Lil was scrambling the facts as though they were alt-eggs. "No!" Astra flashed. "Some aglabs hid in Is-Land, but no Gaian would *ever* have helped them. The Non-Landers were attacking us in the Belt. Remember: Hokma lost her eye on patrol. *That* was why we had to close the Boundary. Then the *infiltrators* swarmed up to the mountains and dug tunnels and smuggled *nano-explosives* into Is-Land. That's why Klor only has one leg. His daughter died too—*my* Shelter sister. At a bus stop in Sippur. I *saw* it."

She was almost panting with the effort to correct Lil's warped views. In response, Lil reached over and stroked the teaby vaccination scar on her arm. "You're right," she said lightly, mockingly, "I shouldn't talk like this. You're a poor little Sec Gen drone. You'll probably have to report me."

Lil's fingertip was an electric needle, sending a sizzle of fury to Astra's heart. She opened her mouth to blast Lil off the cliff—

But as she did so, Lil looked her right in the eyes and smirked.

A cold, feverish knowledge crawled over Astra's skin. Lil knew she wasn't Sec Gen. She clamped her mouth shut.

"I'm Sec Gen," she said, finally, each word an iron spike to kill this argument dead. "That means I care about my friends. Even if you're not Sec Gen too. Even if you don't love Gaia enough to die for Her."

But she'd given it away, she knew. Just like on the sunlit strip of the ledge, she'd wobbled. She'd been about to yell, "I'm not Sec Gen, so shut up and listen to me!" and even though she hadn't, the intention had hurtled out of her at the speed of light and struck Lil right between the eyes. Lil's flashing, smug expression said as much and more.

"I'd die for Gaia," Lil said grandly. "Just not for CONC."

"Is-Land *is* Gaia." Astra batted Lil's jibe away with another Imprint. The crisis had passed. So what if Lil knew she wasn't Sec Gen? No one would believe her if she said so, especially not considering all the other crazy things she was spouting today.

"No it isn't. There are Gaians in Asfar, you know."

"There aren't," she replied flatly. It had somehow become her duty today to disagree with Lil and she wanted her shift to end.

"There *are*. They wear clothes; that's the only difference. Even some of the Southern Belters are clothed Gaians too, now. They converted, but IMBOD still won't let them in. *I* think there's room here for all the Non-Landers. They can live in the cities and eat alt-meat."

Astra was bored now. Lil was trying to goad her with heretical remarks, but these were ancient Year Four arguments that everybody knew the answer to. "They don't want to live in cities. They want to live in villages and slaughter sheep and cows. Which reminds me: I'm *hungry*," she complained, opening her pac.

"Me too." It was surprising to hear Lil agree, for the first time all day. She pulled out the hummus and tomato sandwiches Hokma had made for them that morning, and the two green apples. The sandwiches were a little squashed, perhaps because of Lil's cartwheel. Astra had a salad box to share: lettuce, cucumber slices and toasted hazelnuts, with a small bottle of lemon dressing. She also had forks and napkins, and some carrot cake Nimma had given her. She brought everything out, drizzled the salad dressing over the leaves and gave Lil a fork. They ate in silence, apart from the munching of the apples. When she'd finished hers, Lil got up and hurled the core off the cliff. It sailed in a high curve through the air, tracing an arc like an invisible rainbow.

Watching the apple core disappear, Astra suddenly felt incredibly lonely—lonelier even than the ancestors, who were somehow together, privately alike, even if locked in their own separate prayers. Why couldn't she tell Lil she wasn't Sec Gen? Lil said whatever she liked, all the time. She had just spouted off all that absurd, exhausting stuff about the Pioneers and IMBOD and CONC without a single worry that Astra might tell Hokma or Nimma or Klor.

But that was the problem. Lil didn't respect any rules and so you couldn't trust her to keep a secret. And she wouldn't understand, anyway, that you could be like Hokma and question some of IMBOD's decisions without being a *dissident*.

She chucked her own apple core into the undergrowth. She was done competing with Lil for today.

They had both saved the cake for last. Lil picked up her piece, sniffed it and examined it closely. "Is it made out of *carrots*?" she exclaimed.

At last, something Lil didn't know. "Yeah," Astra said. "And walnuts and soy-butter icing. Nimma made it."

"It must have taken a long time to cut the carrots up so small." Lil actually sounded impressed now.

"She didn't cut them up. She grated them."

Lil didn't want to, Astra could tell, but grudgingly she asked, "What does 'grated' mean?"

Astra thought about it. "A grater is a kitchen utensil. It looks like . . . a metal cylinder with lots of little moon-shaped knives cut into it. The knives have holes behind them for the grated bits to fall through. You can do apples and beetroots too, for salads."

Lil was staring at the cake in her hand. "I've never had carrot cake before." Without warning, her whisper edged into a whimper.

Nimma and Hokma had badgered her to play with Lil, to be kind to her. "She's never had a friend," they'd said. Lil had won her over with her games and stories, and gradually Astra had forgotten how desperately sad she could be. Now, for the first time, Astra felt the enormity of everything Lil had missed out on: friends, cakes, a kitchen, a Shelter mother. The emptiness was huge, bigger even than the emptiness of the ancestors. It sucked her appetite away.

"I guess you couldn't do any baking in the cave," she offered, awkwardly. Lil ignored her. For a moment Astra thought she was going to give the cake back, but she didn't. She took a bite and ate, slowly, expressionlessly, her jaw methodically churning. Astra started eating her piece too. The aroma of cloves and nutmeg was calming, and Nimma's rich, creamy icing stuck to the roof of her mouth, absorbing her attention. As she chewed the cake, its honeyed syrup flowed steadily into her veins.

Beside her, Lil was licking her fingers, one by one. When she'd finished, she turned to Astra with a radiant smile. She had a dab of icing on her chin. "That was *good*."

"Nimma's carrot cakes are the best." Astra grinned too, and popped the last crumb from her palm into her mouth.

"I need a nap now, and then we can go." Lil stretched out on her back and closed her eyes. Her nipples puckered into hard brown walnuts. As Astra watched her ribs rise and fall, a fleet of dandelion seeds drifted over Lil's ribcage. It was a Gaia vision, she could tell, but what it meant, she didn't know.

When she woke up, Lil's face was next to hers.

"I'm sorry I said mean things," she said quietly. "I like you being Sec Gen. It makes you benevolent."

The sun was lower in the sky and its lengthening rays were traveling up Astra's legs to her thighs. Lil's breath smelled of the carrot cake, sweet and spicy, and her breasts were brushing against Astra's arm. They felt soft and mysterious, as if even Lil didn't know what they were doing. Astra didn't move.

"That's okay," she said. "I like you not being Sec Gen." *It makes you magnificent* she almost, but didn't, say. "Thank you for showing me the ancestors," she whispered instead.

Then the palm of Lil's hand was grazing her chest and Lil's chin was on her shoulder and Lil's voice was in her ear. "Your skin is my skin," she said, and then she was kissing Astra's face, and Astra was turning toward her and kissing Lil too.

That was how her first Gaia play started, and though at first she was anxious in case she broke any rules without knowing it, and a little irritated, because Lil kept murmuring instructions and she didn't see why *Lil* should take charge of what was supposed to be a cooperative game, eventually something shifted. A little voice in her head told her that if she was Sec Gen she would enjoy following orders, and anyway, everything Lil told her to do felt good. Then Lil was quiet at last, and for a long time it was as if they were shaking a long, shimmering flag out over the steppes, their skins a sateen pathway unrolling toward the faint puffy clouds on the horizon.

Afterward, Lil smiled down at her. "You know all my secrets now," she said.

2.6

The next day was Arkaday, but Astra wasn't allowed to go up to Wise House. In the morning she had to help clean and decorate Core House because tomorrow was the official results ceremony of the five-yearly IMBOD Or inspection and three officers were coming up from Sippur for a special evening assembly and banquet. The Or-kids had to recite Gaia hymns for the officers and rehearsing for that took all afternoon. After dinner, Nimma said she and Yoki had to sit in the Earthship living room and do at least two hours' sewing. Tomorrow's hymns had to be *word-perfect*, so she and Yoki had better wear their Tablette earphones while they sewed. "No ifs, ands or buts, butterbean," Klor had said when Astra started to protest.

Astra knew the Gaia hymn back to front, so after Nimma left, she switched channels and listened to music instead, a birdsong, brook-babble and flute tapestry that gently pulled her thoughts back to the forest. As she sewed petal after petal she roamed back over her afternoon with Lil, revisiting the ancestors and the arrowpain, and what had happened on the ledge. Soon, although her fingers were cramped and her vision blurred from squinting, in her mind she was floating above the steppes in a sunburst of Gaia Power and giggles.

It hadn't all been wonderful, though. She still didn't know if she and Lil had broken any Gaia-play rules, and that worry was nibbling away at her now like a rat in a kitchen storeroom. And earlier in the afternoon, she couldn't forget, they'd fought: a horrible fight. Lil had said stupid, nasty things and Astra had felt a million *negative emotions*, emotions no Sec Gen ever had to worry about. When she remembered that part of the afternoon, how exposed she'd felt, it was as if the rat inside her had spilled a whole winter's granary into a sewer: her stomach panged and churned all over again. She should have kept calm; she shouldn't have let Lil get to her like that.

But the horrible part had passed, hadn't it, she thought, as nightingales warbled over a high lilting flute. When? After they'd eaten, and after she'd seen her Gaia vision: the dandelion seed heads blowing over Lil's sleeping body. Finally, as she finished her twentieth petal of the evening, Astra realized what the vision meant.

Lil had wanted to see balloons—balloons her dad had told her brought Non-Landers to Is-Land, like viruses or germs. She thought that the Pioneers were baby-killers and IMBOD was brainwashing everyone in Is-Land. But the flying seeds said that she was wrong. The flying seeds were Gaia's messengers: they were saying that Is-Land was a peaceful, beautiful country that sent seeds of hope out into the world— but Lil's eyes were closed to them. Gaia had let Astra see them because Astra's job was to teach Lil the truth: that Is-Land was Gaia's guardian, and IMBOD existed to protect the protectors.

Understanding a Gaia vision was like watching an Owleon fly for the first time: your heart went soaring with the bird, riding the invisible currents of Gaia's warm breath. Everything was perfect. Everything made sense. Her blood singing, Astra sat back on the sofa and tenderly watched Yoki sewing, his earphones shutting him off in his own tranquil, orderly Sec Gen world. As he mouthed his hymn, she experienced a second slow but dazzling wave of revelation: the Gaia vision wasn't finished with her yet. Watching Yoki concentrate, his lips silently moving, his head rocking, for the first time in her life she realized *why she wasn't Sec Gen.*

For Sec Gens, she suddenly understood with infinite clarity, visions weren't puzzles: visions were simply images that illustrated Imprints. None of them would have turned a vision around in their mind like a pebble in the hand, feeling for the perfect fit to their fingers. Yoki and Meem learned their hymns and sang them gladly, with pure voices; Peat studied his laws and fitted them together like soilbags, one on top of each other, to make a solid barricade against uncertainty and fear. Her Shelter siblings weren't *drones*; they weren't worker bees or sacrificial worms, but if faced with a dangerous idea, like starlings they would immediately retreat into the strength of the murmuration. If Lil had said all the crazy things she'd said yesterday to any of them, they wouldn't have tried to argue with her. Yoki would have got upset and refused to listen: he would have closed his eyes, plugged his ears and started chanting Imprints to calm himself down; Meem would have been perplexed, perhaps would have tried to get Lil to eat her lunch; and Peat, well Peat might have been *benevolent*—yes, he might have said to Lil kindly (and a little pompously) that she was mistaken. But later on, all of them would have told Nimma and Klor that Lil was saying bad things about IMBOD, and they would have expected her to be disciplined or removed from their company.

She, Astra, had been open to Lil and all the different feelings she'd provoked. It had been a painful experience but as a result, she had learned something a Sec Gen would never have understood. She'd been able to see, at last, when Lil ate the cake, that she wasn't dangerous. She was strange and uneducated, sad and confused, not because she was bad, but because she'd never had a Tablette or a Shelter mother, and because her dad—well, Astra still didn't really understand Lil's dad. Frowning, she returned to her petal. Possibly, it occurred to her as she bit off a knot, he really was crazy: maybe he'd had a *mental illness*.

It was such a stunning thought she dropped her sewing in her lap. *Of course*: why else would Lil be saying such crazy things? Craziness didn't just mean things being jumbled and random, like one of Nimma's quilts—it was also scientific: it meant having a mental illness. No one in Or had a mental illness because the adults were screened before they were allowed to live here and their Code children were safe from genetic disorders. But in cities like Sippur and Atourne, even in New Bangor, people still suffered from conditions that thanks to the Serum would soon be a thing of the past: depression, bipolar disorder,

claustrophobia, and—*oh!*—there was one that made you paranoid! Yes—
schizophrenia!

It was like solving a Code Thought or Logic problem after you'd
struggled with it for ages. Astra wanted to throw her petals and needle
aside and jump up and shout *Yes!* Maybe Lil had inherited schizophrenia from her dad. That would explain everything: why he'd taken Lil
away in the first place, her lightning-fast changes of mood, her paranoid
fantasies, her suspicion of Tabby and IMBOD, the absolute impossibil-
ity of explaining anything to her.

The music was quickening to a new rhythmic line of woodstick on
stone. Her heart pattering, Astra stared unseeing over Yoki's shoulder
into the row of fruit trees in the greenhouse corridor. Nimma said Gaia
had sent Lil here. Gaia had done that so Astra could watch over her. No
Sec Gen would have the understanding or patience or curiosity to keep
one step ahead of Lil's unpredictable mind. She would have to watch Lil
carefully now. She might ask Hokma about paranoia—one day when
Lil was doing chores in the garden, perhaps. And she would stay open
to more Gaia visions, because it was clear that Gaia wanted her to help
Lil recover. Otherwise Lil might have to have a brain implant, like the
people on the bus to Sippur. Astra had seen them since, over the years,
shopping together in New Bangor, carefully stroking the vegetables at
the market before putting them into their basket, and once she'd almost
run into one of the women on her own. She was talking rapidly to herself and barging past people on the sidewalk, rudely, just like Lil—

"Dreaming, Astra?" Nimma came bustling into the room with a
feather duster and clicked her fingers under Astra's nose. As Astra started,
one of her earphones fell out and the music leaked into the room.

"What on Gaia's green earth are you listening to? No wonder you're
distracted! You should be learning your hymn for tomorrow."

"I know it already," Astra mumbled automatically, turning the
music off.

Nimma began flicking the duster over Sheba's photo on the mantelpiece. "Then you should be learning your Blood & Seed chant, or at least
sewing your petals. Look at Yoki, he's charging ahead. *And* he's memorizing his hymns."

"Sorry, Nimma." Astra picked up her sewing again. For once, she didn't mind being told off. Telling you off was just what Nimma did. It was her pattern, just like memorizing laws was Peat's pattern and protecting Gaia's creatures was Yoki's. Up until now, Astra's pattern— her special melody in Gaia's symphony, as Hokma called it—had been training the Owleons, but that had kept her apart, up at Wise House, as though she didn't really belong with her Shelter siblings and the other Sec Gens at school. In fact, she realized from her new vantage point high above the world, up until now her special melody had been yoked to a discordant counterpoint: a turmoil of unspeakable emotions. Now, though, Gaia was hinting that Hokma was right: because of this hidden turmoil, her human harmonies ran deeper than the Sec Gens'. She was able to *understand* people, even strange and difficult people, and one day she might become a genius at curing mental illness. The thought was so exciting it almost banished the very possibility of negative emotions.

As Nimma dusted around her and Yoki, Astra finished expertly edging her two-hundred-and-eighty-second petal.

"I put sequins on this one." She showed Nimma her handiwork.

"Oh, so you did. That's lovely, darling," Nimma cooed. "Now just another hour, and then bed. You've got a big day tomorrow—an important Gaia-play lesson, Vishnu said, and then the hymn ceremony and banquet. You'll want to be wide awake for all of that, won't you?"

No she *didn't* want to be awake for the Gaia-play lesson. For one thing, she didn't want to learn that she had broken a rule already, or to say anything by mistake that might betray what she and Lil had done on the ledge. For all she knew, being an early starter at Gaia play was a sign that a person wasn't Sec Gen. But almost worse than these fears was the painful pressure she awoke to the next day, building on her cheek—a *pimple*.

A pimple was an Old World stigmata, an Abrahamic mark of disgrace. None of the Sec Gens got pimples, and when Astra's first one had erupted, Nimma had almost taken her to the doctor. Klor had saved her, saying that surely IMBOD hadn't entirely solved the problem of puberty yet, and wasn't it better just to let Astra get some sun? But the sun didn't help. Like scarlet volcanoes, the pimples throbbed beneath her skin until, despite everything Nimma and Klor said, she was forced to squeeze them, making the yellow, custardy pus spatter the mirror and a bitter wash of saliva rise in the back of her throat. She could almost taste it, this vile, alien fluid her own body was manufacturing to humiliate and betray her.

For after being squeezed the pimples didn't disappear, but sprawled on her face like Dark Time bomb craters, and everyone who saw her looked first at the absolute mess she'd made of herself. On the first day you could even see the marks of her fingernails, two red crescent moons digging into her skin. The adults silently pitied or condemned her while the Sec Gens examined her closely—never unkindly—in awe of her difference and debating the cause of her plague. Silvie favored diet, though Astra ate exactly the same food as her siblings, while Tedis thought she wasn't peaking enough and prescribed twice-daily sessions of self-Gaia play. Nimma, of course, blamed Astra's dread, saying it was greasy and telling her not to let it touch her face or the pimples would spread. Astra would mutter, "I washed my loc yesterday!" but the most painful thing about the pimples was the lurking feeling in her stomach that Nimma was right: she *should* wash her hair more and she *shouldn't* pick at her skin. The curse of the pimples really was her own fault.

Today she had controlled herself and the pimple was still just a painful red bump. She still didn't want anyone to see it, but she'd had no choice. She wasn't ill and she had to go to school. As the Gaia-play class settled in the cherry orchard, she kept her head down, her dread dangling over her face. It was an inadequate shield—she'd rather be wearing a beekeeping hat or a fencing mask—but it would have to do. Tedis, thank Gaia, was sitting on her good side and Sultana, on her left, would be entirely focused on the lesson. Just to be on the safe side, she avoided everyone's gaze, concentrating on the scent of dry earth, the skittery sounds the squirrels made as they investigated the trees and the way the light slanting through the branches struck the brand on Mr. Ripenson's chest. The scarification was in the shape of a pair of crossed staffs, the four heads each embellished with a different design: a lotus opposite a discus, and a conch shell opposite a mace head. The symbol had been burned with a laser by a Craft worker in Atourne, he'd told her one evening at dinner, and represented the Old World god Vishnu he was named for, whose motto was "to maintain and preserve." The lotus meant spiritual purity, the mace head was a mighty weapon and the conch was not only a trumpet but the home of the god's Gaia partner Lakshmi. The shell was now the CONC emblem, of course, but Astra especially liked the discus: it was a Sudarshana Chakra, a spinning blade with 108 teeth that would destroy your enemy forever.

Mr. Ripenson smiled around at everyone. "Good morning everybody, and welcome to the lesson we've all been waiting for: Woodland Siesta and Gaia-play rules."

Interest rustled around the circle. Tedis exclaimed "all *right*" under his breath and Sultana had her Tablette out already. Yoki, opposite Astra, grinned as Acorn cleverly twirled a stick between his fingers.

"As you know, in high school you'll take siesta in the woods. There's a main shelter there with mats and hammocks, where you can sleep if you like, or play Tablette games, but there are also huts and clearings spread throughout the bushes for private Gaia play. It's school and a game, so it's only natural that there will be *rules*. The good news is that Sec Gens won't generally feel any urge to violate most of these rules. But"—he lifted a finger, quelling the playful groan that had arisen at his joke— "this is extremely important, everyone: Woodland Siesta rules are also Is-Land laws and you can be punished severely for breaking them. In order to graduate, you will need to pass a written exam on them, so I advise you to take detailed notes today. Turn to the lesson page, please."

The rules were *Is-land laws*? Why hadn't he told them that before? Her stomach clenching, Astra pulled her hydropac onto her lap and took out her Tablette. The circle of students fell quiet as everyone bent their heads over their screens and read.

New Bangor Schools

Years 8–12 Woodland Siesta

Gaia Play Rules

Gaia play is an important part of a child's development. In conformity with the National Curriculum, our aim at all New Bangor schools is to allow a safe environment for such play. Gaia play at school may only take place during Woodland Siesta and is subject to the National Law Code. It is therefore strictly forbidden, at any time on school property:

1) to insult someone's Gaia Power;
2) to pester another child to Gaia-play;
3) for anyone to watch Gaia play without the participants' knowledge or consent;
4) for anyone under the age of fifteen to penetrate a vagina, throat or anus with any object or part of the body; and similarly for anyone under the age of fifteen to allow such penetration;
5) to force another child to Gaia-play;
6) for anyone under the age of twenty to Gaia-play with anyone more than three years (36 months) older or younger than themselves.

Enforcement

Woodland Siesta will be supervised by two teachers at all times. However, Gaia play is by its nature private and the teachers will be based in the main shelter. Students will therefore be responsible for monitoring their own and others' behavior, and are expected to report any infractions immediately to the supervisors. In addition, all Gaia play in the Woodland huts and clearings will be recorded by unmanned closed-circuit cameras. Footage will be auto-scanned by the latest Gaia play recognition software and images that pass inspection will be immediately erased. If infractions of the rules are detected, the footage will be watched by the school doctor, and relevant teachers and Shelter parents will be informed.

Infractions of Rules 1, 2 and 3 will be addressed by immediate suspension of Woodland Privileges for the offender, and counseling for both the violator and the victim. In addition, at the Head's discretion, violators may be required to make a public apology to the victim at School Assembly. Infractions of Rule 4 will result in the separation of the offending parties, who will also be given counseling and, for a specified period, be required to attend siesta on alternate days. Future infractions of Rules 1, 2, 3 and 4 may also result in exclusion and transfer to a Bioregional IMBOD Shelter School. Infractions of Rules 5 and 6 will result in immediate exclusion; transfer to the Bioregional IMBOD Shelter School, and legal proceedings.

It was hard to concentrate when she felt so anxious. Astra skimmed the page, and then went back and read again. She had to stop and think about the math in Rule 6 for a second but, thank Gaia, it was clear that she and Lil hadn't committed any infractions. Yet.

"Let's go through these one at a time," Mr. Ripenson said. "No insulting anyone's Gaia Power. We all know that already, don't we?"

Astra opened a new window on her Tablette. *Rule One*, she typed. But she didn't know what else to put. She didn't think she'd ever heard any one insult someone's Gaia Power. The very concept was bizarre. Around the circle, her classmates exchanged puzzled glances.

"Does it mean no making jokes about Gaia parts?" Silvie ventured.

"Bad luck, Baz," Tedis crowed. As well as top run-scorer and chief detumescencer, Tedis was the self-declared king of armpit farts and as the class laughed, he raised his elbow and trumpeted victory now. Basil mimed shooting an arrow back at him and Tedis lowered his arm, grinning.

"Tedis, can I ask you to take this class seriously, please?" It wasn't like the teacher to speak sharply; everyone stopped giggling.

"Sorry, Mr. Ripenson," Tedis said, surprisingly meekly. Astra knew he liked the teacher. He'd been talking about getting his own chest scarified when he was eighteen—not the same design, of course, but a Gaia hymn in Braille. Girls would want to touch it, he said.

"Thank you." Mr. Ripenson raised his voice. "Listen up, everyone. Bodies can be very funny. Especially Tedis's." People laughed and relaxed: Tedis was clearly forgiven. "Bodies make noises or smells or disgusting liquids at the wrong time," he went on, to more giggles. "They wobble or bounce when people run. It's okay to laugh then. No one minds a little affectionate teasing. But when people Gaia-play, they are often extra sensitive to criticism. So teasing someone in a way that belittles their body—that tries to make the person feel small, or different from others—is never allowed."

Beside Astra, Sultana's fingers were racing over her keyboard, taking notes word for word. Astra's page was still blank. It was just difficult to even imagine trying to make someone feeling bad about their body. It went without saying that the human body was Gaia's creation, and as with all Her creations, diversity was the key to survival. Fat bodies were soft and nurturing and well insulated. Thin bodies were agile and energetic and didn't need to consume many resources. Muscular bodies were strong and impressive and useful for all sorts of practical tasks. Young bodies were sleek like seals; old bodies were wrinkled and delicate, like the piece of antique silk Nimma kept at Craft House, even though worms had died to make it. Gaia parts too came in all sizes and shapes, but that was a cause for fascination, not belittlement. Leaf's growing breasts and miniature Gaia pepper had been the subject of much playground interest lately, and heesh had responded with all manner of information about the important historical role of the boy-girl and girl-boy as a kind of cross between a fortune teller and Wheel Meet Supreme Court Judge. Leaf had even volunteered to settle petty disputes arising between boys and girls, though Astra privately thought heesh was just as likely to play favorites as anyone.

No, as Klor always said, the Sec Gens were all happy as clams in their skins. Still, a rule was a rule. You had to learn it and obey it, even if—like some of Klor's sayings—it made no sense. *No belittling people's bodies*, she typed, at last. Beside her Tedis wrote, *No Gaia shrimp jokes*, but when Silvie checked his Tablette screen and whispered "*Tedis!*" he deleted it.

"But," Mr. Ripenson went on, "though this rule is obvious, nevertheless, it is possible to break it without meaning to. Listen carefully, everyone. When you start Gaia play, you might discover that you prefer some types of bodies—or kinds of play—to others. That's part of the magic of Gaia Power: it draws certain people together. But this also means that you will sometimes want to decline an offer to play. In order not to insult the other person, it is *very important* to decline invitations in a kind manner. If you are cruel or thoughtless, the other person could feel deeply wounded and it might even become difficult for them to worship Gaia in the future. Gaia would suffer then, as well as the person you rejected."

This was serious, she could tell from his tone. Astra typed, *Decline all invites politely*. But what did that mean? From other people's faces, she could see she wasn't the only person with questions.

"How exactly would the person suffer?" Sultana asked, with her characteristic desire for precision. Astra sometimes discussed the intricacies of Gaia hymns with her, but it wasn't like talking with Lil. Sultana's thoughts were occasionally beautiful, but they were never wild or daring.

"Excellent question, Sultana. For one thing, they might become afraid to approach others. They might even start to find it hard to peak."

Afraid to invite play. Difficulty peaking. Astra typed slowly as, opposite, Baz put up his hand. "But we're Sec Gens. So we won't ever feel wounded like that, right?"

"That's correct, Baz: Sec Gens are emotionally robust and resilient, so you're unlikely to sustain any damage from isolated insults, but remember that the older students in Woodland Siesta or people you meet later in life won't be so lucky. So you have to get into the habit of following this rule with everyone."

Astra stared at her Tablette. Her pimple was throbbing like a warning light. She had been far too confident, she realized. These rules didn't matter to Sec Gens but they contained all sorts of secret traps for her. What if she kept Gaia-playing with Lil—or didn't want to anymore—and she insulted Lil by mistake—or, more likely, Lil insulted her? Would she end up *not being able to peak*? It was a terrifying thought. Her eyes stung with tears.

Frigging Gaia. She couldn't *cry* during Gaia-play lessons. Panicked, she reached into her hydropac, took out a hanky and blew her nose.

"Are you okay?" Sultana whispered.

"Just hayfever."

Sultana patted her on the arm. It was a good lie; she'd used it before. Crisis past, Astra stuffed the hanky back into her pac. Her pimple was pulsing like a miniature heartbeat, but she resisted the temptation to finger it. Sultana was probably feeling extra sorry for her dual affliction.

Leaf put up hir hand. "What if someone *says* you insulted them, but you didn't?"

"You needn't worry about false accusations, Leaf. The cameras will show what happened."

"But what if you say the wrong thing by mistake and someone's feelings get hurt? Is that still your fault?"

Sometimes Leaf's probing manner got on Astra's nerves, but today she was grateful to the girl-boy. Maybe if she was lucky, the Sec Gens would ask all her questions for her.

"Look, everyone," Mr. Ripenson raised his voice again, "don't be scared. I know this rule sounds a bit alarming, but there is an Imprint to deal with it. If you don't want to play with someone, all you have to say is, 'I'm sorry, you're really beautiful, but I don't feel like Gaia-playing with you today.' If you say that to a person on three separate occasions, then they have to stop approaching you. If they keep on trying, it's a violation of Rule 2. Okay? We'll set the Imprint in another lesson, but we need to move on now. So, Rules 2 and 3. These are pretty self-explanatory, aren't they?"

Astra wrote out the invitation-declining Imprint in full while beside her, Tedis typed, *No pestering, no spying.*

The teacher was swaying slightly as he went over the next two rules, Astra noticed, as if he were gently rotating on his sacral node. That had happened to her once while she was meditating, a comforting motion that seemed to connect her to Gaia's own axis. Could he be meditating and teaching *at the same time*? If anyone could, it was him. Back at Or, he meditated every morning before breakfast in the fruit orchard. Watching him now made her feel calmer. Law is a cultural Code, she remembered Peat telling her once; just like biological Code, it forms who we are. Maybe if she memorized the Imprint and obeyed the rules exactly, she might even start to fit in.

"Rule 4. No vaginal, anal or oral penetration until the age of fifteen. Why do you think this rule exists?"

"So the school garden always has enough cucumbers for lunch?" Tedis stage-whispered. Laughter erupted on their side of the circle. "Sorry, Mr. Ripenson." He slapped his palm over his mouth. "I forgot."

This time he didn't reprimand Tedis for being crude. "Nice try, Tedis," he smiled. "But no. If fifteen-year-olds want to use cucumbers, they have to bring their own. Anyone else?"

Sometimes Astra wanted to impress the teacher and answer a question, but she was always afraid that if she got it wrong and was overcome by embarrassment or envy of a smarter student he would notice her struggling with negative emotions. This question, being hard, risked such exposure. Boy-girl penetration, Astra knew, was one cause of pregnancy. But as soon as a girl got her Gaia-blood the school clinic gave her a hormone implant, so that couldn't be the reason for the rule. You could also get diseases from Gaia plow penetration, but there were vaccinations and treatments for all of them, and as long as you got tested regularly, they weren't a big deal. And she had no idea at all why fingers would be forbidden. She kept quiet and waited for a Sec Gen to venture a response.

"So that *boys*"—Silvie poked Tedis in the thigh—"have to learn how to play with the clitoris."

"Yes, Silvie, encouraging the development of foreplay skills is one reason for the rule. But there's another very important reason for the ban on penetration."

At last Acorn put up his hand. A thoughtful boy, he could often make interesting links between concepts. "Penetration promotes Gaia-bonding?" he hazarded.

"Very good, Acorn; exactly. Studies have demonstrated that the practice of penetration is closely linked to Gaia-bonding, and premature bonding is not advised for teenagers. Why is that, do you think?"

At last: a topic Astra knew something about. The main problem with Torrent and Stream's Gaia bond—as far as she understood Nimma's complaints about it—was that their treatment of Congruence had split the Or-teens into two factions. Torrent was now the eldest child in Or, Astra had overheard Nimma saying to Klor, and he ought to be setting an example for the others, not dividing them into camps with his petty exclusivity.

"Pah. Some people are naturally monogamous," Klor had snorted. "Look at us, woman! Forty years together and still at it like Gaia's own gibbons."

"Thirty-nine years," Nimma had corrected him primly. "And *we* met in our twenties, while I was still seeing that biochemist from North Atourne—a situation that continued for two years, as I recall."

Klor had conceded defeat. But it was true, Astra had observed, that two cliques had hived off from the main mass of older Or-teens. Congruence was never seen without Holaa and Ariel, her guard of honor, while Brook and Drake appeared to admire Torrent for inspiring such rampant adoration in Stream; the foursome were often together, the twins practicing their gymnastics to entertain the canoodling couple. Mr. Ripenson, Nimma had said, had offered to give all the older Or-teens group counseling, but the Parents' Committee, by a narrow margin, had voted against this course of action. It was clearly a topic the teacher cared a lot about, and to answer the question correctly would surely impress him.

She put up her hand. "Because it makes people selfish," she said. "We should all be playing together, not in couples or little groups."

"Great answer, Astra." He beamed at her and Sultana made a note of her words and she glowed inside. She might not be Sec Gen, but sometimes, when the teacher or the others praised her, she almost felt as if she was. "That's one reason, yes," he addressed the group again. "This should be a time when you forge social networks that will support you throughout your lifespan. But there's another reason too. Anyone?"

Oh. The glow dimmed. She'd only got it half-right. Careful not to let her disappointment show, she kept her own smile plastered to her face. Around her, the other children were silent.

"Play should be fun, shouldn't it? Something we do for its own sake, not for any long-term goals. Your first experiences of Gaia play should not be pressured by the need to make long-term promises to anyone else."

"But bonding is good, right?" Yoki sounded confused. "It makes you feel secure, that's what my Birth-Code mother says."

A prickly feeling stole over Astra. Why was Yoki able to express vulnerability without arousing suspicions? Why, she wondered miserably for the millionth time, was life so easy for the Sec Gens and so difficult for her?

"Absolutely, Yoki: bonding is healthy and normal. But it's also a serious commitment. Bonded couples make promises to each other. They also make sacrifices. At the heart of bonding is a complex relationship between two different people's sets of evolving needs. Children, even older teens, simply don't have enough self-knowledge to make such calculations accurately. For one thing, you will change so rapidly in the next few years that it's impossible for you to know what you'll want to be doing or who you'll want to be with a year or two from now. So until you are twenty and ready to start making plans for work and study and travel, you are not encouraged to make long-term Gaia commitments. Think of it this way: holding back from penetration is good practice for holding back emotionally from deeper involvement with a Gaia play pal."

"But you could Gaia-bond without penetrative play, couldn't you?" Sultana piped up, a tinny note of anxiety in her voice. "By kissing and peaking? Or just by holding hands?"

Mr. Ripenson adopted a reassuring tone. "Yes, theoretically you could—but let's be clear about two things. First, you're Sec Gens: you get your emotional security from being a member of a group and you probably won't feel the need to seek an early exclusive commitment. Second, while Gaia-bonding is discouraged, it is not against the rules. If you do end up bonding, you won't be in trouble, but your teachers and Shelter parents will keep an eye on you both to make sure that your work and other friendships don't suffer. Okay?"

Sultana and Yoki might be soothed now, but Astra was on the verge of bursting open. Yet again the rules had revealed her calamitous deficiencies: Sec Gens wouldn't bond prematurely, but she might—a one-sided bond that would leave her clingy and bad-tempered like Stream, or terribly hurt, like Congruence. And what if the studies also showed that *Gaia-bonding promoted penetration*? She might break Rule 4 and be forced into counseling, into an IMBOD Special School. The thought made her break out in sweat, made her want to shut down her Tablette screen and walk away from Gaia-play class forever.

But she had to stay put, her face burning, watching Sultana underline _We are Sec Gens_ in her notes. "Now," the teacher rolled on, "Rules 5 and 6. These are very serious offenses which can be punished by prison. Why is that? What's wrong with forcing someone to Gaia-play with you?"

"It's what the oil junkies did to the planet," Yoki declared. "Just taking what you want, what makes you feel good, without caring about Gaia or Her creatures."

There he was again, showing anger, to the approval of Acorn and the others around him. She should mimic her brother, she knew, and channel her own anger and fears into a heated defense of Gaia. But she was so choked up she couldn't risk speaking at all.

"Exactly," Mr. Ripenson said, the gravity in his voice according Yoki full credit. "Fortunately, forced Gaia play is rare in Is-Land. It does happen, very occasionally, when men, mostly—though sometimes women or two-sex people—feel angry or upset or are simply being very selfish. Upon investigation, it is often discovered that these people themselves were victims of forced Gaia play in their childhoods. That is why counseling is needed whenever any violation of the rules occur."

"But Sec Gens don't get angry or upset," Silvie commented. "And we're never selfish. So we'll be okay, right?"

"Over time the Security Serum will reduce or even eliminate the danger of this crime, but there are still occasions when in the natural course of Gaia play you need to be aware of the rule. You could already be Gaia-playing, and really enjoying yourself, when suddenly, for whatever reason, the other person wants to stop. Sometimes, for example, if a girl is having her Gaia-blood, her stomach might start to hurt. In those cases, regardless of how nice you're feeling, _you have to stop_."

That's just a normal play rule, she wanted to shout. _You always stop a game if people get hurt or upset_. But what if _she_ couldn't, she thought, panic scrambling through her again. When she was peaking, it was impossible to stop. What if not being Sec Gen meant she would force someone to peak with her and break Rule 5 too? Astra couldn't bear it any longer. She reached for her hydropac—but Sultana had got to hers first and offered her a hanky. She took it, and pressed it against her wet eyes.

"What if you feel *really* close to peaking, though?" Tedis asked. "Like you *can't* stop."

It was as though he'd read her mind. Some adults said Sec Gens might be able to do that, one day. Balling Sultana's hanky in her fist, she stared down at Tedis's sculptured thigh. *Please, Gaia, let me not be different from everyone else*, she prayed. *Let me not be selfish*, please!

"Good question. If you feel that close to peaking, it's allowed to keep playing with yourself. But you should ask if the other person minds. Often, they won't, but if they do you should leave them and finish playing somewhere else."

The answer satisfied Tedis. It was reasonable: fair and do-able, like all Mr. Ripenson's suggestions so far. Astra drew a deep breath. She would learn them all, all the required behaviors and emergency responses, and she would follow them precisely, every time. She would be okay. She would ask Tedis or Silvie or Sultana if she had any doubts. With a grateful little smile, she gave the hanky back to Sultana.

"Okay, let's move on. Rule 6. No Gaia-playing with older or younger people. Now this rule Sec Gens do need to pay attention to. Sec Gen kids like to make adults happy, and you might therefore find yourself in a situation where you don't know if you should obey an older person. You won't be allowed to leave the main shelter with anyone who is too old or too young for you, so you don't need to worry about this rule during Woodland Siesta. In your community, though, there might be an older child or adult who wants to play with you. You already know that if someone tries to touch your Gaia parts, you should tell your Shelter parents. As you get older, though, you might be tempted not to tell. You might actually want to play with the person. But even if you like them very much, you mustn't do so. Why is that?"

"Because they're bigger than us?" Leaf ventured. "They might hurt us without meaning to?"

"Yes, Leaf. Exactly. You might get physically hurt by the size and strength of an older person's body, but an older person is stronger *emotionally* as well; they know more about themselves and about the world. They are more likely to want to form a Gaia bond, but it would be very wrong for them to do so with a child. It would be like pitting someone who had just learned how to play chess against a Grandmaster. They might let you win a few games to be nice, but ultimately, they would be in control of your emotions during a time when you should be having fun."

Fun? Chewing her dread, Astra made the note. Gaia play didn't look very much like fun anymore. All in all, the rules were extremely serious, and it was clear that some of them would affect her far more than the Sec Gens. She would have to talk to Hokma about them, maybe when Lil was around so that she could learn the rules too. Though Lil wouldn't think school rules applied to her—she would probably have some outlandish argument against each one, arguments that no one could ever think of in a million years. Then they might fight, and who knows, maybe end up insulting one another.

"Don't panic!" Tedis whispered. "There isn't a physical exam." Her face flaring, she folded up her Tablette and stuffed it back in her hydropac. Tedis probably thought she was a study-bee, like Sultana. Well, let him. She didn't care.

"Well done, folks," Mr. Ripenson said. "You've all worked hard today, dealing with some complicated concepts and questions. Shall we finish with a Murmuration Swim?"

He stood up and stretched, his own Gaia plow a soft, thick vine drooping over its seed pouches. Everyone cheered and jumped up for the Starling game: running together through the practice lawn to the school brook, arms outstretched, swooping and leaping and swerving, always keeping half a yard between your fingertips and those of the other players. As they tumbled out of the orchard, Yoki and Acorn running together, Sultana squealing with delight beside her, Astra kept Tedis in sight. He wasn't allowed to run the fastest in the game, but he always tried to steer—she could tell—and she liked to be next to him and steer too, to make him follow her direction as often as she followed his. In the hubbub of positioning, Tedis brushed against her, surprising her hip with the warmth of his thigh, holding it near hers a second longer than necessary. A flush of heat charged her nerves. You weren't allowed to touch each other in the game. As she stared after his retreating back, he turned and winked.

She was rooted to the spot. Tedis had never winked at her before. Was he trying to distract her from the game? But Mr. Ripenson was clapping and she had to stop thinking and start moving. As always, once the Murmuration game got underway, you soon lost track of who was playing incorrectly or trying to cheat. The sun gilding her skin, her feet pounding over the lawn, Astra relinquished her desire to be fastest or best, to make Tedis follow her, even to reach the brook; her fear, envy and anger melted away and she felt briefly, helplessly, one of the Sec Gens, forever enveloped in a magical, ever-flowing wave of love and togetherness. Why couldn't Gaia play be like this, Astra wondered as she splashed, finally, with Tedis and Silvie and Sultana and Acorn and Yoki, into the warm water: not riddled with questions and rules, but exhilarating, soothing, refreshing and unanswerably whole.

2.7

After school the Or-kids lined up behind the marquee that had been erected in front of Core House. There were rows of chairs inside for the adults, facing a trestle table covered with Nimma's best embroidered linen cloth, where the three IMBOD officers would sit and deliver their report. Ahn and Nimma would sit with them, representing Code House and Craft House and jointly, Core House. Behind the table was a tall rail where all the Owleons would perch: Helium, Silver, the two IMBOD trainees and the three Code House birds. The children would enter from the back and process down the center aisle reciting their hymns; then they'd gracefully turn and form a semicircle in front of the trestle table and sit down on the grass. They needed to perform perfectly because the procession was being filmed: Ahn would be operating the Kezcams, one stationary throughout, suspended behind the lead IMBOD officer, and two moving above the procession, and later, as the Inspection Report was read, the audience.

Astra had been seven at the last Inspection Report Ceremony and she vaguely remembered it had been long and boring, but Or had done very well, and Ahn especially had been praised for his consultancy work for two Bioregional Councils, the dry forest and the Steppes. She'd wondered why Hokma didn't get to sit at the long table, representing

Wise House, but Hokma had said the birds were her representatives and anyway, Wise House was an office of Code House. There had been lots of clapping, Astra remembered, and afterward the banquet had been amazing, even better than the Winter Solstice feast because more vegetables were in season. They'd had her absolute favorite, rostis, which Moon didn't put on the menu very often because peeling and grating enough potatoes for everyone took a long time. The menu for today was a secret, but Astra and Meem were both hoping rostis would feature again.

The procession was beautiful. There were fifty-eight Or-kids over the age of three now, and they entered in pairs, the little ones first, holding flowers and singing the simplest hymn: "Gaia, We Love You." The older children followed, all the way up to the seventeen-year-olds, chanting "Like a Hawk She Watches Us." Astra walked in beside Yoki, head high. Nimma had been kind for once and had patted a little tinted herbal cream on her cheek, hiding the red swelling. The cream smelled of calendula and witch hazel and had a drying, tightening effect on the pimple. In general, she felt good. The buoyant effect of the Murmuration Swim had lasted and now the chanting had begun she was swept up in the momentous sense of occasion here at Or.

Over the last two months everyone had had shorter showers than usual so that the rain tanks could be used to water the grass on the lawn; now the blades were long and lush beneath Astra's feet. The sun was bright, and passing into the marquee was like entering a glowing lantern or a shadow theater, the seven birds perched darkly at the opposite end of the tent like cutout silhouettes. She raised her voice:

> *Like a hawk She watches us*
> *Scurry to and fro*
> *It matters not who we are*
> *Or what we think we know*

Some of the adults turned in their chairs to admire them, but the children weren't supposed to smile or wave. They had to keep their heads high and eyes forward and walk in time with the recitation. Astra kept her vision fixed on the Owleons: Helium in the middle of the rail, the larger Code House birds on either side of him, then Silver to the left and the small trainees on either end. Silver was watching her; she had to do him proud.

If we forget to worship Her
She'll swoop down from the sky
Rip us from Her feathered nest
And cast us out to die

She was nearing the table now. The three IMBOD officers occupied the center, flanked by Nimma and Ahn. The officer beside Ahn was a thin, pale, blond woman, and the one beside Nimma was a broad-shouldered, coffee-colored man. The man in the center was taller than his colleagues, olive-skinned with a hairy chest. He had a high forehead and was wearing rectangular rimless glasses. He looked familiar. As Astra reached the front of the aisle she realized why.

Sometimes Astra and the other Or-kids played a game in the kitchen with the walk-in freezer, opening it to let a blast of ice vapor sear their skin. Right now, Dr. Samrod Blesserson could have been that open freezer door. For a second, every muscle in her body stiffened and her flesh felt as though it was shriveling on her bones. Miraculously, the moment passed; she realized her legs were somehow still pacing forward to the rhythm of the chant, but inside her thoughts were chattering like her teeth had done the day Torrent had dared her to stand inside the freezer for as long as she could. Dr. Blesserson had said he didn't want to have anything to do with Or anymore. Why was he here? Where was Hokma?

She and Yoki reached the head of the aisle; in front of her, Meem turned left. Above Dr. Blesserson the Kezcam was recording the procession. She drew herself up, focused on a point a short distance ahead and chanted as loudly as possible. She wasn't sure, but possibly Dr. Blesserson's gaze clicked on her. Then she was following Meem into the grassy space in front of the table. From the corner of her eye she could see Hokma in the second row of chairs. Beside her was Lil.

Hokma nodded at her. Then she was out of sight, unless Astra turned her head, and she wasn't allowed to do that. She joined Meem, standing with her back to the adults and Lil and facing the table: fortunately not directly in front of Dr. Blesserson. It was agonizing, not being able to turn and see Hokma—but she had smiled. Did that mean everything was okay? And why was Lil here? Was she coming to the banquet too? No one ever told her frigging *anything*.

The female officer was practically ogling her and Meem, head tilted as if to say "what adorable children." Beside her, Ahn was unobtrusively swiping his Tablette, his hair a springy puffball in the yellowish glow of the marquee. Above him, Silver was preening, using his beak to rehook the barbules on a flight feather, realigning it into a perfectly smooth surface. If she clicked her tongue he would look at her, but she was on no account allowed to do that, and nor did she want to attract Dr. Blesserson's attention. Torrent and Stream processed in front of the table, the last strains of the hymn died away and as applause filled the tent, the Or-kids, as one, bowed to the table. Then, still as one, they turned and acknowledged the Or-adults. Completing the circle, they faced front again and sat down on the grass.

At the table, Nimma leaned into her microphone. "Thank you, Or-kids," she proclaimed, "for that stirring welcome to our distinguished guests. I'm honored to introduce our IMBOD panel, who have worked so hard with us over the last six months, combing through our records and inspecting every last inch of Or. We're so looking forward to their response, and learning from experts how to improve all of the work we do here. I am especially pleased to welcome IMBOD Chief Inspector Dr. Samrod Blesserson. We are all grateful for Dr. Blesserson's profound work on psychological recovery from IMBOD Service. Not everyone may yet know of his current return to the GeneIsis project, developing new National Service training methods for the Sec Gens, for which he has—very reluctantly, he tells me—taken up the honor and responsibility of a full IMBOD officership. Community inspection isn't his normal field of duties, but as many of you know, our original lead officer had to step down due to illness, so we are deeply grateful to Dr. Blesserson for taking time out of his invaluable research to step in at the last moment to deliver our Report."

Dr. Blesserson—*Chief Inspector* Blesserson—leaned forward into his microphone. "Thank you, Nimma, for the gracious welcome," he said. Astra could see his IMBOD boots and bare calves under the table: he wasn't wearing long pants today. "First, please let me assure you all that this Inspection has given me invaluable insights into Sec Gen behavioral patterns that will contribute greatly to my own ongoing research. But we all know that the health of our own careers depends on the health of our nation, and it was my honor to be asked to help monitor and nurture the overall performance of one of the bioregion's top-performing communities. Let me introduce my esteemed colleagues, who after all have done all the work on this report!"

People laughed and the other officers smiled, acknowledging the compliment. Behind them, Helium, as if alarmed, raised his wings. Dr. Blesserson introduced his fellow officers, reeling off lists of their accomplishments, and the marquee fell quiet again.

Beside Astra, Meem's breath had slowed. She was probably meditating, as Modem, with a wink, had suggested they do during the reading of the report. The best thing to do, Astra decided, was to concentrate on her own breath and keep watching Silver. If she never caught Dr. Blesserson's eye the whole ceremony could pass without any trouble. He might not even recognize her, after all. She must look very different now she was nearly thirteen.

The other two officers were Inspectors, a rank below Dr. Blesserson, but clearly experienced community investigators. The woman gave her report on Code House, talking about each team and praising their biggest commercial successes, including the gro-light sensitive fruit trees for north-facing balconies. These, she said, had made a significant contribution to Or's financial stability. She named the top members of the urbag team, including Sorrel, who all stood up to be applauded. She also named Klor, for his work on the Visitor team. Or, she said, was fast becoming a must-see spot on a national tour, extending the average length of Is-Land visits by 1.63 days and bringing valuable tourist revenues to the bioregion. Klor stood up to receive his accolades and Meem and Astra both turned and craned to see him. On the other side of the aisle, he rose above the sea of bodies, his face creased up in a big Klor smile. He nodded at the officer, then waved his hand dismissively at his Or colleagues as if batting away a fly. You could almost hear him thinking, *Pah! I did nothing! They came to see the apple trees, not me!* People laughed, and Meem and Astra hugged each other, only stifling their giggles when Nimma shot them a warning look from the table.

Silver finished preening and hunched on the rail. The Owleons were so striking, overlooking the tent, totems of Or's exceptional role in the bioregion and beyond. Astra was expecting Hokma to be named next, for her work with the Edition Four birds, but the female officer concluded with some words of general appreciation for Wise House, which continued to contribute greatly to the vital work of national defense, not to mention—and here she turned and gestured up at the birds— ceremonial marquee decoration.

As if on cue, Helium let loose a dropping, a white streak that hurtled to the grass behind Dr. Blesserson. The tent exploded with laughter, startling the birds, who flapped up from the rail, straining at their leads. Silver squawked and molted, losing a feather, which floated down to the ground behind the female officer, who was explaining the joke to her colleagues. Dr. Blesserson grinned and placed his hand on his head, as if for protection.

Astra frowned. The Owleons weren't *decorations*. They were here representing Gaia's creatures. It wasn't funny if they had to shit, and it wasn't right to scare them. But the adults clapped loudly, the female officer bowed her head and then the tall male Inspector, who was also a top woodsman, was giving his report on Craft House. He praised Or's national reputation for excellence in fabric work, and named Nimma and her team, who stood and bobbed quickly, clapping each other. The officer concluded by commenting that, considering its forest location and fine stands of lacebark, Craft House could offer more in the way of woodwork, but he noted that Or had recently made an application to IMBOD to fund two new woodcarvers and a studio extension, and he assured Craft House that he would personally recommend that this funding was approved. This announcement was met with the biggest round of applause yet.

Now it was Dr. Blesserson's turn. Astra knew she ought to look at him now, in case later, on the Kezcam video, her head was out of line with the other children's. She tried to focus, not on his face but on the marquee flap behind him. Dr. Blesserson tapped his Tablette screen, glanced up over his glasses and began.

"To me falls the honor of delivering the report's overall conclusions, and the final recommendations of the panel. The full text will be available on your Tablettes tomorrow, and we are all understandably looking forward to one of Or's mouth-watering banquets, so you will be delighted to hear that I am going to keep this brief." Again, people chuckled. Even though he was head and shoulders taller than most people, and a genius, Dr. Blesserson, Astra realized, had a way of making himself seem unimportant.

"I am delighted to report that Or has excelled in nearly all of its long-term objectives, and indeed has surpassed several not even dreamt of at the time of the last Inspection. The committee has no hesitation in awarding another Outstanding result."

A tumult of applause shook the marquee. Nimma was beaming like a sunflower, and Ahn looked up from his Tablette to cast one of his pale, crooked smiles over the audience. Meem threw herself at Astra and nearly knocked her over with a hug. Behind them adults were whispering, *Well done!* and, *Oh, what a relief.*

Dr. Blesserson raised his hands and waited for silence. "I must add, however," he went on, "that the committee is concerned that Or's high performance to date may be in part due to the heavy workloads undertaken by some of the founding members. While dedication and commitment are of course to be commended, we note that over time such work rates may paradoxically result in a drop-off of efficiency. We note, for example, that attendance at Or Parents' Committee meetings has recently been, shall we say, less than consistent. We therefore recommend that the position of School Spoke be offered to a new member of the community, allowing Dr. Hokma Blesser to concentrate on the Code work for which she is justly renowned."

A man behind Astra made a little "hmp" sound in his throat. Otherwise you could have heard a sparrow's heartbeat in the tent. Nimma was still smiling, but she wasn't looking in Hokma's direction; Ahn was back at his Kezcamming. Astra's face flooded with rage. She wanted to run up to the table and bang her fists on the cloth and shout at Dr. Blesserson: *Hokma works all day, and she looks after me and Lil at night. She knows all about Or-kid education and who cares if she doesn't have time to go to frigging meetings to talk about washing frigging diapers.*

She wanted Helium and Silver to shit all over the head table, but the meeting was rolling smoothly on, like a granite boulder crushing wildflowers in its path. "Thank you, Dr. Blesserson," Nimma said. "We of course take the committee's recommendation in the generous spirit in which it is offered, and will act on it immediately."

"I have no doubt that you will." Dr. Blesserson addressed the audience, looking out into the middle distance, although he must have been perfectly aware that his sister was sitting in the second row. "Just as I have no doubt that Dr. Hokma Blesser's achievements will figure prominently again in the next Inspection Report. But let me finish on an uplifting note. I once again offer my congratulations to you all for maintaining your stellar position in the IMBOD Community Rankings. I have also been asked to make a special announcement on behalf of the Or Steering Committee. It therefore gives me huge pleasure to officially announce that just this morning in Sippur the Steppes Wheel Meet awarded the contract for the design of its new Bioregional Arts and Crafts Gallery to your Founding Member Ahn Orson, who has beaten out top candidates from all over the country. This prize is another gilded laurel leaf in Or's crown, and I can think of no better way to end this meeting than with a standing ovation to Ahn, and to you all."

Dr. Blesserson and the two Inspectors stood up and clapped vigorously, raising their hands above their heads. They were sky-clad except for their armbands, hydrobelts and boots. Wearing shorts or a dhoti in Or, Astra realized, as she and everyone in the tent got to their feet, would have been a big mistake. Dr. Blesserson had come to Or to attack his own sister, to tell the Or Steering and Parents' Committees what to do. He needed to pretend he was one of the team, not a city Gaian who thought he was smarter and more sophisticated than mountain Is-Landers. But that, Astra now knew, was *exactly* what he was.

2.8

Astra trailed out of the marquee side exit with the other Or-kids. Meem and Yoki were mimicking Klor's funny hand wave, and Peat was enthusing about the possible new woodcarving studio. Astra detached herself and searched on the lawn for Hokma. There she was: standing at the side exit talking to her brother. *How could she do that?* He had just humiliated her in front of the whole of Or. All over the lawn adults were sneaking glances at her Shelter mother. "Our first recommendation," an urbagger near Astra murmured. "Well, I suppose it had to happen sometime."

"She *has* looked tired lately," one of Klor's team replied, sympathetically.

"She's up at Wise House the whole time with that feral child," another man commented. "Seems like a sensible decision to me."

Lil was clinging to Hokma's hand, her legs crossed as if she were a seven-year-old who needed to pee. As Astra watched, Hokma pushed her forward and introduced her to Dr. Blesserson. He did exactly what he'd done to Astra at his house: glance briefly at her as if she were an inconvenience. Lil leaned against Hokma and averted her head. Her eyes met Astra's and she stuck out her tongue.

It was one thing to observe Lil's mental illness when they were alone. It was entirely another to have to cope with it in public, especially in front of Dr. Blesserson. Astra stepped back quickly into the warm crush of adults milling on the lawn. But it was too late: Hokma had seen her and was waving her over.

She trudged across the grass back toward the tent. Hokma reached out and pulled her into the circle.

"You remember Astra, don't you?" she asked her brother. Her tone was clipped.

"How could I forget your charming Shelter daughter, Hokma?" Dr. Blesserson gave a wince of a smile. "And how is Astra?"

"She's *fine*," Astra snarled. Beside her, Lil emitted a delighted little grunt.

"Ah, not so emotionally composed today, are we, Astra?" Dr. Blesserson examined her coolly. "Isn't it a shame, Hokma, that she hasn't turned out as even-tempered as her peers." He reached forward, took Astra by the chin and twisted her face into the light. "And the Serum hasn't prevented her acne. Such a rare case. *What* a pity."

"I don't have frigging *acne*!" Astra wrenched herself away and stood shuddering beside Lil. Acne was when you had pimples *everywhere*. It was an Old World disease, like teaby and HIV and cold sores. No one in Is-Land had acne anymore because the oatmilk was treated to prevent it. She just had the occasional pimple, that was all. Maybe the Sec Gens didn't get them, but Torrent did sometimes, and so did Holaa. She'd bet anything that Dr. Blesserson had had pimples too. When you looked close up, he had little indents in his cheeks, pockmarks that definitely weren't frigging happy-face *dimples*.

"Astra," Hokma said sharply. "She can be a little testy when she's hungry," she said to her brother in that same taut voice. "She's doing very well at school, you'll be pleased to know. Top of the class in Language Skills, and top ten percent in Code."

"Impressive." Dr. Blesserson didn't sound impressed. He sounded like he was taunting her. "Let's hear some of those Language Skills then, Astra."

Her face was hot and her palms were damp. She didn't want to recite a poem in Asfarian: she wanted to kick his shins.

Dr. Blesserson chuckled. "Don't worry, Astra. Language Skills are always the first to desert us when we're nervous."

She wasn't going to let him think she couldn't speak. She drew herself up and threw out her chest. "You shouldn't have demoted Hokma," she declared. "She was doing a good job. She only didn't come to meetings because she was looking after me and Lil."

"*Demoted.*" He smiled a big smile now. His teeth were exceedingly white and shiny, as if fresh from a kiln. "That *is* top flight vocabulary for a little girl. Well done, Astra."

Little girl. She opened her mouth to fire back, but Hokma squeezed her hand and spoke first. "Dr. Blesserson didn't demote me, Astra," she said brusquely. "The committee made a recommendation and he delivered it, that's all."

"*I'm* hungry," Lil butted in. "You said there was going to be a *banquet.*" She was lolling against Hokma now, and pulling on her arm. It was impossible to believe she was the same person Astra had argued with and Gaia-played with two days before. Astra folded her own arms across her chest. Hokma was defending her worst enemy and Lil was acting like a spoiled infant. *Both* of them must be mentally ill.

"Ah, the joys of parenthood. Shall I let you fill these rude little stomachs, then, Hokma?" Dr. Blesserson was scanning the lawn. "I should really have a word with Dr. Grassmere."

"Of course, Samrod. And congratulations again on your appointment." Hokma stood aside and he strode off without so much as a goodbye glance at Astra or Lil.

"You've got a rude tummy," Lil crowed, poking her in the belly.

Astra swatted her hand away. "*He's* the rude one."

"Astra," Hokma spoke in a low voice. "He's just doing his job. I don't want you to go complaining about him to *anyone.* Understand?"

Astra toed the dirt. "I'm *not* testy when I'm hungry. I'm not even hungry." Her stomach was, in fact, grumbling, but she didn't feel like going into Core House. Was Lil going to sit with her and the Or-kids? What if she said crazy things? Right now she was swinging off Hokma's arm like . . . like a *chimpanzee,* pulling at an angle to the lawn and attracting the attention of the adults. Why didn't Hokma tell her to behave?

But Hokma was laughing at *her.* "Oh?" She tousled Astra's hair. "Sounds like someone's tummy thinks differently."

Lil shot her a knowing look. *They speak to you like you're kids*, she'd said on the ledge.

"I want to take the birds back to Wise House," Astra complained. "They were frightened in the tent."

"They'll be fine. Lil and I will take the trainees later, and Helium and Silver can fly back. Do you want to sit with the Or-kids at dinner, or with me and Lil?"

Lil got to sit with the adults? At a table with *candles*? "With *you*," Astra muttered.

She was afraid that Dr. Blesserson would be at their table, but he and the other IMBOD officers were seated at an oval table at the top end of the room with Nimma and Klor and other members of the Steering Committee. Normally this table held flowers, but when guests came it was put into service for dinner. In front of it, the trestle tables were draped with white cloths and the older Or-kids were helping the kitchen team put bread rolls and roasted nuts and seeds on all the tables, and wine flagons, candles and tinderboxes out for the adults. Astra was too short to see if there were empty chairs anywhere, but Hokma said there was space at the table that ran along the far left wall of the room, beneath the high windows with Sorrel and Mr. Ripenson and Moon and Aesop. As Astra passed the Sec Gen table, she gave Meem and Yoki a little wave. They waved back, Meem's face lighting up with amazement as she realized Astra was sitting with the adults today. Yoki's expression hardened, though, when he saw Lil.

Nimma's team had specially washed the long white dining-hall curtains for today and they floated gauzily down behind the table like angel wings from a fairy tale. In front of them, Mr. Ripenson and Sorrel were lighting the candles, Mr. Ripenson flicking the tinderbox wheel with his thumb and Sorrel catching the spark with long, green-tipped matches that released the scent of sulfur when they flared. You learned how to make matches and work the tinderbox when you were fourteen and joined the kitchen team. Until then, candle paraphernalia was strictly off-limits. Fascinated, Astra nudged Lil, but she gave Mr. Ripenson a disdainful glance and craned her neck up at the high timbered ceiling. Just because she could start a flame with her breath.

"A little fire and brimstone," Mr. Ripenson said to Hokma. "Seems suitable for a visit from the avenging technocrats."

She laughed. "Oh, Samrod's always been a stickler for the rules. You should have seen the way he ran our dolls' hospital. Woe betide me if I ran out of bandages."

The other adults laughed too, but Astra stood awkwardly at the top of the table. There were five empty seats, three on one side and two on the other. Was she allowed to sit where she liked?

"You two go in first." Hokma nodded at the three chairs on the far side of the table. "Astra, sit next to Sorrel."

"I don't want to sit in the middle," Lil whined. "I want to sit at the end. Next to Astra."

Whining never got you anywhere with Hokma. Astra waited for her to tell Lil to do as she was told. But Hokma, unbelievably, sighed and said, "Okay. I'll sit next to Sorrel. Lil, if you need to use the bathroom, it's over there." She pointed across the dining hall at the washroom door. "If you want to leave Core House, you can wait for me at the swings and I'll come and take you back to Wise House."

"But—" Astra protested. She didn't want to sit beside Lil if the girl was going to act like a poorly trained simian the whole time. If she was sitting at the adults' table, she wanted to sit among the *adults*.

"Astra. It's her first time at table. Cooperate, please."

Hokma squeezed in between the chairs and the curtains to take the seat next to Sorrel and her enormous baby belly. Lil grabbed Astra's arm and gave a triumphant little hop. Astra pulled away and dragged out her own chair.

"Hi, Astra. Hi, Lil." The adults greeted the girls, and Astra muttered hellos back. Lil sat down beside her and bounced on her chair. Hokma reached over and pulled the candlestick away from Lil, putting it right in front of Astra, which was a relief. The two seats opposite her were empty and beyond the flame she had a full view of the near end of the oval table. If it wasn't for the candle she'd be staring at Dr. Blesserson the whole meal. At least he had his back to her, thank Gaia.

"Anyone sitting here?" Russett was towering over the table. Russett was Torrent's Code-Shelter father, tall like his son, but bulky. His broad chest was covered with curly silver hair and his brown skin was freckled and reddish in places: he was really light-skinned, but deeply tanned. The hair on his head was short and thinning, but Nimma had told Astra that when he was younger it had been even longer than Torrent's. Russett was good at archery—he had coached the Or-kid team a few years ago and Astra had liked all the exercises he'd made them do to strengthen their back, shoulder and abdominal muscles. But he could get angry if the team lost and in the end the Parents' Committee had decided that the younger children needed a more "philosophical" coach. Now he helped train the older children for their IMBOD Service fitness exams.

"You are, friend." Mr. Ripenson pulled out the chair next to him, opposite Astra.

"Hello, Astra," Russett said, sliding the candle back up toward the top of the table so he could see her face. "How's the petal-sewing going?"

Hokma had noted the candle move; she caught Russett's eye and jerked her chin toward Lil, who was kicking her chair leg with her heel. The knocking vibrations were extremely annoying. "Okay," Astra replied, but Russett wasn't looking at her anymore.

"So this is the famous Lil," he said, moving the candle back a fraction. "How do you do, Lil?"

Lil didn't raise her head; she just started twiddling her bread knife on the table in time to the thud of her heels against her chair legs. Astra trod on her foot and she stopped the kicking at last.

"Shy, hey?" Mr. Ripenson laughed.

"First time at adult table." Russett poured himself a glass of red wine from the flagon beside the candle. "Bound to be tongue-tied. Are they allowed some wine, Hokma? That'll get 'em talking."

"No," Hokma said firmly. "Torrent, please take these away."

Torrent had arrived at the end of the table with a serving cart. Hokma reached in front of the candle and pushed the wine glass that had been set for Astra up toward Lil's. As the kitchen team always did when preparing or serving food, Torrent was wearing a red handspun linen apron, which he'd folded down over his waist to show off his pecs and abs. He put the glasses on the bottom shelf of the cart, then gave Lil and Astra a wink.

"Come and help do the dishes later, Astra," he said, "and we'll crack open the sloe gin."

"Torrent," Russett reproved, but the other adults were laughing. The joke was on her, though, and Astra glowered down at the tablecloth. Beside her, Torrent filled a plate with beetroot, apple and walnut salad and handed it to Lil. She grasped it in both hands and set it down in front of her.

"We pass the plates down the table, Lil," Hokma said. Staring openly back at Torrent, who was taking full advantage of the opportunity to inspect her, Lil plucked a slice of beetroot from the plate and popped it into her mouth.

"*Mmmm*," she declared.

Astra didn't know if she wanted to giggle or jab Lil with her elbow.

"Okay, never mind for today," Hokma said. "Torrent, just pass the plates to Astra please. Lil, use your knife and fork. And wait until everyone's got their salad to start."

"Isn't Astra teaching Lil how to behave?" Torrent asked breezily as he passed her a salad. "She's been minding my manners for years."

Hokma and Moon chuckled, but Russett was not amused. "Torrent, you're serving. This is not the time for jokes."

Astra passed the plate down and made a face at Torrent, who just grinned and cast more curious looks over Lil as he finished serving. Russett was the last to get a plate, and when he raised his wine glass and announced, "To Gaia," everyone began eating.

The starter was good, especially with the crusty bread to mop up the horseradish and honey dressing, but soon the adults were ignoring her and Lil was still keeping mum, finger-picking at her food. She should have chosen to eat with the Sec Gens. This was boring. Russett and Sorrel were talking urbag business, and Hokma was explaining something to Mr. Ripenson, drawing an invisible diagram on the tabletop with her finger as Moon listened in. The teacher smiled at her, and for a moment she hoped he might tell Hokma about Gaia-play lessons and how she'd contributed to the discussion today. Then she could explain further what she'd meant, and call him *Vishnu*, which she was ordinarily too shy to do. But at the same time she didn't want Mr. Ripenson to talk about school, not in front of Lil. The adults' conversations melded with the general hubbub of voices and chiming of cutlery on plates.

Lil turned to Astra and nodded toward the head table, where the members of the Steering Committee were sitting with the IMBOD officers. "*Someone* likes Dr. Blesserson," she whispered.

Looking around the candle flame, Astra followed Lil's gaze. Dr. Blesserson and Ahn were laughing loudly. Ahn was throwing his head back and Dr. Blesserson briefly put his hand on Ahn's shoulder. Across the table, Nimma was smiling at them and saying something in the ear of the female Inspector; Klor was grinning and wagging his bushy eyebrows.

"Drink up, girls." Hokma refilled their water glasses.

"Thank you, Hokma," Lil said brightly. They were the first polite words she had said at table. The adults smiled broadly at her and each other.

"You're welcome, Lil," Hokma replied. Under the table Lil nudged Astra's leg with her knee.

"Thank you, Hokma." Astra reached for her glass and took a sip.

She understood now. *It was all an act.* Lil was playing the adults like a game, acting like an infant so that she could get her own way, sit in the best vantage point and observe the room without distraction. She and Lil finished their salads in silence, but it was a purposeful silence now. They were alert to the Steering Committee table, to the way Dr. Blesserson was dominating the conversation, using his hand gestures to attract everyone's attention, but turning respectfully to Ahn every few minutes to allow him to address the group as well. Congruence was serving their table, and when she came to dish out the main course, Ahn placed his hand on the small of her back and pushed her toward Dr. Blesserson, who looked up at her and said something that made her smile. Ahn gave her back a little pat and dropped his arm.

"Enjoyed that salad?" Hokma asked.

"Yes, thanks," they replied in unison.

"Good girls."

Then Torrent was back, collecting their salad dishes and passing out bowls of tofu and alt-prawn gumbo with brown rice.

"There's brandy in the broth," he said as Astra took her own bowl and set it down in front of her. "Better keep an eye on the girls."

"*Thank* you, Torrent," Russett said. Astra remembered that tone from archery coaching. He didn't mean "thank you," he meant "*that's frigging enough*." Torrent was silent as he passed around the rest of the dishes.

"He's a bold one, that boy," Sorrel said as Torrent trundled the cart back to the kitchen.

"Takes after his Code father, does he?" Mr. Ripenson joked.

"Takes after his Code mother, actually," Russett replied, shortly.

Mr. Ripenson glanced over the table at Sorrel, and Astra remembered that Torrent's Code mother had gone to work in New Zonia and never come back; that was why Russett had come to live in Or. Torrent had two Shared Shelter mothers now, a pair of Gaia-bonded women he stayed with in New Bangor every other week, but Russett never settled long; he had had various Gaia partners.

"I like gumbo," Lil announced. She had saffron-colored spots on her chin and her eyes were gleaming.

"Yes, gumbo's good, Lil," Mr. Ripenson agreed as Russett drained his wine glass. "I'm glad you're here to share it with us." Lil didn't reply. She was lifting another brimming spoonful to her lips.

"She's very helpful in the kitchen," Hokma said approvingly. "She'll be a good cook herself one day."

The broth was rich and spicy, and maybe it did go to Astra's head a little. Spoon in hand, she forgot to spy on Ahn and Dr. Blesserson and instead concentrated on not spilling a drop. Beside her, Lil was doing the same. Her leg was still pressed against Astra's and as their spoons dipped in the gumbo and the chilies and brandy warmed her blood, it began to feel as though they were one being: a strange three-legged, two-headed creature, its life force swirling between its two hearts. By the time Torrent arrived to take the dishes away and bring them their dessert, Astra's Gaia garden was humming.

Dessert was a slice of chocolate torte with raspberry sauce. It was almost unbearable to have to wait to eat it until Torrent's cart was empty.

At last he was offering the last slice to Russett. "*Voilà, Papa,*" he said, flourishing the dish.

"*Ooh la la.*" Moon laughed. "Who says French is a dead language?"

Russett raised his hands to take the plate. Torrent pulled it away. "Or are you still on a diet?" he asked.

"*Boy!*" Russett slammed his palm down on the table. "If I have to tell you one more time to show some *respect* for the table, you'll be running Kinbat laps for a *month.*"

The candlestick was trembling and Hokma's hand shot out to steady the base. Lil dropped her spoon on the tablecloth and put her hands over her mouth. Her body was shaking. Astra couldn't look at her.

"I thought you wanted to lose weight." Torrent's tone was hurt, that of the unjustly accused, but his eyes were silently laughing with Lil.

"Your father's right, Torrent," Hokma said. "Servers shouldn't make personal remarks to table-sitters. Please apologize to Russett or I'll have to make a note of this in your school file."

Torrent raised his eyebrows. "Sorry, Hokma. I thought you weren't the—"

"She's the School Spoke until the Parents' Committee appoints her successor," Russett thundered. "Now you apologize to her too, you insolent cub!"

Torrent gave a little bow. "*Mesdames et Messieurs,* your banquet waiter enjoyed your company so much he forgot he wasn't at home with his esteemed Code father. He unreservedly apologizes for any misunderstanding, offense or inconvenience caused."

Torrent turned on his heel and wheeled the cart away. Russett shook his head, like a dog clearing its ears of water. "If I'd known what he'd be like at this age," he declared, "I'd have volunteered him for the Security Serum trials when he was a baby."

The adults laughed, but Astra wasn't sure Russett was joking. His cheeks were red and his eyes were hard blue stones.

"He's a bright boy," Hokma said. "He's just trying out a bit of banter."

"Fine for you to say," Russett barked. "You don't have to worry about Astra talking back every chance she gets. She was a handful as a youngster, but look at her now. Good as gold."

Mr. Ripenson looked troubled. "Perhaps we shouldn't talk about the children's behavior in front of—" he began, but Hokma cut him off.

"If you're having difficulties with Torrent, Russett," she said, "you can always talk to the Parents' Committee."

"Kids don't listen to *committees*," Russett bellowed. Beside Mr. Ripenson, Aesop started to cry. Russett lowered his voice. "And I don't appreciate being told how to bring up my Code child by someone who doesn't even go to half the meetings."

Moon's eyes widened. Mr. Ripenson made a little moue at Hokma, as if to say "don't worry." Russett stabbed his torte with his fork, took a big mouthful and washed it down with more wine. He clunked the glass back down on the table and the wine sloshed up the edges. Aesop's wails subsided as Moon pressed him to her chest.

"I'm *full*." Lil broke the silence. "Can I eat my cake at Wise House?"

Or-kids never got to take Core House food home with them. That rule existed so that Core House plates and mugs didn't end up in bedrooms or under bushes all over the bioregion. But Hokma drained her wine glass and pushed her own torte aside.

"You've done very well, Lil. If you can carry your plate all the way without dropping it, you can eat your cake at home. Astra, you can take yours to the Or-kids' table if you like."

Hokma and Lil stood up. They were leaving. Astra got to her feet too. She wanted to go with them and talk with Lil about what they'd seen, but it was clear that she was being ordered to join Meem, Yoki and Peat and the other Sec Gens. Trailing behind Hokma and Lil with her dessert plate, she noticed Dr. Blesserson's head watching his sister's departure. Hokma didn't acknowledge anyone sitting at the oval table. She kissed Astra goodbye at the Or-kids' table and Lil, suddenly, leaned forward and kissed Astra too, lightly on the corner of the mouth. Then she stared intently into Astra's eyes as if sealing a pact. Something had been definitely been decided between them, though watching Lil leave, Astra had no idea what. She sat down, a tremor running through her. Maybe Lil didn't have schizophrenia. Maybe she was just very good at lying.

"She doesn't look feral," Peat said. Astra realized he was talking about Lil.

"She's got tidier hair than Astra," Meem laughed.

To be fair, thanks to all the stuff her dad had told her, Lil probably didn't know half the time that she was lying. "She's not *feral*," Astra said haughtily, spearing the last piece of torte with her fork. "She just isn't educated yet, that's all."

2.9

"Hokma's going to Gaia-worship with Ahn tonight," Lil whispered, her breath caressing Astra's ear. "In the meadow. Do you want to sneak out and watch?"

It was Wise House siesta time and they were lying in Astra's bed, which they now shared when Astra was staying. Hokma was in the lab, doing her weekend clean. Astra shifted onto her side. Lil's eyes were glinting, daring her to say yes.

"How do you know that?" she asked, sharply.

"They did last night. I followed her when she went to meet him. They argued first, but then they lay down. And last Full Moon she went out for three nights in a row."

Astra raised herself on her elbow. "You've been watching them Gaia-play?"

Lil rolled onto her back and idly stretched her arms up to the ceiling. "Not yet. I was too far away. But I checked today and I found a spot we can see from."

"No we can't," Astra said firmly. "Gaia play is private. You're not allowed to watch other people doing it." That was Rule 3: an Is-Land law. She'd tried to tell Lil the rules but as she'd suspected, Lil hadn't been a bit interested. Still, it wasn't against the rules to get a head start on

Gaia play—Tedis had asked Mr. Ripenson, and then the next week told the class that he had been playing with the daughter of an international long-stay visitor. The daughter was fifteen, he'd said, and had already been penetrated, but he, of course, had practiced self-control, even though he knew he wouldn't bond with her because she was going back to New Zonia soon. Everyone had been impressed and for a moment Astra had itched to tell the class about her and Lil. That would show Tedis he wasn't the only one ahead of his age group. She had suppressed the temptation, though. Yoki hated Lil and she didn't want to upset him or inadvertently say anything that might make Mr. Ripenson suspect she was bonding.

Because she wasn't. She and Lil didn't make plans together, or promises or sacrifices, they just played again—out by the watercress stream, or quietly in the loft during siesta when Hokma was sleeping, with Astra making sure they didn't break any of the rules. Yesterday, by the stream, she had even tested Lil, pretending to feel ill and saying she wanted to stop. Lil hadn't been very sympathetic, but she had stopped kissing her. She'd rolled on her back, twirled a strand of her hair in the air and said, "You should go and ask Hokma for some medicine, then." Astra had waited a minute and then said she felt better, and they'd continued.

Later, though, Lil had whispered, "If I was a boy I would stick my Gaia plow right inside you, whenever I wanted," and afterward she'd asked Astra if there was a boy at school she liked, all of which made Astra feel uncomfortable. She'd said no, but when Lil pressed she said that Tedis Sonnenson was a good cricketer, but he told a lot of stupid jokes. Lil had nodded and said sagely, "My dad said boys are stupid. He said they don't grow up until they have a baby, so if I bonded with one I might have to put up with him being an idiot for a while." It was stupid, of course, to say that all boys were stupid just because they were boys; Astra had tried to tell Lil about gender then, but Lil didn't know any boys so they couldn't have a proper discussion. Astra had given up and they'd lain in silence on the warm rocks until Astra had suggested going back to see the ancestors again. Lil had refused to take her. She said they had to wait until the autumn. The ancestors needed lots of time alone to talk with Gaia.

"Gaia play isn't private everywhere." Lil sniffed her armpit, then folded her arms behind her head. "In other countries people make Tablette videos of themselves Gaia-playing and put them on the internet for everyone to see."

"They do *not*," Astra scoffed. Lil had said a lot of preposterous things over the last few weeks, but this really took the spelled cake.

"They do." Lil sat up, her head grazing the low ceiling of the loft. "It's called borno. My dad told me. Before he returned to Gaia. I told you: he said I had to know everything about the world."

My dad said this. My dad said that. Astra was getting sick of it. Lil's dad had apparently traveled for three years after Code College and had returned to Is-Land oozing bizarre and unnecessary information. Admittedly, some of the things he'd told Lil were interesting: men who wore white dresses and danced in whirling circles to worship the moon; Old World communities where people rolled cheeses down hills and chased them with a wooden spoon; a hotel made of glass and shaped like a ship, where twenty thousand people had survived the Dark Time drinking fizzy wine that Lil swore tasted like berry biscuits. But others were horrific: countries where people sucked sheep brains through straws, or lived in underground cities where they never saw the sun; cities where women paid doctors to stuff their breasts with plastic bags to make them look bigger. She didn't want to hear any more of that stuff. "Yeah, well," she snorted, "that's the reason we're Gaians, isn't it, so we don't have to do disgusting things like play borno, or—or—or eat megafauna."

It was mean, she knew, to throw the hunting in Lil's face, but it was the only way to shut her up. She'd done it once before and Lil had looked furious and not spoken for an hour, until Astra had been afraid she would tell Hokma. But she hadn't squealed, and this time she didn't react with hurt. Instead she narrowed her eyes and curled her upper lip. "If you ever tasted real spit-roast chicken you'd never eat that pathetic alt-chicken again," she declared.

Astra drew breath to reply, but as she was trying to think what to say, she heard the lab doors grumbling open onto the veranda. The girls froze, then rapidly slid back down between the sheets. The bathroom door clicked shut and a minute later the faint sound of the shower came whistling through the thick straw-bale walls.

Astra's heart was galloping in her chest. How did Lil always do this to her? Spin things around, make her feel flushed and disoriented, like she was running a race with no finish line. As she was trying to sort out her thinking, Lil slipped her fingers into the crease of her elbow. "I'm sorry, Astra," she whispered. "You're right. My dad said that borno is bad, and if I ever go to New Zonia when I grow up I must be careful not to do it by accident."

Lil nudged closer so her bare leg was touching Astra's and her chin was resting on Astra's shoulder. Lil's nipple was hard now. The feeling of it there, pressing into her arm, was like a button: a Gaia button, stitched on Gaia's eternal shawl. Between Astra's legs there was another button, and it was quietly throbbing.

"That's okay," she whispered back. "You didn't have a Tablette, so he had to give you lessons from what he remembered."

"But it's not always wrong to watch other people Gaia-play." Lil's mouth was in Astra's hair and her hand was drifting down Astra's arm. "My dad said that before, way before the Non-Landers and the Pioneers, there were temples to Gaia all over Is-Land. To celebrate Her, the temple priests and priestesses Gaia-played in front of everyone. You could come and watch them, or you could come and play with someone too."

Lil's hand slipped under the sheet and settled lightly on Astra's stomach, light as a butterfly on a petal.

"But that's with permission," Astra objected weakly.

"Don't you ever like to play pretend?"

The pulse between Astra's legs had quickened. It was shooting tendrils of heat through her belly. Astra placed her hand on Lil's. "Sometimes," she whispered.

Lil stroked Astra's fingers. "Ahn and Hokma are the high priest and high priestess," she crooned. "We're the new young priestesses who have to learn how to worship Gaia."

Astra wanted to play pretend, wanted to say that Lil should stand behind her while they watched and kiss her neck and cup her breasts in her hands. But the Tablette video playing in her head got stuck when the camera pointed at Hokma and Ahn. Hokma was her Shelter mother. She was solid and logical and always the same and her job was to look after Astra. She knew that Astra and Lil were Gaia-playing—yesterday she'd asked Astra if things were going better now with Lil and when Astra had nodded, she'd said, "If you have any questions about Gaia play, come and ask me. It isn't always as natural as it seems." But Hokma hadn't asked to watch them, and Astra didn't want to watch her with Ahn either. Ahn was skinny, so skinny he was almost an ancestor already. You could see his bones through his skin, his gray eyes were always look-ing somewhere far away and his Gaia plow was pale pink like a worm. She didn't want to see him clutching Hokma, leeching her of all her Gaia Power. What if Ahn infected her with his emptiness and Hokma started looking like an ancestor too?

Except Lil wanted to see Ahn and Hokma together, and Lil was somehow making her feel good. Good and bad at the same time. Why did Lil always start a war inside her?

"I don't know," she whimpered.

Lil squeezed her hand. "We can watch for just five minutes. Just to see his Gaia plow get big. Then we can come back here and practice."

In the bathroom, the shower stopped. Astra's heart stopped with it. "She's coming," she gasped. She twisted onto her side away from Lil and pulled her knees up to her chest.

Lil curled herself around Astra's back. "She's still in the shower. She's touching herself and thinking about him."

"He won't come tonight. He never comes when I'm here."

Lil draped her arm around Astra's waist. "I bet he will. He'll meet her in the flying field like he did last night."

"Well, I'm not going."

Lil removed her arm, and rolled onto her back. "Fine. I'll go with-out you."

The bathroom door opened and shut and Hokma trod down the veranda toward the living room. She entered quietly and climbed the ladder to her own loft. Through half-shut lashes, Astra watched her ascend. She was wrapped in a blue towel, and her wet hair was neatly combed. Her eyepatch was hanging around her wrist; up in the loft she set it on the little table by the futon, then undid her towel. For a moment Astra could see the strong curves of her belly, and her lolling breasts with their spreading brown nipples. Then she lay down with her back to the room and pulled the sheet up to her waist.

That was Hokma: clean and cool and calm. She would wake up at exactly half past three and fix them all a pitcher of ice water. Then she would feed and fly the Owleons and work on her Code research. After dinner she would tell Astra and Lil Old World fairy tales on the veranda and then put them to bed. All of those things were ways of worshipping Gaia, but if she also wanted to go off to the meadow and do sticky, noisy things with Ahn, that was her business. Lil shouldn't be following her. And if she tried to, Astra would have to stop her.

After siesta Lil acted like nothing was wrong. She was chirpy with Hokma and helped bring the Owleons onto the lawn for their afternoon perch. Astra tethered Silver, stalked back to the veranda and commandeered the hammock. When Lil asked if she could join her, Astra refused. Hokma took her side for once and asked Lil to help her in the vegetable garden.

Astra watched them from the hammock, a lump rising in her throat. How had it happened? How had Lil picked her up higher than anyone ever had and then, in the same swinging arc, dumped her in a nest of brambles?

Hokma and Lil returned with armfuls of lettuce. "Don't forget you've got an appointment with Nimma this afternoon," Hokma said.

She *had* forgotten. It was a Blood & Seed ceremony hipbeads fitting and she hadn't wanted to mention it to Lil. Well, good, it would get her out of here, at least. She flipped herself out of the hammock and put on her hydropac.

"I'll walk with you, as far as West Gate," Lil said, following her around Wise House.

Astra shrugged. "Can't stop you."

They scrambled down the steep slope in silence, Lil's feet above her dislodging little stones that tumbled down around Astra's shoulders. At the crossroads, Astra turned toward Or and picked up her pace.

"Are you mad at me?" Lil's legs were longer, and she was right at Astra's shoulder.

"No."

"Then how come you're not talking?"

"I think you're stupid, that's all."

"Ooo-oh." Lil skipped over a branch in the path.

Astra was walking as fast as she could without breaking into a run. "Yes. It's stupid to watch them. It's *illegal*. They could catch you and then you'll be in big trouble. Where would you live if Hokma kicked you out?"

"I can live in the woods."

"No you can't. Not without your dad to help you."

"Yes I *can*. He taught me how." Lil's breath was on her neck, her voice a taunting gloat. "And he showed me how to get out of Is-Land if I want."

Astra spun around to face Lil. "You can't get past the Boundary. IMBOD would stop you."

"I can," Lil crowed. "He showed me a *secret* way."

Astra opened her mouth to spit, "He did *not*," but she hesitated. Lil's dad had shown her the ancestors. He did know secrets.

"It's a tunnel. If we go out tonight and watch, just for *five* minutes," Lil wheedled, "I'll show you."

"You said the tunnels were all blocked up," Astra challenged.

"I had to say that, didn't I? The tunnel is a *secret*."

"Where is it? What direction?" Astra asked suspiciously.

"It's two days' walking, northeast."

"We can't go out overnight."

"We can ask Hokma. I bet she'll let us."

"No, she won't. Northeast is the off-limits woodlands."

"Yeah, I know." Lil's eyes glittered. "I can show you the otters. We can tell Hokma we're camping by the stream."

Astra paused. She really wanted to see the otters. But there were bears in the off-limits woodlands, and wolves too, and everything Lil said was leading her deeper into potential big trouble. "I'm not lying to Hokma," she declared. Lil found it so easy to lie—she was probably lying about the otters *and* the tunnel. It was a trap—just a story, to get her to break the law. "You're making it up, anyway, to make me go with you tonight," she accused.

Lil regarded her with an expression of contempt. "You're scared," she said.

"I am not."

"Yes you are. You're scared of growing up."

"*What?*"

"All of you are, so cozy cozy. You're scared of being lonely or hungry or invaded. I'm not. I'm not scared of *anything*."

Astra gave her a scathing look. "You were scared when you came here asking for food. You were scared of living in the woods then."

"I wasn't scared. My dad told me to pretend I was, so that . . ." Lil trailed off.

"So that what?"

Lil tossed her head. "So that you'd feel sorry for me and be my new family."

"Yeah, well, it looks like you don't have *any* family and we're stuck with you, that's all. So don't go messing things up here."

Lil dug her heel into the dirt. She jutted her chin out at Astra. "I could really mess things up for you."

"Yeah? How?"

"I could tell Ahn that you haven't had your Security shot."

Astra's stomach seized and her heart boomed in her chest. For a sickening moment she thought she might pee right down her leg and into her sandal. But she didn't. Somehow she had known the threat was coming. She had been on her guard ever since the cliff—that was why she hadn't bonded with Lil. And that was why, even though her blood was flaring cold in her veins, she was able to control her bladder and her voice. "I have so had my shot," she replied.

"No, you haven't. You don't act like you're supposed to. You fight back and get upset easily. That's why you spend so much time with Hokma, away from the other kids. That's why Hokma wanted me to be your friend."

"You're nuts, Lil. You don't know any of the other Or-kids. Yoki gets way more upset than I do. No one will believe you."

"See. You're not even denying it. You're a terrible liar, Astra."

"I'm not *lying*." Her fists were clenched now.

"Yes you are. And you're getting upset. If I tell Ahn the truth he'll know right away that you're scared of being found out. He'll get you tested and then everyone will know I'm right."

"He won't." Astra took a deep breath. "He'll get *you* tested. For a *mental illness*. I'll tell him what you said to me on the cliff. I'll tell him you're *schizophrenic* and *paranoid*, like your dad, and you'll have to go and live in a neurohospice in Atourne."

Lil shrugged. "All the Or-adults will know that what I said is true. You'll find out in your IMBOD Service—if they even let you do your IMBOD Service once they find out you haven't had your shot."

Astra took a step closer, tapping her temple with her finger. "You know why you're nuts, Lil? Because if you tell Ahn I didn't have my shot, he and Dr. Blesserson will blame Hokma. Hokma's already in trouble. What if they punish her? What if they *lock her up*? Who'll look after you then? Huh?"

"I can look after myself. Anyway, they're going to find my family soon. Hokma told me."

"No, they're not. You don't have a family. You just have me and Hokma. You're crazy, Lil. *Crazy*."

Lil's face was pinched up like a lump of brown dough and her eyes were two narrow knife-slits. "You have to come and watch with me tomorrow night or I'm going to tell Ahn about you." She spun away and ran back up the path toward the crossroads. Astra stood looking after her, her heart thumping in her chest, tears boiling in the corners of her eyes.

2.10

"Stop fidgeting, Astra." Nimma tried to fasten the hipbeads around her back, but the two ends wouldn't meet. "Goodness! You're growing so fast. I'll have to add another inch before the clasp."

Astra was standing on a three-legged stool in Craft House. She shifted her weight again from one foot to the other. The fitting was supposed to be fun. She'd wanted to see all the different beads and help choose them and admire herself in the mirror wearing the sample string, but now the beads were digging into her flesh, her head was racing with furious thoughts and Nimma was annoyed with her.

"Nimma," she wheedled.

"Yes, dear?"

"Can I stay at the Earthship tonight?"

Nimma sighed. "I thought you were going back to Hokma, darling. I've said Meem can have her friends over. What's the matter with Wise House? You always stay there at the weekend."

She hadn't considered the possibility that Nimma would say no. Mostly Nimma complained that she never saw Astra anymore. "Lil's acting funny," she floundered. "It's because she isn't Sec Gen. She says mean things sometimes."

"Mean things—like what?"

This was dangerous. "I dunno—things I don't like—about Gaia play in New Zonia." It was the best she could do.

Nimma tutted. "Do you want me to talk to Hokma about it?"

She shouldn't have said anything. She shouldn't ask Nimma and Klor about anything Lil had said or did because any strange stories coming out of Wise House about IMBOD or broken Gaia-play rules might get her and Hokma into serious trouble. And she couldn't tell Hokma what Lil had threatened because the punishment for breaking Rule 3 was going into counseling, and if Lil was forced into counseling there was no telling what she might do. She might even tell the doctor about Astra's shot instead of Ahn.

She'd have to handle this herself. "No, it's okay. I'll go back. She changes her mind all the time, anyway. She's probably forgotten what she said by now."

"Good. You just try and forget it too. She had a very hard childhood and it's going to take her time to adjust to the way normal people live." Nimma put the sample string back in her sewing bag and slapped Astra gently on the hip. "You can get down now, darling. Why don't you stay here with me and do some petals before you go back up? That will calm you down."

It was like doing a scene in Role-Play class, eating dinner at Wise House that night. She and Lil said all the right words—"pass the salt please"; "what should we do tomorrow morning?"—but they were just acting, pretending, so that Hokma would think everything was normal. Afterward Hokma made them mugs of hot barley and oatmilk, and they sat on the veranda playing whist. They played three rounds, as usual, and everyone won once.

"Bedtime, girls." Hokma gathered the cards back together.

Lil flicked a little look at Astra, then gave a big yawn. "Okay, Hokma," she agreed.

Perhaps Lil really was tired. They'd hardly slept at all during siesta, after all. And surely Ahn would come very late, if he came at all. But though Astra closed her eyes immediately when she got into bed, she just lay awake on the edge of the futon, her body tense, Lil's breathing beside her stealthy and light, not hoarse and slow like it was when she was sleeping.

After what seemed like forever, she heard Hokma's loft ladder creak.

She sat up. "Where are you going?" she asked.

"Shh. I'm just getting a glass of water. I might sit on the veranda for a while. You go back to sleep."

Hokma padded out onto the veranda and shut the door softly behind her.

"She's going to meet him outside," Lil whispered triumphantly. "We can watch from the window and when they go into the woods, we can follow them."

Lil was clambering over her to the loft ladder.

Astra grabbed her leg. "Stay here, Lil. We can play priest and priestess while they're gone."

Lil shook her off. "They'll be gone for hours. We've got lots of time to come back and play."

She was halfway down the ladder. Astra lay in bed, clutching the sheet in her fists. She could just stay here—but then Lil might make good her threat and tell Ahn that she hadn't had her shot. And anyway, she couldn't let Lil spy on Hokma during Gaia worship. She'd been thinking hard all evening, and she had come up with a plan to stop her; two plans in fact. She would now have to put at least one of them into action.

"There he is." Lil was crouching at the back window, peering out across the lawn. Astra's fingers were gripping the sill. Over them she could see Ahn's head, his blond hair luminous and floating in the trees. Hokma was striding across the lawn toward him, her bottom like two bronze orbs in the glow from the veranda nightlight. There was an unfamiliar thin dark line around her hips. Was *Hokma* wearing *hipbeads*?

"As soon as she gets to the woods, we can leave," Lil instructed.

"They'll hear us. Let's just stay here."

"Stay if you want, but if you do I'll find Ahn tomorrow and tell him what I know."

Even though there was zero chance of being seen inside Wise House, Lil crept to the veranda door, hunched close to the wall, like a Boundary constable. She opened the door a crack and slipped out. Astra had no choice but to follow.

Outside, Lil ducked right to avoid the pool of light spilling onto the lawn. Keeping low to the ground, Astra went left. She was going to do this her way.

They met at the edge of the wood. Moonlight speckled the leaves and it was just possible to make out the glimmering shapes of individual trees. Lil put her finger to her lips and pointed at the path to the flying field. If Hokma and Ahn had gone down it, they must be nearly at the gate by now.

Lil took the lead, Astra close behind as they passed the back of the Owleon aviary and penetrated the forest. If only she could somehow fly Silver to Hokma, send her a message. But what would she say? And she couldn't stop, she had to keep close to Lil. The important thing was not to be heard. *Not yet.* It was impossible to move silently: twigs and leaves crunched underfoot and her breathing was a roar in her ears. But there were other noises in the forest too: distant screechings and abrupt scurryings, and everywhere the hushed sway of branches in the canopy. Surely Hokma and Ahn would be listening to each other. She had to reach them soon, before it was too late to interrupt.

The cedar hedge was towering ahead of them. There was the gate, a tall frame of silver bars. Between them, Astra could see Hokma and Ahn silhouetted in the moonlight flooding the field. They were standing up to their waists in the long grass, holding hands and stretching their arms up to the night sky. She moved back behind a pine trunk.

"They go to the top of the field, by the juniper tree," Lil whispered. "I saw where the grass is all flattened."

Lil hadn't gone further than this before. Maybe they could still go back. "They'll see us if we go through the gate," Astra objected. "It squeaks, and we'll be right in the open. C'mon, Lil, we've seen them Gaia-worshipping. We can go back now." That was Plan A: to convince Lil to abandon the mission.

"That was *nothing*. They'll be doing way better stuff than that. I bet she hangs off the tree. There's a hole in the hedge, further up, and then we can come up the dark side of the hill and watch from behind the rock pile."

It was like being in Debating class. You had to reject everything your opponent said. "What if they go to the rocks too?"

"We'll see them coming. We'll hide in the grass."

"What if they—?"

But Lil had set off up along the hedge. Astra kept pace. She was going too fast now to feel frightened.

"Here," Lil hissed. At their feet, there was a small gap between the hedge and the soil. Astra knelt. The soil had been dug out as if by animals, perhaps dogs, years ago when Or was new and community mammals were still allowed. There was fine dry dirt in the air; it tickled her nostrils and she stifled a sneeze.

There *had* to be a way to talk Lil out of this. "It's way too small for us," she claimed. "It's for . . . I dunno . . . *rats*."

Lil was on her knees, peering into the hole. "We'll crawl on our bellies, like snakes," she crooned, placing her palms together and waving them around in the dirt.

"We'll get scratched," Astra insisted. "Then Hokma will know we were out."

"If we get scratched we can wear our housecoats in Wise House and our hydropacs outside. We can go for a walk in the morning and say it happened then."

Lil threw herself down on the ground and began inching through the hole. Her head and her slim back disappeared, swallowed up by the hedge. Then her legs wriggled through, and finally the soles of her feet.

"C'mon, Astra. It's easy. I didn't get scratched one bit." Lil's whisper echoed back through the twiggy tunnel. "Okay. Maybe the tip of my left shoulder blade."

There was no help for it. Astra lowered herself to the earth and entered the black bush.

She had to grab in the dark for roots and branches, drag her chin through the dirt and propel herself forward with her toes. Lil had lied, of course: the poky fingers of the hedge *did* carve into her back, and there was a rock in the dirt that scraped her chest until she stopped and reached beneath herself to dig it out. She was going to be grazed and bruised all over tomorrow. There was no way Hokma wouldn't see the marks.

But once she had started, she had to continue. At last her head was out the other side and Lil was pulling at her armpits, tugging her through into the moonlit field.

"My knee hurts," Astra scowled, fingering the tender spot. She was sure it was bleeding.

"Oh, it'll be all right. You'll soon forget about it. Look—"

They were at the foot of the slow rise to the center of the field. Astra followed Lil's finger. She could see the solitary juniper, a writhing black mass sucking the moonlight out of the night air, and in front, their bodies barely visible against a smear of stars, Hokma and Ahn. They were embracing, their silhouette like a broken column, jagged at the top. Hokma's head, Astra realized, was pressed against Ahn's chest and his face was in her hair. Why was she doing that? She looked small in Ahn's arms. But Hokma wasn't small: she was a giant. Then, in a slow slithery motion, Ahn slid down Hokma's body and began sucking one of her nipples. Hokma threw her head back to stare at the stars.

Astra had seen enough. She picked at a twig that had got caught between her foot and her sandal and threw it back under the hedge.

"Wow." Lil exhaled. "We're just in time."

"I don't like it," Astra muttered. "Why is she letting him act like a baby?"

"C'mon, let's go to the rocks. They'll be lying down soon." Lil was scrambling to her feet. Her back hunched, she sneaked left, along the edge of the field as it curved behind the tree. Astra watched her go, moonlight grazing her hair, her body flowing into the dark crescent of the slope.

She had tried everything, but Plan A had failed. Lil had left her no other choice. Astra got to her feet and crept after the small, intent figure, letting the gap between them widen until she could barely see the gleaming curve of Lil's shoulders, the silver ghost of her hair. When Lil reached the path to the rocks, she looked back once, pointed into the field then turned and disappeared into the grass. Astra stopped and breathed in the dusty scent of soil and wild grains. Plan B depended on her and Lil not being together. She placed both palms on the earth. *Please Gaia, help me protect your secret mysteries.*

She continued to the path, and entered the field. Lil would be nearly at the rocks by now. She stood up and started running.

"*STOP, LIL, STOP,*" she yelled. "*Hokma, Lil's running away!*"

"Okay, girls. What was going on out there? One at a time. Astra, you first."

Hokma and Ahn were sitting on one sofa, Astra and Lil on the other. There were four mugs of hot barley oatmilk with honey on the table. Lil was scrunched up against the sofa arm, refusing to look at anyone; Astra was perched on the edge of her cushion. Hokma was unsmiling, but Ahn was regarding her and Lil with an almost amused expression. Astra didn't like his look at all. Why did he think this was *funny*?

"I woke up," she started, addressing Hokma, "and Lil was getting out of bed. I thought she was going to the bathroom. But she didn't come back, so I got up too. She wasn't in the bathroom, so I went to tell you. You weren't there either. So I put on my shoes and went outside. I thought maybe you were night-flying an Owleon, so I went to the field. Then I saw Lil, and she was standing at the gate, I didn't know why. But she didn't open the gate. She went along the hedge and crawled under it, so I followed her. When I got into the field I saw you and Ahn standing by the tree. Lil was going in the other direction. I thought she was running away."

She'd devised most of the story beforehand and rehearsed it in her head. It sounded true, she thought. In fact, all the actions in the story were true, which made it easy to say with conviction. That would show Lil: she *wasn't* a lousy liar.

"Thank you, Astra. Lil?"

Lil was twirling a strand of her hair with her finger. She stopped, picked up her drink, took a sip, then set the mug back down on the table.

"I'm not *stupid*," she said, airily. "If I wanted to run away, I'd have taken my hydropac and some food. I wanted to watch you and Ahn Gaia-worshipping. Astra said she wanted to watch too, but then she changed her mind because she didn't like seeing Ahn acting like a baby. So she decided to try and stop me and be a *hero* at the same time."

The corners of Ahn's mouth turned down for a moment and at the same time his eyebrows raised. It was a strange expression. He seemed not just amused now, but almost . . . *impressed*. He looked at Astra next, as if to say . . . *so?*

Hokma sucked her lips, and sighed. "Okay, folks, I'm hearing two different stories. Astra?"

"She's *lying*. I would *never* want to watch you and Ahn doing stuff like that. That's *illegal*."

Ahn laughed. Hokma shot him a stern look and he leaned back against the cushions, his hands clasped behind his head.

"Full moon, Hokma," he said. Astra hadn't heard him speak for so long she'd forgotten how raspy his voice was, as if he had a permanent sore throat. "Gaia plays tricks on us all. There's no harm done. Let them go back to bed."

"No, Ahn, I want to get to the bottom of this. One of them is lying."

Lil plucked at a splinter in the sofa arm. "Okay. I didn't *exactly* tell the truth. Astra didn't want to watch you Gaia-play, but I said that if she didn't come with me I would tell Ahn that she never had her Security shot."

It was the risk she had taken: that Lil would make good her threat. All Astra had hoped to do was establish her own innocence and Lil's guilt, and thereby cast doubt on any accusation that might follow.

"See? She's crazy! She's a total liar!" she shouted, bouncing on her cushion.

Hokma's face was immobile and her gaze was trained on Lil. Beside her, Ahn lowered his arms and leaned forward. His mouth was a still, thin line and his eyes were darting between Hokma and Astra and Lil like quick colorless minnows.

"What do you mean, Lil?" he asked in his fine, sandpapery voice.

"I mean she's not like the other kids, is she? Look at her now. She's getting upset. And she asks me lots of questions about everything. She's curious, but my dad said he didn't want me to have the shot because then I would just accept everything I was told. He said he wanted me to think for myself, even if it meant I felt sad or angry sometimes."

Lil sounded so smug, Astra wanted to punch her. "I did so have my shot," she yelled. "Hokma was *there*. It just affects kids differently, that's all. Yoki still cries sometimes, and I still get angry. Especially when people *lie* about me. Hokma, make her *shut up*." She slammed her fist into the sofa arm and burst into tears.

Hokma was still staring at Lil. Ahn, though, leaned forward and watched Astra cry. Aware of his gaze, she dried her eyes and stuffed her hands down into her lap.

"Hokma?" Ahn's elbows were resting on his knees and the tips of his forefingers were pressed together like a steeple at his lips. "Lil's made some observations. What's your hypothesis?"

"It's true Astra's different from the other Sec Gens," Hokma said slowly. "I've often wondered about it. I think she was immune to the emotional component of the shot. Do you remember, she ate poison berries that day and was sick at school? Maybe that interfered with the uptake levels. Lil," she addressed the girl, "Dr. Blesserson gave Astra the shot in his office. Ahn can check the records if he likes."

Lil stood up. "No, Dr. Blesserson didn't. You made him pretend that he did. That's why he doesn't like you. I can prove it."

Lil walked to the foyer door and left the room. They could hear her enter the lab.

"What exactly is going on here, Hokma?" Ahn's dry voice had hardened now.

"I don't know," she replied.

Astra wiped her eyes. "I did *so* have my shot," she repeated, bitterly.

Lil returned, gripping a long thin object, dusted with ice. She thrust it in front of Ahn.

"This is Astra's shot. It's been in the freezer. My *hypothesis* is that Hokma was keeping it in case Astra ever got tested."

"Thank you, Lil. Please sit down." Ahn took the needle and examined it carefully. Lil walked around the table and sat back down, this time in the middle of her cushion.

"Hokma," Ahn said. "This is a Security Serum shot. It is dated 77 RE. That was the first year of GeneIsis. Why do you have it in your freezer?"

"Samrod gave it to me," Hokma replied.

"Why?" Ahn rotated the needle slowly in his hands, scrutinizing it again from every angle. It was still in its original sealed bioplastic sleeve, which was shedding ice crystals onto his thighs.

"Because I was interested in the Serum."

"All the Serum research is available online to a scientist of your standing. And you haven't even opened this hypodermic."

"I thought I might be able to develop something for the Owleons based on the Serum principles. But it was low-priority and I forgot about it. That's the truth, Ahn."

Ahn put the needle down on the table, stood up and walked to Hokma's desk. His back to the sofas, he picked up one of her pens, tapped it twice on the desktop and put it back in its mug. Then he turned and leaning on the edge of the desk, said as if to no one in particular, "Owleons don't have emotional thresholds or intellectual capacities worth molding, do they? Help me out, Hokma. Tell me something I can believe, why don't you?"

Astra was shivering and a salty trail of snot was running down her upper lip.

Beside her, Hokma swallowed. "I didn't want her to have the shot, Ahn. Her Birth-Code mother wouldn't have wanted it. And she's got too good a mind to dull."

The words hung in the air like a flag on a windless day. "And Samrod?" Ahn asked.

"He didn't want to, but he helped me. You know he owed me a favor."

Ahn placed his fingertips on his temples now, and closed his eyes.

"Who are her other Shelter parents? Nimma and Klor?"

"Yes."

"Do *they* know?"

"No. No one knows."

He wiped his cheeks with his hands now, and opened his eyes. "And this other child. Yoki? Is he another of your projects?"

"She's not a project. And Yoki had the shot. He was just hypersensitive to begin with."

Hokma was speaking reasonably, but Ahn wasn't even *trying* to understand. "So Astra is the only one you've *interfered* with," he sneered.

He was gripping the edge of the desk now so his rangy body looked bigger, blocking the window behind him. Astra longed to run from the room, far from Wise House, but she was glued to the sofa, riveted to the fight the adults were having about her.

"I didn't *interfere* with her, Ahn—quite the opposite." He'd got to Hokma now; her voice was tense and hostile too. "She's exactly the same as the older children; as *you and me*."

Hokma's voice broke then, and she stood and took a step forward, her arms out, but Ahn was looking at her as if she'd committed the worst crime in Is-Land. "Is this why Samrod relieved you of your position?" he snapped. "It is, isn't it?"

"Ahn, no!" Now Hokma did nearly shout. "I missed a few meetings. It was time to move on anyway. You know I only had the job for so long because no one else wanted to stand for it!"

But Ahn wasn't listening at all now. He had closed his eyes again and was pressing his fist into his forehead. "What have you done, Hokma? What in Gaia's holy name have you done?"

Hokma turned to Astra. "Girls—go to bed. Astra, sleep in my loft. I'm going outside with Ahn for a minute."

"Isn't *she* in trouble?" Astra hissed. "She *told*!"

"We'll talk about it in the morning. Now do as I say."

Lil was already climbing the ladder to Astra's bedloft. Astra watched her ascend, her steps almost jaunty as if she were performing a dance exercise. From the desk, Ahn was watching her too. His gray eyes were sharp as quartz now, as if Lil were a member of some volatile species who might suddenly grow wings and fly through the ceiling.

"*Now*, Astra," Hokma ordered.

Astra stood up. She climbed Hokma's ladder and got under the covers. There was a cup of cold herbal tea by the futon and the loft smelled of cinnamon, and Hokma's skin. She curled up on the edge of the bed closest to the wall, her back to Lil's loft. Beneath her, the door to the foyer swished open and closed, and then the front door to Wise House clunked shut.

"'That's the *truth*, Ahn?'" Ahn's explosion was muffled by the straw-bale walls. "How frigging long have you been frigging *lying* to me, Hokma?"

The two adults moved away, down the path to the front gate, and though she could hear them shouting at each other for a while she couldn't make out what they were saying. Eventually she couldn't hear anything except Lil's breathing, a gentle rasping wheeze far away on the other side of the room.

In the morning, apart from Hokma's breakfast commands, no one spoke for a long time. Astra made berry and almond porridge and Lil laid the table. After they'd eaten and washed the dishes, Hokma took Astra and Lil outside to the veranda to talk. They sat in a semicircle on the three wicker chairs.

"Astra," Hokma began, "don't worry. Ahn isn't going to tell anyone. I've told him how dangerous that would be for me, and he won't do it."

"Did he promise?"

"He doesn't have to promise, Astra. As long as we're Gaia-bonded, he won't do it. A bond of our duration is worth protecting. So he won't tell, okay?"

Hokma's bond with Ahn hadn't seemed very strong to Astra last night. Right now though, she had a more pressing anxiety. "But what about *Lil?* She could tell *everyone!*"

"I don't think Lil will. For two reasons. Lil, let me know if I'm right. First, I think you didn't know quite how much trouble Astra and I could get into if other people knew she didn't have her shot. Did you?"

Lil was looking out over the lawn as if she were bored.

"She *did* know," Astra burst in. "I *told* her!" Now she'd blown her cover story, but it didn't matter. Hokma didn't seem to care anymore about who was lying last night.

"All right, Astra," Hokma quieted her. "Lil?"

Lil scowled. "Astra said you could get taken away," she muttered at last. "But I didn't think Ahn would tell anyone. Not if you're Gaia-bonded."

"You took a big risk there, Lil. Ahn and I have a long relationship, but he has a career to think about and if anyone finds out he's covering up for me, he could get into a lot of trouble too."

"Then he'll keep it secret, won't he?" Lil scowled and folded her arms.

"Yes, he will—and so will you, won't you, Lil? Because you don't want Astra and me to get taken away, do you? I don't think so. I think what you wanted was to see Ahn and me Gaia-play."

Astra sat up. At last, Lil was going to get punished. "She tried to make me watch too," she informed Hokma. "I told her it was illegal!"

"Thank you, Astra. I'm sure you did. But let's all remember that Lil hasn't had Gaia-play education at school, like you're getting. She doesn't have any Shelter siblings and she doesn't know any boys, or even any girls apart from you. She probably has a lot of perfectly natural questions about Gaia play and she just wanted to see how it worked."

It was unbelievable. Lil could scratch Hokma's other eye out and Hokma would say that she just wanted to see how the retina worked.

"She *knows* how it works! She did it with *me*!" She was blubbing again. Her vision was blurry, her voice choked. She stood up and marched to the end of the veranda. At the living room door she turned and shouted, "She probably did it with her *dad* too! She's mentally *ill* and she wants to star in *borno* in New Zonia when she grows up." Then she slammed the door, went inside and threw herself on the sofa, crying.

"Astra, I'm sorry. All right? I'm sorry." Hokma was sitting beside her, awkwardly patting her shoulder as she wailed into a cushion. "But why didn't you tell me what was going on? We could have talked about it, worked it all out."

No we couldn't. Astra couldn't explain that if she'd run like a baby to Hokma, telling tales on Lil, even if Hokma didn't force Lil into counseling, at the very best Lil would never take her to see the ancestors again, and at the worst Lil would be furious and tell *everyone* about her shot, and she and Hokma would be taken away. She couldn't say anything. She could only keep crying into the wet cushion beneath her cheek.

"Astra," Hokma said wearily, removing her hand, "talk to me, please. You're nearly thirteen. You can't keep having tantrums like this."

She was to blame? *She* was being told off? The injustice triggered a fresh round of sobs. Finally, over the edge of the cushion, she managed to sputter "She's *huh-huh-huh-horrible*. I *hate* her. Look what she *did*. Why isn't *she* in *trouble*?"

"Lil's in big enough trouble already. She grew up in the woods, her dad's died, and we still don't know if she has a family."

"Her dad was *crazy*." Astra wriggled around and scrunched up against the sofa arm, hugging the cushion to her stomach. "He taught her hunting and told her weird things. I think he Gaia-played with her, because"—she didn't know exactly and faltered—"because she wants to play like a boy sometimes," she finished lamely.

Hokma regarded her calmly. "Lots of girls like to play like boys. That's normal. We especially asked Lil about her dad, and she said he never Gaia-played with her. It sounds to me that when he got ill and knew he might be dying, he told her some things she was really too young to hear. Some of them are nasty, I know, but they are mostly true, and you'll learn about them in high school. In the meantime, we need to be kind to Lil and give her a home and then she'll learn how to be nice to us too."

Astra wiped her face. "She *won't*," she whispered ferociously. "She found the needle. She'll tell Nimma and Klor."

Hokma took her by the chin and looked into her face. "Astra, listen to me. You don't need to worry about anything. Lil's going to say sorry to you, I promise. She was mean to you and you're right, she should be punished. She'll have to do extra chores so that you can concentrate on your sewing this week. And she definitely can't go to the Blood & Seed ceremony. How's that?"

Extra chores and missing a ceremony she hadn't even asked to go to? It wasn't a harsh enough punishment—not nearly enough. Lil had Gaia-played with her and then she had betrayed her biggest secret to Ahn. She had hurt Astra. Hurt her *heart*.

Astra shook her head, tears spilling down her face again.

"Oh, I know." Hokma sighed. "She was a Gaia playmate, wasn't she? But that's what happens sometimes: Gaia playmates aren't always nice to us all the time. That's why we don't Gaia-bond until we're much older."

It wasn't fair. Now she was being accused of breaking the rules. "I *didn't* Gaia-bond with her. I *didn't*. It was just Gaia play, that's all."

"I know you thought you were just playing. But maybe you bonded a little, without knowing it. It can sneak up on you, especially if you're not playing with anyone else. You'll have other Gaia play pals soon at school. Let's just try and keep working with her here, okay? You had good times on your walks, didn't you? She's taught us lots about foraging and she knows all the Gaia hymns."

She almost did tell Hokma about the ancestors then, and what Lil had said about Is-Land and Non-Landers. But what was the point? Hokma would just take Lil's side and Lil would never take her back to see the arrowpain. She kept crying, the tears dripping off the end of her nose as she balled her fists in her eyes, dumbly shaking her head.

"I know, I know," Hokma kept repeating, but *no*, no she *didn't*. She didn't know anything at all. At last Hokma pulled Astra into her lap, like she was seven again, and whispered into the top of her hair, "Look, I really am sorry, Astra. Maybe I did the wrong thing taking her in. Let's make a deal. You give her a week to show you she's sorry too, and if you're not friends again by then, I'll find somewhere else for her to live. How's that?"

Hokma brought a damp cloth for Astra to wash her face and Lil came in and said she was sorry. She brought a bunch of wildflowers for Astra and said she hadn't known how important it was to keep the secret, but she did now. She said she would do all the cleaning this week, so Astra could sew. Then Lil went out to the aviary with a bucket and brushes and Astra got to sit on the veranda with Hokma and rehearse all her lines for the Blood & Seed ceremony, which Hokma remembered word for word from her own ceremony all those years ago. At lunch Astra and Lil said "please" and "thank you," and in the afternoon she went back down to Or for the hymn rehearsal.

When Nimma asked her if everything was okay at Wise House she nodded, and said "Hokma just needed to tell Lil off, that's all." Then she got in line with Meem and Yoki and said all her lines perfectly, in a high, piercing voice.

2.11

Over the next week, most of Astra's free time was taken up with Blood & Seed sewing and rehearsals. The ceremony was to be held on Arkaday, at the Bioregional Congregation Site northwest of New Bangor. Year Seven students from all the dry forest Foundation schools would be there: three from New Bangor, four from Vanapur and seven from Cedaria. There would be smaller ceremonies in the ash fields and the white desert, which didn't have many schools, and larger ones in Bracelet Valley and the steppes, where the Congregation Site was massive. The Blood & Seed ceremony lit the five beacons of the Boundary. It was one of the biggest nights of the year. There would be bioregional prizes for the most polished appearance from a school, so all the celebrants needed to practice their choral hymns until they were word-perfect.

Astra stayed late after school all week, and because Lil was doing her Owleon chores, she didn't go up to Wise House in the evenings when she got home. She had dinner with the Sec Gens, avoiding Ahn—who ignored her even more than usual, so that was easy—and then she went straight up to the Earthship. She'd made Hokma promise that she wouldn't let Lil fly Silver. Instead, Hokma sent Silver to the Earthship every evening with a memory stick full of "work hard" and "good luck" messages, and Astra sent him back with footage of the rehearsals and her growing pile of petals.

On Veneday evening she finally finished her petals, only a day after Yoki, so on Sabbaday Nimma allowed her to go back to Wise House to show Lil her hipbeads.

"Just for a couple of hours, darling. You need to bond with the others today. Come back for a swim at four, okay?"

Astra nodded and set off, her hipbeads tucked into a hydropac pocket. When she got to Wise House she saw her name had been spelled out in white pebbles on the path to the front door. Beside it a trail of more white pebbles was leading right. She followed it around the side of the house to the roosting lawn. Silver was there, resting, and the three new Owleons were stretching their wings, trilling and crooning in the strange new oboe-like way IMBOD, for some top secret reason, had ordered Hokma to Code for. In the middle of the lawn Hokma and Lil were waiting with a picnic, spread out on a gold cloth Astra had never seen before.

"Happy Blood & Seed Ceremony, Astra!" Lil jumped up and ran toward her carrying a big white daisy chain. "You're the Queen of Wise House today!"

Astra let her place the crown in her hair. "Thanks," she mumbled.

"Come and eat." Hokma waved them over. The cloth was filled with plates of alt-egg and cress sandwiches, long carrot and cucumber sticks, hummus and cherry tomatoes, and toasted seeds and pine nuts to sprinkle on everything. There were sweet crunchy peapods too, and elderflower cordial, and biscuits with silvery sparkles on top. In the middle, arranged in a triangle, were three dishes of soy yogurt swirled with strawberry jam.

"They were my idea," Lil said proudly. "Blood and Seed pudding."

Astra sat down. "It looks nice," she said, grudgingly.

"The whole picnic was Lil's idea, and the pebble path too," Hokma said. "She's been getting things ready all morning."

Astra took a plate. "Have you flown the Owleons yet?"

Lil shook her head. "No, we waited for you. Did you bring your hipbeads?"

"Yeah."

"Excellent! I want to see you wear them after. I won't touch, I promise."

Over lunch, Lil told Astra about all the chores she'd done that week: as well as weeding and cleaning, she'd woven a new side-panel for the compost, fixed the leak in Helium's roof, gathered worms for the vermicompost and oiled the squeak in the flying-field gate. As Lil chattered, Astra began to feel almost sorry for her. *She'd* spent the week getting ready for her Blood & Seed ceremony, a national event the whole country stopped for. Lil might never be able to take part in anything as important. She didn't fit in, and no one knew what to do with her or where to put her. Astra was her only friend and she'd tried to bully her. Now, though she would never say so, Lil was obviously scared she wouldn't ever have any friends, so she was trying to make it up to Astra. Maybe she had learned her lesson.

After the savories Hokma stacked the empty plates on the lawn so the three red and white puddings were the only dishes left on the gold cloth. Astra stood up and put on her hipbeads. The long string wrapped three times around her waist and belly. Most of the beads were small, and strung in an alternating pattern of rich polished rosewood and golden seeds, but every thirteenth bead was bigger and made of crimson glass. The largest red bead was a garnet; it was set between two tumbled moonstones and hung right over her Gaia mound.

"They're beautiful." Lil's voice was tinged not with envy but awe.

Carefully, one foot after the other, her arms raised in front of her, Astra circumambulated the gold cloth. When she returned to her place, she sat down in the way she'd been taught: feet crossed and then slowly lowering herself, thighs aching, to the grass.

Hokma and Lil applauded. "That was amazing, Astra," Lil said, as Hokma passed out the puddings. "You were like an Old World ballet dancer."

If she was the Queen, she could make announcements. Astra finished her pudding and put the bowl down on the cloth. "Next week I'll ask Nimma to make Lil a hipbead string too," she said.

"That's kind of you, Astra," Hokma commented.

"*Really?*" Lil's eyes shone like polished tiger stones. "Thanks, Astra."

A shadow beat down from the sky and beside them Helium landed on a perch, his enormous wings casting a breeze over Astra's shoulders. He had a ribbon around his memory-clip leg: a message from Or, red for urgent. Hokma got up.

"I'd better check this, girls."

"The Queen desires to inspect the compost panel," Astra proclaimed. Leaving Hokma to take the memory clip into Wise House, she and Lil raced over to the garden. The new panel was woven tightly, preventing the compost from bulging and spilling out like it used to.

"You did a good job," she said.

"My dad taught me weaving." Lil picked up the compost stick and rested it on the fence.

Astra plucked at the edge of a bark slat. "I'm sorry I said that about you and your dad. And borno."

"That's okay." Lil poked the stick through the top layer of dried grasses. "I'm sorry I messed everything up. I just wanted to see Hokma and Ahn Gaia-worship. I thought you wanted to too, but you were scared."

There was an ant crawling over Lil's forearm, weaving between the light golden hairs on her skin. "I wasn't scared," Astra said.

"No. I know you weren't." Lil was methodically stirring the food scraps, her triceps rippling as the ant began to ascend toward her shoulder. "Hokma said if we make friends again I can stay here this summer and maybe go to high school in New Bangor in the new term," she stated flatly. "I can study with you and her and catch up on my lessons. Then I can join the class of the last year of non-Sec Gens. They'll be older than me, but Hokma said as long as I can do the work, they'll accept me."

The ripe, sweaty smell of the compost was blooming in Astra's nostrils, making her mouth water unpleasantly. If Lil came to her high school, would Astra have to deal with her strange behavior, introduce her to Tedis and Silvie, try to explain her to the Sec Gens? Lil would be in Year Ten, but she'd be a year younger than her classmates so would that mean she'd Gaia-play with the under-fifteens? Astra didn't know at all if she wanted that to happen. She should be saying "That's great," but the words stuck in her throat.

"What if we don't get along?" she asked instead.

"Then I have to go to an IMBOD Shelter school in Cedaria, for non-Sec Gen kids who need special care. Ahn and Hokma will tell them that I'm mentally ill, so even if I tell them about you, they won't believe me." Lil stabbed the stick deep into the mulch. "I would *never* tell anyone about you, Astra. I *hate* IMBOD. I don't want to go to their stupid school. I want to stay here and go for walks with you and fly the Owleons and meet the other Or-kids. I just want everything to be like it was before, only better."

It was as if Lil were stabbing the stick into her heart. Lil was crazy but she was her friend and her fate, suddenly, was in Astra's hands. She couldn't let Lil go to an IMBOD school. She didn't want that power. "Me too," she whispered.

The ant disappeared into the small, sweaty cave of Lil's armpit. She scratched, flicked the dead ant away, then turned and examined Astra's face. "No, you don't," she said.

Astra was affronted. "Yes I do."

"No, you don't. You don't want me to go to your high school. You don't want me to Gaia-play with Tedis Sonnenson."

It was too close to what Astra had been thinking to admit it. "I don't care who you play with," she said haughtily. "We're supposed to play with lots of people. Anyway, you think boys are stupid."

Lil returned to churning the compost. Astra leaned against the panel. The rough slats pressed into her chest and her hipbeads dug into her stomach, making little indentations that would collect water if she and Lil ever lay down in the rain together. Lil was scared, she understood that: scared of starting high school and scared of meeting boys.

"Lil," she said slowly, "tomorrow night in the ceremony, I have to ask Gaia to help me let go of childishness. I'll ask Her to help me let go of our fight, and when I come back, we can start again."

Lil gave the compost one last thrust. She withdrew the stick from the mulch, wiped it clean on the edge of the fence and turned to Astra. "Promise?"

"I promise. On the ancestors."

"Good." Lil nodded. Then she tossed the stick aside. "Gallop-twist you to the bird-roosts!" she cried.

Gallop-twist? What was—?

Lil was prancing and twirling across the lawn, making snorting noises. "Not fair, not fair!" Astra shouted. Laughing and whinnying, her hand clamped to her head to keep her daisy crown from slipping, she skipped and pirouetted after Lil until they had both collapsed in giggles on Hokma's gold cloth. Clutching their sides, they rolled about, knocking knees, as Silver spread his sun-glinting wings, the trainees warbled and Helium swiveled his head 180 degrees to watch them, blinking his wild planet eyes.

"My darling Shelter daughter. My precious Shelter son." Klor stood up as Astra and Yoki entered the living room. "Here you are, tall and bronzed on your Blood & Seed Day. Could I be more proud of you? Not if you won an IMBOD medal. Not if you swam an ocean. Not if you discovered how to milk moonbeams and feed all of Nuafrica with their rich goodness."

Klor's craggy face was as warm as a sunlit cliff. Beside him, Nimma's eyes were moist.

"Oh darlings. Don't you look wonderful?"

It was late Arkaday afternoon. Astra and Yoki had had an extra-big lunch and a long siesta and were now wide awake. They had spent the last hour showering and dressing for the ceremony, which started at dusk. Astra was wearing a pair of brand-new boots, her first ever knee-high pair, and a new solo-purpose hydropac—a small one made entirely of tubing that sat high on her back so the straps didn't detract from her hipbeads. Yoki was also wearing a hydropac, boots and a beaded necklace which complemented her string's design—his mother-of-pearl center bead was flanked by two small garnets. They were both carrying cherrywood staffs, from the tops of which dangled their white and crimson petal bags. Klor had carved Astra's staff with a spiraling pattern of feathers to represent the Owleons, and he'd whittled the head into the shape of a heart. Yoki's Code-Shelter father Pan had carved his with four bands of animal footprints and a flame on the top. Klor and Pan had given them the staffs in a special presentation after lunch in the dining hall. They'd also received an orchid each from the Code House teams and then, to the applause of the whole of Or, Nimma had fastened on Astra's hipbeads and Yoki's necklace.

Afterward, Klor and Nimma had also given Astra Eya's bracelet to keep in her box in her room, saying she didn't have to wait until her birthday because she would become a woman tonight. She had wanted to wear it for the ceremony but it was the wrong colors. She'd pleaded to wear it just in the van, but it was still large for her wrist and Nimma was afraid it would fall off. She'd been upset, but then Nimma had also given her three glass beads for her hair: two blood red and one creamy white.

The beads were big and looked like sweets. They were very special glass, Nimma said: Murano glass, from Atlantis. Kali had bought them a very long time ago and Nimma had worn them at her own Blood & Seed. Then Klor had put his arm around Nimma and said, Sheba had loved looking at the beads, though she always had to be stopped from trying to eat them, hadn't she, Nimma? Nimma hadn't smiled. She'd said that Astra couldn't keep the beads, but she was allowed to wear them today. Astra had wanted to thread them into her dread, but Nimma had refused; instead, she'd worked them into a braid on the other side of Astra's head and they hung there now, beautiful but heavy, like the responsibility of remembering Sheba today.

"Your chariot awaits, my noble young warriors." Klor gestured to the front door and Yoki and Astra led the way out of the Earthship and down the path through Or. Beyond Core House, a crowd had gathered—children and adults—all waving and clapping as they approached West Gate. Out on the road, the minivan was waiting, its side door open.

"Happy Blood & Seed Day," everyone was calling. Torrent was making a war whoop with his hand patting his open mouth, Meem and Peat were throwing flowers in their path, and Congruence and her friends were dancing in their honor, swaying like waterweeds to aid their procession. As she passed through the gate to the minivan, Astra's heart fluttered into the sky like a lark.

Pan was sitting in the driver's seat beside Freyja, Yoki's Code-Shelter mother. Nimma was in the middle pair of passenger seats and Hokma was opposite her on the single. Between them, at the end of the galley, someone else was sitting alone in the back row.

It was Ahn.

"Hello, Astra," Ahn said. "Hello, Yoki. Happy Blood & Seed Day."

Astra paused on the step of the van.

"Come on, Or-child, in you go." Klor put a hand on her back.

"You and Yoki sit at the front." Nimma patted the backs of the first row of passenger seats.

Astra turned around to Klor. "Why is Ahn coming?" she whispered.

"He's filming the ceremony, angel. Now step up, we don't want to be late."

She had no choice. Astra heaved herself into the interior. She took the window seat behind Pan and tucked her staff between her knees. Freyja and Pan turned to exclaim over Yoki, giving him hugs and a kiss as he sat down too. "Do you want me to pass your staff to the back of the van?" Hokma asked.

"No."

"Don't you look beautiful, Astra," Freyja cooed. "Oh! Are those Kali's beads, Nimma?"

"We thought she should have them for today," Klor said from his seat beside Nimma. Astra waited for Nimma to reply too, but she didn't.

"Oh, I'm so glad." Freyja stroked one of the beads. "They're such a wonderful gift from Elpis too, aren't they, Astra?"

She couldn't speak. The glass beads felt like lumps of cast iron on her head. Why had Nimma given them to her if she didn't really want her to wear them? And why was Ahn here? The ceremony was for children and parents and teachers—Hokma hadn't said anything about Ahn coming.

"Everyone in?" Pan called.

"Everyone in!" Klor reached over and rolled the passenger door shut, Pan started the engine and they were off.

They sang Gaia hymns on the way, and in between the adults reminisced about their own Blood & Seed Days. When Klor and Nimma were young there weren't any bioregional ceremonies, or even petal-sewing tasks. The ceremonies were held within the community and were all slightly different. Sometimes there were only one or two children involved, though, and so neighboring communities often joined forces and created local gatherings. Gradually, as people realized that it was important for Is-Land to have stable traditions, IMBOD had made Blood & Seed Day part of the national curriculum. The petal-sewing had been assigned, and the hymns and bead-strings standardized. Hokma, Ahn, Freyja and Pan all had memories of their schools being transformed on the day, and the older and younger children watching them weave around on the lawns or in the woodlands. Then, as the Boundary had grown more secure, IMBOD had established the five Congregation Sites and given the Bioregional Wheel Meets control over the ceremonies. It was also decided not to invite other children anymore: until you had children of your own, Blood & Seed Day should be a unique event in your life. You weren't allowed to talk about it with younger children, so Astra and Yoki had only a general idea of what to expect. They did know that the laser ritual had been added especially for the Sec Gens, bringing an extra dimension of importance to the night. Klor and Nimma had attended Peat's ceremony last year, of course; they said that although he'd been nervous at first, he'd shone with excitement from beginning to end.

"Will Blood & Seed Day ever evolve into a *national* ceremony?" Yoki asked. "All the different Congregation Sites could take turns, and everyone could come from all over Is-Land."

The van bumped over a rut in the road and Kali's beads knocked against Astra's temple. She wanted to undo the braid and take them off, but that was impossible—*unthinkable*—like putting Sheba's photo into the manufacture-loop recycle bin.

"It's been talked about," Pan told Yoki. "But something similar was tried once and it was a logistical nightmare, so the idea was dropped."

Freyja coughed.

"What do you mean?" Yoki asked. "When was it tried?"

Pan's eyes were on the road and his shoulders were square at the wheel. After a second, Freyja replied, "During the Eastern infiltration, in the year of Klor and Nimma and Sheba's great sacrifice, IMBOD decided that it was too dangerous to have the ceremony at the dry forest site. So the dry forest schools joined the ash fields ceremony. It was the year after my own ceremony, so I remember it well."

Yoki, sitting beside Astra, gripped his staff tighter. Astra knew why. Apart from Hokma, she couldn't remember another Or adult ever mentioning Sheba in front of Nimma. Neither she nor Yoki turned around. Behind her, Nimma's grief was like a forest cobweb in the night: she couldn't see it, but it was drifting over her, getting stuck in her hair, caught in her breath.

Suddenly she felt smothered in guilt. Of course Nimma would feel sad tonight.

"It was a seven- or eight-hour journey, Yoki," Klor said into the silence. "People had to stay overnight, so their work and other Shelter children suffered. Some mothers with infants stayed behind and missed the ceremony altogether."

"A national ceremony would be far too long," Hokma said firmly. "I've never thought it was a good idea."

"Sec Gens would probably have the stamina for it," Ahn said from the back, "but having so many people drawn to one location could make Is-Land vulnerable, Yoki."

Yoki swung around. "Could Non-Landers attack the *Blood & Seed ceremony*?"

"Is-Land isn't vulnerable, Yoki." Astra raised her voice but kept the tone level. She wasn't contradicting Ahn, she hoped, but reassuring her Shelter sibling. That would show Nimma she was a good sister, worthy of the beads Sheba had loved. And it would also show Ahn that she could fit in with the Sec Gens. "The Boundary is well defended."

"Of course it is, Astra." From behind her, Nimma spoke crisply. "But we don't want the roads blocked, causing chaos that Non-Landers could scheme to take advantage of."

"Oh, politics! Let's not talk politics for once, my darling," Klor exclaimed beside her. "Look, Or-kids. A gap in the trees—there's the steppes! Gaia's stubbly cheeks!"

"Klor!" Nimma protested, and all the adults laughed. Yoki giggled too, and bounced in his seat, and Astra relaxed. The bead braid was heavy, yes, but she didn't mind. She wasn't going to spoil tonight by being a selfish non-Sec Gen. Tonight was going to be perfect. Tonight she was going to belong.

They were leaving New Bangor, now, taking the road to Sippur. As twilight began to fall, the adults started singing "Gaia's Endless Bounty" and soon they were all harmonizing. Then, suddenly, the glint of the Boundary was visible on the right. Instead of sailing past it, as she and Hokma had done in the bus so long ago, Pan turned up into the mountains and joined a stream of traffic flowing toward the Blood & Seed ceremony: buses, cars, minivans and horse-drawn carts full of children and their parents.

They drove into a big field filled with vehicles and people. Just inside the entrance a parking steward in a bright yellow tabard flashed a STOP sign at them. Pan unrolled the window.

"Happy Blood & Seed Day," the steward greeted him. Pan told him which school they were from and the steward pointed at a tall blue flag in the corner of the field.

"Golden Bough's over there. Most of the schools are here now. When everyone's gathered and ready, you'll hear the signal to enter the site at the foot of the flag."

The fourteen school flags were lined up along the edge of the wood that protected the Boundary. More parking stewards helped direct the van across the bumpy field, down a double row of vehicles parked in front of the blue flag and into a space beside a wooden cart and horse. It was Silvie's Shelter mothers' cart, Astra knew, the one they sometimes brought from Higgs to New Bangor laden with produce. Today it was decorated with bright green boughs and lengths of silver-and-red rope Silvie and her community siblings had knitted. Yoki slid out of the van and Astra joined him on the grass. Ahead of them, their friends from school were milling around on the verge of the field, examining each other's hipbeads, necklaces and staffs. Their parents and some of the teachers were there too, chatting. Mr. Ripenson had come earlier to help set up; he was standing next to Mrs. Raintree at a folding table, pouring cups of tea from a flask. He noticed Astra and Yoki and waved.

"Go on then," Nimma said, "join the others—but don't wander off. We'll be going in soon."

Astra, shiny and strong in her hipbeads and brand-new boots, carrying her staff with its beautiful heart-shaped knob, with all her Shelter parents beaming at her, strode with Yoki down the avenue of vehicles to join their classmates. The braid beads swung gently from her head and the hipbeads rolled over her skin and clicked lightly against each other.

As her friends parted to let her and Yoki join their Murmuration, Leaf reached out to finger Kali's beads. "O Gaia, those are so gorgeous. I just want to suck them!"

Soon Astra was right in the middle of the crush, telling the story of Kali and Atlantis, and checking out everyone else's hipbeads. All the strings had to be made of at least three IMBOD-recognized Blood & Seed beads, one brown, one red and one white, from a choice of wooden, nut, bone, glass, mother-of-pearl or ceramic beads and a range of semi-precious stones: garnets, dark carnelian, red jasper, rubies, moonstones, opals and pearls. No one in the Golden Bough Murmuration had a ruby—those were for wealthy urban children—but the school had decided that all the girls should have a garnet as a center stone and the boys a moonstone, and Leaf one of each. Some of the larger beads were carved into lacy patterns, others were painted with tiny dotted or flowered patterns. Even the smaller beads were all different: translucent or opaque, flat disks or spheres, faceted or smooth. Tedis's necklace alternated moonstone cubes with carved round oakwood beads. Leaf's divider beads were white ceramic, hand-painted with red petals. Each bead string was a power cord that connected you with Gaia. You would keep it forever, and wear it in your Gaia-bonding ceremonies, when a loved one died and during the birth of your children. At the end, you would be burned or buried in it.

The sun was setting now. To the west the sky was flushed. The evening air was warm and supple. Rubbing everyone else's beads between her fingertips, explaining over and over how Kali had worn a rubber wetsuit and iron lungs to buy her Murano beads in Neuropa's famous underwater city, Astra almost forgot about Ahn. There was great excitement too over Silvie and Sultana, who were both wearing blood panties, Sultana having had her first bleed in sync with the ceremony. The school would score points for this. Tedis was wondering if they had time to send scouts to check out the other schools and see how many blood-panty girls they had when Baz pointed into the air and asked, "What's that?"

A Kezcam was swiveling above them, a small black ball punctuating the deepening blue heavens.

"It's the camera," Astra said. "We're not supposed to look at it, remember."

"Yeah, Baz." Tedis punched his arm. "Was that you at rehearsal or did you send your Green Spoon Room clone?"

"Ha ha. I didn't think it would look like a burned testicle."

Everyone laughed. Carefully, Astra cast an eye out over the field. Ahn was standing by a horse and cart, the Kezcam bag on his hip and Tablette in hand. He was swiping the screen and scanning the air above the crowd in his practiced way. Hokma and Mr. Ripenson were in front of the tea table and they were watching Ahn too. Then Mr. Ripenson raised his hand and as if jerking herself awake, Hokma stepped over to join Nimma and Klor.

The sun had set. *Whooo hooo. Whooo hooo.* Mr. Ripenson made the call of an owl and the children rushed to line up behind him in order of height, shortest to tallest, alternating staff hands like rowers with their oars on a scull. The other teachers and parents following in single file, they entered the paperbark woods along the edge of the field and passed into the Congregation Site.

The Congregation Site was a clearing between the woods and the Boundary. From the road it was a golden wink, but here the Boundary was a towering screen, a gilded curtain of swooning light running between two dark mountains and disappearing at either end into the woods. The Boundary was imposing, impenetrable: two watchtowers jutted up either side of the clearing and IMBOD soldiers, Astra knew, were patrolling the parapets behind its fiery veil. But at the same time the Boundary was enchanting, intoxicating, exhilarating. Beneath the royal blue twilight sky its bright yellow and orange flames mingled and rippled to the ground like an endlessly falling bolt of sateen. Looking at it was like watching a cascade of golden salmon leaping down a waterfall. The Boundary was the Or Story Fountain, but ten times higher and infinitely longer. It was Tabby held under the covers at night when you were little, filling your vision with soothing colors and ushering your brainwaves into Beta-flow. It was the flare inside you when you peaked and remained peaking for an eternity—but it was there for everyone to see and share. The Boundary was Gaia's sacred girdle, Her holy ring of fire.

Moving toward the Boundary, Astra felt her legs begin to drag, as if a magnet in the earth was pulling her to the ground to worship Gaia right here, right now. But she couldn't stop: she had to keep walking, following Leaf down the center aisle between the site's amphitheater seating toward the Blood & Seed labyrinth.

The fourteen schools were to stand in rows, seven on the right side of the labyrinth entrance and seven on the left; their parents and teachers sat on the benches behind them. Mr. Ripenson was ushering the children into their row, behind a school from Cedaria.

Peat had not been allowed to tell her and Yoki what the labyrinth looked like, only that it was awesome. All Astra knew was that it was set out in a Chakravyuha pattern, an ancient Hindu battle formation. The first time the children walked the labyrinth would be at the ceremony—in rehearsal they had simply walked around in a circle, chanting their hymns. Here, as she took her place in the row and peered between the heads of the students from Cedaria, she could see the pattern for the first time. The Bioregional Wheel Meet had paved it with red marble stones, bordered with beds of white irises and lilies. Solar garden lamps planted at regular intervals between the flowers lit the path, which doubled back on itself in wide circles until it reached a tight spiral at the center. It was supposed to look like a blooming lotus or a spinning chakra. Warriors on the rim protected their leaders in the center, and if the enemy somehow did manage to penetrate, they would find it impossible to escape.

Though the labyrinth looked like a maze, there was only the one path to the center and back. If you met celebrants coming the other way, you were to step around them. The marble was glossy and the stones, though flat, might be uneven and slippery to walk on, so you had to walk slowly and use your staff for balance. Fundamentally, though, you didn't have to worry about anything as you walked the labyrinth. It would pull you to the center and then release you.

Everyone had entered the site now. The sky was darkening and the Boundary flames were shading from orange to crimson. Mr. Ripenson had gone to join the Golden Bough parents and teachers in the seats. Four IMBOD officers, two men and two women, all tall and toned, processed down the center aisle and took their places either side of the labyrinth entrance. Behind them, the Boundary imagery morphed from fire to liquid. Now it was as if waves of blood and milk were washing down the screen. Beneath it, the labyrinth shone with an eerie glimmer, the faint auras of the solar lamps almost absorbed by the Boundary's deepening ambient light. Against the spectacle, the IMBOD officers were dark silhouettes, four black outlines against the pouring wall, the two men facing the two women on either side of the entrance. Then, from the watchtowers, two spears of bright white light struck the two officers nearest the entrance. Bleached in the beams, they lifted their arms, each bearing aloft a chalice.

"Blood & Seed Day," the four IMBOD officers began to chant. Astra heard the adults behind her rise to their feet.

There were no speeches here, no master or mistress of ceremonies, no one telling you where the restrooms were, or the order of events. Everyone had rehearsed; everyone knew what to do. She opened her mouth and joined the hymn.

Blood & Seed Day
Blood & Seed Day
Day of Sowing
Day of Growing
Day of Ripeness
Red and Whiteness
Youth abloom
Spilling, spooling

Powering, pouring
Into Gaia's
Sacred Womb

The words were simple, but they were repeated in different patterns, in counterpoint to the other schools, and many hours had been spent rehearsing the full cycle with recordings of the other parts, and once with a Tablette connection between the fourteen schools. Sewing petals in the Earthship, Astra had tried changing the words to "Day of Snoring, Day of Boring." But though Yoki had giggled, he'd caught himself and shaken his head. "Don't make fun of Gaia, Astra," he'd ordered. And now, hearing the hymn in its full-throated glory, rising into the evening sky above the Boundary, she forgot that she'd ever resented having to learn it, forgot the times she'd pricked her finger sewing, forgot about all the petals she'd sewn only for Nimma to say *not good enough, unpick it and start again*.

The row ahead of her was moving now as the children from Nīrāgā began to walk toward the entrance to the labyrinth. She was nervous, she realized, suddenly pierced with the dreadful feeling that *she* wasn't good enough to be here, she hadn't practiced hard enough, she wasn't Sec Gen, she had let herself get woefully distracted by Lil. But she couldn't give in to the fear; she couldn't let anyone know. She had to concentrate on the hymn, not let the school down. If you forgot your place, it was better to mouth the words until you found it again. Right now they were repeating each couplet five times: *Day of Sowing, Day of Growing, Day of Sowing, Day of Growing . . .* She *knew* this. Repeating it, she felt her tremor of panic subside.

At last her school line began to move too, starting from the innermost child—the tallest, Tedis—and then she was turning and following Fox on her way to the heart of Gaia's womb. The beams of light were moving over the labyrinth now, and the IMBOD officers were as tall as trees in the night. Astra hardly noticed them, focused as she was on counting phrases and moving one slow step after another in time to the hymn. At the labyrinth threshold Fox stopped and took a sip from the chalice offered by the man on the right, and another from the one held by the woman on the left. That was the beginning of the ceremony. Without Fox, she might have forgotten. As Fox stepped over the threshold and into the labyrinth, the two Chalice Officers turned to their Second Officers, the flagon-bearers, who refilled the goblets. Astra remembered to face the female First Officer first. The officer was dressed in full uniform: boots, knife belt, hydrobelt, medpac and peaked cap. She lifted the silver chalice to Astra's lips. It was filled with a dark liquid she knew was red, though it looked black in the weird mixture of light swirling over the clearing. She took a scant mouthful of sour cherry juice, then turned to the male officer. His chalice was full of liquid that should have looked white but didn't; it was gray and shadowy, streaked with the red light of the Boundary, but it tasted exactly like what it was, her favorite drink, gorgeous rich coconut cream.

Day of Ripeness.
Red and Whiteness.

Now she was chanting again as she stepped over the threshold. She didn't need to watch Fox anymore; though he was only a pace ahead of her, he was in his own world and she was in hers. She plunged her hand into the drawstring bag hanging from her staff and withdrew a fistful of petals. As she placed her boot on the first red marble paving stone, she let one fall. The path was already scattered with red and white drops of embroidery and hers was immediately lost in the drift. It didn't matter: she was in the labyrinth now. The path turned sharp right, not around the edge of the labyrinth, but into one of its middle rings. As she stepped on, other celebrants moving either side of her, she allowed more petals to trickle through her fist. Some fell in the cracks between the stones, others wafted into the flowerbeds, their sequins glimmering in the soft glare of the solar lamps. Ahead of her, Fox was chanting loudly and shaking his fist like a silent rattle in time to the hymn. In the glow cast by the Boundary his back was marbled like the paving stones. So was her own skin, she noticed vaguely, as the red streaks veining her forearms deepened to crimson. Then a beam of hot white light poured over her, draining everyone near her of all color. Everyone was bathed in an ever-fluctuating stream of womb-blood and semen.

Youth abloom
Youth abloom

It took longer than you thought to walk a labyrinth; that was what Mr. Ripenson had said; but at the same time it took no time, because it took you *outside* time. In her peripheral vision Astra could see the empty center, but as she reached the end of her first near-navigation around it, the path doubled back on itself, taking her one ring closer to the outer edge. She was walking back alongside the path she had just trodden, further from her destination than she had been before. She was a petal in an eddy of chanting and as she walked the wider ring, planting her staff, dipping into her bag, shedding her petal-seeds, singing her monotonous songlines, she began to understand what it meant to be letting go of childish desires. The hymn was rising and ahead and behind her the celebrants were steadily pouring into Gaia's womb. She didn't need to be first to the center. She would get there in time. She didn't need to be faster than the others. Their steps gave hers fraternity, sorority, solidity, strength. She didn't rue the spilling of her petals, the weeks of painstaking work they represented. She wanted to offer them to Gaia, to the feet of her brothers and sisters, to the vision field of her parents and everyone's parents, sitting in the darkness outside the rim of the labyrinth. And she didn't want to be angry with Lil anymore. She wished now that Lil could be here too, except she was, because she was in Astra's heart and her rough tears were staining Astra's petals and falling softly down to the path too. She was shedding Lil's anguish for her and letting it mulch into the mystery of Gaia's benevolence, Gaia's offer of renewal to every broken, damaged, wounded generation through their children and their children and theirs.

Spilling, spooling
Powering, pouring

She was on the outer rim of the labyrinth now. If she were in battle, she would be one of the bravest warriors, facing the enemy, baring her teeth, lunging and stabbing, never losing formation. But she was safe, shielded by the Boundary, its wealth of ruby and silver illumination coating her from braid bead to toenail as she walked the far edge of the circle, back yet again to near the entrance, where the path made a wider loop inwards, up past the middle rings she'd already walked and into a simple spiral, its coils tightening toward the center of the labyrinth. From the corner of her eye she could see the Cedaria had reached the center. The girl paused, only for a moment, then turned and began to spin back out again onto the path. As Astra made the dizzying rotations toward the core, she met the girl returning, and then her train of Cedaria celebrants. One by one they stepped carefully around her. The prospect of this interweaving had concerned her when it was explained in rehearsal, but now it was occurring she realized the path was wide enough and the brush of flesh on flesh a signal of the energy building in the labyrinth. She had wanted to be the first student, hers the first school to enter; she had thought that being first was a privilege, she had wanted the whole labyrinth to herself; but she now understood it was more powerful to be lost in Gaia's eternal turning. She dug deeper into her petal bag: she had to cast away all her petals, all her childish doubts, desires and fears, before she reached the center.

Into Gaia's
Sacred Womb

Even though she had been spying it the whole way, that pivotal space—Gaia's womb-heart, the battle vortex, last standing ground of mighty Warrior Kings and Queens—when the center of the labyrinth was finally there, underfoot, its arrival surprised her. A tiny part of her mind had been worrying that it was too small, too crowded, her time in it would be too short—and she *was* briefly crushed up against Fox and Leaf as she entered and left, the line bunching and inching to accommodate her—but in the moment that she stood and planted her staff in the soil between the three paving stones that marked the center, she felt as open as the steppes. Her petal bag was empty, her head sang with understanding, her heart was winging in her chest. She whirled once around her staff and began to retrace her steps back to an entirely new world. As she placed one poised foot after another, lightly maneuvering around celebrants still journeying to the center, still shedding petals, still burdened with childish desires, she felt her stomach wrench and liquid trickled down her thigh.

She kept walking, but when the blazing white beam passed over her again, she glanced down. It wasn't pee. It wasn't Gaia-play juice. It was black.

She finished the labyrinth walk with tears brimming in her eyes, blood pouring down her legs. Gaia had visited her in the Blood & Seed ceremony. Gaia had *chosen* her. She chose girls rarely, not every year, and when She did it was a great blessing, not only on the girl's school, but on the whole bioregion. Astra knew exactly what to do. When she exited the labyrinth, instead of following Fox back into their school row, she presented herself to the two female IMBOD officers still standing sentinel at the entrance. In the spill of light between their two erect figures, she patted her leg and showed them her dark wet palm.

Silently, her back straight, the chalice-bearer strapped the chalice into her hydrobelt, retrieved her Tablette and handed it to Astra. Astra wiped her hand on her belly and touch-typed her name into the screen. Her photo came up, with three rows of text beneath it:

Astra Ordott

Golden Bough School

New Bangor

Not Gaia-bled

This was the official IMBOD Gaia-blood database. Girls who had already begun bleeding were listed with the date of their first Gaia-blood. If their cycle coincided with the ceremony, they had to wear blood panties, like Silvie. The only way to possibly cheat the system was for a girl who had only just begun bleeding to keep the fact secret, then wear a mooncup or a tampon and pull it out and discard it while in the labyrinth. But because of the penetration rule even small tampons and mooncups weren't allowed until at least age fifteen, so the girl would be breaking *two* laws. Besides, she would have her staff in one hand and all the other celebrants would see her grappling with her Gaia garden with the other as she walked. Even if the girl had somehow connived to gain glory for her school by asking her friends not to report her, celebrants from other schools would see her, and so would the IMBOD officers in the watchtowers, passing their bright beams over the labyrinth in search of any such desecrating act. And later, of course, the site gardeners would find the evidence, even if the girl had managed to tread her tampon or mooncup down into the earth with her heel. So in fact, cheating was impossible—but naturally the officer had to check the records.

The Chalice Officer examined her Tablette, rapidly thumb-swiping and tapping the screen. The swirling light from the Boundary was haloing her thick hair and the screen up-glow coated her face with a greenish patina. She smiled, and her teeth glinted like emeralds. For a moment, she looked like the ancestor in the far seat of the arrowpain. Then she put a hand on Astra's shoulder and gripped it in a half-shake, half-hug. Beside her, the Second Officer raised her flagon in the air. The Chalice Officer shoved her Tablette back in her belt and twisted Astra around to face the stands of parents and teachers. As the two watchtower beams converged on them she grabbed Astra's staff-hand wrist and lifted it high in the air.

Astra was quaking and a lathe of pain was rotating in her stomach. The bright white lights were cascading over her, delineating every blade of grass at her feet, sending long black shadows crisscrossing down toward the school rows, striping the celebrants still processing out of the labyrinth, still chanting the Blood & Seed hymn. Over the choral tapestry of interweaving voices, a roar rose up from the stands. The adults were applauding. They were calling *Gaia Gaia Gaia*.

The officer was yanking her arm out of its socket and her gut was wound tight as a scarf caught in a bicycle chain. Her face contorted with pain and she was afraid she might drop her staff. When she opened her eyes, a Kezcam was dropping out of the sky. With a tiny shudder, the black ball stopped directly in front of her, on the edge of the spotlight.

Astra stared into the lens and placed her free hand between her legs. She thrust her dripping red palm out toward the camera and up into the air. The cheer of the crowd intensified and their clapping became rhythmic in time to the chant. The spotlights swerved back to the labyrinth, the applause ended with a final full-throated GAIA, and she and the officers were left in the dark.

As her eyes adjusted back to the marbling Boundary light, the Chalice Officer dropped her arm and bent down to shout in her ear, "Go back to your place in your row."

She was a woman now—but like a child, she wanted to find Nimma and curl up in her cushiony lap, or go and lie in the long grass on the edge of the woods. Instead, she rejoined the line of exiting celebrants, strange students from another New Bangor school who parted to let her in, and when the line reached her row she peeled off and slipped back to her place next to Fox, walking slowly with head held high past all her friends, who couldn't reach out and pat her on the back or hug her because the Kezcam was following her and any breach of protocol would subtract from the points she had just earned, but whose sweet, kind, familiar faces radiated joy for her and pride for Golden Bough School.

They stood tall, chanting and waiting for the labyrinth to empty of students. The blood was crawling down her leg, tickling her as it reached a sensitive spot just above the knee, but Astra didn't dare wipe it away. When all the schools were back in their rows, the watchtower lights strobed rapidly, then cut off. This was it, the signal for the final act of the ceremony: the Sec Gen laser ritual.

Everyone stopped chanting. The Pilgrimage site was lit only by the four officer spotlights and the ghostly glow of the Boundary. In one fluid movement, the students of all fourteen schools knelt on the ground. Just as they'd rehearsed, Astra paused for the count of three, then placed her staff to her right and lay back on the grass, her feet on the earth, knees in the air, hydropac coiled like a mat between her shoulder blades. She reached out for Leaf and Fox's hands and held them loosely, her right wrist resting on her staff. She was a link in a chain of children staring up at the stars, waiting, hearts steady as pulsars, to take the final step into adulthood. From the Boundary, a single soprano voice soared over the site, a high keening wail of aspiration, followed by a deep male bass, a rumbling counterpoint that answered the soprano's cry for knowledge with a fathomless echo of the night's impenetrable mysteries.

Astra's skin erupted in a cold rash of joy. The sacred singers of Vanapur Temple had emerged from the watchtower to serenade her and her generation. The singers, in their high traditional headdresses and woven wrist- and ankle-wraps, were standing on the parapets of the Boundary, arms raised to the sky, embracing the watching parents and teachers. The labyrinth officers were securing their chalices and flagons into their hydrobelts and taking their square black medpacs from their shoulders. Ensconced in the light of the four spotlights, they were leaving the entrance to the Chakravyuha and marching down the central aisle, medpacs in their hands, each stopping before one of the first four schools, pausing, bowing to the parents. They were turning into the rows, kneeling before the first students, unbuttoning the medpacs. How long would it take for an officer to reach Golden Bough School? Her knees trembled and she inhaled and focused on stilling the tremor. She couldn't let everyone down, not after being Chosen.

The singing continued, monotonous, swelling, hypnotic, punctuated only by the occasional random yelp or moan. When it was her turn, Astra wasn't going to utter even a gasp. Her fingers were entwined with Leaf's and Fox's and her legs were firm now, the soles of her feet planted securely in the grass. Her eyes were filled with the dazzling smear of the Milky Way, her nostrils hummed with the scent of sweat, earth, lily pollen and the faint tang of blood, her blood, now tracing a line down her legs, seeping into the soil. Her body was not her own: her body belonged to Gaia, to Is-Land, to her generation. She ached for the consummation of all that she was.

After she didn't know how long, the officer was there, in their row. Beside her, the light beam was flooding Leaf's body and the officer was kneeling between hir legs. She caught a whiff of an intense, acrid smell that nearly turned her stomach and Leaf was gripping her hand until she thought her finger bones would break. But heesh didn't cry, didn't make a single sound.

And now it was her turn.

The officer was between her knees. She mustn't look up, would never know if her initiator was a male or a female officer, a chalice- or a flagon-bearer. The officer was snapping on a new pair of latex gloves, spreading her buttocks apart and rubbing her Gaia garden with a wet sponge, all the way down to her anus. Just as they'd practiced, she opened her legs as wide as she could, raising her buttocks and exposing her perineum. The scent of alcohol wafted up to her nose and the air cooled her damp genitals. Then the officer was drying her quickly with a flannel, not removing it, but plugging her slightly, pushing the cloth a fingertip into her Gaia garden, just enough to prevent the blood from flowing out. It was coming now. She clenched Leaf's and Fox's hands and they squeezed back, Fox with more strength than Leaf.

The officer was smoothing the stencil over her perineum now, holding it down with two fingers. Then, with the other hand, heesh was taking the laser gun from hir belt. The spotlight was blinding her, bleaching her body. Everyone in the stands, every Golden Bough parent and teacher, was watching her, all holding their breath for the Chosen one, begging her not to fail them now. She tensed, squeezed her eyes shut, gritted her teeth. *It will hurt you more than the others*, Hokma had said. *Anything I give for the pain will wear off before the ceremony starts. You will have to cope with it yourself. Count to ten. Breathe deeply. Release the air slowly. Clench your feet inside the boots. Press your wrist against your staff. Create another pain.*

ONE—

A pinball of fire rocketed up her spine, dislocating her bones, rattling her teeth. She dragged a breath . . .

TWO—

. . . of charred air into her lungs. The pain was slowly circling her root chakra. A sickening stench . . .

THREE—

. . . invaded her mouth, a sulfurous cloud of rotten alt-meat, struck matches, sucked pennies. The flames crawled up her nerves . . .

FOUR—

. . . and it was all she could do not to shake her legs and throw her hips in the air. There was bile in her throat, the searing circle of pain . . .

FIVE—

...joining like a snake, tail to mouth, complete. She choked back the vomit. A thin red-hot bar began to ...

SIX—

...traverse her. She rammed wrist against staff, bone against wood, two crossed dorjes welded together. Now ...

SEVEN—

...a downward whiplash began and ...

EIGHT—

...another, meeting in a point on the still-burning circle and now ...

NINE—

...at last, the vertical gash, dividing the triangle, back down to the ...

TEN—

...point of worst pain ...

Just when she thought she had to scream or pass out or die, it was over. The IMBOD shield was branded at the root of her Gaia garden and the officer was spraying her with cooling anesthetic. Leaf and Fox were pumping her hands. Her eyes burned. She was Sec Gen now, in everything but Code.

2.12

No one had giggled, no one had faltered; everyone had remembered their lines. No one had cried or screamed during the Branding. No points had been deducted for any part of their performance. Silvie and Sultana had been Gaia-bleeding, and Astra had been Gaia-Chosen, and thanks to the extra points she'd earned them, Golden Bough School won the Congregation Site prize for Best Performance at the Blood & Seed ceremony. As the bioregional medals were being hung around their necks, the results of the other four ceremonies came in to the officers' Tablettes. Incredibly, another girl—from Atourne—had also been Gaia-Chosen that year, but no girls in her school had been bleeding at the start of the ceremony, so thanks to Silvie and Sultana, Golden Bough had also taken the *National* Blood & Seed prize. The female chalice-bearer announced the amazing news, and everyone at the Congregation Site leapt to their feet and cheered until Astra worried that their throats were being stripped of their linings.

Afterward, Astra's classmates mobbed her, desperate to touch and hug and kiss her. Just as she thought she might be crushed, Tedis and Baz lifted her on their shoulders and paraded her up and down the central aisle between the stands, Yoki jumping along by her legs. Tablette cameras flashed everywhere—the parents and students of the other schools were as ecstatic as her own friends and community. Gaia had chosen their ceremony, and they would remember all their lives the moment when their labyrinth walk was transformed by the convergence of the watch-tower lights on the girl who had become a woman among them. When the boys finally let her down, Tedis hugged her. Her nipples pressed hard as acorns against his chest, but then strange adults were falling over themselves to hug her and Nimma was rushing over, pushing them away.

"Astra, oh my darling! Let me look at you!" Her Shelter mother cupped Astra's face in her hands and kissed it all over. Then she sank to her knees, pulled a damp cloth out of her hydropac and began rubbing at the dried blood streaks on Astra's calves.

"Good Gaia, woman, don't wipe it away," Klor boomed behind her. "Gaia has marked her twice tonight: let her stay marked."

"She can shower at home, Nimma," Hokma chimed in.

There was a severe, tugging feeling in Astra's stomach. Lil had told her about this. "I've got cramps," she moaned.

"Nimma," Hokma asked, "did you bring any aspirin?"

"Only enough for two bioregions." Nimma rummaged again in her pac and handed Hokma a bottle. Hokma gave Astra two pills and helped her fumble for her hydro-tubing. She sucked and swallowed. "My brand hurts too," she whispered. It was burning again, a lancing, almost intolerable pain, traveling in spurts up to her coccyx.

"The aspirin will help," Klor soothed.

"Oh, Klor, it's not nearly strong enough," Nimma snapped. "Astra, lie down."

Astra obeyed, opening her knees to let Nimma spray her again with anesthetic. Klor knelt at her side and stroked her forehead with his gnarly knuckles.

"Brave Astra," he smiled.

"I don't see why they couldn't have been injected," Nimma grumbled. "It's all right for the robust ones, but Yoki's in tears."

"They have to learn to take a little pain," Klor said. "That's what the Sec Gens do for us all. Isn't that right, angel?"

"Well, they've done a good job, at least," Nimma added. "The circle is round as the moon, Astra. You must have held perfectly still."

Astra nodded dumbly. Nimma was pulling a pair of blood panties up around her waist, flipping the hipbeads out so the three ropes hung over the red absorbent cloth. The spray was working, her stomach felt better and she thought that in a minute or two she would be able to walk again. As she lay there, dazed and catching her breath, a shadow blocked the light: Ahn, Tablette in hand, a Kezcam hovering at his shoulder, was standing over her, smiling his thin smile.

"So. The Gaia Girl," he greeted her. "Well done, Astra. Well done, Hokma."

Astra shut her knees and Hokma said quietly, "Thank you, Ahn, but I had nothing to do with it."

The traffic was bumper to bumper leaving the parking field, but the cars rolled down their windows so people could keep waving at each other, all singing the Blood & Seed hymn as they inched toward the main road. In the minivan, Mr. Ripenson had joined them, sitting in the back next to Ahn; Freyja's arm was resting across the back of the front seat, stroking Pan's shoulder and from her seat behind Yoki and Astra, Nimma asked if anyone was hungry and brought out a picnic hamper filled with soy yogurts, bananas and berry biscuits. Yoki was hugging Astra, saying, "You're my sister. I *love* you!" over and over and she was squeezing him back saying, "You're my brother. I love *you*." Then right outside Astra's window Silvie's carthorse lifted his tail and dropped a big ploppy poo pile on the road and everyone started laughing, even Ahn.

After the picnic, the van picked up speed and Astra and Yoki stretched out on their seats, head to toe. Her brand was burning, but only slightly now, a constant reminder of the enormous change she had undergone tonight. Yoki fell asleep, but Astra lay happily imagining telling Lil everything that had happened. Tonight, she would send Silver with the news. Back at the Earthship, she would unclasp Silver's memory clip from his leg, plug it into Klor's Tablette and download a photo of her between the two officers, one of her on Tedis's shoulders, and another of the whole school getting their medals. Then she'd send Silver ahead of Hokma, back to Wise House, so if Lil was up she could see the photos right away.

"Hokma," she whispered.

"Yes, Gaia Girl?"

"I want to send Silver to Lil. Promise you won't tell her anything first?"

"I promise."

But when she woke up, she wasn't being gently shaken by the shoulder and told to get up for the walk to the Earthship. The van was squealing up the road and adults were exclaiming, "What in Gaia's name?" and, "Careful, Pan, there are *children* in here." She raised her head groggily as the van screeched to a halt.

"What's the matter?"

"It's okay, Astra," Freyja said. "We don't know yet."

"Astra," Nimma ordered, opening her hydropac, "lie still." She opened her legs to let Nimma spray her, craning her neck to see what was happening. Klor was wrenching the door open and he and Ahn and Hokma and Mr. Ripenson were pouring out and up the path through East Gate. Pan was slamming his door shut and following them. Freyja was looking anxiously at Yoki.

"Are we home now?" Yoki asked, rubbing his eyes.

"Yes, but we have to wait here for a minute," Nimma said. "Here, let me spray you again."

"Why do we have to wait?" Astra demanded. She stuck her head out of the van. The air was filled with a commotion of calls and cries, and another burning smell met her nostrils—not nauseating, like the laser gun on her genitals, or cozy, like the kitchen stove when you opened the door to add a log. She peered up through East Gate. At the top of the lawn, blooms of smoke were billowing into the night. Beneath the huge ash-gray blossom, flames were leaping like tigers from a black, broken cage. Against their violent orange glow she could see the silhouettes of people, a chain of bodies, as though the Or-adults were all holding hands and dancing around the blaze.

Core House was on fire.

Nimma reached for her and started, "Astra, stay here—" but she was already off, sprinting up the path after Hokma. Everyone in Or was out on the lawn, she could see them now, dark shapes dashing back and forth, shouting instructions, wailing. Shelter parents were holding crying children, and now she could see the chain of people weren't dancing: they were lifting the hose from the swimming-pool pump and spraying it over the flames. But it was too late: the cedar roof and walls of the dining-hall extension had been incinerated, leaving only the stone wall of the original building and the timber frame of the hall still standing. As she surged up the path, a great roof beam crashed down into the fire.

Astra caught up to Hokma and skirted around her, running as close as she could to the blaze. The heat on her face was unbearable: a furnace, worse than the hottest day of summer. It stung her eyes, and the smoke made her want to cough. Around her, people in heavy boots were stamping on the lawn, extinguishing sparks that were spitting and shooting out from the fire, tracing golden arcs through the air as they descended to the dry grass.

"*Astra.*" Hokma grabbed her from behind. "Step back. Let the fire team do their work."

Hokma pulled her back onto the lawn, and then Yoki and Nimma were there too, Yoki crying and Nimma squawking, "Hokma, where's Klor? *Where's Klor?*"

"He's there." Astra pointed. "Look!" Klor was near the front, shouldering the hosepipe, giving it some of his height. "He shouldn't be *doing* that. Let the younger men play the daredevil. Oh Klor, what are you *doing?*"

"Everything's under control, Nimma," Hokma assured her. "It won't spread. There's no wind tonight."

But Nimma wasn't listening; she was repeating herself, her head swiveling about like a weathervane in a gale. "Where's Meem? Where's Peat?" she demanded, as if Hokma could possibly know. "Have they taken a headcount? Why aren't people at the fire point?"

There was a fire plan, Astra remembered; they were supposed to meet at the swimming pool. But it looked to her as if anyone not in the hosepipe chain was milling around, watching the inferno. For it was a mesmerizing sight: a raging cavern of timber and flames with a white-hot sanctum of ashes swirling at its heart. Most marvelously, the heat almost generated space: what had once been a reasonably large hall was now monumental, a roaring galaxy, a new dimension of the universe being born and dying in one eternal, expansive, suffering explosion. Astra could have watched it all night.

"Is everyone okay?" Yoki's lower lip was trembling.

"Let's go and find out," Hokma said firmly. With Yoki trotting behind, she and Nimma dragged Astra away from the thunderous sight of the dining hall collapsing, one beam at a time. They hurried across the lawn to the swimming pool, stepping around the black scorch marks in the grass. There were Meem and Peat, standing in a huddle with their Birth-Code mother Honey, Moon and Aesop, Tulsi and Flint, one of her Shelter fathers, and a slew of other children and parents. Congruence was between Gloria and Luna, and on the edge of the circle Mr. Ripenson was hugging Sorrel. A few feet away, Ahn was filming, sending the Kezcams careering around the lawn. "*Meem, Peat,*" Nimma cried, and Astra's Shelter siblings ran from their Code mother's arms to be hugged. Everyone reached out to embrace Astra and Yoki too. Astra wanted the adults to notice her blood panties, but they were too busy talking about the fire.

"Moon!" Nimma pulled the younger woman to her, embracing Aesop too, snuggled in his wrap between their breasts. "Is everyone safe? Is everyone accounted for?"

"Arjun's doing the headcount now," Moon told them. "Russett's looking for people too."

"Oh, please Gaia, everyone be safe," Nimma cried, placing her palms together, her fingertips at her lips.

"How did it start?" Hokma asked brusquely.

"No one knows." Moon turned and gazed at the fire as if she still couldn't believe it was there. "It started about an hour ago. Most people had gone to bed. Arjun and Russett were playing chess in the Quiet Room when they smelled smoke. They thought it must be coming from the stove, but the kitchen was fine, so they looked in the dining hall. Arjun said it had already caught hold by then: the curtains had burned all the way up to the roof and the tables and chairs were ablaze. It was too late for the fire extinguishers so they raised the alarm and got the pump team going. We called the fire station too, but the roads in and out of New Bangor are so busy they haven't got here yet."

"But how could—?" Nimma flashed with anger. "Did someone leave a candle burning?"

"No," declared Flint, who was a full-time member of the kitchen team, "they were all blown out after dinner and taken back to the kitchen, like always."

"I *said* we should build the dining hall in stone," Nimma said angrily. "But people didn't listen. They just wanted to get it up quickly and cheaply."

Astra tugged at Moon's arm. "Did you count Lil?"

Moon looked anxiously at Hokma. "Lil's at Wise House, isn't she? We didn't go up there, no. We needed everyone here. Maybe we should have." Her face crumpled. "I'm sorry, Hokma. I just wasn't thinking straight."

"We have to count Lil," Astra insisted.

"I'll go now," Hokma said.

"I'm coming too!"

Hokma and Nimma exchanged glances. "No, darling," Nimma said. "I want you here with me tonight."

"Why can't I come? Lil's my friend."

"Lil will be fine, Astra," Hokma said. "She'll be in bed sleeping. I don't want you to wake her up and spend all night talking."

"You have to get up early, remember." Nimma seamlessly took the baton. "The journalists are coming to see the Gaia Girl."

"The Gaia Girl?" For the first time Moon and the other Shelter parents looked properly down at her. "Oh, Astra!" Moon exclaimed. "You're wearing *blood pants*! I can't believe I didn't notice—what a night! *Congratulations*, sweetheart. Nimma, Hokma, how exciting!"

Then it was like the Congregation Site all over again, with the Or parents hugging her and ruffling her hair, and Yoki standing proudly at her side, telling Peat and Meem how all the other schools had clapped and taken photos. Astra looked around for Ahn. Shouldn't he be filming this? But he had wandered back near the blaze, the Kezcams invisible above him.

"Shh now, Yoki," Nimma said. "You can't say anything about the ceremony, remember."

"I wasn't! Just the parade."

"Okay, Astra." Hokma rubbed her back. "I'm off now."

It wasn't fair, but there was nothing she could do about it. "Will you take Silver and send him back to say Lil's okay?"

"Astra, Lil is fine—and if she's not, then I'll come back and tell you, okay?"

She was going to keep arguing, but Hokma had already stood up and Russett was pounding over the lawn toward the pool.

"Is Torrent here?" he panted, his face red with exertion. "Or Stream?"

"Torrent?" Moon looked around. "No. Isn't he in the pump team?"

Tulsi pulled at Flint's hand. "Daddy?" she pleaded. "Where's Stream?"

Russett shook his head, impatiently, as if he was wasting his time with them all. He made as if to go, but Nimma took his arm. "Russett, slow down. Where did you last see him?"

"*I* last saw him in the Earthship, refusing to study. Arjun last saw him in the dining hall," Russett said shortly, shaking off her hand. "After dinner. With Stream."

Nimma gasped.

Hokma stayed put. Astra took her hand.

"But the hall was empty when you and Arjun—" Moon started.

"*I don't know!*" Russett exploded. "It *looked* empty! We didn't look under the frigging tables, did we? I've looked every-frigging-where else, and so has her Shelter father. We can't find them. They're not in their Earthships, and they're not on the grounds."

"Maybe they're in the woods," Hokma suggested, "Gaia-playing?"

"Gaia-playing?" Russett turned on her. "While Or is on fire?"

Flint stepped forward. He swallowed before he spoke. "Russett," he said quietly, "I caught them Gaia-playing in the dining hall last month—behind the curtains. I said if they did it again I'd tell you. I'm sorry, I should have—"

"You said *what*?" Russett raised his fist. "You let him get away with that? You *idiot*, you—"

"Russett!" Hokma dropped Astra's hand and stepped between the two men. "*Calm down.*"

Nimma pulled Astra and Yoki against her, but Astra reached up and tugged at Nimma's arm. "We have to find Lil," she insisted.

"Shh," Nimma ordered. Around them Tulsi was shrieking, begging to be picked up, and the younger children were crying, "Mama, where's Torrent? Where's Stream?" Flint bent and gathered Tulsi in his arms.

Russett was shaking. "If they were in that hall, Flint," he said in a low voice, "I'll kill you. I'll frigging kill you." Then he turned and stalked off toward the Kinbat track, bellowing, "*Torrent. Stream.*"

"Oh dear." Nimma stared after him. "And in front of Tulsi!"

"He's worried to death," Hokma said flatly.

"I should have told him." Flint looked sick. His arms were wrapped tightly around Tulsi, who was crying into his shoulder. Congruence was sobbing too, and Gloria and Luna were holding her tightly now.

"No, Flint," Moon reassured him, "Torrent's seventeen. Russett can't control everything he does."

"I want to see Lil!" Astra shouted.

"Astra, be quiet," Hokma commanded. "I'm going to find her now. You do what Nimma tells you. Luna," she said more softly, her hand on the Shelter mother's shoulder, "why don't you take Congruence home? Gloria should be resting too."

Hokma strode off to East Gate and Gloria and Luna took the still-weeping Congruence back to their Earthship. Nimma and Moon wouldn't let Astra leave the swimming pool so she stood watching the fine, ineffectual stream of water fall over the flames until there was no more water left in the tanks. Just as the flames had subsided into small flickering fingers and the dining hall had disintegrated into a black mess of charred wet wood, the New Bangor fire truck arrived, its sirens screaming up the hill and through East Gate. Most of the younger children had fallen asleep, curled up on the ground or in their parents' arms; the noise woke some of them, but no one took them back to their Earthships. Klor was striding over to the pool, his face, arms and chest smudged with soot. He hugged everybody, getting them all sooty too, and when Astra asked if they could go down and see the truck now it was safe, he said no, the larger beams were still smoldering and the fire team didn't need an audience of over-excited children. When Nimma and Flint asked, he said no, Torrent and Stream hadn't been found. "They'll be in the woods," he said. "They'll stroll up for breakfast and get the shock of their lives."

It was agonizing, not knowing where Torrent and Stream were, but they couldn't stand around on the lawn all night. Flint's Gaia partner Thor arrived and the fathers took Tulsi back to bed. Meem and Peat went back to Honey's Earthship, Yoki went to stay with Pan and Freyja and Astra walked back home with Nimma and Klor. She wanted to wait up for Helium, but he hadn't come by the time she'd finished her shower. Then she was yawning and Nimma said Hokma would probably send him in the morning, so after she had learned how to change the pad in her blood pants and had sprayed her brand with more anesthetic, she had at last to go to bed.

Without her Shelter siblings there, Nimma hovered over her the whole time. She even insisted on brushing her hair. Astra thought she would take the braid beads back, but Nimma said, no, the Gaia Girl could keep wearing them for the journalists tomorrow. The big hard beads were uncomfortable against her head, but Astra flipped the braid up over the pillow and before she knew it, she was fast asleep.

But Helium didn't come in the morning. He wasn't waiting for her on his Earthship perch beside Silver with a memory clip full of congratulations tied to his leg. Instead, Hokma—who never came down to Or before noon anymore—was sitting in the guest's chair in the living room. Klor was standing by the mantelpiece and Nimma was perched on the sofa. Hokma's face was drawn and rumpled, and there were shiny red pouches under her eye and her patch. Nimma's eyes were bright pink and her face was puffy. Klor looked gray, as though he hadn't had a shower last night but had rubbed the soot into his skin.

"Astra," he said, "come and sit down. We have some very sad news."

Astra sat down on the sofa, an arm's length from Nimma. This wasn't about *Lil*. Nimma wouldn't cry over Lil.

"What happened to Torrent and Stream?" she asked.

It was the worst thing she'd ever heard—even worse than hearing about Sheba. The fire team had found Torrent and Stream. They had been under one of the tables. It looked like they'd fallen asleep after Gaia-playing and had breathed in the smoke. They had been poisoned by the carbon monoxide and had died in each other's arms.

She looked from one adult to another. "Did they wake up?" she demanded. "Did they try to escape?"

"No, they didn't wake up," Klor said. "They died in their sleep."

He was lying, she knew from the way Nimma was sitting stock-still, not meeting her eyes but staring at the photo of Sheba on the mantelpiece. Torrent and Stream had been *burned alive*. While she was being branded, they were roasting, their flesh spitting and blistering off their bones as they tried to fight their way through the flames to the door. Stream's hair had been on fire and Torrent had taken her hand, tried to pull her through the chairs, but it was too late. The flames were too high and they couldn't get out. They had screamed and screamed, but the beams were crashing down around them and no one could hear them. Astra, though, had watched: she'd gazed into the heart of the furnace, watching Torrent and Stream burn to death, wishing the fire could go on forever. She'd thought their blazing tomb was *beautiful*. The memory rose inside her like boiling water, scalding her face.

"What's left?" she whispered. "What's left of them?"

Nimma edged close and put her arm around her. "The fire team found some bones, darling. And Stream's jewelry."

"They didn't know what was happening, Astra," Hokma said. Her voice was hoarse. "They were together. Gaia took them back together."

"The fire team said they died peacefully, Astra," Klor repeated.

It was lies: all lies. The stench was in her nose; the galaxy of fire was consuming her head. She rose in her seat. "What about Lil? Where's Lil?"

Hokma cleared her throat. "Astra," she said, then stopped and covered her face with her hand.

Astra stood. "Where's *Lil*?" she screamed.

"You must stay calm, Astra," Klor said, "or we can't tell you anything."

"Drink some water, darling." Nimma pushed a glass toward her.

They weren't going to tell her anything unless she drank it, so she did. Breathing heavily, she put the glass back on the table and waited for Hokma to speak.

Lil was gone. She wasn't at Wise House when Hokma had returned. She had obviously decided to leave, because she had taken her hydropac and her knife and Hokma's tinderbox, a small pan and a bag of vegetables from the garden. She had left behind her Gaia hymnbook with a handwritten poem for Astra. Hokma handed it to her.

"She took a *tinderbox*?" Nimma gasped.

Hokma nodded.

"Hokma," Klor sounded shocked, "do you think she could have—?"

"I don't know." The vertical furrow between Hokma's eyebrows looked for a moment as black as a burn mark. "I ran back here last night and asked if people had seen her. No one remembers her. The fire team didn't find the frying pan, or"—she paused—"any other bones."

Everyone was silent. Astra looked down at the hymnbook. A piece of folded handmade paper was tucked inside the front cover. She pulled it out and opened it. In blocky red ink, surrounded by a border of stars and flowers, the poem read:

> Astra
> Like a hymn
> yore in my heart
> even when we are apart.
>
> Yore the star-girl
> yore my fire
> when I'm roaming
> in my bones
> I'll follow you
> to my onely home.
> Lil xx

Yore my fire. What did that mean? Was the dining-hall fire a message for *her*?

"Can we see, darling?" Nimma asked, holding out her hand.

"*No*." Astra refolded the poem and clapped it back inside the book. "It's mine!"

"Did you read it, Hokma?" Nimma asked sharply.

Hokma paused. "It's a friendship poem. There's a reference to fire, but it's emotional. I don't think we can infer—"

Astra was outraged. "You read *my poem*?"

"I had to, Astra. Lil might have set the fire. I had to see what she was thinking."

Astra gripped the hymnbook. "Why did she go?" she demanded. "Why did she set the fire? She said she wanted to stay with me."

"We don't know that she did set the fire, Astra," Klor said. "It could just be a coincidence."

"A highly unlikely coincidence," Nimma scoffed. "Especially after—" She stopped and looked at Hokma.

"After *what*?" Astra insisted.

Now Hokma glanced at Klor. It was as if none of them could talk without asking each other's permission. Klor sighed heavily, as if giving assent only because of exceptional circumstances.

"Astra," Hokma said, "do you remember during our picnic, Helium had an urgent message for me? The message was from IMBOD. It was about Lil's family."

"You didn't tell—"

"*Shhh*." Nimma cut her off. "We weren't allowed to tell you. We probably shouldn't be telling you now. So be quiet and listen, my Gaia Girl, or you'll have to wait for the official announcement like everyone else."

Hokma was rubbing her face, exposing the scar tissue beneath her eyepatch.

Klor took over. "IMBOD has found Lil's family," he said. "They live in a community on the steppes, at the foot of the dry forest."

"So maybe she went to find them. We can look there."

For the first time, Hokma looked at her straight. "She doesn't know they've been found, Astra. At least, *I* didn't tell her. I wanted to come to your ceremony and I didn't want to leave her feeling upset or confused. I shouldn't have left her by herself. I should have asked an adult to stay with her. I'm sorry." She addressed Nimma and Klor. "I'll never forgive myself—she must have sensed I was anxious after I got the message."

"Oh, Hokma, no." Nimma reached for her hand. "You couldn't have missed Astra's Blood & Seed."

Astra looked suspiciously at the three adults. "Why were you anxious?" she demanded. "Why would Lil be upset that they found her family?"

Hokma shook herself back into the room. "It's very complicated, Astra. Lil's mother died when she was little, like she said—but Lil's grandmother told IMBOD that—"

She stopped and looked at Klor for support again. He looked at Nimma, then said gently, "Lil's Code-Shelter father wasn't an Is-Lander, Astra. He was a Non-Lander—an aglab. He bonded with Lil's mother, and when the Southern Boundary closed, her community protected him. He lived in a cave in the forest—that's why there was no record of him."

Astra clutched the hymnbook to her chest. "*Lil's not a Non-Lander*," she hissed. "She knows all her Gaia hymns! We—" She halted. A cold, clanging feeling was running through her, a paralyzing mix of guilt, shame and fear. However strenuously she denied it, part of her knew it was true. Lil's dad had told her bad stuff about Is-Land, stuff only a Non-Lander would think. Astra had tried to pretend Lil had a mental illness, that she was uneducated, but she should have known. *She should have reported Lil*. How could she have been so stupid? She sat quaking, her breath shallow, scared to look up.

"I know it's difficult, darling." Nimma stroked Astra's hand. "She was a good friend to you, wasn't she? You did all that foraging, and you Gaia-played with her—Hokma told us. She can't help who her father was. But still, she's not one of us, is she?"

Astra wrested her hand away. "You said Elpis sent her," she accused.

"I know I did." Nimma's voice was strained. "And maybe Elpis did. But perhaps we misinterpreted her intention. Maybe we were supposed to give Lil to IMBOD, to keep Or safe." Now her voice broke entirely. "Oh, Klor, it's true: I *wanted* her here. And now she's set this terrible fire."

Then Klor and Hokma were comforting Nimma, saying, no, no, it had been a collective decision; how could anyone have known what the girl was thinking? Astra let the adults dither on because it wasn't true. Lil *couldn't* have set the fire. Lil *couldn't* have killed Torrent and Stream. Even if Lil's dad was a Non-Lander, *Lil* was a Gaian, and she wanted to stay in Or and go to school.

But if Lil hadn't known about her family, she must have left for another reason. Lil had wanted to go to high school, but what had Astra said? Not "Great," but "What if we don't get along?" That's when Lil had got upset. That's when she'd felt unwanted, scared, *belittled*. If she'd set the fire, she'd done it because she was angry with Astra. Because she thought IMBOD was going to take her away.

"It's *my fault*," she moaned. "I was *mean* to her at the compost. I should have invited her to the Blood & Seed ceremony. Then she wouldn't have burned down the dining hall."

"It's *not* your fault." Now Hokma leaned over and took Astra's hand. "Lil could be very difficult sometimes, couldn't she? You couldn't always be nice to her."

"It *is* my fault," Astra screamed, pushing Hokma away.

Beside her, Nimma was getting agitated. "This is what she's like, Hokma. This is what I mean."

"Maybe it's her Gaia-blood," Klor offered.

"Oh, *Klor*—" Nimma turned on him in exasperation. "Her hormones are supposed to be *balanced*."

Hokma reached for her shoulder. Dimly, Astra recognized that she should make an effort to calm down, but it was easier to descend into a state of dry, shuddering sobbing, dragging one long harsh breath after another into her lungs. She had driven Lil away. She had made Lil feel so bad she'd set fire to Core House.

"*I k-k-killed her*," she howled. "*I killed T-t-torrent and S-s-s-stream*."

"No, you didn't," Hokma urged, shaking her shoulder. "We don't know that Lil set the fire. Maybe Torrent and Stream were smoking a cigarette and fell asleep before they put it out."

"Astra, darling," Klor said loudly, crouching before her and placing his hands on her knees, "we know it's a shock. But Lil has a frying pan and a knife. She won't be hungry. There's nothing to worry about, is there?"

"She's hyperventilating, Klor." Nimma sounded angry now, as though Astra were a malfunctioning Craft machine. "Why is she like this? None of the others ever behave like this."

"She's in shock, darling," Klor said. "Give her a minute. Astra, calm down."

Hokma was gripping her shoulder, her fingers fierce as Helium's claws. *You're nearly thirteen*, they said. *You can't keep having tantrums anymore. Not in front of Nimma*. Astra forced her breathing back under control. Between her legs the Shield was beginning to burn again. She was Sec Gen now—branded. She had to be rational. She had to find out exactly what was going on. "Why is it c-c-complicated?" she stammered, drying her eyes. "Why couldn't you tell her? Why can't she go and live with her *f-f-family*?"

Hokma patted her on the back and stood up. There was another silent team-talk pause as with tiny flicks of their eyes and imperceptible nods of their heads, her Shelter parents codecided to release another piece of classified information. "She's not allowed to live with her family, Astra," Hokma said at last. "Her family is going to be punished for hiding her father, so she can't go back to them. IMBOD wanted her to go to a special school in Cedaria where she could be properly reeducated. I had requested a Steering Committee meeting for today so that Or could vote on making a counter-offer, to keep her here."

Astra couldn't speak. She stared at Lil's hymnbook and tried to take it all in. IMBOD had wanted to put Lil in the special school. Ahn, and probably most other Or-adults, would have voted against Hokma. It didn't matter what Astra had said at the compost heap; somehow, Lil had known that she had to escape. Her dad had shown her a tunnel out of Is-Land. But Astra would never tell anyone about that—that, or about the ancestors and the arrowpain.

Lil was gone. The tears brimmed again in her eyes.

Klor stood up. "Come, come, Gaia Girl. There's nothing we can do for Lil right now. We have to be strong and help Russett and Stream's family and show the world our resilience. A journalist is coming today from Sippur to write a story about the fire and take pictures of you. We want to be ready for her, don't we?"

"Astra." Hokma leaned close to her again. "Klor's right: Lil can look after herself. And you're growing up now. Last night you let go of childish attachments, didn't you?"

Astra was exhausted. She wiped her nose with the back of her hand. It was true: last night she had become not only Sec Gen but the Gaia Girl. No one could take that away from her—not Ahn, not Lil, not Nimma, not anyone. Reluctantly, she nodded.

"Gaia Chose you," Hokma continued softly. "You have responsibilities now."

Klor was at the front door. "Oh my dewy meadow!" he called back into the Earthship. "What do I see? Everyone's waiting down at East Gate. They want to see Astra wearing her blood panties!"

"Klor!" Nimma stood up, shaking out her faux-grass skirt. "Weren't you there last night, my man? She's not seven anymore."

"She'll always be my little angel," Klor beamed. "Won't you, Astra?"

Astra dried her hands on her legs. "I'm coming in a minute. I'm just going to put Lil's book in my room."

And that was what she did: she put the poem in the secret prayer pocket in the hymnbook and the hymnbook away in her Belonging Box with Eya's bracelet; she put the box back high on the shelf above her bed and she went down to have breakfast in the marquee the adults had erected on the lawn in front of the remains of Core House. Russett wasn't there, or Stream's family, or Congruence, and everyone else was either quietly sobbing, or tired and silent and red-eyed. But one by one they hugged her, and then Mr. Ripenson stood up and said that Astra had been Gaia-Chosen to help them cope with this terrible tragedy.

At noon, the journalist came and took pictures of her in her hip-beads and blood panties, with Silver on her wrist and Klor and Nimma and Hokma standing close around her. Astra answered questions about Torrent and Stream and repeated the story that the adults were starting to tell: that while no one in Or had understood why the two teenagers had bonded so early, now it was clear that as Gaia was going to take them

back to Her so soon, She had wanted them to experience that closeness
before they returned to Her. She also talked about growing up in Or,
and said she wanted to be a Code worker when she grew up, but in the
meantime she was looking forward to going to high school and starting
Woodland Siesta. She said that of course she was deeply honored to be
the Gaia Girl and would do her best to represent her community in her
appearances at bioregional festivals and ceremonies this year.

The story appeared on everyone's Tablettes that evening, along with
photos of Torrent and Stream. After she read it, Stream's Shelter mother
asked Nimma if Astra would recite a Gaia hymn at the Birth House ceremony for the two teens, and Nimma said of course she would. Congruence spoke too, briefly but very touchingly, saying how she would never
forget the pure love she had felt for Torrent, and Russett sat crying like a
baby with Flint, Tulsi and Thor at his side.

The following week, the IMBOD officer came to interview her
about Lil. She did a calming meditation beforehand and even though
Ahn was sitting across the table, filming the interview, she held her
nerve and acted like a perfect Sec Gen. She said she missed Lil and she
hoped Lil hadn't set the fire, but if she did, then she should be punished.
When the officer asked her if Lil ever talked about Non-Landers, she
said no. She said that Lil was a good forager and could sing the Gaia
hymnbook from start to finish, but she wasn't Sec Gen and didn't know
any other kids, and probably she was scared of starting high school so
she'd gone to try to find her family, because everyone needed their family. Hokma sat beside her, and when she'd finished, Hokma said, "Very
good, Astra. Can she go now, officer?" The officer said, "Thank you, and
enjoy your year, Gaia Girl." Ahn didn't say anything, but as she stood to
leave the room his steady, colorless gaze swept up and down her body,
then dropped back to his Tablette screen as she passed.

Part Three

Autumn 86 re–Spring 87 re

3.1

It didn't come when she expected it. Not during Year Eight, her year as the Gaia Girl, when she appeared at all the bioregional seasonal celebrations and was interviewed for the national news on Founding Day; when she buried her memories of Lil, Torrent and Stream in the drifts of leaves that rustled beneath her and Tedis, or Sultana, or Forager, or Leaf, entangled for hours in Woodland Siesta; the year Hokma and Ahn dissolved their Gaia bond and—though Hokma said the breakup had nothing to do with her or the shot, and that she was still very good friends with Ahn—she would sometimes turn at dinner to find him scrutinizing her with those pale gray eyes, and the danger of exposure felt like a cold wind stealing up her spine. It didn't come in Year Nine either, when the thin cloak of protection her fame had provided began to fray and she became just Astra again, a student of slightly less than average height and weight, not-quite-significantly higher than average language skills and a perfectly average number of Gaia play pals—six. Year Nine was the year her long-simmering battles with Nimma erupted into all-out war, provoked by her decision that after a year of Nimma insisting she stick to just one loc, pinned back for Gaia Girl photos, she was going to dread the rest of her head. The war raged for a week until the evening Hokma got angrier than Astra had ever seen her and shouted, "*What's* wrong *with you, Astra? You* must *be more careful! She's working with Ahn now—do you* want *them to talk about you?*"

Which was how Astra learned that Ahn had sub-contracted Nimma to design the curtains and upholstery for the Arts and Crafts Gallery in Sippur, and though she screamed at Hokma in return—"*You try living with the frigging bitch!*"—in the end her fury was swamped by her fear and she returned to the Earthship to say sorry, promising to be content with one dread until she had finished her IMBOD Service, inwardly resolving to trudge on through Nimma's petty restrictions and blatant favoritisms until that magic time Hokma had promised her: when she'd be at college in Atourne and could make new non-Sec Gen friends, people with questioning minds and independent spirits, just like her.

It helped that Nimma was busy, commandeering the kitchen table to cover with swatches of fabric and blueprints of Ahn's temple she would pore over until late into the night. The threat of Ahn receded too, as he spent more and more time in Sippur at the gallery building site, until, when Astra started Year Ten, he moved there entirely, visiting Or only on occasional weekends. In Year Ten Wise House, while comfortingly familiar, began to feel boring in comparison with the challenges of school, the pleasure-pull of Woodland Siesta, the engrossing discovery of penetrative Gaia play and the urgent necessity of Tablette talk with her school friends late into the night. In Year Ten she began to feel safe again, and in Year Eleven she forgot to worry entirely. Year Eleven started with the spectacular opening of the Arts and Crafts Gallery, with Nimma pink-cheeked with pride at the national reviews of her curtains and upholstery. Ahn came striding triumphantly back into Or, but Astra barely saw him. He reestablished his long working hours at Code House, and otherwise he and Nimma were often in Sippur now, giving talks at the Gallery, while as Year Eleven rolled on Astra herself learned what it meant to have a full schedule. She had to study and fitness-train around the clock now; she couldn't visit Wise House every evening—or even every weekend—but had to leave the Owleons to Hokma. And when she did visit, Hokma spoke less and less often about anything interesting, and Silver was like a toy she'd outgrown.

It came when she had stopped expecting it. It came in Year Twelve: the year that began with the crushing introduction of a nearly doubled school workload, a roster of deadlines the Sec Gens managed like clockwork but she struggled to cope with, harnessed like a *mule* to a chafing routine of studying for college aptitude tests and training for IMBOD Service fitness exams, the joys of eating, sleeping and Gaia play just briefly scheduled feedbags in the whole draining ordeal. It came when she was ground down, short-fused, her entire life stifling, her dreams insignificant; when Nimma had started to turn her critical attention back to Astra's study habits, the state of her room, what she ate for frigging breakfast. It didn't come as she had always imagined it would, in one fell swoop, with a thunder of horse hooves and boot steps and a circle of IMBOD officers blocking out the light. It came, not like a hawk seizing a chick, but incrementally, like a crow trapping a wounded rabbit and then, with beak and claws, tearing its guts out in a slow, inexorable flaying of hope. It started with a meeting.

Hokma hadn't been at breakfast, but that was nothing unusual. Now she was looking after the Owleons on her own again, Hokma came down to Or just once or twice a week. Her eccentricities had multiplied over the last two years; she lived on a diet of raw fruit and vegetables now, drank only water, and kept her salt-and-pepper hair shaved to within an inch of her scalp. The Owleons still brought IMBOD funding into the coffers, and most Or-adults spoke of her as if she were a legend, but some people called her *la hermitrice*, not always respectfully—and something had soured between her and Nimma. Astra had noticed the rift two years ago on Is-Land Founding Day, when Hokma had refused Nimma's gift of a new sateen housecoat, saying she preferred to mend the old one. In front of everyone at the celebration, she'd given the hand-embroidered emerald coat to Sorrel. After that, Nimma had begun grumbling about the state of Hokma's boots and hipbelt, saying they were an embarrassment to Or. The alt-leather was scuffed and worn and their cuts were out of date, that was true, but when did Hokma ever go to meetings outside Or? Astra hadn't paid much attention, but then one day she'd tried to invoke Hokma's productive seclusion to justify taking some time for herself. Brandishing her fabric scissors, Nimma had launched into a stream of bitter complaint.

"No you *can't* eat breakfast in the Earthship on school days," she'd snapped. "I know *Hokma* doesn't eat meals with us, but look what that's led to. She's stepped down from all her committees; she barely shows her face in Or anymore—what kind of community member is she? You'd think she'd try a bit harder after the last inspection, but no, her attendance points are going to be even lower next year, and Gaia knows what she'll look like if she does turn up to the banquet. She's expecting my work and Ahn's to make up for her negligence, that's what she's bargaining on. Her isolationism is setting a terrible example for you, Astra. What's wrong with eating with all the other Sec Gens anyway? None of them ever want to squirrel themselves away."

Astra had remained clamp-lipped under this tirade, then mumbled something about having just wanted more quiet time to study, but she herself increasingly felt frustrated by Hokma. Her Shelter mother was useless to talk to about homework, she still wouldn't reveal any of her Owleon Code breakthroughs, and when Astra tried to ask her about Is-Land history—even once broaching Lil's balloon story—she'd assume a professorial tone, saying there were different points of view about certain events, but it was best to wait until college to explore them. Hokma was mainly wrapped up in the Owleons as usual, working with a composer in Atourne, trying to Code them to sing in harmony, which might have been interesting, but when Astra had asked if there would be a concert she'd snorted, "They're not performing seals, Astra." The reason for the research was classified, as usual, and Astra resented being kept out of the loop. She'd kept the biggest secret of all tight shut, hadn't she? So she cleaned the cages and flew Silver once a week and stopped asking questions.

Otherwise, Hokma treated Astra like a little girl still: she sometimes sent Silver down to Or with cutesy messages—pictures of the new chicks or plants flowering in the garden. But when Astra looked for him that morning, he wasn't on his Earthship perch. The sky was dark—the cyclone season was arriving, and probably Hokma hadn't wanted to risk him getting whisked away by the wind.

She devoured her bowl of muesli and dried fruit, her Tablette hidden on her lap so she could review the Code equations she'd fallen asleep memorizing the night before. Beside her Yoki was doing the same. They took the bus into New Bangor together, sitting at the back, away from the noisy excitement of the younger children up near the driver. For some, it was the first time on the cyclone school bus, with its heavy reinforced frame, huge wheels and set of high steps at the door. Meem was tired too; she leaned her head against the window in the seat in front of Astra, catching a nap before another long day of lessons. Meem's hair was freshly styled in a cornrow-and-flat-twist updo; Astra had refused Nimma's offer to French-braid her own. French braid pigtails and a dread? Did Nimma think she was an Old World scarecrow?

The cyclone started at noon. Whirling skirts of high wind tore over the steppes as a fringed hem of rain whipped the mountains. Astra spent Woodland Siesta in a rocking treehouse, water rushing from the banana-leaf roof. She had been Gaia-playing with a Year Eleven girl recently, but Cotton was sidling up to a boy pal today and Astra was drooping so she slept the full two hours nestled on a mat between Tedis and Leaf, who stayed awake reviewing their Law lessons. Being in Year Twelve put Gaia play in perspective. Soon you would be gone, and in the meantime you were preoccupied with tests and exams and thoughts of leaving home. Now it made sense, the way that in Year Nine and Ten your older play pals had ignored you in the hallways and returned your long romantic Tablette-talk messages with a bare minimum of greetings. She and Yoki walked back to the school building together in what had become a torrential downpour, dried off beneath the hot-air fans in the gym and took two more hours of classes before the bus came to take them back to Or.

The rain had stopped by the time she arrived home. Pendulous drops of water glistened on the trees and the air was laden with the smell of warm, steaming earth. Strangely, the lawn and gardens were empty; perhaps the teams were all working to deadlines, or in a meeting. The clutch of Or-kids dispersed through the silence to their various destinations, Astra walking with her Shelter siblings along the Kinbat track toward the East Slope Earthships. She enjoyed it, in a strange way, the feeling of wandering through a deserted community. It reminded her of training for the dry forest marathon last year, when she and Yoki and a few others got up early to put in a few miles along the Kinbat track before anyone else was awake, caught up in a brief spell of solitude before the hectic day began.

Though the track wasn't completely empty—Vishnu was striding quickly ahead of them. That was also unusual. Normally he hared straight to the Core House daycare to pick up his two young daughters. He and Sorrel must have a different arrangement today for some reason—perhaps Florence, the girls' other Shelter mother, was looking after them this afternoon.

"Vishnu's in a hurry," Meem remarked. "I hope the girls are okay."

"Yeah, weird," Yoki commented as the teacher began to jog.

"If one of the kids were sick, he'd be going to his Earthship," Astra pointed out. "They're probably with Florence and he's just going to see Sorrel."

"But the urbaggers are really busy right now," Yoki said reasonably. "Why would they want Vishnu hanging around?"

It was a favorite game, sitting on the Earthship living roof and guessing where everyone was going; sometimes they even bet on it—Meem had won big when she realized before anyone else that Florence had bonded with the new Craft worker Blossom. You could also score points for funny answers. As Astra was trying to think of one, someone came pounding up the track behind them. It was Congruence.

Astra and her siblings moved aside. Congruence was a dedicated distance runner, doing twenty Kinbat laps a day while listening to music on her Tablette armband. Astra liked pacing herself against her, but the older girl didn't mingle with the high school Or-kids. Congruence had finished her IMBOD Service last summer and returned to Or with the other twenty-year-olds. But instead of starting Biotecture College in Atourne in the autumn, she had stayed on, helping Luna and her Shelter father care for Gloria, her Shelter mother, who was dying. This summer she had begun working as Ahn's apprentice. Now that the Steppes Arts and Craft Gallery had been received with such acclaim, he had started preparing a design submission for the new National History Museum in

Atourne, and after some negotiations, the college had agreed that Congruence could get credit for the work she did to help him. Astra rarely saw either of them, but Nimma, who was advising on interiors, said the designs were coming along beautifully and Congruence had a real gift for siting and landscaping.

Congruence backhanded a greeting and ran on, her long black braid swaying like a bell rope down her back.

"Nimma said Gloria wants to go to a neurohospice soon," Meem reported when the girl was out of earshot.

"Really?" Yoki stared after Congruence. "That's sad."

"Yes," Meem agreed. "But she'll return to Gaia at peace then. And that will help Congruence be at peace too."

"We'll all go to a neurohospice one day," Yoki agreed. "As long as we return to Gaia in Is-Land."

Astra couldn't contribute to the Sec Gen platitude-fest. Gloria had cancer—not skin cancer, which did still occur sometimes, but a tumor in her stomach which had been treated but then returned, spreading to her lymph system. No one knew why, when everyone in Is-Land was Coded against cellular malignancies, but sometimes, Klor had said, like damp against damp-proofing, cancer found a way through. He had been troubled though, Astra could tell. It was wrong to have cancer in Is-Land; it might be a sign that one of the crop Codes was faulty—or that Gloria had a hidden genetic weakness, one Congruence might have inherited. The Sec Gens knew all this, but they blithely assumed the best: Gloria was an isolated case. Still, they loitered with Astra, watching Congruence, hands at her waist, slow to a walk. At the exit to Code House she showered quickly with a hose, stripped off her running bra, wrung it out and stuck it in a hydrobelt pocket. Then she trotted up the steps. Vishnu was ahead of her. As she passed, the teacher reached forward and touched her arm.

Congruence wrested her elbow away. She took the next four steps two at a time, then she turned and tapped her Tablette—*I'm late*—and resumed normal-but-speedy step climbing. Vishnu stopped to observe her. Then he climbed on too, steadily, not attempting to catch up.

"Whay hey. What's Vishnu done to her?" Yoki wondered.

"Nothing. She's just jumpy," Meem explained. "I said hi to her the other day and she nearly dropped her dinner tray. Nimma says it's because she's not Sec Gen and she's finding saying goodbye to Gloria very difficult."

"Come on," Astra said. Talk of non-Sec Gens still made her nervous. It was nice to not have so many of them around in Or anymore to confuse her. "We shouldn't be wasting time like this. She's just late for Ahn. You know what he's like."

They headed up the path to the Earthship. Silver wasn't there, but Astra didn't register even mild disappointment at his empty perch. Sometimes filling his memory clip with bland news to send back to Hokma was just another chore. Right now, she was hungry. When they were small, Nimma used to take a break and meet them at home; she'd stopped doing that when Meem started high school, but she still left out a plate of fruit and biscuits every day. They had their snack, then Yoki and Astra turned on their Tablettes and Meem left to visit Honey, who had just started Sheltering Dew, her bond partner's Code baby with a professional Birth mother from New Bangor. It was better without her: Year Elevens didn't fully understand the pressure yet and Meem would often ask for help with her own homework, a distraction Yoki didn't mind, but Astra resented. At last, after a set of mind-splitting equations, it was time to head down to Core House for dinner.

Because of Ahn's commitment to the gallery project, it had taken nine months to design and erect the new dining hall, but he had insisted on creating a memorial to Torrent and Stream and the new building had been amply worth the wait. Its skylights and white wood beams pressed a healing poultice of light and space to the wound of the fire. The official cause of the blaze was still *Accidental; herbal cigarette suspected*, but just in case, there were now metal slat blinds instead of curtains and the candles were all in glass jars. A wood sculpture of a young man and woman entwined stood in the corner, and at the request of the Parents' Committee the seating was more varied: there was a row of banquette booths along one wall, to encourage adults to sit in small groups and play games or chat after dinner, reducing the noise levels in the Quiet Room and ensuring that children or young people would not play unattended here again.

Today, though, the dining hall was empty, no clacking of serving spoon on pan or nostril-perking scent of garlic emanating from the kitchen, and there wasn't a member of the kitchen team in sight.

"We're not early, are we?" Astra asked, puzzled.

Yoki checked the wall clock. "No—"

Behind them the door opened and they turned to see Meem lunging into the room.

"*Astra*. You're *here*." Meem flung her arms around Astra, nearly knocking her backward. This was peculiar too. She and Meem had hardly been parted an hour.

Awkwardly she patted her Shelter sister on the back. "Yeah—but where's everyone else?"

Meem peeled away from the embrace but gripped Astra's hand and Yoki's and started tugging them toward the top end of the children's table. "They're in a meeting. Yoki, we have to sit with Astra tonight."

"Okay." Yoki, accommodating as always, fell in step with Meem. "Why?"

"I can't tell you. Honey made me promise."

Meem's tone was playful, but Astra was confused and getting irritated. She resisted Meem's insistent pull. "*Meem. Tell us.* What's going on? Why are they *all* in a meeting?"

She was pushing it, she knew. When they were younger, her Sec Gen friends and siblings had never questioned an adult's authority, and as a group, her schoolmates were still slavishly obedient. But lately Astra had found that if she got a Sec Gen on their own, simple curiosity could sometimes get them to override a promise to a parent or teacher. She had to sound confident, that was the trick. It was almost as though the Sec Gens responded to a certain tone of voice. She didn't push often, in case people noticed, and it was risky to try it in front of Yoki, who could corroborate any story of coercion, but a spiral of annoyance and anxiety was rising in her torso and she needed to know what was happening.

"I can't. And anyway, they're going to tell us all together. After dinner."

The Sec Gens were all bigger and stronger than she was. Astra had little choice but to let herself be dragged across the floor.

"So why do you know now, then?"

"Honey and Storm were talking about it when I came in. They left the meeting early because Dew was crying. They think he's sick."

"If *you* know now, why can't we?" Yoki asked, very reasonably, Astra thought.

"Because..." Meem hesitated. "Because if I tell you that, Astra might get upset."

The irritation was shrinking now and the anxiety was swelling, pressing against her ribs. *Was the meeting about me?* she wanted to ask, but she couldn't. And anyway, Meem couldn't know she wasn't Sec Gen or she wouldn't have hugged her. "Why would I get upset?" she probed cautiously. "Were Honey and Storm talking about me?"

"No." Meem sat down. But Sec Gens couldn't lie. "Well, yes. A bit."

It was like "Animal, Vegetable, Mineral." As she said the words she knew they were the answer. "They were talking about Hokma."

Meem pulled her hand, hard. "Sit down, Astra. They're going to tell us soon. I just wanted to make sure you were here, that's all."

Astra yanked her hand away. "Where's Hokma?"

Meem looked pleadingly at Yoki. "I didn't mean to break my promise, did I?"

"You didn't break it."

"I'm going to Wise House," Astra announced, heading for the door.

"*No.*" Meem stood up, and snatched at her elbow. "She's not there. IMBOD took her. Last night. They took her and Helium and all the Owleons away."

She was running like a river, frothing over rocks and surging around bends, churning under bridges, charging against banks. Her right arm was pumping the air, grabbing at vines and branches, her left was clamping her breasts to her chest. Her throat was scorched, her lungs burning as the soles of her feet went blazing over roots and stones. Meem and Yoki were far away, tiny bewildered figures clinging to the door of Core House; the adults coming down en masse from Code House were a clump of insentient beings, oblivious to her escape from the lies they were bringing for dinner. She was going to find Hokma: Hokma and Helium and Silver and the chicks.

Up ahead was the crossroads, and someone was there. Not Hokma: someone tall and pale-skinned, who ducked back into the trees as Astra approached. She cut up through the stringybarks, flitting like a bat between the trees. *Someone was guarding the path to Wise House.* Her heart was a chiseled flint, scraping at her chest. There was a roaring in her ears, muffling the sound of the world. *IMBOD had taken Hokma away.* She crept forward at an angle, plotting her way up the slope, aiming to emerge at the gate. It was twilight now and she could slip among the shadows heading for the ghostly trunks of the lacebarks ahead.

"*Astraaa. Aaaastra.*" Below her on the path, adults were calling her name. She pressed on through gray veils of dimming light. She could hear people following her now, their heavy boots squelching and cracking through the mulch, swearing as they slipped on the steep muddy slope. They would catch her, but first she was going to see for herself what IMBOD had done to Wise House.

But she couldn't see Wise House. She was crouching behind a lacebark and she could only see the fence. It was wrapped in a long yellow and black ribbon and guarded by two IMBOD officers. One was talking into her armband Tablette, the other was standing in front of the gate, scanning the woods. They both had pistols strapped to their thighs. One was holding the lead of a straining Alsatian.

"Understood," the dogless officer said, and clicked off her Tablette talk. "*Astra,*" she called, "you can come out now. You're not in any trouble."

She couldn't go forward. She couldn't go back. She sank to her knees behind the tree and flattened herself into its roots like a hare into her form. Her cheek was rubbed raw against the scabrous gray bark, her breast was squashed on top of a spongy tree fungus. Her face was a silent monsoon. That was how Vishnu found her.

"Astra. Oh thank Gaia." He knelt and put his arms around her. "Come, Astra, come home."

Then Russett was there, and Moon, and others too, vague figures hanging back in the trees.

"Sweetie." Moon stroked her back. "You must come home now. Hokma's not there. Come home and we'll explain."

Russett and Vishnu hooked their elbows beneath her armpits, helped
her to her feet and showed her to the IMBOD officers. Then as the dark
clouds reopened, they escorted her down the steep path and back to
Core House.

"*Why?* Why did they *take her*?" They were in the Quiet Room but she
was bellowing like a bull. She knew that she shouldn't be shouting, but
she didn't know how to behave anymore. She couldn't pretend. How
would a Sec Gen kid act if IMBOD took their Shelter mother away?
Did anyone know? Had they done tests? She wasn't in trouble, the
adults kept saying, their faces blanched with concern as they cosseted
her with pillows and glasses of water. She could just feel what she felt for
once, couldn't she?

"Hush, hush," Vishnu fretted. You'd never guess he was a teacher and
a father of two, or branded for an invincible god; he was floundering like
an international visitor confronted with an upset Or-kid. Beside him on
the sofa, Nimma was dabbing her eyes with a hanky; Klor had his arm
around her and looked too dazed to speak.

"You *let them*!" She accused the circle. "You let them take her!" They
shrank back, a confused woolly ball of theories and responses—except
for Ahn, of course. He was sitting on a chair between Congruence and
Moon, and though each woman had at one point been stroking his
arm—obviously considering that as Hokma's ex-Gaia partner he was in
need of support—he was now doing that steeple thing again with his
fingers at his lips, his expression tight and alert, his reptilian eyes flickering between Astra, Nimma and Klor.

Russett was the only one unperturbed. Since the deaths of Torrent and Stream he had changed. At first, people had thought he
would leave Or, but he'd said he had nowhere to go. He had undergone two years of therapy: not only bereavement counseling, but
anger management and parental skills lessons. Flint and Thor and
Tulsi's Birth-Shelter mother had accompanied him on his journey, and Russett was now Tulsi's Shared Shelter father. He was
also back coaching the under-ten archery team. As Astra's scream
reached glass-shattering pitch he stepped forward; looming over the

armchair, he leaned down so his pouchy, broken-veined face was bang up against hers.

"Astra, *be quiet*," he ordered in a low voice, "or you are going to your Earthship and no one is going to be telling you *anything* for a very long time."

His voice vibrated through her like a gong. The men, and Moon, had dragged her down from Wise House. They could drag her away from Core House too. She gulped for air and shut up.

Russett turned back to the other adults. "Now tell her. She has the right to know."

People looked at Nimma and Klor, but Nimma was sobbing now and Klor shook his head helplessly. "Vishnu, you tell her," he croaked.

Vishnu sucked his lower lip. It was so strange to see him so anxious. The only time Astra had ever seen him close to distress was the evening Sorrel had collapsed in the Quiet Room, going into labor early with their second Code daughter Kishar, and he'd come barreling from his Earthship down to Core House. "It was Helium, Astra," her old teacher said at last. "He died on a flight back from Atourne and a farmer found his body on the steppes. He turned it in to IMBOD and when they checked his memory clip they found some things that shouldn't have been there."

Helium was dead? Astra choked—but the adults weren't grieving, she suddenly realized; they were *afraid*. At the sight of Moon's drawn face, a trickle of fear crept into her too. "What do you mean?" she asked. "*What* shouldn't have been there?"

"We don't know, darling," Sorrel said. "We just know that IMBOD has taken Hokma in for questioning. They couldn't leave Silver and the other Owleons there by themselves so they've taken them too."

"We're sure there's an explanation," Pan spoke brightly, with faux-confidence, as if she were a child. "She probably had permission from Dr. Blesserson or the National Wheel Meet—she'll tell IMBOD what she was doing and she'll be back soon."

At the mention of Dr. Blesserson the alarm in Astra's belly twanged up a note. *Your little experiment*, Hokma's brother had called her all those years ago. *Your project*, Ahn had sneered. But Hokma couldn't possibly have been keeping records of Astra's behavior, could she? Or sending information about her over the steppes?

"Astra," Vishnu asked, "you don't know what she could have been working on, do you? Anything unusual at all?"

The fear was rising in her throat now. Astra glanced at Ahn. He wasn't saying anything; he was *watching*, she realized. Beside him, Congruence's face was scrunched up like a sponge, positioned to soak up the tension misting from his frame.

Ahn was a snake and she wasn't going to give him the pleasure of seeing her panic. She folded her arms. "Erm, the *Owleons*?"

"Leave the girl alone, Vishnu," Ahn said, his soft, loathsome voice sprinkled with threat Astra knew was intended for her. "She's not on trial."

"Of course not," Vishnu replied shortly, not looking at Ahn, "but she's in a better position than most of us to know what Hokma may have been doing lately. I'm sure we'd all rather know what was going on, wouldn't we?"

"Ahn's right, sweetie. No one's on trial," Sorrel gently corrected Vishnu, who lapsed back into silence.

Astra avoided everyone's gaze and forced herself to remain calm. There was *no way* Hokma would fly information about her shot across the country, and if she had, IMBOD would have arrested her too. So this was something to do with the Owleons, though she didn't know what. Ahn was a malevolent *wasp*, waiting to sting her, and the rest of them were useless grubs. They hadn't got a clue; they didn't know an Owleon from an oil junkie and they couldn't chuck an alt-chicken across a road. Look at Vishnu, sulking after one sly rebuke from Ahn. And Congruence—what was she even doing here, anyway? She wasn't an adult. She didn't know anything about Hokma or the Owleons or Wise House, none of them did. And if they thought that just because Astra didn't stay there much anymore, she'd stopped caring about Wise House, they were *wrong*.

"What about the worms?" she demanded.

"What worms, darling?" Klor asked.

"The vermicompost wigglers. Who's going to feed them? I have to stay up there and take care of them."

"No, you can't do that, angel. IMBOD is looking after Wise House. They'll look after the worms too."

"Oh Klor," Nimma sniffled, and then burst into a fresh round of sobs. "What did I say? What did I say? We let her isolate herself from us. We have no idea what she was doing up there."

Astra stopped, then, and refused to listen or speak any more. Soon she couldn't tell who was talking; she was trapped in a hollow, inter-weaving round of adult voices, all saying *no, no, whatever Hokma might have done wasn't Nimma's fault or anyone else's—and besides, they didn't know anything yet; everything was going to be okay, Hokma would be back in a day or two, just you wait and see.*

But their stringybark basket of reassurances was full of holes, each one larger than the crater Hokma had once shown her on the edge of Sippur.

3.2

The next week the winds ripped through Or. The urbaggers and stap-croppers had to peg covers down over the Code House roof plots to protect the topsoil and small plants, and every day Astra had to battle to and from school, squinting against the dust and enduring Nimma's constant nagging about her "bird's nest" of hair. But though the winds brought signposts down on the New Bangor main road, sent veranda chairs tumbling over the grass and whisked flap-hats off children's heads and up into the treetops, it didn't bring Hokma back. IMBOD was holding her in Atourne, Klor said, and right now she wasn't allowed to Tablette-talk or email Or, and no one knew when she would be able to communicate again. Their faces were anxious and tight-lipped, but still all the Or-adults kept on saying not to worry: IMBOD was just making sure Hokma hadn't broken any rules by mistake. As soon as Hokma explained things to their satisfaction, they would let her go.

Yoki and Meem hugged Astra, then carried on with their studies and social lives as normal. Though her Shelter siblings' calm acceptance of uncertainty was infuriating, their unchanging routines were a handrail Astra clung to that week, going to school, running laps, doing chores with a tumor of fear bulging inside. If Hokma hadn't been sending infor-mation about Astra—which, given that no IMBOD officer had even come to test her, seemed more and more unlikely—what in Gaia's name *had* she been doing? Suppose she had been helping other children avoid the shot? In which case, would IMBOD also find out about Astra? Ahn hadn't told on her at the Or meeting: did that mean he wouldn't tell IMBOD either? Surely not—if he did they'd ask how he'd found out and why he hadn't told them before, and they might suspect that he knew more of Hokma's secrets. He might be frightened too, she realized at last: frightened even that she would tell IMBOD that he had known about her. That was why he'd defended her from Vishnu. But for how long would he continue to protect her?

The endless permutations of uncertainty were intolerable. Once she even wondered if she should go and see Ahn and ask him for help—but no, that was crazy, why would Ahn help her? He wasn't helping Hokma. When Vishnu insisted on calling a small meeting in the Quiet Room "to discuss what might be done for Hokma," Ahn showed up late, and when Vishnu suggested he use his position to write to IMBOD, he'd said he doubted the word of a biotect would make any difference to an IMBOD classified secrets investigation. Nimma had backed him, of course. As she was browbeating Vishnu, Ahn shot a look at Astra, a piercing look of resentment that sent his own fear traveling through her. They were both Hokma's accomplices, Ahn's glance said, him thanks to her. Then the next day he and Congruence went off to Sippur, to work at the museum—"until there was news," Nimma said—and the opportunity to confide in him was lost.

At last Peat Tablette-talked her from his IMBOD Service barracks near Atourne. He said that legally IMBOD had a month to question Hokma and then they had to decide if they were going to charge her, release her or place her under Concernful Detention. Astra had found Year Eleven Law tedious and this year she had specialized in Code and Global Languages. Now she wished she knew more about the Wheel Meet justice system.

"Concernful Detention—what's that?"

The internet connection in the barracks was poor and Peat's face kept losing definition. As he blew out his cheeks he became a blobby brown balloon on her screen. "It's when someone's behavior is . . . *concerning.*

They can be kept in prison until circumstances change and they aren't considered a worry anymore."

"But that could be anything!"

"Technically it's pretty broad but IMBOD only invokes it when someone is a national security threat or seriously mentally ill. Hokma was probably just involved in some petty illegal Code sharing. I doubt it would apply."

She couldn't share his confidence. "But IMBOD owns the Owleons. What if sharing their Code *is* considered a national security threat?"

He pouted, his lower lip a briefly shining crescent on her screen. "Okay, so it's a gray area—but as long as she has a good lawyer, she should be fine. Anyway, don't worry, Astra, they'll probably just release her with a reprimand. She's been working for them for years."

Don't worry: that's what they all kept saying. The short-tempered, absentminded, distant adults, who were clearly worried to death themselves; the placid, kind, sweet-natured Sec Gens who wouldn't, *couldn't* worry, even if they were facing a quadruple amputation. But there was nothing to do but worry. And miss Hokma.

In fact, there was something enormous to worry about. On the seventh day after Hokma's arrest, IMBOD charged her with treason.

Klor broke the news to Astra and her Shelter siblings. Peat was present on Libby. Meem and Yoki put their arms around Astra. She didn't push them away.

"Treason," she repeated dumbly. She had come to the meeting convinced that IMBOD had discovered that she hadn't had her shot, but this news was even worse. The word was like a hammer cracking down on her head, pulverizing everything inside it. Treason was the worst crime you could be accused of. The punishment was life imprisonment in solitary confinement, at the bottom of a cement well. The wells were located in a heavily guarded site in the ash fields, and the tops were covered with a black waterproof cloth so the prisoners could never see the sunlight or the stars, or feel the wind or rain. The light was artificial and the air was pumped in, dusty from the pipes. Liquid food was hoisted down on ropes, and the prisoners lived with the constant smell of their toilets. Those who sought to betray Is-Land were guilty of attacking Gaia Herself and did not deserve to enjoy a single pleasure of her bounty. When Astra was little she'd had nightmares about being locked away like that. The thought of Hokma being confined in a traitor's well made her want to run through the greenhouse corridor window.

"It's a very serious charge," Klor said needlessly as Nimma reached forward to comfort her. "We can't believe it either. But IMBOD have told us they have substantial evidence."

Nimma gripped her knee. "Darling, we know this must be so hard for you."

Astra ignored Nimma's hand. Hard for *her*? Wasn't it hard for Nimma too?

"*What* evidence?" she demanded of Klor. Now the initial shock had drummed through her, her mind was whirring again. *She* hadn't been tested or arrested, so IMBOD didn't know about her shot—so what else had Hokma done?

"They can't tell us," Klor sighed. "It's confidential. Think, Astra: are you *sure* you don't know anything about what Helium might have been carrying? Why was he over the steppes?"

They'd had this conversation a hundred times already. "How am *I* supposed to know?" she snapped. "He flew to Atourne once a season to take seeds to Hokma's friend at Code College. Maybe *she* knows."

Nimma withdrew, her eyes flashing. "There's no need to display such a temper, Astra. We're trying to—"

She hadn't been shouting! She'd—

"Astra's just anxious, aren't you darling?" Klor attempted, but Nimma was just warming up. Behind Astra, Meem and Yoki's arms dropped to the sofa. They were still touching her, but lightly, passively, as they waited for the storm to pass.

"I'm not the one who's brought all this trouble down on our heads, Astra." She was speaking quickly: the rain pattering on the window before the thunder broke. "Don't punish *me* with your rudeness. If you—"

"Hang on," Peat interrupted before Astra could stand up and stalk out. "Sorry, Nimma. It's just there was an IMBOD arrest in Atourne yesterday—a Seed Coder. It was in the latest city news bulletin—here, I'll find it."

Astra focused on Libby. The wallscreen went gray, then reloaded with a webpage from the *Atourne Times*. It was a small article, no photo, just a few lines of text.

> Code College researcher Dr. Cora Pollen was taken into IMBOD custody today. Officers arrived at 1 p.m. and escorted Dr. Pollen from her offices. Colleagues say she is a private woman, well respected for her work on radiation-resistant wild rice, which entailed frequent trips to the dangerous Southern Belt. An IMBOD spokesperson stated that Dr. Pollen is being detained for questioning on a highly classified matter.

"That name sounds familiar," Klor mused.

Nimma replied, staring at Astra, "Don't you remember, dear? She's Hokma's Birth-Code niece. The friend of Astra's Birth-Code mother."

Cora. The name turned around slowly in Astra's mind: yes, Cora was Eya's friend in the story. The story she had loved as a child but hadn't heard now for years. Was Hokma still in touch with Cora? If so, she thought with a surge of hurt, why hadn't she ever said anything about her to Astra?

"Astra? Was Hokma sending Helium to Dr. Pollen?" Nimma's voice scraped like a steel nit comb over Astra's scalp.

"I said, I don't know," she muttered, folding her arms. "She never talked to me about Cora, or Eya. *You* told me that story."

She was controlling her temper, but Nimma was shaking. "I'm trying to get to the bottom of something very very serious and you are being *insolent*, Astra. Why do you *always* talk back to me? I see you, don't think I don't—even if your lips aren't moving, you're talking back to me *in your head.* The others never do that. Klor"—oh for Gaia's sake, her voice was trembling now, she was going all little girlie, like she did when she wanted Klor to put his arms around her and make like she was a friggin' pink princess—"what's *wrong* with her? They were supposed to be lovely, like little fawns . . . Why does she *hate* me?"

"Nimma, darling—" Klor sounded as shocked as everyone else looked. Meem and Yoki had sidled to the corners of the sofa and the whites of Peat's eyes were gleaming on the screen. "Astra doesn't hate you. We're all just very upset, that's all. It's stress, playing havoc with our emotions. Even the Sec Gens get stressed under extreme circumstances. Isn't that right, Astra? Yoki?"

Nimma was looking up at the mantelpiece. Here it came: the ultimate comparison. Well not this time. *Frig Nimma. Frig Klor*, always trying to calm everyone down. It didn't matter if she was calm or angry, Nimma would find a way to get at her. She wasn't Sheba, that was the problem, wasn't it? She wasn't Sheba who had died before she could do a single thing wrong.

"I don't frigging *hate you*!" Astra yelled, jumping up. "I just hate being the *suspect* around here all of a sudden. First *Ahn*, and now *you*—you're my frigging *Shelter mother*. Why don't you just try *believing me* for a change?"

"*Language*, Astra! *Language!*" Nimma screamed.

"Whoah," she heard Peat breathe as she stormed out of the room. "Did Astra skip dinner tonight?"

The next day the two IMBOD officers arrived. They were staying for three days, Klor said, sleeping at Wise House and occupying a Code House office from 9 a.m. to 9 p.m., during which time they were scheduled to interview every Or-adult and child over the age of six. Astra was scheduled for the first day. Because she was under eighteen, at least one Shelter parent had to be present. She didn't want Nimma to come, but Nimma, sticking hairpins in her braid coil in front of the mantelpiece mirror, insisted.

"I know you think that I don't care about you, Astra, but I do. We're both going with you and that's final."

So she marched over to Code House with Nimma in her second-best faux-grass hipskirt swishing behind her. Klor met them in the lobby and took them upstairs and into the back corridor, where they waited on a bench outside an urbag office. Through the glass wall of the corridor, water was trickling down the cliff face of the hill behind Code House.

She concentrated on one small dripping outcrop of rock, timing soft, inaudible kicks against the bench leg in sync with the fall of the drops.

"Stop that, Astra," Nimma snapped. "Anyone would think you were ten."

Klor patted Astra's hand. "She's just nervous, aren't you, darling?"

"We're all nervous. But we don't have to damage the furniture. If you could just make an effort to control your emotions you would be much happier, Astra. Klor—"

"*You* don't—" Astra started, but the door opened beside her and Ahn stepped out.

"Thank you again, Ahn," a man with a deep voice was saying as he pumped Ahn's scrawny arm practically off his shoulder. "That is extremely helpful. We'll let you know the results of our investigation."

"My pleasure, Dr. Wolfson," Ahn said, toadying up to him. "I'm only too glad to be of help."

The IMBOD officer stuck his head around the door. It was a handsome head: the man had mahogany skin, a wind-grooved forehead and aquiline nose, framed by thick white hair, a closely clipped white beard and a pair of rectangular spectacles.

"Ah there she is. With two parents. Excellent. So sorry to keep you all waiting." He was addressing the adults, not her. "We'll be with you in a just another moment."

The door clicked shut behind the officer. Klor stroked her hand again, but Nimma jumped up and took Ahn's arm. "Ahn, how was it? Are you all right?"

Ahn's shoulders shook and he gave a peculiar cough. Was he *laughing*? Astra seethed. The coward couldn't wait for Hokma to go down that well. "Not the most pleasant experience of my life, but I'm fine, thank you Nimma." Then he shook Klor's hand and in a second smooth, unreadable Ahn was back. "The officers are very understanding. They know Hokma let us all down, and now they just want the best for Astra. Like we all do. How are you, Astra?"

Ahn's smoky quartz eyes were unusually bright. Why was he pretending to be nice? And why had he and the officers been talking about *her*?

In a chill instant Astra realized her error. She'd been so afraid for Hokma and so angry with Nimma that she'd forgotten to be afraid for herself. Her heart seizing up, she stared past Ahn's fleecy thighs to the cliff.

"She's impossible right now, Ahn," Nimma apologized. "They'll be lucky to get a civil word out of her."

"We were all like that at her age, weren't we?" Ahn's voice was swirling in her head like dried leaves. He couldn't have. He *couldn't* have.

"*We* were," Nimma agreed. "But she's not supposed to be like this."

"She *has* had a shock," Klor contributed, mildly. "I expect her system's on overload, isn't that right, Astra?"

If Ahn had told on her, she'd *kill* him. She back-kicked the bench leg so hard her heel hurt.

"I said *stop that*, Astra," Nimma flared.

"Perhaps the officers can give you something to help calm her down," Ahn suggested.

She wasn't going to let him think he had won. "They can give us Hokma back," Astra retorted.

"We all love Hokma, Astra," Ahn said, another flicker of threat now driving his dry-as-dirt voice, "but we have to be prepared for the possibility that she might not be the person we thought she was."

Who was she to you? she wanted to yell. *Just a pit stop? A convenient play pal you frig for twenty years then drop when she gets old and turn your back on as soon as she actually needs you?* But his eyes still held that triumphant glint. If he'd told, she would have to deny it. She couldn't lose her temper. She had to be incredibly careful now. She held her tongue as Nimma clutched Ahn's arm.

"All those years together—I mean, I know things had changed recently, but still . . . What you must be going through, Ahn—if there's anything we can do, you must just ask."

He patted her hand. "Thank you, Nimma. It's been a shock, of course, Klor, to everyone, but what's important is that we cooperate fully with the investigation and not blame ourselves for its results." Aiming one more gloating look at Astra, he bowed slightly to them all and loped back down the corridor toward his office, his limbs long and loose, his springy hair, Astra noticed for the first time, haloing a bald patch on the back of his head.

"He's so brave," Nimma sniffled. "Astra, he's right. I know it's hard, but we have to be prepared for any eventuality."

Astra barely registered Nimma's obsequious drivel, or Klor's warm hand on her back. Her pulse was racing and she had to calm herself down. She relaxed her shoulders and breathed slowly into her abdomen, as she'd learned to do over the years. If Ahn had told, she would deny it. Dr. Blesserson had given her the shot. But what if IMBOD tested her? Then Blesserson would be in trouble—Ahn wouldn't risk that, would he? No, he couldn't have told. But—an image of Ahn at the banquet table flashed into her mind—what if Samrod and he had concocted a plan together?

There were too many sickening possibilities to prepare for and no time to do it in. She had never rehearsed for this. Hokma had always said not to worry, just tell the truth and she would take the blame. But she hadn't ever said that she might end up in a traitor's well.

The door opened and the IMBOD officer reappeared, Tablette in his hand.

"Astra Ordott, Nimma Shipdott and Klor Grunerdeson, please come in."

The officers sat behind a desk beneath a massive wallscreen displaying the IMBOD Shield. Astra and Nimma and Klor sat in three chairs facing them. The window-wall was to her right, but the urbaggers out unrolling the lower chamber roof cover were a world away.

"Good to meet you, Astra," said the bearded officer, who was hairy all over, with a broad furry chest and barrel belly. "I'm Dr. Wolfson, and this is my colleague Dr. Petaldott. We're IMBOD Chief Inspectors and we're here to ask you a few questions about Hokma, to help us understand her behavior. We're also concerned that you may have suffered from her actions, and if that's the case, we're here to put that right."

Dr. Petaldott was a middle-aged black woman with a neat pixie cut, silver hoop earrings and impressively veined biceps. "What Dr. Wolfson is saying, Astra," she said smoothly, "is that you're not in any trouble. You just have to answer fully and honestly, and we'll take care of everything."

Astra stared at the floor. There was a knot in one of the floorboards that looked as if you could poke it out with your finger. The knot had once been a branch. Tree branches grew incrementally from the tips of their twigs, the buds elongating and widening in diameter. Some buds, though, remained buried in the bark until the right weather came and helped them sprout blossoms and leaves. Hokma had once asked her to think of her emotions like that: dormant, waiting for their season. The knot in the floorboard, she realized with a slight fizzing sensation in her forehead, was a Gaia vision: it was reminding her to keep her feelings hidden.

"Thank you, Dr. Petaldott. I'll do my best," she said. Her voice was shaky, but expressing vulnerability when away from the group was normal for Sec Gens. Perhaps if she just stayed calm, at most expressed a little sadness and anxiety, she would get through this okay.

"Good," Dr. Wolfson smiled at her. "First of all, Astra, we'd like to ask you about Helium. As far as you knew, for how long had he been making flights to Atourne?"

Was it a trick question? Everyone knew Helium was Coded to fly between Or and Atourne. Didn't they? She didn't know if she should lie or not. She settled on shrugging. Around her, the adults exchanged glances.

"Okay." Dr. Petaldott made a note on her Tablette. "Does that mean you don't know or that you don't want to tell us?"

Astra swallowed. "I don't know."

Dr. Petaldott cocked her head. "You don't know how long Helium had been flying to Atourne; or you don't know whether you don't know or you don't want to tell us?"

Astra shook her head.

"She was very close to Hokma," Klor spoke up for her. "I expect she's afraid she's going to get her into trouble."

"Oh darling, no, that's not just it," Nimma interrupted. "She's been so difficult since the arrest, officers." She pouted at the officers. "Half the time you can't get a word out of her, the other half she's screaming at you. My husband thinks perhaps the stress is interfering with the Serum settings. We—well, *I*—wondered if she could have a booster shot. It would help her cope better with this dreadful situation, I am sure."

The problem with Hokma's request had always been that Astra's emotions weren't like oak buds; they were more like the pimples that still occasionally throbbed on her face, sprouting white shiny heads and begging to be squeezed. Right now her heart was pumping so hard she thought it might explode. But she had to keep very still. She focused on the knot in the floorboard.

"That's interesting. Thank you, Ms. Shipdott," Dr. Wolfson replied. "In fact, we are ourselves concerned about Astra's emotional well-being. We understand from her school records that the circumstances surrounding her Security shot were irregular, and that Hokma was responsible for making sure she had it in the end. Given the current situation, we are required to investigate further."

It was happening. She was unbelievably calm. It was like playing cricket, when you had taken your guard at the crease and the bowler had released a spinball and you could see every stitch on it hurtling toward you in crisp, clear slow-motion as you—seeing yourself too, as if from above—watched your body flex into action, every muscle poised to cut the ball away, out of danger, a long, low, rolling cherry disappearing between the legs of the fielders so you could keep making your runs.

"Dr. Blesserson gave me the shot," Astra said in a tone of astonished innocence. "Samrod Blesserson. Hokma took me to Sippur. You can ask him."

"Yes, that's right." Klor, thank Gaia, backed her up. "Isn't it, Nimma? We all picked flowers for Astra to take to Sheba's fountain—my late Code daughter, Doctors. It was such a poignant departure. I remember it as if it were yesterday."

"My condolences on the loss of your Code daughter, Dr. Grunerdeson, Ms. Shipdott," Dr. Wolfson said. "I have quenched my thirst at her fountain often. However, while it is clear Astra went to Sippur, significant questions still remain about her shot."

Dr. Petaldott addressed Nimma and Klor. "We have spoken to Superintendent Blesserson about Astra's shot, and with your permission he's agreed to Flock-Talk with us this afternoon. Would that be acceptable to you?"

Astra's moment of clarity popped like a soap bubble. She had to *think*: think what to say next. Did they know Ahn knew? Maybe they had just told him their suspicions and he'd been secretly glad that she and Hokma would be found out without him. Right now, it would be her word against Dr. Blesserson's—somehow he'd clawed his way up to a Superintendentship, so definitely no one would believe her. But whatever *he* said, she couldn't say anything that would get Hokma into trouble. Calm. *Stay calm.* She had gone to the clinic, and Dr. Blesserson had given her the shot. That's all she had to say. He had signed her certificate, emailed the school. He couldn't argue with that.

"Yes, of course," Klor was saying.

"Goodness." Nimma sat up in alarm. "Hokma hasn't got Dr. Blesserson into any trouble, has she?"

"Not at all," Dr. Petaldott reassured her. "We are extremely grateful to the Superintendent for his assistance. Indeed, he's also agreed to act as a key witness in the trial. I think you'll be very interested in what he has to say."

Dr. Blesserson was going to testify against Hokma? Astra wanted to spit on the screen. She swallowed down the bile. It mingled with fear in her stomach. The knot in the floor was no help at all, a shorn weapon floating out of reach. Dr. Blesserson and IMBOD were in this together, against her and Hokma. All she had in her defense was a faraway half-truth: Dr. Blesserson had given her a shot.

Dr. Petaldott and Dr. Wolfson readied their Tablettes for a Flock-Talk. Behind them, the Shield disappeared from the wallscreen, three camera indicator lights flashed on the frame and five Flock boxes appeared along the bottom of the screen: the two officers and close-ups of Astra, Nimma and Klor. Then Dr. Petaldott placed the call. After two short rings, the face of Dr. Samrod Blesserson was looming over the room like a bloated green moon. He'd put on weight since Astra had last seen him. His face was fleshy now, and his new round gold-rimmed glasses were digging into his cheeks, which were beginning to sag over his jaw. The resolution was low, so at least you weren't confronted with every last blackhead on his nose, but the light in his office was filtered through some kind of hanging vine or a trellis wall and cast a sickly green pall across his skin. Despite the unflattering hue, his features were still sensual—and still oozed arrogance. He had grown heavier from indulgence, it was clear, from tasting whatever—*who*ever—he liked, whenever he wanted to. His tongue made a deliberate, sly appearance, moistening his lower lip like a blood-red slug rolling out onto a leaf, then back under its rock. His eyes lazily scanned his own Flock boxes then met his camera. Astra thought he looked distinctly entertained.

"Good afternoon, Superintendent Blesserson," Dr. Wolfson greeted him. "Thank you for agreeing to meet with us at such short notice."

"Not at all, Dr. Wolfson." Dr. Blesserson smiled. His teeth were as impossibly shiny as ever; for the first time Astra wondered if they were implants. "As I said earlier, naturally Hokma's case is my urgent priority. Nimma, Klor, Astra," he addressed, "what a difficult time it is for us all. But please, let's not make this experience any more official than it needs to be. Do call me Samrod."

"Samrod. Indeed," Klor said. "It is such a hard time—for Astra especially. It's very kind of you to join us."

"Oh my dewy meadow, Samrod, you must be sleepless with worry," Nimma gushed. "And now you're being dragged into this side of things. I'm so sorry."

"Not at all, Nimma. Not at all. It's only right we're all given the chance to tell the officers what we know. I'm just sorry I can't make it to Or in person."

All these odious pleasantries. Anyone could tell Samrod Blesserson couldn't wait for his sister to be convicted of the gravest crime in Is-Land. Astra toed the useless knot in the wood.

"As we discussed, Dr. Blesserson, we won't keep you long," Dr. Wolfson purred. "For the benefit of Astra and her Shelter parents, we simply need to confirm the circumstances surrounding Astra's Security Serum shot. According to the records," he consulted his Tablette, "she was violently ill at school, and rather than take her to the next town in the mobile clinic's schedule—admittedly, a fair distance—Hokma Blesser brought her to you, in Sippur. You filed a report indicating that you had given her the shot."

"That is correct." His voice dripped with languor. He clearly wasn't scared of Astra, or anything she might say.

"We are entirely confident that you did so. It has been noted from more than one source, however, that Astra's behavior over the years has not been entirely consistent with that of a child who received a full dose of the Serum. According to her school reports, her verbal grades occasionally peak over the expected upper limit, while her teachers often comment on her apparent intensity of emotion. Physically, she is slightly smaller and lighter than was to be expected. Her Shelter mother Nimma has today noted her high degree of discontent and uncooperative behavior. We were wondering if you could suggest any reason why the shot might not have taken effect. Could her illness of the day before have interfered with the uptake, for example?"

"That is highly unlikely." Dr. Blesserson paused. Astra tensed. It was coming now: whatever lie he was going to spin. "Nimma, Klor," he continued, greasing the lie with his fat unctuous tone, "forgive me if I have been remiss in not mentioning my concerns before today, but I must confess that I have sometimes wondered about Astra myself. When I visited Or in 82 RE, I found her to be an intelligent but somewhat, shall we say, *confrontational* child. Naturally the Serum has different uptake levels, and as I had delivered the shot myself I assumed Astra was just naturally resistant to some of its effects. Nevertheless, when Dr. Wolfson called me earlier, I was not surprised to hear his report. I have been dwelling on the matter since, and given the recent revelations of my Code sister's activities, the only conclusion I can draw is that she had some kind of secret plan in mind for Astra. It would be simple enough to give the girl an emetic and then contrive to be with her when I gave her the shot. It transpires, you see, that there is an antidote. If taken within an hour of the shot, it neutralizes the effects completely."

"An *antidote*." Nimma's hand flew to Klor's wrist. "Oh, Klor—that would explain everything."

Klor clasped her fingers. "Forgive me, Samrod," he said. "I hadn't heard of an antidote."

"No. For obvious reasons, we haven't wanted to publicize its existence. It was developed by a renegade scientist on the GeneIsis team who made it available for a fee to a handful of misguided parents. They have all been appropriately dealt with now, and the children involved re-Sheltered. We thought we had rounded up everyone, but I worry now that Astra was carefully schooled to avoid triggering an automatic investigation. All her anomalies are very slight, but taken together, especially in light of the current situation, they are deeply suspicious."

No one spoke. Nimma's chest was heaving. Astra could barely breathe and her hand felt like granite beneath Klor's. The antidote story: she remembered now, that's what Hokma had told her to say. But she couldn't do it—if she did, Hokma would go to the well.

"You must forgive me, Klor and Nimma," Dr. Blesserson went on, "for not reaching out to you after the banquet. But for all that Hokma and I have had our differences over the years, it honestly didn't occur to me that she would have deceived us like this. Though, looking back now, I suppose when I relieved her of her School Spoke position I was unconsciously registering alarm at the amount of power she had accrued over Astra."

"It is almost impossible to investigate family members," Dr. Wolfson said as Dr. Petaldott lifted a black briefcase onto the table. "We are entirely unsurprised that the Superintendent suppressed that particular hunch. But I hope you'll both agree that the use of an antidote is an entirely reasonable hypothesis. Astra, did Hokma give you anything to eat or drink right after you left Dr. Blesserson's office?"

"No," she declared, pulling her hand out from Klor's and gripping his arm. "Everything was *fine*. I had my shot, then we came back to Or. I didn't eat anything."

But her voice sounded tinny and Klor was staring at the table, where Dr. Petaldott was clicking open the briefcase, taking out a syringe. "It was a long time ago, Astra," she said. "You might easily have forgotten. Or perhaps Hokma doctored your hydropac. To confirm that you had the full dosage of Serum, we would like to take some blood samples today."

Her last shred of poise had been blasted away. Astra was trapped in her chair, trapped in the room. She pushed herself backward, the chair teetering on its back legs. "*Klor*," she begged, "don't let them put a needle in me. I don't want a booster shot."

"Astra, you're not a little girl anymore," Nimma hissed. Dr. Petaldott unwrapped the needle and examined the tip. Behind the IMBOD officers, Dr. Blesserson's green face gleamed with sour satisfaction.

Klor reached for the back of the chair. "Come, Astra. We have to cooperate," he murmured.

Dr. Petaldott stood up. "We're not going to inject you with anything, Astra. It's just a blood test."

"*No*." She leapt up, knocked Klor's arm away and swung the chair in front of her, a shield against the advance of the needle.

"Astra?" Nimma's voice sheared through the air. "Why don't you want them to test you? If you've really had your shot, everything will be fine."

She flung the chair aside, ran to the door and shook the handle. It was locked. She couldn't get out. Dr. Wolfson was standing up now too, and Klor was reaching for her, to hold her down while she was punctured. She was a wounded animal, surrounded by hunters aiming bows and arrows at her heart. All she could do was lash out, try to hurt them too before they closed in.

"*Okay*," she shouted, "okay. *I didn't have it*. I didn't have my shot. But Dr. Blesserson *helped* Hokma. He gave me a teaby injection instead. You can test me for that!" She held out her arm, with the scar from the injection. "Go on, *test me for teaby antibodies*. And ask *Ahn*—he knew too. Lil figured it out, she told him. Go and ask Ahn—he's been keeping it secret for years. Why isn't he in trouble too?"

No one was listening to her. Dr. Blesserson's smug smile flinched not a fraction of an inch as her accusations splattered the walls. Dr. Petaldott walked smartly back to the table and exchanged knowing glances with Dr. Wolfson, who made a note on his Tablette.

Nimma was virtually hyperventilating, slumped back in her seat, her hands crossed on her chest. "You didn't have your shot! I knew it. I *knew* it! All these years, all these years . . ."

Klor tried to put his arm around her, but she elbowed him away and, sobbing, buried her face in her hands. Dr. Petaldott returned the needle to her briefcase and closed it with another slick click. Dr. Wolfson took off his glasses and rubbed the bridge of his nose, waiting for Nimma's hiccoughs to subside. Klor started toward Astra, but she backed against the wall, her arm in front of her in a judo defense position. He implored her with his eyes, but she held the pose.

He turned back to the officers. "Dr. Wolfson—" He sighed. "How could we not have known? What must you think of us?"

"Dr. Grunerdeson," Dr. Wolfson said warmly, replacing his glasses, "please, don't worry. I appreciate that this comes as a terrible surprise to you and Ms. Shipdott."

"It's not a surprise to *Dr. Blesserson*. It's not a surprise to *Ahn*," Astra hissed. "*They knew. Ahn knew.* If Hokma's a traitor, *they're* traitors too."

"Astra, stop trying to get other people in trouble!" Nimma's voice was rough with phlegm. She cleared her throat. "Samrod, I'm so sorry. She's always been jealous of Ahn. Perhaps she was jealous of your relationship with Hokma too."

Dr. Blesserson shook his head, as if to say, "Not at all."

"That may be," Dr. Wolfson said kindly, "but in fact, Astra's right. Ahn did know about her condition."

"Ahn knew?" Nimma blanched. Klor turned to Astra, his eyebrows knit together in a thick, tufty rope.

"I told you!" Astra shouted triumphantly. "Why don't you arrest *him* too?"

"No, Astra." Beneath Dr. Blesserson's massive, bilious smirk, Dr. Wolfson regarded her indulgently. "Ahn's not in trouble." He turned to Nimma and Klor. "As a matter of course, we investigated Astra's records and when we discovered these anomalies we discussed them with Superintendent Blesserson. In his interview today, we asked Ahn his opinion. Ahn was hugely relieved—he told us he had discovered the truth when Astra was twelve, but Hokma begged him to keep Astra's condition secret. He was deeply worried and conflicted, of course—he thought it was atrocious that Klor and Nimma didn't know, but he had a long bond with Hokma, who worked hard to convince him that hers was a 'victimless crime.' He's not a father or a Code scientist, and the whole situation felt far beyond his capabilities to judge. He agonized over reporting it, but when Astra became the Gaia Girl, he felt that she was sufficiently integrated into Is-Land life not to pose a threat to her siblings. At the same time, he couldn't trust Hokma any longer and as you know, their bond irretrievably broke down. He's apologized profusely for his error of judgment, an apology we've happily accepted. Ahn, of course, knows a great deal about Hokma's character and motivations, and he's also going to give evidence in court that will help us understand the extent of her animosity against the state."

She was speechless. *Ahn had told*, just as she had known he would—but on top of that, just like that gloating, *carnivorous* Dr. Blesserson, he was going to help *convict Hokma*—help condemn her to a life sentence in the worst jail on earth. She wanted to smash something against Dr. Blesserson's monstrous visage, but there was nothing to throw, no vase, no sculpture, no lamp, just a potted orchid, and even in her fury, even to rip that sick triumphant mask down from the wall, she couldn't kill a helpless plant. She stood there shaking, impotent, the adrenalin coursing in her ears.

"How could she have done this to us?" Nimma was bleating. "We've been raising a *cuckoo*, Klor. A cuckoo in our nest."

"Shh, darling, shhh," Klor hushed. "Dr. Wolfson," he beseeched, "Dr. Petaldott, this is a grave shock, a grave shock indeed—but surely it's not Astra's fault?"

"No, of course not," Dr. Petaldott replied. "Astra, you are the victim here. Why don't you come and sit down and let us take care of you?"

"I don't want to sit down."

"Astra," Dr. Petaldott repeated, "Hokma exploited you when you were far too young to understand the implications of your actions. What did she tell you? That the Security shot would limit your chances in life?"

Klor and Nimma had turned in their seats and everyone was looking at her now. She had no exit, no option except silence—but she couldn't let anyone think that she was a victim, or Hokma a *criminal*.

"She was trying to *help* me," she declared. "Look at the Sec Gens: they're happy, but they never ask questions, they never have an original thought, they just do what they're told. They're not like me."

"I'm sorry to hear you say that, Astra," Dr. Wolfson interrupted. "The success of the Security Generation depends on trust. By instilling in you contempt for your siblings and friends, Hokma has ripped you out of this circle of trust. She has damaged not only your own chances at happiness, but theirs too."

Her words were being twisted. She addressed Klor. "I love Yoki and Meem—you know I do. But I'm not like them, am I? I'm the same as the older kids."

"No, Astra, you're not," Dr. Petaldott answered, in a tone of icy finality. "The older children haven't been living a terrible lie."

Nimma was weeping again, her face buried in a hanky, but Klor put up his hand as if to halt the advancing glacier of IMBOD logic. "Dr. Wolfson," he asked, "what's going to happen to Astra?"

"Dr. Grunerdeson, Astra is not culpable for Hokma's abuse of her parental role—but Dr. Blesserson is correct: this crime has caused unknown damage. Astra will need to be quarantined while we assess her and her siblings."

It was a punch in the solar plexus. "*What?*" she whispered.

Klor stood up again, and came toward her. "Astra," he said. She didn't return his embrace, but hugged herself and let him put his arms around her. His touch was light and dry on her shoulders. His chin rested briefly on the top of her head. He smelled of Klor: of warm stone, of afternoons in the sun. He was the wise old man of the woods. Somehow, even in this terrible, endlessly escalating trial, he was still Klor.

"Astra won't be able to continue at school or do her IMBOD Service with the rest of her Year," Dr. Wolfson continued. "If, Klor and Nimma, you both agree to continue in your roles as Shelter parents and Astra's Shelter siblings are rehoused, Astra may keep living in Or and finish Year Twelve via Tablette learning. She will also have to have daily sessions with an IMBOD psychologist. If Sheltering her is too difficult under the circumstances, she will have to go to an IMBOD school in Sippur for reeducation."

"Rehouse Yoki and Meem?" Nimma gawked over her hanky. "But—"

"Of course we agree," Klor immediately overrode her, giving Astra a little squeeze. "Yoki and Meem can live with their Code parents. Astra's a good girl, officers, and we love her. Of course we'll look after her during her rehabilitation."

The assault was too relentless, too well coordinated. She stood in Klor's arms, trembling, no longer able to rebel.

"Is it really too late?" Nimma pleaded. "Can't she have the shot now?"

"It wouldn't be effective, I'm afraid."

It couldn't be happening. Why was only *she* being punished? "What about Dr. Blesserson?" she pleaded, breaking out of Klor's embrace to thrust her arm toward the table. "You haven't taken my blood. *Test it—* you'll see. He gave me a teaby injection. *He knew the whole time.*"

Dr. Wolfson shook his head. "There's no need to test your blood, Astra. It's clear from your behavior that you didn't have your shot. Dr. Blesserson has agreed to also act as a witness for the prosecution. He's certainly not on trial here."

Dr. Blesserson's impassive face was an enormous toad waiting for its next fly. Klor put a hand on her shoulder and squeezed it. Once. A warning. Somehow she knew she should heed it.

"Astra," Dr. Petaldott said, "you were only seven when Hokma abused you and your memory of events is unreliable. As you've heard, your choices now are to cooperate with your Shelter parents and stay at home, or resist them and be taken to the IMBOD Shelter school in Sippur. I suggest that you consider these options very carefully."

"What about the questioning?" Nimma had stuffed her hanky in her hipskirt band, ready for her next set of histrionics. She twisted her emerald ring around and around on her finger. "Are you going to call her in again?"

"We appreciate that she will be hostile to questioning about her Shelter mother," Dr. Wolfson said, "but at the same time, we are concerned that Hokma may have misled her in serious ways. The purpose of the counseling will be to ascertain the extent of the damage she has sustained. In the meantime, if she tells you anything we ought to know, then you are duty-bound to report it."

The IMBOD officers stood up. "Of course we will." Nimma clasped Dr. Petaldott's hand and shook it until the officer's teeth must have been rattling in her head. "Thank you, Dr. Petaldott, thank you, Dr. Wolfson, thank you *so much*, Dr. Blesserson."

"I'm sure Astra will benefit from having her secret out in the open at last," Dr. Blesserson pompously intoned. "My best wishes to you all." Then his face was gone, replaced at last by the pastel yellow standby screen.

Klor pulled Astra to him. "Come on, Astra, let's go home and have a cup of hot chocolate," he said as Dr. Wolfson crossed the room and unlocked the door.

Back at the Earthship Nimma flew into a tornado-sized fit. "All these years," she announced, her arthritic forefinger ripping through the air as she paced in front of the sofa where Astra sat huddled with a cushion in her lap beside Klor. "All these years, you've been *lying* to us. Staying up there with Hokma, laughing at us, laughing at Yoki and Meem. Who do you think you are? Who *are* you? Klor, I can't look at her, I can't look at her anymore."

"I *wasn't* lying," Astra pleaded. "You never asked me if I had the Serum. You just asked if the needle hurt. *Dr. Blesserson's* lying—test me for the teaby shot, *please*, Klor."

"*Ohhh*. Don't you ask *Klor* to accuse *Samrod* of *Hokma's* crime!" Nimma punctuated each name with a finger jab. "She's embroiled enough people in her schemes already. Poor Ahn—burdened with *your* secret all these years."

"Poor *Ahn?*" Klor said it for Astra. "Darling, it would have saved a lot of trouble if he'd—"

But Nimma was having none of it. "That man's a complete innocent, Klor. I've worked with him, I know. He's an *artist*. He lives on another plane entirely. Has he ever even had another Gaia partner? He was *devoted* to Hokma, and she betrayed and manipulated him just like she did us. What an *impossible* position she put him in."

"Surely that's not Astra's fault, is it?" Klor stood and opened his arms. "Nimma, let me hold you. We must deal with this together. All together. All three of us. Astra, you too."

"No, Klor. I can't hug her now. Don't ask me to hug her." Nimma let him hold her and he made a kind face at Astra over her head. Then she burst into tears and pushed him away. "It's *not* just all three of us. It's everyone. Astra's been lying to everyone."

"I haven't been *lying*," Astra repeated dully. "I've been trying so hard, Nimma—"

"Don't you wiggle words, young lady. Your *whole life* is a lie and now *ours* is too."

"Darling, darling," Klor implored, reaching for her shoulders. "It's the same Astra—*our* Astra. She should have told us, Nimma—of course she should have. But she was afraid to, weren't you, my angel?"

Nimma brushed him aside like a ratty bead curtain. "I can't believe this is happening. What about the others, Klor? Yoki and Meem and Peat? How will it affect them? And what if it makes the news? How will it affect our Or inspection next year? And the National History Museum? Will they disqualify Ahn's submission now? Did you ever think of that, Astra? All the people you were getting in trouble?"

On and on she went. Astra stared at the llama wool carpet, a gift to Nimma from the Gallery directors. "She said if I wanted to be a great scientist I shouldn't have the shot," she muttered. "She said Eya wouldn't want me to have it. How was *I* supposed to know it would be such a big deal? I was only *seven*."

"You're not seven now! You should have told us, years ago."

"And then what? What would you have done? You would've told on Hokma and she would have been taken away!"

"Darling, she's right. She was only a child."

But Nimma ignored him. She drew herself up. "We would have spoken to Hokma," she said regally, "and perhaps saved her from herself. We would have reported the situation to IMBOD, of course, but we would have supported Hokma too. We would have said that she'd made the wrong decision for the right reasons. Perhaps then she would have realized that not everyone in Or is against her. Perhaps she would have decided to stop betraying us and Is-Land with whatever she was doing with Cora Pollen. Perhaps we could have prevented this whole disastrous course of events."

It was unbearable. "Oh, so it's *my fault* again?" Astra implored Klor. "My fault she sent Helium to Atourne?"

"Now, now, darling." Klor was rubbing his forehead. "We don't know what would have happened if we'd discovered the truth earlier. It isn't fair to—"

"For Gaia's sake, Klor, stop *defending* her. Can't you see the trouble she's caused? Now we have to babysit her all through Year Twelve—and Yoki and Meem have to suffer too! Why should they lose their Shelter home because of her?"

"They can still come here. We'll work out a schedule. I'm sure IMBOD will relax the quarantine if Astra cooperates with the counselor."

"Look at her: sullen, surly, utterly unrepentant. Is she going to cooperate with anyone? I don't think so."

"I'm sure—" Klor began again.

"We took her in after our own Birth-Code daughter died." Nimma's voice split. "And this is how she repays us. I'm tired of struggling with her, Klor. I'm sixty-three and I'm tired. If you want to keep her in Or, you look after her. You can stay at Wise House or in a tent, I don't care—just not here. Yoki and Meem and I aren't going anywhere."

"Yes, dear, that's a good solution. It won't be for long, will it, Astra?" But Nimma was already sailing out of the room.

3.3

Sometimes—*before*—she had imagined that telling everyone would be a relief. But every day the worst thing about her situation changed. First came the three days spent getting IMBOD approval for Klor and Nimma's custody plan, during which Yoki and Meem were barred from the Earthship and Nimma refused to speak to her. Then IMBOD rejected Klor's application to stay at Wise House with her on the grounds that Astra needed to make a clean break with Hokma and everything Hokma represented. And besides, Nimma argued vociferously to Klor, ignoring Astra even though she was sitting right beside him, Wise House was impractical. The climb was too steep for Klor, and he needed to visit the Earthship every morning and evening. So he and Astra pitched a visitors' yurt behind the Kinbat track and IMBOD approved a schedule which accounted for every frigging millisecond of her day.

In the morning, while the Or-kids were having breakfast, she was to do yoga; after they had gone to school she was allowed to eat their leftovers at Core House. Then she was to go to Code House for her counseling sessions; her downtime and studies would be in the same spare office. She could go outside in the afternoon, to garden or swim, but she was not allowed to mix with the younger children. After the

Or-kids got back from school she had to return to Code House to study. While they were eating dinner, she was to do her Kinbat laps. She was not allowed to visit the Quiet Room after her own late-shift meal at a table across the hall from the kitchen staff; instead she had to return to the yurt for meditation or studying. Her Tablette would be monitored, and under no circumstances was she to Tablette-talk any of her siblings or schoolmates. Any infraction of these rules would be treated very seriously. If she were found attempting to communicate with another Or-kid she would be removed from Or and placed in the special school in Sippur. In addition, Klor, as her guardian, would be punished with a heavy fine.

It was crazy—even Klor said so. Well, "an understandable overreaction" was how he put it, but when he wrote to IMBOD attesting that Astra's siblings hadn't been harmed by her so far, and suggesting she be permitted supervised contact with them for an hour a day, he was rebuffed by a firm letter from Dr. Wolfson saying that the effects of such a prolonged and intimate deception on the Sec Gen loyalty trait had not yet been tested, and absolutely no chances were to be taken. If Astra wanted to protect her siblings and classmates, she would willingly keep away from them. Isolation was also in her own best interests: she needed time to think deeply about her options, and she couldn't do that if she was caught up in the turmoil of explaining her situation to everyone and coping with all their responses. She was to consider the period a welcome rest and retreat that would benefit her immensely in the long run.

And in fact it was a relief to be away from Nimma and her constant accusatory silence, and that first evening in the yurt Astra slept long and dreamlessly.

But in the morning came her meeting with the counselor, with Klor, to hear the rehabilitation plan.

The office she'd been allocated was on Klor's side of the upper chamber. It overlooked the Staple Crops plots, now harvested for the year, beyond which the mountains opened out onto the steppes. Other than the minor variations in the view, it was exactly like the room where the IMBOD interview had been held. The only furniture was a table and several chairs, and the obligatory orchid.

The counselor was an older woman with heavily lined olive skin and greying hair cut in a short bob. She stood up when they entered and shook Klor's hand. "Good morning, Dr. Grunerdeson. Good morning, Astra. I'm Dr. Greenleafdott. Well, Astra," she said as they all sat down, "it's been an eventful few days, hasn't it? How are you feeling?"

Astra rubbed her hands together in her lap. She had to play this right—but what was right?

"Yes, Dr. Petaldott told me you didn't feel like talking. Not to worry. The purpose of these sessions is to help you open up and return as soon as possible to normal life. You'd like that, wouldn't you?"

Return to normal life? Her life had never been normal.

They sat for ten minutes in silence. This was ridiculous. Why wasn't this woman asking her anything? "Why am I in quarantine?" she asked at last. "I didn't do anything wrong. Why am I in *jail*?"

"Quarantine isn't jail, Astra. You're still at home in Or, aren't you? You can still go outside."

"I can't go to school," Astra pointed out, "or see anyone, and they said I can't do my IMBOD Service. So what's going to happen to me? Am I going to be punished my whole life?"

"Not at all, Astra: this period of solitude is designed to help you reflect on what's happened to you, to think about who you are—and who you want to be. Your future is yours to decide. You have many options, and that's what I want to discuss with you and your Shelter father today."

Dr. Greenleafdott explained that Astra was currently in distress, for many reasons and at many levels, but the depth and complexity of her emotional crisis was being masked by the volatility of her anger. Astra, it had been observed, was a person with a powerful sense of anger, and currently that anger was being misdirected toward the people who loved and cared for her, causing her and her family conflict and pain. This was not Astra's fault; she should not have been burdened with the capacity for uncontrolled anger in the first place. For Sec Gen children, anger was a short-term emotion triggered only by urgent, life-threatening situations. For Astra, though, anger appeared to be a chronic condition, triggered by insignificant conflicts. Fortunately, psychological techniques existed to help her control her temper—but first, she needed to channel that anger toward the source of her current difficulties: Hokma. Once Astra was able to recognize that Hokma had abused her, she could begin to work on her anger management and start the journey of reintegration into Is-Land society. She would never be able to fully bond with the Sec Gens, of course, and she would have to perform special duties during her IMBOD Service, but she could certainly take up a place at a college in Atourne, and as she was just a couple of years younger than the non-Sec Gens, she would certainly find suitable friends and colleagues and Gaia partners in the future.

If, however, these sessions failed and Astra was unable to distance herself from Hokma, then the situation would become very compli-cated. Astra could not perform IMBOD Service if she was known to harbor feelings of loyalty to a traitor, and though she would be able to work as an aglab during those two years, without completing IMBOD Service she would not be qualified to attend college, and that would mean all high-level jobs would be closed to her. She wouldn't be able to remain in Or, because her siblings would be distressed by the conflict she posed to their own loyalty, so she would have to work in another bioregion as a basic-rate member of a domestic team all her life, in the kitchen or gardens. Of course, this kind of work was a valuable service to Gaia, but Astra was intelligent and surely she wanted to do more with her life than weed and wash dishes.

Essentially, the counselor explained in calm, professional tones, Astra needed to come to a personal understanding of her rightful place in family and national life. That was the first step. Then she needed to make a public statement renouncing Hokma and her malign influence; this statement would be read at Hokma's trial. A date for the trial had not yet been set, but certainly Astra would want to make her statement in time to start her IMBOD Service. That gave her a maximum of six months to work with Dr. Greenleafdott—although breakthroughs could often occur early in the process, and perhaps Astra could even make her statement this week.

"I see. I see." Klor was straight-backed on his chair, his hands on his knees. "And the trial? Will Astra have to appear?"

"No, the statement will be sufficient. Though if Astra does choose to testify in person, that of course would be looked upon very favorably by IMBOD. As would her willingness to be interviewed for the media."

"Of course. We understand, don't we, Astra?"

Anger: where was it when she needed it? She was drained of all force, an empty kinbattery. "But . . ." She turned to Klor. "Hokma could go to jail forever."

"Astra." Dr. Greenleafdott regarded her firmly. "Hokma's sentence is not your responsibility, and it will not rest on your statement. The charges against her extend far beyond her manipulation of you."

"What did she do?"

"I don't know the evidence against her but we all have to trust that IMBOD would not happily charge one of their star researchers with treason. There is a solid case against her and sadly, you and everyone at Or must now come to terms with her betrayal."

She was talking as if Hokma had already been convicted—but no one had heard Hokma's side of the story. Perhaps she had a defense; perhaps there had been a mistake—perhaps someone had planted a memory clip on Helium's corpse, or perhaps Hokma had just thought another IMBOD ruling was ill-conceived and was trying to help Dr. Pollen with alternative research. Surely her lawyers might argue that Hokma was well intentioned but misguided? If Astra testified against her, Hokma's defense would be weakened. She couldn't do it, no matter how many greasy pots she had to wash or brambles she had to pull up with her bare hands.

She scrutinized Dr. Greenleafdott. "What happens if I don't feel like answering your questions?"

"You're not on trial, Astra. These sessions are to help you. If you don't want to cooperate, that is up to you. But I do suggest that you think about your options very carefully, and discuss them with your Shelter father if you don't yet feel ready to talk with me."

Klor put his arm around the back of her chair. "We'll do that, won't we, Astra?"

"I think that's probably enough for today, isn't it?" Dr. Greenleafdott tapped her Tablette screen. "I'll email you both the sessions plan and see Astra back here tomorrow."

She needed time: time to think, time for things to change, for the decision she was being forced to make to alter its shape, become possible.
But the problem with time was that it wasn't making her decisions easier; it was making all her problems grow. Every day, the pain of being
separated from everyone else intensified, like a spike twisting slowly in
her chest. Every day she had to watch Meem and Yoki and the other
children pour in and out of Core House without her; every day she had
to sit for hours with Dr. Greenleafdott, giving monosyllabic answers to
her repetitive questions. But worst of all were the moments, and then,
gradually, the hours, when she felt that perhaps it was true: perhaps she
did hate Hokma for what she'd done.

Until now she had thought she couldn't hate anyone more than she
hated Ahn and Dr. Blesserson. They were lizards who soaked up the heat
of other people's passions to warm their own blood, maggots who fed
off the rotting flesh of other people's dreams, and in the end they had
betrayed Hokma—and worse, Ahn had done so gratuitously. There
had been no need for him to help IMBOD investigate her shot; Hokma
was in enough trouble already and no one except Astra and Lil knew that
he knew the truth. Her first week in the yurt, Astra spent hours every
night dwelling on his motives. She ached to know how the topic of her
shot had come up in Ahn's interview. Part of her was convinced that Ahn
had instigated the whole line of the inquiry, right from the beginning,
warning Samrod to prepare a case against her—but why? He must have
been afraid that if IMBOD did decide to test her, she would have exposed
him—which was, after all, exactly what she had done. So perhaps, she concluded dully, she was just as vindictive as he was; he was just smarter than
her: he'd thought ahead and she hadn't. By confessing first, he'd become
the witness, not the suspect. And she'd been stupid. She could have stuck
to her story, pretended that she didn't know she'd never had the shot. She
could have let them test her and then feigned surprise at the results—
she could have claimed she'd always believed Dr. Blesserson had given her
the Serum in his office. They would still have assumed Hokma had given
her the antidote, but at least she would have kept Nimma on her side.

She realized how quickly she'd fallen into IMBOD's trap, how her
panic and quick temper had damaged and undermined her, blunted and

baffled what had always been her keen, searing hatred of Ahn and Samrod Blesserson. Maybe they hadn't conspired against her. Maybe Dr. Blesserson had long ago prepared a story to protect himself—and Ahn was just frightened, he had panicked too, thinking somehow IMBOD knew he knew, and had grassed her up in return for legal protection.

Whatever had happened behind IMBOD's closed doors, neither of the men cared a pomegranate seed about her or Hokma. She detested them, but she could live with that; in a strange way, her contempt for the two men had started to sustain her. It set her pulse throbbing in a steady rhythm that would one day, she swore, propel her toward her revenge. What she couldn't live with were her feelings about Hokma. Hokma was her Shelter mother. *Hokma*, Dr. Greenleafdott repeated in every session, *should have looked after her. Hokma should have always acted in her best interests.* As the weeks wore on and the loneliness accumulated beneath her ribs, Astra could feel the counselor wearing her down.

She could be happy right now. She could be Gaia-playing in Woodland Siesta, her legs wrapped around Tedis's smooth flanks, her mouth buried in Sultana's sweet garden, tracing her Shield brand with her tongue; she could be running in berserker Murmurations, practicing patrol moves, preparing for IMBOD Service with everyone else. Instead, she was alone, rejected, facing a future of isolation and menial work: all because Hokma had forced her to make a decision she was too young to understand. She had bribed her with the Owleons and the promise of being a genius one day. But she wasn't a genius, and even if she was, IMBOD would never let her run a lab now. Hokma hadn't even prepared her for the possibility of her arrest. She hadn't told Astra what to say; she'd just left her to flail, helpless, on her own, against IMBOD and the world. *Why did you do it?* she would cry to herself when Klor was out of the yurt, the javelin spike of Hokma's betrayal piercing her chest. *Why did you experiment on me?*

She would awaken feeling heavy and foggy and ashamed—ashamed of her own betrayal of Hokma. Hokma hadn't experimented on her; the opposite was true. Hokma had wanted to *preserve* her from alteration, to allow her to reach her Birth-Code potential. Then, if Astra let it, a squirming would begin in her stomach: a sly worm emerging from the past to whisper, *It's all your fault. If you had told Hokma when Lil threatened you, Ahn would never have found out about the shot . . .*

She'd have to get up then and scrub her face and do kick-boxing warm-ups or double-time sun salutations. She was being weak, failing the test. Hokma wasn't in prison because of her or Lil; she was there because of Helium. Hokma, she knew, wouldn't be crying in prison. She would be strong and patient, she would do yoga during the day, and at night she would lie in bed thinking about the Owleons, or solving Code problems. There was no way she was going to tell Dr. Greenleafdott she hated Hokma.

Except that the only way she had any chance to rejoin her siblings and school friends and go to college and have a job she enjoyed would be to do just that. She was paralyzed by the choice. Perhaps if she held out, something else would happen to change the game again.

She doubled her resolve to clam up again, to never respond to Dr. Greenleafdott's questions with more than a grunt or a denial. Every day when she got back to the yurt after a session Klor would ask her how it went and she'd shrug and mutter, "Okay."

"Hokma would understand, darling," he said finally, one evening when the rain was drizzling down the yurt flaps and the moldy smell of wet canvas was starting to make her feel ill.

She didn't reply.

"She wants you to have a future—any loving parent would happily give their own future for their child's."

She knew what he was saying: *Just lie. You're good at lying. Lie a little more. Tell Dr. Greenleafdott you wish you were Sec Gen; that you feel abused, exploited, betrayed. Tell her you'll testify against Hokma, you'll tell a story the journalists can embellish with lurid headlines: "Ex-Gaia Girl Secret Victim of Is-Land Traitor," "Stranded: Sec Gen Castaway Reveals Lonely Struggle to Fit In." In return, you'll get back your family and your celebrity and with them hook a cushy, non-frontline IMBOD Service position and later, a place at Code College and a job somewhere with older Is-Landers—and there, at last, you might find a way of belonging. Hokma's future is over. Your future is right there in front of you. Reach out and take it.*

But *he* was a loving parent. Why couldn't *he* help her?

She rolled around on her bedmat and whispered across the yurt, "Will you test me for the teaby shot? Please? We could go now, to Code House."

Klor was silent for a very long time. She flopped over on her back again and shut her eyes.

"I would give my other leg for you, my darling." His voice pushed through the rain, then faltered. "But I can't destroy Nimma."

No. She had known that battle was lost before it began. But Klor had *wanted* to help her fight Dr. Blesserson. She clung to that thought like a walking staff. "He's lying though," she insisted. "You know he's lying, don't you?"

Klor sat up, reached over and turned on his solar lamp. "Astra, I believe that you believe in your story."

What? She raised herself too, but he stopped her with a palm. "But even if Dr. Blesserson did know what he was doing," he continued, "Hokma was his *sister*. And she saved his bond partner's life. I can't blame the man for trying to help her, or for protecting himself now. We just have to cooperate, darling. They do want what's best for you in the end."

It was hopeless. She was just running Kinbat laps with an empty hydropac. She sank back on the bed. Klor lay back down but kept the light on. He was looking at her, she could tell.

"You've been so brave, Astra. Just be brave a little longer."

She stared up at the circle of light dancing on the yurt canopy above their heads. How long would she and Klor be here? Everything could all change again tomorrow. And there was something she hadn't told anyone yet—would never tell IMBOD, or Nimma—but she had to tell someone.

"Klor?"

"Yes, darling."

"I had a Gaia vision. That's why I did it."

"Did you now? What kind of a vision?"

So she told him about the living roof, and Hokma's poppies, and the orchids. Klor listened, and thought, and then he said, "Maybe the vision was right, maybe Gaia does want you to stand apart."

Stand apart. Behind his bed, the aluminum joints and segments of his intelligent leg were quietly reflecting the lamplight. The mechatronic limb could have been made of knotted gold.

"Gaia told you to stand up," she said. "That's what you told all the visitors."

"She did, many times, until I finally listened. But standing apart, even on your own two feet, is much harder."

"Why did She choose me?" Her voice broke, and she gulped back the salty self-pity.

"Because She admires you, Astra, just like I do. But I know She doesn't want you to sacrifice yourself on Hokma's pyre. Listen to the rain. Isn't it saying be gentle with yourself?"

She didn't know what the rain was saying. There were thousands of drops falling on the tent, each one canceling the next one out. *Stop stop stop*, they were saying. *Stop thinking, stop talking.* She'd thought she understood Gaia visions, but maybe Nimma was right: maybe they were just a way of telling yourself what you wanted to hear.

"All they want you to do is express loyalty to Or, darling," Klor urged, "so as not to confuse the Sec Gens. You can still feel loyal to Hokma in your heart. Then you can come back and visit here after college, even live nearby, if you like. And maybe Hokma will serve her time and come out. There are sure to be appeals."

The wind rose outside, and a branch crashed to the ground. Traitors were never let out.

She was going to do it: she would save herself and help destroy Hokma. Then she wasn't going to do it. Then she was. And though in the end she didn't have to, in her heart—in the wet, raw wound gouged out by the whittled tip of the pain Hokma had persuaded her to risk—she understood that if the game hadn't changed the way it had, she would eventually have said the words IMBOD wanted to hear.

And so the fact she hadn't was no comfort at all.

It was their fifteenth session. That morning the counselor had Tablette-texted Nimma and Klor, asking them to join the meeting. Klor came in with Astra to find Nimma already there, sitting next to

Dr. Greenleafdott in one of four chairs arranged in a circle. Astra sat beside Nimma just so that she didn't have to look at her. Nimma would expect to see progress, and even though she did often wish she was Sec Gen now, she didn't want to say that in front of Nimma yet. *Probably*, she thought, *the counselor has some trick in mind, to use my Shelter mother's presence to get me to say how much I miss the Earthship, how much I want to come home.*

"This is not my usual way of working," Dr. Greenleafdott began. "Normally I wouldn't bring parents into a session without my client's permission. But I'm afraid to say that this is not a session. IMBOD has asked me to break some sad news to you all. Astra, Dr. Grunerdeson, Ms. Shipdott, I regret to inform you that, tragically, Dr. Hokma Blesser died in her cell last night. She appears to have had a stroke. That was always a possibility for her, ever since the head injury that cost her her eye."

"Ohh," Nimma gasped.

"Astra, darling, I'm so sorry—" Klor reached for her hand, but the four chairs were on a merry-go-round, spinning faster and faster, and Astra's head was bursting and her vision was a blur and the adults' voices were streaming away in the wind. It wasn't real here anymore—nothing was real; nothing was true . . .

She got up to walk out, to walk away from this woman and her dizzying lies, but her knees had disappeared and instead she collapsed back against the edge of her seat. Klor was there, his arm supporting her.

Somehow, she found her voice. "Where is she? I want to see her," she whispered.

"She's in Atourne still," Dr. Greenleafdott said, "but I'm afraid she won't be released to Or. The day before she died, Dr. Blesser signed a full confession to treason, so her body is now IMBOD property. The autopsy is being performed today, and when the results have been documented, she will be cremated and her ashes will be used as fertilizer for farm animal feedage, following standard IMBOD procedure for the bodies of traitors."

Astra was barely listening. She'd been flung from the whirligig onto the hard stony dirt and now she was limping in the wilderness, holding her head. There was a rushing sensation in her ears and her eyes hurt as if the sun were blinding them. Her skin was a crust of ice, her teeth were chattering and she was rocking back and forth, clutching her ribs.

Hokma was dead.

Klor leaned forward. "What exactly did she confess to, Doctor? What did she say?"

"I don't have a copy of her statement, I'm afraid. But I understand that among other misdeeds, she did confess to abusing Astra and manipulating the trust of her brother and Gaia partner. She begged for everyone's forgiveness."

"Do you hear that, Astra?" Nimma hissed. "She knows she did you a great wrong. Why can't *you* see that?"

Her hands were over her face. She couldn't look at any of them.

"We'll take her home," Klor said. "Doctor, please, may we take her to the Earthship?"

"Yes, you may. The quarantine and counseling are suspended for two days."

"Klor!" There was a note of panic in Nimma's voice. "What about the other children? Doctor—can we tell them?"

"Yes, the news is now public. I have called a meeting for the rest of the Or-adults this morning and a press release will go out this afternoon."

Astra was at the door, with Klor. She turned to him: her only ally.

"I don't want to go to the Earthship. I want to go to Wise House."

3.4

They couldn't stop her. They told her Wise House was boarded up and the gates were locked and it would be detrimental to her treatment, but she tore herself free from their lame chorus of warnings and stumbled across the Kinbat track and over to West Gate, and in the end, though Nimma fell away, Klor walked behind her until she slowed to let him catch up, pacing in silence as far as the crossroads, where he sat at the top of the steps to the Fountain and waited for her to return.

Her vision was streaked, the world was wobbling and her tears splashed on the roots and leaves like fat drops of rain. Hokma was dead. IMBOD *said* Hokma was dead. They *said* she had confessed. But she *couldn't* be dead—she *couldn't* be guilty. She *couldn't* be a traitor. She would be waiting for Astra at Wise House with Helium and Silver and a plate of berry biscuits and a list of chores. She just had to reach the crest of the slope and she would see the open gate ahead and the path leading to the yellow front door, and Hokma would be on the living roof, picking wildflowers for the table. The Owleons would be on their perches and after tea she and Hokma would take them out to the field and fly them. Then they'd clean the aviary and work in the garden and play whist and fill the antique pens with ink and write in Hokma's homemade notebooks. *Hokma's notebooks.* Why couldn't she have one?

IMBOD had taken them all away in big boxes. Why couldn't she have a small one, with recipes or poems? She wanted something to hold, to keep forever—one of Hokma's eyepatches; a talon from the coat rack; one of Helium's feather quills; a snippet of Hokma's brushcut.

But the gate was locked and the fingercode had been changed and barbed wire looped along the top of the fence. She couldn't even see Wise House through the trees. She clung to the wire and pressed her body against the links as though her flesh might squeeze through, like clay through a sieve. Then she remembered: there *was* a way through.

She ran right along the fence until it met the cedar hedge. The barbed wire above her head turned the corner too, a coiled ridge of sharp metal teeth biting into the foliage. She ran through the lacebarks, tripping over roots, and out into the flying field. A veil of sunlight was falling through the clouds over the wild grass, bronzing the juniper tree and the rocks at the top of the slope. She picked up speed as she passed the gate, not even bothering to try it, and headed for the gap where she had wormed through on her belly after Lil.

She missed it on the way up, but when she realized she'd overshot she retraced her steps, crouching and patting the ground, and she found it. The lower branches had grown down to the earth, but beneath them the soil was still scooped out and she recognized the place: her rough passageway into disaster, betrayal and exile. IMBOD had missed it.

A reintroduced fox could slip through, and maybe a small child, but she was far too big now. She needed garden shears. She would have to come back—or, *wait*—the earth was soft from the rains; could she dig out the hole? She hunted in the field for a sharp stone the right shape and heft and when she'd found one she knelt and began to scrape at the soil, which came up easily in great lumpy handfuls she flung behind her like a dog digging for a bone. For a minute or two it felt as though she could dig down to Gaia's molten core, but then she hit a rocky layer and as she pushed her head into the hedge to gain leverage, she saw that the trunks were closer together than she'd remembered. She'd never get her shoulders and hips past them.

No. She *would*. She would dig deeper, that was all, until she could squeeze through on her side. She redoubled her efforts with the stone, scrambling at rocks, picking away worms and a large green beetle, until her fingernails were torn and a mealy grit coated her lips.

But there was a massive rock at the base of the hole and she couldn't find its edges. She slammed her stone against it and the stone broke in two and she dropped her head, sobbing in frustration.

That was when it fell, chinking against the rock, from the depths of the hedge, into the hole in front of her: a *jar*. She recognized the lid: it was Hokma's berry jar—but the berries were gone, replaced by a thick roll of hemp paper. She seized the jar and brought it out into the light. Through the glass, in Hokma's handwriting, in peacock-blue ink, was her name: *ASTRA*.

She took the jar to the rocks, the glass feeling smooth and calm in the palm of her hand. She sat with her back against the largest rock, facing the hedge, so she could see if Klor came looking for her. She opened the jar, pulled out the roll of paper and unfurled it. The paper was covered in small, spidery handwriting—carefully printed, not joined up or rushed—and it was wrapped around a downy white feather.

Dear Astra,

Helium has not returned from his Atourne flight and I fear his absence will lead to mine. If you are reading this, then I expect you are facing a crisis, one you may think I should have prepared you for. I am sorry for your pain and confusion, but I decided it was better you had nothing to hide except the Serum Shot decision. Astra, I am not afraid of IMBOD. They will never believe that Samrod helped us, so you should tell them that I gave you the antidote, no matter what the consequences may be for me.

I want to tell you that I love you. Though I am not a natural mother, caring for you has been the greatest joy of my life. I know people will think I have deprived you of belonging to the next stage in human evolution; perhaps you yourself will come to hate me for your impossible choice when you were only 7. I take full responsibility, for you were too young and I knew that. But I was compelled to act out of love for you and respect for your Birth-Code parents. I planned to tell you your parents' full story when you were 20, but I will have to do so here, and trust that Gaia will lead you to this letter. If She does not, then She does not want you to know.

You are like Lil, in more ways than one. Your father, Zizi Kataru, is a Non-Lander. Eya swore me to secrecy; even Nimma and Klor do not know. Zizi was an aglab from the Southern Belt who stayed in Is-Land when the Boundary was closed. Gaian dissidents helped him get forged Is-Land identity documents, those of a petty criminal who hadn't been allowed to do IMBOD Service, and he worked in a restaurant as a dishwasher and later a prep chef. Those same dissidents sent Cora and Eya to me, because I share their vision of what Is-Land should be: not a walled-in land filled with child soldiers and wounded veterans but part of a borderless world, sharing Gaia's beauty and abundance. I do not believe Non-Landers are our enemies, or that it would be impossible for us to live together. Some of their customs are different, but there is room for all of us. Many Non-Landers, including your Code father, share this vision of peaceful coexistence. Gaia knows, it is a difficult hope to sustain, but if we abandon it we abandon our humanity too.

Zizi was not an "infiltrator" but a man who wanted to live in the land of his grandparents, even though this cut him off from his family. His name, Kataru, means "alliance" in his language, and from a young age he felt he was destined to form a strong bond with Gaian people. He adapted to our ways and wanted to marry Eya, but this was impossible. When she returned from Or after your birth, he had disappeared; he had been arrested and expelled to the Southern Belt, where he still lives. Lil is there too, reunited with her father's family. She used a tunnel under the Eastern Boundary and people living in the Barren Mountains helped her get to the Belt. I told Zizi about her and I understand that they now see each other often.

Zizi will always welcome you, Astra. Tragically though, I must tell you that your Birth-Code mother is no longer alive; Eya died 15 years ago after the difficult birth of your half-Birth-Code sister, Halja. Halja lives in Bracelet Valley still, but I don't advise you to try and find her.

Her community's rules are very different from ours, and her father and grandfather would be furious if they knew about you.

I know this must all come as a terrible shock, but a shock can be transformative; it can expose painful truths our everyday lives disguise. You know I lost my eye trying to protect Samrod's Gaia partner. The time has come for me to tell you exactly what happened. The boy who shot me was 15. Our troops interrogated him for information. IMBOD thought I would like to see his body when they were done with him. He was slender, just a whelp. His hair was thickly curled, like Drake's and Brook's. His eyes were swollen and purple, like baby eggplants left to rot in the sun. His fingers were broken like kindling snapped for the fire. His skin was polka-dotted with burn marks, and his Gaia plow was charred black. I was never told his name. I was supposed to be glad he had suffered, but that night I wept for him. I vowed never to wear a prosthetic eye. My wound would speak—silently, just to me—of his gaping pain. He had taken my sight, but he had also given me a vision: I would never see Is-Land in the same light again.

IMBOD will tell you this kind of treatment is necessary to prevent greater atrocities against us and against Gaia. That is not true. The Non-Landers are not a cruel people. The original returnees were unarmed. Their violence has only ever been a weak echo of ours. I intended to tell you our true history after your IMBOD Service, when you had seen the conditions in the Belt for yourself: the acres of faded tents and open sewers; the toxic mines that supply the rare earths for our Tablettes; the lines of Non-Lander women and their scrawny, often deformed babies, waiting patiently for parcels of dried food from CONC medics. You would have seen the IMBOD snipers patrolling the Boundary, aiming at old men with the scent of mint on their fingers and children playing soccer with tin cans for goalposts. You would have seen those same old men and children lying lifeless on the dirt roads of the Belt.

I ran the risk that you would have believed IMBOD's lies about the reasons for these horrors, but I gambled that these lies would be so simplistic, crudely tailored for gullible Sec Gen minds, that you would have begun secretly to doubt them. If not, if you had become a good

Is-Land soldier—for make no mistake, it is a war we are waging in the Belt—I would have accepted that I deserved to lose you, precious child, for the crime of forcing you to grow up far too soon.

If you are reading this, then we have been separated by forces stronger than us both. I am sorry if you have lost Silver too; here is the chick feather I meant to give you on your 18th birthday. But no gift can express my love for you. Every day watching you grow has been a privilege I thank Gaia for, and memories of you will sustain me as I await the greatest challenge of my life. My trial will be an opportunity to speak openly about my vision for Is-Land and my disagreements with the dark direction IMBOD and the National Wheel Meet have been taking us since you were born.

You must not worry about me, or try to protect me. But I must warn you: do not trust Samrod or Ahn. I know there is no love lost between you and them, but they may try and win you over in order to hurt me, or to neutralize any threat they believe you pose to them. Whatever they do or say, believe me, they do not have your best interests at heart. Samrod took a huge risk for us and I never expected him to sacrifice himself for me, but over the years he has ingratiated himself with IMBOD to an extent I could never have believed possible. To be frank, I simply don't recognize him now. He's not the person I grew up with anymore and I cannot predict his actions.

Ahn is a different matter. I am afraid you were right: he has always resented you. When we were young he wanted to have a child with me, but I refused; I had no interest in pregnancy or babies. But then Eya arrived and left you—a child of two lands and no home. Ahn could never understand why I chose to Shelter you; he was hurt and jealous and I can't blame him for being angry with me. I tried to give you both the best of my attention over the years, but things were never the same between us and we started to argue more, sometimes bitterly. Still, we gave each other pleasure, and when you get older you'll understand that no matter how things change, it's very hard to leave someone you've bonded with. When he discovered that I had been lying to him about you he was furious with me. He thought I should tell Nimma and Klor, and he was also afraid that he would be punished for keeping our secret.

Though I told him how dangerous exposure would be for both you and me, I was terribly afraid he would do it anyway. Then a kind of awful miracle occurred: Astra, I learned that he had committed a serious crime, and in exchange for his silence I protected him.

I would so much rather not tell you this story, which shames me every time I think of it. But I don't want you to ever think that Ahn bears me any love or loyalty: he doesn't. Everything went disastrously wrong between us, and he may well still want to punish you for that. Astra, I saw Ahn touch Congruence at the Inspection Report banquet and I confronted him about it at Wise House, the night before you and Lil followed us. He finally admitted that after the Fountain film she had turned to him for help with her studies and—he said—for some adult affection while her Shelter parents were dealing with Gloria's illness. He swore blind there was nothing wrong with his interest in her, but I knew he was lying, and I know how young girls think. That summer I walked every day to the paperbark grove and, finally, I caught them Gaia-playing. I took a photograph. I feel so dirty writing that down, but I did it gladly because I knew I had saved you. Then I let them continue their affair, though it hurt far more than I thought it would. He may have been an old shoe, but he fit my foot, Astra.

Still, as the other saying goes, time softens all cries and proves all ties. She came back to him after her IMBOD Service and she is now of age. Don't mistake me: Ahn did her a great wrong. It doesn't matter that she wanted to be with him: she was young and vulnerable, and I believe he was only attracted to her because he was angry with me. But they have bonded now, and last month he told me he's not afraid of the photograph anymore. Congruence knows about you, Astra, and she has said that if he wants to tell Nimma and Klor and I make good my threat, she would defend him in any trial, and wait for his return should he be jailed for his offense.

Such cases often attract a degree of public sympathy, and can even lead to calls to lower the age of legal consent; still I know that neither of them desire to bring such scandal and deprivation down upon their heads and he has remained silent for that reason. But I also know that the other charges against me will be so grave, and the need to convict me so strong, that IMBOD is likely to grant Ahn immunity from prosecution in exchange for testifying that I also betrayed Project Genelsis. I have kept the photograph hidden behind a Code wall, to access if I need it, but I'm afraid it may now cause more harm than good to reveal it. My crimes dwarf Ahn's, and playing the blackmail card may well just be used against me.

I know this is very worrying, but what I am hoping is that Ahn simply wants to be left alone with Congruence. Perhaps Gaia wants them to be together. Maybe she will give him the child he always desired, or maybe she will milk him of his knowledge and leave him to desiccate in that airless office of his. I don't know, and I don't care; I only care about you. Though I am desolate to leave you, I know that Klor and Vishnu and Sorrel will always look after you. Just ignore Ahn, Astra, and let them protect you.

I think my bond with Ahn failed because I could never tell him about my belief that you, part Non-Lander, have a special role to play in the struggle to unite your two peoples. Astra, you are the Gaia Girl, and I believe you were chosen for more than just blessing bioregional fairs. But whatever my own dreams for you and Is-Land, only you can decide the purpose of your life. I tried to ensure that you could dream freely, as my generation and all our ancestors have.

I wish I could be there to answer all your questions, about Helium and Cora, and Zizi and Lil, but you should face IMBOD in innocence, not stained with my guilt. If you find this letter before they question you, I urge you to pretend you've never read it. And please believe me that whatever happens to me, Astra, <u>it's not because of you</u>. I have only one other piece of advice for you: trust Gaia. She wants all Her children to live as one family, under Her wings. That was Her message to us in the Dark Time and we must not misinterpret it. You are my brave, strong, beautiful Shelter daughter, but your true Mother is Gaia, and if you turn to Her when you are uncertain or afraid, She will always guide and protect you.

All my love
Hokma

She let the letter drop to the ground and sat staring blindly out over the field. Part of her mind was numb, as if it had been sprayed with anesthetic. Part of it was inflamed, raging at Ahn. But beneath the stupor and the fury an awakening pulsed: *Hokma was a dissident*. She had said so, proudly, in the letter. This was no forced confession; this was her statement: what she believed, why she lived on her own in the woods—why she'd stopped Astra from getting the Security Serum shot—*why she had been arrested*. Cora Pollen was a dissident too. She and Hokma had helped Eya because... her stomach turned... because *Astra's Code father was a Non-Lander*.

She knew it was true. It explained everything—why she didn't belong, why she had never fit in. She dug her fingernails into her scalp and rubbed hard, as if her head were infested with nits. She had her Code father's hair. She had a head of Non-Lander hair and a false stamp of IMBOD approval burned on her root chakra. She was a freak—a *fraud*. She was a cross-Coded bitch, half-criminal, half-untouchable. Hokma might know who her parents were, but her dreams were delusional—fairy tale horseshit. Even if what she'd said about Non-Land was true, Astra was no frigging savior. She was a pariah, and she would be wherever she went.

She sat breathing hard, her scalp burning, blood rising beneath her ragged fingernails, staring down at the letter on the ground. Had she always suspected this? When she was a child, she had always begged to hear the worst part of any story: the ending of her Birth-Code mother story, when Eya went away; the part in Kali's story when the prisoners were left to starve on the Death Ships; exactly how Torrent and Stream had died. She had always pressed and poked and squeezed until she was told the ugliest truths, or until she had seized them for herself from the adults' pile of lies—except, she remembered with a sick streak of shame, on the ledge with Lil, when she had retreated into Sec Gen dreams of safety, into Woodland Siesta, battle sports, Code study.

But she wasn't Sec Gen—she had *never* been Sec Gen. And now, no matter how much she wanted to, she couldn't live that lie anymore.

A trail of ants crawled over the scroll of paper: workers, carrying on, just like the Sec Gens. But who was she? She'd been a worm, squirming beneath the rock of Hokma's love, Hokma's authority—but not anymore. She was exposed now, and Hokma was right: whatever it was Astra had been chosen for, she would have to decide for herself. The throbbing in her head intensified and she squeezed her eyes shut. Something was coming: something else, something not in the letter. The letter was finished now, and proved false in the most basic way, for in the letter Hokma was alive—but Hokma was *dead*: killed for saving Astra from the Serum, for daring to dream her own dreams about Is- Land, for wanting to speak out against IMBOD. Hokma hadn't had a stroke; only a Sec Gen would believe that. IMBOD had murdered her, with the help of Dr. Blesserson and that malicious, festering, *child- frigging* pus-maggot Ahn.

She opened her eyes and looked up to see a kestrel hovering over the field. She stood and put Silver's feather in the pouch on her hipbelt. Walking in a circle around the rocks, she read the letter again, this time out loud, feeling the rhythm of Hokma's voice in her mouth, tasting the love in her words, testing Hokma's implacable confidence against her own knowledge, her own strength, her own self. When she had finished, she looked up at the kestrel, and as she watched, the raptor plummeted to the ground, hunting a mouse or a vole. She rolled up the letter and slid it back in the jar then found another stone and dug a hole between two rocks. She buried the letter, then camouflaged the site, piling on some of the earth and stones she'd dug out.

She turned around and marched across the field into the woods, the stone still clutched in her hand. Klor was at the crossroads. If she cut through the lacebarks and then the stringybarks and pines below them, she could veer back down the slope to the path and leave him stranded far behind.

3.5

Her mind was whirring like a circular blade, clear and sharp as broken glass. Her boots were kinetic battery packs, each pounding step she took charging her body with the heat of Gaia's molten core. Her limbs were pistons, pumping acid through her veins. The stone clenched in her hand chanted *kill kill kill*. The leaves on the trees whispered *now now now*.

She surged through West Gate and onto the Kinbat track. Behind her, Moon was power-walking; she called out "Astra—?" but Astra ignored her. Her heart rate accelerating, her ears roaring like the wind around the yurt at night, she pounded around the track, past the vegetable garden, past East Gate, past the swimming pool and then, her muscles glowing, her pace slowing to a brisk walk, she swerved up the path to Code House. Her heart was thumping in her throat as she took the steps two at a time, passing Sorrel on her way down, absorbed in her Tablette screen. "Astra?" She looked up, a startled expression on her face, but Astra was already crossing the deck and pulling the cedar doors open. *Yes yes yes* the stone hissed. The dark, brooding clouds overhead murmured *calm calm calm*.

A couple of Code House guides were herding a group of visitors around the lobby, their chatter bouncing off the high glass walls and roof. She elbowed her way through to the staircase. "Hey," one of the guides, a bony Seed Coder in red-rimmed glasses complained, "watch where you're going, Astra." She ascended the staircase one solid step after another, breaking the skin of the lobby's bubble of commotion, leaving the din of exclamations far behind her. On the second floor she turned right down the back corridor; picking up speed again she passed the gushing cliff waterfall and swerved around Russett, who lifted his coffee mug in the air to avoid her. "Klor's not in," he called over his shoulder, but she was striding past Klor's office and at last arrived in front of Ahn's door.

She grabbed the handle. It couldn't be locked, not now. The office couldn't be empty. No. *Slow slow slow* the stone sang.

The door swung open. She shut it tight behind her.

"Hello?" Ahn was standing behind a large screendesk at the other end of the room. The surface was tilted toward him and Congruence was leaning forward to fingerswipe the surface. His hand, Astra could see, was grazing her bottom. As he looked up, he removed it.

"Astra," he frowned. "What are you—?"

She stepped forward, took aim and hurled the stone at his head. Congruence dropped to the floor as it blasted an arc through the air.

"*Good Gaia,*" Ahn shouted, swerving and ducking and shielding his face with his arms. The stone crashed into the shelves behind him, rattling a row of award sculptures and knocking one down to the floor with a deadening clunk.

FRIGGING GAIA—*MISSED*. But target still off-guard. Advantage retained.

She cast around the room for more ammunition. The right wall was sheer gold-tinted glass with a one-way view of the escarpment, stretching out to the steppes beneath the lowering sky. In front of the window-wall, a couple of cushion-chairs were arranged around a low table: she spotted a teapot, two celadon cups and an elegant biolamp. Possible . . . but no, better, right here, closer, sheathed in decorative steel cases and displayed on a candelabra on a shelf beside the door were the three Edition One Kezcams: the perfect ammunition, ripe for the plucking. She snatched one up. Empty of helium, encrusted with enameling, the sphere was not quite a shotput, but it was still promisingly heavy in her hand.

"You let them *kill* her!" Like a nuclear-powered windmill, she fast-bowled the Kezcam at Ahn, aiming this time for his heart. He crossed his arms over his chest and turned sideways, grunting as the missile cannoned into his shoulder.

"*Ahn!*" Congruence shouted from under the screendesk. She was thrusting the fallen award, a planed chunk of bronze, up into Ahn's hand; he grabbed it and moved into the room, sliding in front of the window-wall, his hurt arm across his torso and groin, the award raised in front of his head.

"Stop this *now*, Astra," he demanded, his voice harsh as dried bark.

She snatched up the two remaining Kezcams, one in each hand.

Then everyone shouted all at the same time.

"You *carnivore*," she yelled, charging forward. "You frigging *cannibal*!"

"Astra—don't make me do this." He was backing away, teetering, his face suddenly—gloriously—jaundiced with terror.

"Throw it, Ahn, *throw it*," Congruence urged. She was half-standing herself now, reaching up to the shelf for another weapon. Astra threatened her and she ducked back down. By the window, twisting his hips and leaning back like a bowler, Ahn threw the award at Astra—but Ahn had only ever *filmed* cricket games and he hadn't been in IMBOD training for decades—or maybe she'd lucked out and struck his dominant arm. Whatever the reason, his throw was a wobbler, a dud, with no force behind it.

Astra dodged easily, and the award sailed into something behind her, a ceramic, from the sound of the smash.

"Frig!" Ahn screamed, perhaps at the loss of some expensive vase. He was off-balance, teetering, full-frontal, his Gaia plow swinging like a curtain tassel.

She aimed low and the Kezcam slammed straight into his testicles. With a blood-curdling groan, he fell to his knees, doubling over, clutching his genitals.

"*Ahn*," Congruence screamed again.

In the gleam from the biolamp his thinning hair was a half-blown dandelion seed head, his bald patch a high shiny bull's-eye a child couldn't miss. Breathing heavily, Astra raised her final missile.

The door banged open, startling her.

"*What in Gaia's name is going on in here?*" Russett roared.

"She's ... gone ... crazy!" Ahn gurgled. He was reaching for the arm of the chair now, his face purple and sweaty, contorted with pain. The moment was lost.

In her peripheral vision she saw Congruence leap up from behind the screendesk, her fingers curled around the first thrown Kezcam. As Congruence hurled it at her, Russett barreled across the room, head down. Just before he rammed her against the wall, knocking the wind out of her lungs, she pitched her final Kezcam as hard as she could. Congruence's shot missed, but over Russett's shoulder Astra saw the windowpane shatter as her own hard black missile went sailing out through a golden blizzard of glass and disappeared into the air.

3.6

She was running down a long, bright corridor, the doors flying open on either side. Samrod Blesserson was laughing in the distance, waiting for her to catch up, then disappearing as soon as she reached him. She ran on and on, past rooms full of screens, screens full of rooms, flickering with images of everyone she knew, everyone she could never leave behind, no matter how far or how fast she raced: Nimma making biscuits, her fingers sticky with dough, her eyes sour and red as dried berries, saying, *None for you, Astra, none for you*; Klor tumbling down the slope from Wise House, grasping at roots which came up in his hands, his aluminum leg rolling after him, the foot kicking his temples as he cried out, *Stop, stop*; Lil standing on a chair gyrating her hips, Silver fluttering on her shoulder and then, as Astra moved closer, plucking a hipbead from her string and placing it under Astra's tongue where it dissolved into a bitter, chalky sludge and trickled down her throat until Lil dissolved too and she was watching Russett and Torrent wrestling at the center of the Boundary labyrinth, hands at each other's throat, spotlights raking their contorted faces as an IMBOD officer jabbed them both in the ribs with a stick while in the next room Ahn and Congruence Gaia-bonded, his long blond body covering hers as she lay face down against the screendesk, her fingers gripping the edge, her small breasts flattened against the plans for a circle of traitor wells; and beyond them all, locked, trapped, hidden away, was Hokma . . . Hokma caged in Wise House, the rooms cobwebbed and empty, the lofts broken, the windows boarded up as Hokma stood in the gloom with Helium on her wrist, turning to Astra again and again, saying, *Live the truth, Astra, live the truth*, as Helium spread his wings and pulled her up by the wrist, up to the low, flat ceiling that vanished as they reached it and soared up into a pouring shaft of red light and downy feathers, filling Astra's mouth and nostrils and ears with the dry smell of bird dust and the warbling cries of an orchestra of Owleons. *Whooot-whooot. Coo-loo-loo. Pree-pree-pree.*

Light flooded the room, all the rooms, all the screens, until she was swimming in a sea of pale, translucent, watermelon red. *Kra kra kra. Kra kra kra.* Her ears were whorled echo chambers, a wild carousel of sound. The *whomph whomph* of wingbeats disturbed the air and there was a scuffle of claws on cement. *Ha ha ha. Ha ha ha. Phweeeee. Phweeeeee. Trrrru trrrru.* Birds: an eternal soft cacophony of birds, and, through her nostrils, a trickle of fresh air infiltrating her brain.

She opened her eyes. She was propped up in bed on what appeared to be a balcony. The mattress was raised behind her back and she was looking out over a wrought-iron railing into a large round courtyard tangled with cedars, cypresses, orchids and birds. She couldn't see the ground, but between the trees she could glimpse a far tier of balconies as the building curved around to meet itself. She looked up: above her was a white ceiling with a patch of bubbled paint and a creeping black blossom of damp. Her head felt—not cold, but somehow exposed; there was a slight tension at the base of her skull and between her legs was a faint burning sensation she dimly remembered having experienced before. The courtyard was a deep green well. She had no idea how high up she was, how tall were the trees—she could have been one hundred stories up a hollow tower, or floating in the sky. Her body felt as far away as the invisible sun. She looked down at it, its distant form molded by the damp, wrinkled sheet. Her breasts were blanked out, bandaged tight by the sallow yellow cotton; her arms lay like two dead branches.

Experimentally, she splayed out her fingers. They obeyed the commands of her mind and she lifted them to her head. Her scalp had been shaved. The short hairs were soft, like a pelt. She reached to the back of her head and gently investigated the tense spot at the base of her cranium. A round cloth sticker sprouting a rubber nib was plastered at the top of her neck. She tried to peel it off, but her finger nudged the nib and she experienced a jabbing pain deep inside her head, as if she were threatening to rip a taproot out of her own brain. She smoothed the plaster back down and returned her hands to her lap, palms up, the tips of her fingers gently interlaced. It occurred to her to also probe the dull pain between her buttocks, but lifting the sheets felt like too much effort, so on second thoughts, she left her hands at rest.

There was a Tablette tray, she saw now, mounted on a jointed metal swing-arm to a railing running down the left side of the bed. The tray was nearly vertical and pushed to one side. She pulled it toward her. The screen was flowing with fractals: deep cogs, symmetrical petals, endless spirals. As she studied them a pale but pointed voice swam from the cloth and rubber lilypad at the base of her skull, up to the fine tip of the taproot in her head.

WELCOME ASTRA

"*Gaiaaaaaa. Gaiaaaaaa.*" The voice in her head was drowned out by a woman's cry, a voice traveling from somewhere outside her. She turned her head to the right. Her shoulder burned. About twenty feet away, a woman in a bed just like hers, with a shaved head like hers, was singing and raising her arms to the courtyard. She was straining to lift herself out of the bed but she remained clamped to it. Twisting to observe the woman more intently, Astra realized her own hips were restricted. She wasn't sure if this mattered. The woman wasn't calling to her, after all.

Fwup fwup. Fwup fwup.

A bird arrived: an Owleon—Silver—landing on the sheet, shaking out his feathers, lifting a claw with a memory clip attached. She had no food to give him. She held out her wrist and delicately he climbed onto it. She stroked him. He wasn't Silver. He was young, his white belly feathers still fluffy and full, and his shawl was more amber than gray. He inched up her arm and held out his claw.

She untwisted the memory clip and Not-Silver hopped to the foot of the bed. But what was she to do with it? Oh, yes: the Tablette tray. Later she would insert the clip, but right now the red sea was swimming again in front of her eyes.

When she woke again, it was raining. She was immersed in the glimmer and rush of the downpour and she didn't think to consider where she was. Then she recognized the bed and dimly recalled the visitation of the Owleon. The memory clip, she saw, was now resting on a narrow, slightly battered groove running along the bottom edge of the Tablette tray. She stared at the groove and its dimpled indentations and for the first time it occurred to her: *I am not at home.*

She should get up, go and find someone, but when she tried to slide her legs out of the bed she discovered again that she couldn't. She lifted the sheet. A thick white belt was wrapped around her body, then around the bed itself.

It was all very perplexing. Who could she ask? The woman in the bed to the right was lying with her eyes closed and her knees spread. Her mattress was flat and her right arm was moving beneath her sheet, her hand obviously between her legs. Her lips were moving, but she made no sound.

Astra looked to her left. A similar distance away stood another bed, this one occupied by an elderly man, sitting upright. A few strands of gray hair drifted over his scalp. He had pushed his sheet aside, revealing the full length of his body, a skin-sheathed skeleton, secured by his own white belt. His arms were raised and moving strangely, one fast and zigzaggy, the other slow and swoopy, as if he were conducting the storm. The velocity of the rain increased and the man's Gaia plow stiffened and twitched. With his slow hand he reached down and massaged the tip.

She faced forward into the dark pelting rain. In her peripheral vision the Tablette screen was pulsing with ever-mutating floral geometry.

People Gaia-playing in public—but was she in public? This was a puzzle.

YOU HAVE QUESTIONS.
WE HAVE DELIVERED THE ANSWERS.

The voice was kind and correct: yes, Silver—no, Not-Silver—had brought her a message. She reached for the memory clip. It was grooved and shell-like in her fingers. She mustn't drop it, mustn't let it tumble to the floor. She swung the Tablette in front of her and slid the clip down its frame to the resting notch. It clicked into place. The fractals on the screen fused and shimmered with the voice in her skull.

ASTRA ORDOTT.
ALL IS WELL.
YOU ARE RESTING WITH US.
YOUR MEMORIES ARE OUR MEMORIES
AND OURS ARE YOURS.
TO REQUEST A MEMORY
SWIPETYPE THREE KEYWORDS.

MAXIMUM ORDER:
SIX MEMORIES PER OWLEON VISIT.
ALL MEMORIES WILL BE DELIVERED
IN THE OPTIMUM RATIO
OF ANTICIPATION TO CONSUMMATION.
ALL BODILY NEEDS WILL BE ATTENDED TO
IN FUGUE STATE.
GAIA LOVES YOU.
ALL IS WELL.

All was well. Her memories were safe. Hot liquid filled her eyes, spilled over the rims. She could place an order—when? Now. She pulled the Tablette toward her and thumbprinted the corner. The keyboard appeared. SILVER, she swipetyped. FEEDING. FEATHERS. The words floated on the screen. When the final letter had been inputted they flashed twice and the voice returned.

YOUR MEMORY REQUEST

IS NOW CLIP-LOADED.

YOU MAY REQUEST

FIVE REMAINING MEMORIES

THIS OWLEON VISIT.

TO EDIT ORDERS PRESS "EDIT."

TO CANCEL ORDERS PRESS "CANCEL."

TO SEND CLIP, RELEASE OWLEON.

As the voice spoke, the order command buttons appeared, one by one, on the screen. On the side of the Tablette the memory clip flashed green like . . . like . . . oh yes . . .

EMERALD RING FINGER she input. Then stopped. What else did she need to remember? It was so difficult to think of anything not already encompassed by the courtyard, the bed, the Tablette, the voice in her head. Oh, of course. She flushed. How could she forget to order a Gaia memory? GAIA PLAY . . . PEAK she entered. Then GAIA HYMN . . . FAVORITE.

She had two orders left, the voice reminded her, but surely four memories were enough for today? A shadow was muting the screen: Not-Silver hovered above the bed, his scaly yellow claws massaging the air. She detached the clip and pushed the Tablette tray away and the Owleon dropped to her chest. His feathers were dry. It had stopped raining, she realized; the hushing sound from the courtyard was the wind in the trees and the birds beginning to call to each other again. His eyes, though, were wet: wet black stones in a soft white heart. She could stare into them forever. At last, after she had plunged to the bottom of a black ocean and returned with the moon in her mouth, he lifted his claw, she replaced the clip around his ankle and he flew back into the whispering night.

The light moved slowly across the courtyard, falling over the edge of the balcony, gilding the tips of the railings, then passing on. Not-Silver didn't return. To her left, a large Owleon swooped down onto the old man's chest. The man stroked the bird's feathers, communing with its dignity and grace for what seemed like hours. Finally he unclasped a clip from the bird's claw and attached it to his own Tablette. The golden light from the screen bathed his face and chest and Astra could see that he was smiling. She began to feel light inside, a hollow, brittle, *difficult* feeling that preoccupied her for a time. There was a slight tender swelling in her stomach and as with the burning patch between her legs, which had developed a crust, she sensed it would be dangerous to probe this pain. The only solution to these dilemmas was to sleep again.

When she woke it was twilight and her mouth tasted like—she licked her teeth—like *fennel*. The hurt place between her legs was numb and the pain in her abdomen was gone, replaced by a creamy cushion of pleasure. She put her hands beneath the sheet and felt around her Gaia garden. There was a triangular scab between her anus and vagina: a healing burn mark. No wonder she was in bed, being taken care of. She stroked her stomach in small circles, dipping her fingers into the moist crease above the burn. The bed began to vibrate beneath her, small nodules emerging from the mattress to massage her muscles. After she'd peaked, she lay listening to the whirring tremors and chamber harmonies of the birds, waiting for Not-Silver's return.

She must have closed her eyes again because he came back in bright daylight, bearing a memory clip. Oh yes, the memory clip: her order. She replaced the clip on the Tablette frame and an order icon appeared on the screen.

MEMORY ORDERS

AOA001–AOA004

HAVE BEEN FULFILLED.

YOU MAY DOWNLOAD THESE ORDERS

AND SAVE IN THE FOLDERS PROVIDED.

YOU MAY PLACE

SIX REMAINING MEMORY REQUESTS

THIS OWLEON VISIT.

Order AOA001 was a perfectly hatched memory of Silver on her wrist: the exact patterns delicately brushed on his wings, the curve of his beak, the feeling of luminosity in her chest when she let go of the jesses and he launched his fragile cargo of bones and quills into the air. She replayed it over and over, first watching it on the screen, then closing her eyes to see it in her head. Not-Silver perched on the railing, watching the screen too; sometimes when Silver lifted and stretched, he did too. As she studied the screen, hints of other images edged into her mind: other memories fitted next to this one, she realized; they were clicking against it like beads on a string.

She saved the memory in a folder she named *Silver*, then thumb-printed the keyboard and placed a new order. HELIUM AVIARY CLEAN-ING. HIPBEAD STRING. That would be enough. No, wait. One more. There was a friend she wanted to see again. A girl she'd Gaia-played with. Silvie. That was right. SILVIE WOODLAND SIESTA.

Not-Silver brought her new memories every visit: sometimes just one, sometimes two or three, and not always in the order that she'd requested them. The beautiful and moving memories—SILVER CHICK FEEDING; HOKMA LIVING ROOF; SILVIE GAIA PLAY—arrived just when she thought she couldn't bear being without them for a moment longer. The silly, playful snippets—MEEM BERRY BISCUITS; PEAT EARTH-SHIP DANCING—sometimes came right away and sometimes they were randomly sprinkled with the rest. The painful ones—NIMMA IMBOD INTERVIEW; AHN KEZCAM OFFICE; BOY SOUTHERN BELT—the ones she ordered later, when she felt courageous but at the same time sick with trepidation, came when she'd almost forgotten she'd ordered them. Some of the happy memories were sharp and glorious, triumphs of remembrance, every detail as clear as if trapped beneath a microscope. Some were fuzzy and fleeting, but no less beautiful for that. She fingered them like scraps of cloth, held them to her nose, inhaled the scents of familiar bodies, perfumes, dishes. The painful memories, though, were neither bold nor rich; they had shrunk, somehow, or faded; they were drained of hurt, she learned, and could be watched with an increas-ing sense of relief and then filed on the Tablette with a heartskip of happiness. Once she had ordered her memories, she could reorder them, store them in a hundred different folders and replay them in a hundred different algorithms: GREEK DRAMA MIX; GAIA SYMPHONY MIX; SHAMANIC JAZZ MIX; NORDIC SAGA MIX—the list of show-streams went on and on, endless permutations of memories, countless ways to recognize and relive herself, to see how tiny were her fears and doubts, how powerful and beautiful were her family, her home.

After a time, though—she wasn't sure how many days and nights—the memory-shows began to repeat themes and emotions. While still comforting, they lost their initial sense of revelation. She was happy still, content, but she began to be vaguely aware that something was missing. The consummation was reassuring as always, but the anticipation had faded. She tried to supplement the memory-shows, to order memories she hadn't thought of yet, but that was an impossible task. Memories were like squirrels: they had to come to you; you couldn't run into the forest and grab them. Patiently, for hours, for days, she held out the acorn of her desire for novelty, until finally the voice returned:

YOUR MEMORIES ARE OUR MEMORIES
AND OURS ARE YOURS

Our memories? More memories? Memories from before she was born? Her hand hovered over the keyboard. IS-LAND she swipetyped. 76RE. No: she deleted the date. 10RE: the year of Is-Land's founding. One more keyword . . . ELPIS.

The order was fulfilled more quickly than most—not immediately, not so soon as to render the memory a quick fix, but not after a prolonged, painful wait, and not after so much time had elapsed she had forgotten her request. After two fugue states had passed but the desire was still keen in her stomach, Order AOB337 arrived.

The memory was a mixture of image and sound. For the first time music accompanied the stream of images: Gaians pouring off buses with bags of seeds in their hands; Gaians cleaning streets, building Earthships, joking with CONC soldiers; Gaians laughing and singing—though she couldn't hear the words, just the strains of panpipes floating somewhere overhead. Then one of the women crouched down before a small girl whose face was partially hidden by the small potted sapling she was holding. The girl crooked the tree in one arm and with the other she waved at Astra. She had a round face and blond curly hair. She looked familiar—oh yes, she looked like Sheba . . .

Two men knelt down and joined the image. The man to the right of Elpis was sturdy and weathered, with a strong brow and a tanned, silver-haired chest. The man behind her with his arms on the other adult's shoulders was smooth-skinned and pale, with a sculpted crop of thick black hair. He was wearing a blue-and-gray checkered skirt—no, wait, it was called a *kilt*.

CHARLES MONTERAY, HEW BELSON,

KALI BELDOTT AND ELPIS SHIPDOTT

PLANT THE FIRST OAK TREE

IN THE GROUNDS OF THE NEW

IS-LAND NATIONAL WHEEL MEET.

The images of the tree planting were followed by others: Elpis at school, Elpis riding a pony, Elpis picking tomatoes, Elpis cleaning between her toes with a flannel and looking up giggling. In every shot she looked more and more like Sheba—Sheba, the Shelter sister Astra had never met but knew so well, Sheba dancing, laughing, running through the photoshow on the Earthship mantelpiece: *Sheba*. Now an image of Sheba's Fountain, her delicate tree of tears, rose in her mind, merging with the pictures of the Pioneers, and faintly, oh so faintly, a chorus of young children joined their voices in the "O Shield" hymn. Astra was overwhelmed with yearning. *Sheba. I miss you. Sheba, where are you? Sheba, I need you. Sheba, teach me how to be you.*

When she woke this time, she was in a room with white walls, facing an opaque window. Her head hurt—not the throbbing in her temples she sometimes got when she'd studied too much, but a deep fireball of pain cannoning up from the base of her skull into her frontal lobe. She shut her eyes again. Her throat was fissured, a jagged crevice in a rock face.

"Water," she begged.

"Astra. You're back," Klor said. His spade-callused palm was grasping her wrist and he was pressing a cup into her hand. "It will take a little while for your brain to adjust. This is some medicine to help take the pain away. Just drink slowly. I'll wait."

3.7

"Ugh." She grimaced as she swallowed the bitter chalky-pink mixture. "I was having such weird dreams. Silver was there, but he wasn't Silver, and he was bringing me—I don't know, like a Tablette playlist of my whole life. It went on and on—it felt like I was there for months."

"Astra, darling." Klor was sitting on a chair beside the bed. "What's the last thing you remember?"

She blinked. The dream was still vivid in her mind. "There was a Tablette tray, and it talked to me," she said. It was sore at the base of her skull; as she spoke she reached around and touched the spot. It was covered with a plaster, but she couldn't feel the rubber nib she remembered from the dream . . . She looked around at the stark walls. She wasn't on a balcony but in a small, bare, whitewashed room, facing a window open onto the steppes. The bed had a railing, just like the one in the dream, but not a Tablette tray. "Klor?" she asked. "Where am I?"

"You're in a neurohospice near Atourne. You've been here for three months."

She frowned. "Why am I in a neurohospice?" Her eyes widened. "Am I *dying*?"

"No, no!" Klor leaned forward and took her hand. "Good Gaia, no—this is the best neurotreatment center in Is-Land. You're on the memory reordering ward." Klor's skin was pallid, as if he hadn't had any sun for weeks. He gave her hand a little shake. "Astra, listen to me. I may only be able to visit you this once. You have to tell me: do you remember what happened? What you did in Ahn's office?"

She was on a *memory reordering* ward? Like the women on the bus to Sippur? She sat up, but her movement was restricted. There was something tied around her waist. "I'm in a *madhouse!*" she cried, scrambling at the restraint beneath the sheet.

"No, Astra, that's not a Gaian term—you know we don't call people with mental health issues crazy."

"*Ahn* does. *Ahn* called me crazy." Images came flooding back to her: hurling the Kezcams, Ahn's Gaia plow flopping with fright. "He's had me locked up," she yelped. "He wants me to *die in a madhouse.*"

She retched, and a thin stream of bile emerged from her lips. Klor passed her a bottle of water and she rinsed her mouth and spat over the edge of the bed. She couldn't lean all the way over and some of the water splatted the edge of the mattress and Klor's arm. She bent over, clutching her stomach. She remembered everything now: the meeting with the counselor, her march from Wise House, Hokma's letter—*Hokma's death*.

"No, no he doesn't," Klor urged. "IMBOD put you here, Astra—it was for your own safety. You hurt Ahn very badly. If Russett hadn't stopped you, you could have killed him."

"Then put me on trial!" She tried to rise in the bed, but the belt around her waist prevented her. "Let me stand up and tell everyone what he did. He hated Hokma for Sheltering me. He was jealous of me from when I was a *baby*—so he told IMBOD about my shot. He knew they would kill her, but he didn't care. He wanted to punish her, to get rid of her, so he could have a Code child with Congruence. Klor, he Gaia-played with Congruence when she was *seventeen*."

She was pleading with Klor, but he was regarding her with pity, as if she were a suffering animal. "You're confused, darling, Congruence is twenty-one, not seventeen. Her parents have spoken to her and she says she and Ahn have become close since working together, that's all. It's not ideal, and I know Vishnu was upset with Ahn, but it happens sometimes."

"She's *lying*—" she bleated.

"Astra, *no*. And you mustn't think Ahn would ever try to hurt Hokma. She died of a stroke, sweetheart. No one killed her—and especially not Ahn. He didn't hate her—that's simply not true. He loved her, for many years. We all knew you were a little jealous of *him*, but we thought that was normal. We never dreamed you would attack him the way that you did."

Her—jealous of *Ahn*? She opened her mouth to protest, but Klor shook his head, kindly but firmly. He didn't believe her; he would never believe bad things about Ahn. Not after what she'd done.

She sank back into the pillow. "Did I really hurt him?"

Klor paused. "Astra, you cost Ahn his fertility. He can still Code a child by cloning, but not by Gaia-bonding. It's a psychological wound as much as a physical one. If you were eighteen, you *would* be on trial."

She couldn't meet his eyes—she couldn't show Klor her pleasure, hard and bitter as a cough lozenge. Good: she had done it, she had taken something precious from Ahn, just like he had taken something precious from her: the most important person in her life.

"He didn't love Hokma," she said stubbornly. "He wanted IMBOD to take her away. That's why he—"

"Enough, Astra," Klor interrupted, his voice raised. "I understand that you were angry with Ahn, but he had to tell IMBOD the truth about your Security shot: it's what anyone would have done. And in any case, your shot had nothing to do with Hokma's arrest. It's all come out now, as part of Dr. Pollen's trial."

She punched the bed with the sides of her fists. "What has? What's come out? What does everyone except *me* know?"

His sigh was as heavy as a bag of damp sod. "Hokma *was* a traitor, darling. She was sending top secret Codes to Dr. Pollen in Atourne, and Dr. Pollen smuggled them into the Southern Belt on her field trips. They were part of a cell of dissidents, helping the Non-Landers breed Owleons and grow protein-enhanced grains and drought-resistant vegetables—they were giving away all these things other governments pay a lot of money for—to our *enemies*."

He didn't want to believe it, she could tell, but she had read the letter; she knew it was true. She opened her mouth, then shut it again.

She couldn't mention the letter. There would be hidden cameras in here, microphones, and she couldn't get Klor into trouble. But everything Hokma had written was worming its way back into her mind and there were a thousand things she desperately needed to know: did IMBOD really torture Non-Landers and massacre children? Why had no one ever told her about the rare-earth mines in the Belt? And, above all, why on Gaia's green earth had Hokma confessed? She had said in the letter she was going to use her trial to speak out about her beliefs. There was no way she would *confess*.

"What happened to her?" she demanded. It was too big a question, she knew. "To her *body*?"

Klor sighed. "She was cremated, darling, like Dr. Greenleafdott told us. Her ashes were used for fertilizer."

"Then how do we know she's dead?"

"Oh, Astra . . . They sent us photographs, and the coroner's report. I'm glad you didn't see them, but perhaps you should."

If IMBOD could wipe three months from her life, they could make a drugged woman look like a corpse. But why would they keep a traitor alive? Tears welling in her eyes, Astra slid back down on her pillow. Hokma had been returned to Gaia by anonymous aglabs without anyone to cry over her, without any stories to sail away in.

"Did we have a ceremony for her?" A tear seeped down her cheek into her ear. "At Birth House?"

Klor looked troubled. "No, darling, we weren't allowed. And people didn't want to. But I went to Wise House for you. I climbed onto the roof and picked some wildflowers, and then I went and sprinkled them in the brook."

"You climbed onto the roof?" Astra sniffled.

"I did. I strapped my leg on my back and hopped and hauled myself up."

"Nimma wouldn't like that."

"Ah well. Nimma doesn't know everything this crazy old man does when she's not looking."

It was a Klor eyebrow moment. She smiled weakly, though the relief didn't last long. There was a dead weight on her chest, burning a hole right through it. "What happened to Dr. Pollen?" she asked at last.

Klor was serious again. "She was sentenced to life imprisonment—and not a day too long."

"Did she say anything at her trial?"

"Say anything?" He was puzzled now.

She had to get this right. "About IMBOD? About Hokma?"

"Oh Astra, she was incoherent—she was a *traitor*. You really don't want to think about her right now. We need to think about *you*."

But she wouldn't let him change the subject. "What do you mean, incoherent?" she demanded. "What did she say about Hokma?"

"She accused IMBOD of killing her, of course." Klor shook his head in disgust. "She's delusional, Astra, and deeply misguided. You don't want to defend her or people will start thinking you're their accomplice and not their victim."

It all made sense now. She clutched the sheets in her fists, leaned forward and hissed, "But they *did*. IMBOD killed *Hokma*. She was going to speak out against IMBOD and the Wheel Meet at her trial, and . . . and—" In a rush, she finally understood *everything*. "Ahn and Dr. Blesserson didn't want their reputations to suffer. They only agreed to testify against her as long as she was killed so they would never have to!"

"*Astra*," Klor roared, "you cannot talk like that! It's *wrong*—very wrong. And if you keep accusing people falsely you *will* have to stay in here forever."

He was standing up, pointing his finger at her, and she was breathing at a gallop, but at last she shut up.

Klor sat down again, patting his hair back across his scalp. "Astra, *please* try to understand. You're here because you assaulted Ahn, a grievous attack that permanently damaged him. You were sedated afterward for your own good. Out of his *love for Hokma*, rather than take you to juvenile court, Ahn suggested that you come here for memory pacification treatment. Normally three months would be an effective first course, but frankly, I'm not sure it has helped you at all."

She couldn't blame him for not understanding. She would need proof, hard proof, before she got Klor on her side. Right now, she needed him.

"Three months," she repeated, twisting the sheets. Her fingernails were very short, she realized. Much shorter than she liked to cut them. "But—"

"I know." Klor's anger sank without trace back into his kindness. "It seems like you've been dreaming—that's the nature of the treatment. It helps many people, and it helps Is-Land too, to build a national archive of memories, especially childhood memories still fresh in a young person's mind. That was another reason Ahn wanted you to come here, so you could give something back to us all. But it troubles me, Astra, for you to be getting this treatment. The other patients are old, or have a long history of mental illness: they need to be calmed. But you—" Klor slapped his aluminum knee and stood up. "Oh Gaia," he exclaimed, "you just have a temper and we didn't realize you needed extra discipline. We brought you up like a Sec Gen when we should have been much tougher on you. I blame myself, Astra. I should have known, right from the start. When you came to visit me that day, before your shot, you remember? You were worried, and I understand now: you were worried that I would know you hadn't changed."

She let him pace, though his gait did not lull her. She was in a neurohospice for dying, *mentally incompetent* people, and Ahn had put her here in order to add her like a specimen to his National Museum. Dr. Blesserson had given him the idea, no doubt. She was tied to the bed. And even though she'd been dreaming for *three months*, Hokma was still dead.

"What's going to happen to me?" she asked dully.

His face flushed, Klor sat back down. "I can't get you released, Astra, but you're my legal responsibility until you turn eighteen and until then I have some influence over your treatment. You've had a full introductory course of memory reordering, as we agreed with Ahn, and it's clear to me it didn't work. I'm not going to authorize another treatment course, not unless you want it. But if you don't, your options are limited. Ahn doesn't want you back at Or unless you're cured."

His words whirled in her head. Flying among them was an image of small Elpis, snatched from her dreams. "What about Nimma?" she asked, in a small voice.

Klor hesitated. "Nimma wants you to get better, angel."

"She doesn't want me to come home."

"It's not just Nimma who's concerned, darling. The Parents' Committee is anxious too. It's been agreed that Or isn't the right Shelter home for you right now."

Oh.

"Vishnu too? And Sorrel?"

Klor paused. "Darling, Vishnu and Sorrel have left Or. They're living in New Bangor now and the children are spending weekends with Florence and Blossom. It's a very difficult situation. And given Vishnu's differences with Ahn, he's not the right person to Shelter you."

Vishnu knew about Ahn and Congruence. She clung to that knowledge like she had once clung to Hokma's hand. But Vishnu wasn't allowed to see her, and no one else wanted to. She was determined not to cry. "Where can I go, then?"

"Dr. Greenleafdott has recommended a Shelter school, but you can only stay there until you turn eighteen. Then, if you still aren't cured, you'll have to come back here, or to another neurohospice, and IMBOD will take full control over your treatment."

She wanted to scream—but she couldn't blot this out; she had to listen. She had to *understand.* "How will the school know if I'm cured?" Her voice trembled.

"By your behavior, partly—but also by brain tests, using an implant like the one you've just had to monitor your honesty and loyalty."

She was silent. She knew she would never be cured, and she could never pass their tests. She was *glad* she'd damaged Ahn. If she ever did go back to Or, it would be to finish the job. But first she had to get out of this bed—and not to live in an IMBOD school. There *had* to be somewhere else she could go.

The sun was brightening outside. Beyond the freshly painted window frame, the steppes had vanished in a haze of white light. Slowly she began to realize the only thing she could do; the thing she was born to do.

"What if I want to leave Is-Land?"

It was as if she'd fired a gun. Klor jolted in his seat. "Leave Is-Land?"

"People leave sometimes, don't they? They go to New Zonia, or Neuropa."

"I suppose . . ." It had never occurred to him, she could tell, but, Gaia bless him, he was considering it. But then his face shut down. "No, it's not an option. You're not trained for any job yet."

"I can garden—I can cook. I can speak Asfarian and Inglish. Well, I could soon, if I was living in—"

Klor wagged his finger at her. "Taking a poorly paid job in a world of non-Gaians would not be sensible, Astra."

She raised her voice a notch. "Klor, do you know who my Code father is?"

"We've never known, sweetheart. And even if we did, we can't ask him to—"

"He was a Non-Lander. Hokma told me before she got taken away."

It was as if Klor had bitten into something that was too spicy, too bitter, too sour, too hot. She'd never seen his face host so many expressions at once. "Good Gaia, child," he sputtered at last. "No, no he wasn't. Hokma was very wrong to—"

"He *was*. Eya told her. IMBOD can ask Dr. Pollen." She held out her arm. "You can take my blood and test my Code."

Now he was purely and simply aghast. "What have they done to your mind? Why on Gaia's good earth would you want that kind of stain on your record?"

"I'm half Non-Lander. I want to be expelled to the Southern Belt."

"Astra, you don't know what you're saying—oh Gaia, please help me." His voice was thick and choked. Abruptly, he got up and went to the window and looked out.

She stared at Klor's tufty back, sagging butt, wrinkly elbows. "What do you see, Klor?" she asked, at last.

Without turning, he softly replied. "I see Is-Land, my darling. The land we Gaians brought back to life so that all our children could flourish here."

"I love you, Klor." She had spoken so quietly she thought he hadn't heard her.

But he had. "I love you too, my darling," he said, still gazing out of the window. "Look at those beautiful pink cherry blossoms drifting across the garden. Oh my dewy meadow, you came into my life just like that, like a petal on the breeze."

She gulped, and the words came tumbling out of her. "I'm sorry, Klor. I'm sorry I hurt you . . . Thank you for loving me . . . I wanted to be a great scientist when I grew up—I wanted to learn how to regrow your leg. That's why I didn't want to have the shot."

He turned at last to look at her. "Oh, Astra," he said, his eyes shining. "Angel. Don't ever worry about my leg. You regrew my heart."

She gazed back at his craggy face but he looked away and continued haltingly, as if speaking to himself, "I knew I should love Peat, but Gaia forgive me, I didn't. I knew he needed care, and he was amusing, of course, but I was numb to him. Then you arrived, and oh my dewy meadow, your little face was so curious. Your eyes followed me wherever I went. Sometimes only I could make you stop crying. You liked my rolling gait, and gripping the fur on my shoulders. I tried to resist—I felt I was being disloyal to Sheba. But when you laughed, somewhere far away I could hear Sheba laughing too. And so I thought I should make you happy, if only for her sake. Then . . . well, then I fell in love, in the way only fathers do."

He still wasn't looking at her.

"I don't ever want to leave you, Klor," she said, "but you can't let them keep me here. Please, help me escape."

He was quiet for a moment longer, then he turned back to the window. "You were never mine," he whispered, "just like Sheba was never mine. Look, my darling. The wind is taking the blossoms away."

When he sat back down beside her, he was calm. "I'm going to try my best, Astra. I will tell IMBOD what you've told me and they may test you, I don't know. If it's true, then there is no future for you here, no matter what we try. But Astra"—he broke into a plea—"you don't have to go to the Belt to live with illegal squatters and violent criminals— why? I could petition IMBOD to send you to Neuropa."

"No. I want to find my father."

He was silent as he sat, both hands resting on his knees. Then slowly, he said, "There was a time when Non-Landers came here to work. Some

Gaians, the dissidents, argued that they were peaceful, respectful people. The dissidents were blind to the wider dangers of such attempts at
assimilation, but I will give them this—I have myself met one such Non-
Lander, an aglab with an extraordinary knowledge of fruit trees. Astra,
for the sake of that man, I am going to grant your Code father the benefit
of the doubt. But"—he raised his palm to stop her interrupting—"but
before I let you go to the Belt I'm going to do some research. If CONC
can find a decent job for you, and if they assure me that with IMBOD's
permission you may eventually be able to work elsewhere in the world,
I will recommend your eviction. But you need to know that eviction
doesn't mean freedom from IMBOD. You'll be monitored closely in
the Belt."

She touched the back of her head. "With an implant?"

"I don't think so—not yet, anyway. But you'll certainly have to report
to an officer and stay out of trouble. They don't have neurohospices or
reeducation schools there, darling. They have *prisons*."

"Klor—" Her voice cracked. "Thank you."

"You might not thank me later, Astra. But it's your decision, and I've
always known I must one day live with some version of it. It's natural to
seek your Code roots. You grew up in the richest land on earth, but if
you are cross-bred from a harder soil, you'll survive the transplantation."

"Will you say goodbye to everyone for me? To Yoki and Meem and
Peat." She paused. "And Nimma."

"Of course I will, my angel. Of course." As he reached to embrace her,
his dear face crumpled up like a brown paper bag, and for the second
time in her life, she saw the tears come glistening from his eyes.

3.8

Later, an IMBOD doctor visited the room. He said that her Shelter father had requested an investigation of her Code origins, so he needed to take a blood sample. While they waited for the results, her memory pacification treatment was to be discontinued. Instead she would be put on a light mood elevator and her Tablette would be loaded with a program of gentle entertainment: nature films, Gaia hymns and games. There were other quasi-lucid patients in the hospital and if she behaved and didn't upset the others on her wing, she could play chess and *hnefatafl* with them out on the balcony, exchanging moves by Owleon. She would need a little more physical stimulation now that she was no longer having treatment, so in the evenings her bed would be brought back into the room and she would be allowed to do yoga. She would also be given solid food three times a day.

"Do you feel able to cooperate with this regime, Astra?" he asked.

She nodded dumbly, proffered a vein and watched him suck a thick red jet of blood from her arm.

She was contemplating the courtyard when they came. Two caramel-feathered tumbler birds were bickering on the balcony railings, their beaks clashing and throats purring as they struggled to dislodge each other. As the officers stepped up briskly to the bed, the clicks of their heels startled the birds into flight. One soared briefly, then performed a double somersault before beating off into the trees. The other dipped and disappeared, then reemerged near the trees, wheeting like a wren.

"Astra Ordott." The first officer was not speaking, but reciting. "I am here to inform you that as a result of investigations instigated at the request of your Shelter father, your paternal Code identity as a Non-Lander has been confirmed. Eviction proceedings have begun against you and will conclude with your departure from Is-Land within the next three days. You will be taken to a holding cell where you will be made ready for your deportation to the Southern Belt. You will be provided with clothes and shoes, and with the permission of your Shelter family and in advance of your eighteenth birthday, the contents of your Is-Land child savings account will be released to you. Your Shelter father has made special petition that you be permitted to take up an entry-level position with CONC in the Belt, and that you be allowed to take certain items with you. In consideration of your Shelter father's long service to Is-Land, the judge has granted these dispensations. You are to come quietly now with me. If you do not come quietly, you will be reimplanted and transported in fugue state. Will you come quietly?"

She nodded. The first officer reached beneath the bed to loosen the white belt, and the second officer handed her a metal box—*her* box, from her Earthship bedroom. She pried open the lid. Inside, nestled in a lacy woven red shawl, were Eya's silver bracelet with its five blue lakes, Silver's feather, her hipbeads, the cherrywood heart from the top of her Labyrinth staff and an old Gaia hymnbook like the ones she'd seen in showcases at schools and galleries.

"Astra," said the first IMBOD officer, "it's time to go."

She replaced the lid of the box and swung her legs out of the bed. The soles of her feet met the cool marble floor and she stood. Her calf muscles spasmed, but took her weight. Gripping her Belonging Box, she stepped ahead of the officer, toward the open door.

Acknowledgments

I am deeply grateful to Bejan Matur for her generous permission to open Astra with an extract from "The Sixth Night *growing (up)*," from the poem cycle "The Seven Nights," translated from Turkish by Ruth Christie with Selçuk Berilgen and first published in *How Abraham Abandoned Me* (Arc Publications, 2012). Thanks are also due to Sarah Hymas, who alerted me to this beautiful book when she heard I was traveling to Turkish Kurdistan; and to Arc Editorial Director Tony Ward and his whole team, who continue to publish such fine international translations in a difficult climate.

An early version of Chapters 1.5 and 1.6 appeared under the title "Or Daughter" in the e-journal *MAMSIE: Studies in the Maternal*, 4(1), 2012. I sincerely thank the editors and peer reviewers.

My research for *Astra* was wide-ranging, including trips to South East Anatolia and Iceland where stays at the Kervanseray Hotel in Diyarbakır, the Hacı Abdullah Bey Konaği in Savur and the Kurdish village of Yuvacali; plus visits to the pigeon market at Mardin, the ash fields of Þórsmörk, the historic outdoor parliament at Þingvellir and the Geothermal Energy Exhibition at Hellisheiði Power Plant all made lasting impressions. I am also indebted to the Garbage Warrior and Earthship Creator Michael Reynolds and his team, who are constantly working on radical, sustainable biotectural solutions to the fossil fuel crisis; the Brighton Permaculture Trust 2012 Green Architecture Day, where I learned much about eco-communities in the UK; the Vanderbilt Center for Intelligent Mechatronics, whose revolutionary prosthesis designs inspired my descriptions of Klor's leg; Dr. Hillel Chiel and his team, inventors of an endoscopy camera based on the principles of worm locomotion; the Dark Mountain Project, visionary organizers of the 2012 Uncivilisation Festival; Sally Buckland of West Sussex Falconry, who so memorably introduced me to the heart-shaped world of owls; *The Owl Who Liked Sitting on Caesar: Life with a Loveable Tawny Owl* by Martin Windrow (Bantam Press, 2014), which I read prepublication thanks to the author and his agent, Ian Drury; and last, but far from least, the eye-opening document *GMO Myths and Truths* (*Version 1.2*) by Michael Antoniou, Claire Robinson and John Fagan (Earth Open Source, June 2012). Clearly, none of these innovators, researchers, gate- and raptor-keepers are responsible for any errors of fact or interpretation on my part in these pages.

When it came to writing the book I was enormously assisted by Arts Council England, who provided a grant that enabled me to concentrate fully on the final draft. I must also thank Jo Fletcher for her outstanding editing and mentorship; Nicola Budd for her ever-buoyant support; and John Parker and John Berlyne for enabling my ongoing relationship with JFB. Rowyda Amin, John Atkinson, Hugh Dunkerley, Fawzia Muradali Kane, Mike Kane, Judith Kazantzis, Catherine Lupton, Jennifer Beth Sass, David Swann and Irving Weinman all offered sound literary, scientific and/or eco-critical advice along the way, while special thanks go to James Burt, Rob Hamberger and Sarah Hymas for their extensive feedback on early drafts, with a starry mention to John Luke Chapman for keeping an eagle eye on the text during the last Kinbat laps.

I also wish to thank my aunt Mary Griffiths for her wisdom, humor and love over the years; Stefan, Rebecca and Mason, for teaching me just how deep family runs.

About the Type

Typeset in Garamond Premier Pro at 11.5/15 pt.

Garamond Premier Pro is a product of type designer Robert Slimbach's study of Claude Garamond's type designs. This interpretation of the Garmond extensive typeface is refined, versatile, and yet contemporary with current typography.

Typeset by Scribe Inc., Philadelphia, PA

Gloucester Library
P.O. Box 2380
Gloucester, VA 23061